HARD LUCK HANK

DUMBER THAN DEAD

by
Steven Campbell

web page: http://www.belvaille.com

facebook: http://www.facebook.com/hardluckhank

cover art by Ian Llanas
proofreading by http://lectorsbooks.com/editing

Web links may incur a data charge, may not be available at future dates, and are subject to change.

CHAPTER 1

It was another hot night on the space station Belvaille and I was standing in a cold puddle of sweat.

It wasn't my sweat. It belonged to someone else. Who, I didn't know. But whoever it was left behind more than discarded perspiration.

I stared at the dead body that rested by the foot of the stairs. It was sorely out of place in the otherwise stately home.

The dead man had been shot and stabbed, with the knife left buried in his torso. He had clearly been stabbed many times, which perhaps accounted for the sweat. Hacking at someone was difficult work.

I took some tele pictures of the crime, before anything changed. Before the sweat evaporated. Before the man jumped up and explained he was merely playing a practical joke on me.

The house was exceedingly well furnished. It looked like a shopping catalog they sent to happy couples hoping they would buy something to make themselves even happier. I searched the rest of the home but found nothing out of the ordinary. But a dead body was plenty.

I called up my cop friend, MTB. Told him there was a murder. Gave the address. I asked him to keep it under wraps if he could, but I would understand if he couldn't.

It would take MTB fifteen minutes to get here. I lay down on the nearby couch and tried to go back to sleep. I was still sleep-groggy despite my jolt of adrenaline. However, I found it difficult to snooze while I was twenty feet away from a corpse.

Especially since I had been specifically hired to prevent his murder.

It felt like hours, but MTB finally walked in the front door with gun drawn. MTB was tall, broad, and wore a loose, crumpled suit, years out of fashion. He had a face that looked like it had been punched so many times it was permanently swollen.

"Hank?" he called out in his gravelly voice.

"Yeah," I answered.

He ignored me and went over to the body as I got up from the couch.

MTB had been a cop now for centuries. I'd say it was in his blood, but I'm not sure MTB had blood. I think if you cut him, little cops would spring out and start arresting people. MTB liked to play things strictly by the book. But Belvaille didn't have a book. Not even a brochure. About half the people in the city were criminals. Murders were common. But this was not a common murder.

"What are you doing here?" he finally asked me, after reassuring himself there were no immediate dangers.

"I work here. I am—was—his bodyguard," I said, standing next to MTB but not close enough that I was crowding him.

"I hope he paid in advance," he said absently. I had expected at least one tease, but then MTB shifted into gear. "What were you doing before you found him?"

"Working."

MTB looked over at the couch and saw the piled-up pillows and mess of home-cooked food on the floor.

"You weren't sleeping?"

"Maybe resting my eyes. I'm no good to anyone if I'm too tired to function," I explained.

"So you were 'resting' over there?"

"Yeah."

"You stink like rotten fish," he whispered to me.

"I do?" I asked, sniffing at my shirt, confused.

"Your hearing is okay. And your former employer has three bullet holes and...at least twenty stab wounds. You were either asleep or you're an accomplice. Which is it?"

"I guess I might have been asleep," I admitted.

"What is this water on the ground?"

"I assume it's sweat," I said. "Not much evaporates in this humidity."

MTB dabbed his face with a chillwipe, a chemical towel that maintained a frosty temperature.

"No kidding. I thought it was bad outside. What is it, a hundred degrees in here?"

"A hundred and one. He was really anal about it."

"One bullet went through and hit the stairs. So he must have been standing when he was shot. And it must have been close range," MTB said.

He walked over and examined the hole in the ornate plastic stairs. The base of each stair had little white cherubs sculpted into them. They all smiled contentedly. Like they were happy the homeowner had been killed because he had stepped on them so many times.

"It's a pistol," I said. "I figure a .38."

"Did you check the bullet?"

"No. I've seen enough people shot that I can tell what kind of gun it was," I replied. "Two wide shots in the upper chest, one in the abdomen. That last was probably when he was falling."

"Why the knife? You think he was still alive? Did the shooter suddenly run out of bullets? It doesn't make sense," MTB said.

"None of it makes sense. That's why I called you."

"Okay, so who was this guy you were hired to bodyguard?"

"He's a Damakan," I explained needlessly.

"I could tell by how hot it is in here. And this house isn't gaudy enough to belong to any crime boss you normally work for. Was he an actor?"

"Aren't they all?" I asked.

"Just about. Damakans must have had a traumatic evolution."

"Why do you say that? Because this guy was shot or because they're all actors?"

"Actors. Damakans don't have emotions of their own. They act out scenes for each other to help them feel emotions. That's why they're so good at drama."

"So why would that be traumatic?" I asked.

"Think about it. They must have been going through hell to become like that. You or I see something scary, we get scared. Simple. But you can't frighten a Damakan until another Damakan acts out a scene. A big predator roaring at them won't even raise their blood pressure."

"I don't know if it works exactly like that," I said.

"This dead actor play in anything famous?" MTB asked.

"Maybe. He was in a weekly show about people working as medical technicians."

"A lot of shows like that," MTB said.

"Wednesday night. I think it was called something like, 'Organ Transfer.'"

"'Open Heart.' Holy frack, this is Cousin Randolph." MTB spoke the character's name that the dead actor played.

"Yeah."

"Weelon Poshor," he said. "Was that his real name or a stage name?"

"How should I know?" I asked.

"Did he have any enemies? Did you know this was coming?"

"If I had known, I wouldn't have gone to sleep," I replied.

"The door was unlocked when I came. Did you open it for me or was that the killer?" MTB asked.

"I enter the passcode when I come over. I *think* I locked it. Can't remember."

MTB walked to the door and looked for signs of forced entry or electronic bypass.

* 3 *

"What's the code to the door?" he asked.

I fished in my pocket and pulled out a strip.

"You have it written down?" he asked.

"The code is twelve digits long. I have enough trouble remembering my own name."

MTB returned to the body without trying the code. He studied the dead man's features.

Weelon Poshor had a big brown afro and eyebrows to match, in that they looked like twin bushes planted on his face. His nose hooked and was so long that it made you wonder if he had nibbled on it while he spoke.

"So why do you think someone would kill him? He have a wife? Lover? Kids? Rivals?" MTB asked.

"Not married. No kids that I know. If he was ever threatened or hassled, I never saw and he didn't tell me about it."

MTB glanced at me.

"When you first called, I was surprised. Haven't heard from you in ages. Someone said you got a girl."

"Yeah." I know he's heard about her, but I don't push it. He does.

"She a local gal?"

"This is a space station. No one is local, MTB."

"You and I are local."

"I guess. No, she doesn't come from around here. Look, I get what you're asking. She's a Damakan, too."

"Is that how you got this gig as bodyguard?" he asked.

"No. Just because they're the same species doesn't mean they all know each other. I've been doing security work on pictures for about six months. I get the jobs from Cliston."

"Ah, yeah. That makes sense. Your girl, is she in the entertainment industry?"

"They don't call it that," I said.

"What? Girl?"

"No, entertainment. They call it dramatic industry."

"Why?"

"Because to them it's more than entertainment. Like you said, it's their emotions. She does small theater work. She doesn't want all the big lights and publicity," I said.

"One of those *bashful* Damakans, huh?" MTB asked.

"Wise guy."

"It's none of my business, Hank."

"Then why are you asking?"

"No reason. You got to admit, it's damn unusual for a Colmarian to be dating a Damakan."

"I'm not a Colmarian, I'm an Ontakian. She's my fiancée," I said.

"Oh. Congratulations."

"Well, we're kind of engaged to be engaged," I amended.

"Getting back to the stiff, did you search the rest of the place?"

"Yeah. No windows broken. Nothing taken," I said.

"This isn't a robbery. No one stops to stab someone a couple dozen times if they're looking for quick cash. This was a murder," MTB said. "You work on the other side of the law quite a bit, Hank. You ever heard of someone being hired to kill a big-time Damakan actor?"

"No. Never. Kidnapping, rarely. Extortion. Bribery. But Damakans are like a commodity of the station. They create a lot of jobs and a lot of money. Killing one...I just don't see why anyone would do it," I said.

"Someone who uses a knife when they got a gun is either angry or trying to make a point. Maybe a jilted romance?" MTB asked.

"Damakans aren't violent," I said.

"Everyone is violent with enough motivation," MTB countered. "Besides, maybe it wasn't a Damakan who killed him."

"It definitely wasn't. Whoever did this came in here sweating. This is room temperature to a Damakan."

"Yeah, so maybe a Colmarian did it. I got to call the forensics people to check this place out," MTB said.

"You have forensics people?" I asked, surprised.

"Nah. I guess I'm trying to be cute. We can't do any of that 'angle of attack' or 'time of death' crap. But..." MTB kicked the body twice. "I'd guess he croaked about four hours ago."

"Three, is what I'd say. I don't think I was napping for *that* long. Can you test the sweat?" I asked.

"Test it for what? You think we keep a record of everyone's sweat? This isn't a *real* city, you know."

"It's got real people. Real houses. Real deaths."

"But this space station isn't a part of the PCC empire. We don't pay taxes. We don't have forensics. Hell, we barely have any police. One time I spent three hours collecting fingerprints at a crime scene and the only ones they matched were mine."

"Maybe you were the criminal and didn't know it," I said

"Maybe. But can you promise me that *you* didn't kill this guy? Look, I don't hassle you about the life you lead. You do what you got to do in this city."

"No, MTB. I didn't kill him. If I did, I'd tell you," I said, looking him square in the eyes. He and I go back a long way.

"Good enough for me. Okay. I know you wanted this quiet, Hank, but a Damakan getting iced is a big deal. The gun must have been silenced or you would have woken up."

"And he didn't shout or scream," I said.

"Maybe he knew the killer?"

"Or was taken by surprise coming down the stairs," I said.

"Someone has to talk to his Guild. Can you do that?" MTB asked.

"I suppose. But isn't this just my rotten luck? It's going to do wonders for my reputation as a bodyguard."

"Not such great luck for him either," MTB said.

"In his case, it wasn't luck. He didn't trip and fall on three bullets and then try and stop the bleeding by stabbing himself twenty times. Clearly someone planned this."

CHAPTER 2

I went to City Hall. It was the largest building on Belvaille and seemingly constructed out of pure hubris. If it had only been ten percent taller, the upper stories would extend into outer space.

My apartment was located there and so were the offices of Weelon Poshor's talent agent. I figured I owed the agent a heads-up that one of his actors was dead.

My home was on the 46th floor, not even halfway up the big spire. I ducked inside, splashed some cool water on my face, and put on a fresh shirt. Because the space station was perpetually hot to accommodate the Damakans, I was perpetually stuck to my clothes. On average I took several showers a day and changed my wardrobe at least twice.

I left my apartment and headed to the offices of the Artistry Agency. They were big players when it came to booking acting talent. The agency's job was to pick out the rising Damakan stars for the Guilds. In exchange, they got a piece of the action.

"Can I help you?" the receptionist said in a thick accent. It was a recent fad to have receptionists with thick accents. I think the goal was to make you feel like an outsider.

The lobby of the agency was saturated with hip artwork, sculptures that looked like someone had upturned a dumpster and glued all the trash together. Talent agencies only represented Damakans, so the climate was adjusted for their comfort. I was boiling.

"Is the boss in?" I asked the receptionist.

"Do you have an appointment?" she replied, not looking at me.

"No. But tell him Hank is here and it's urgent. He'll see me," I said.

"I doubt that very much. If you don't have an appointment, you can't go back."

I leaned over, putting my beefy hands on her fashionable desk. The table legs snapped off and ricocheted against the walls. I was a mutant Ontakian who weighed thousands of pounds. I carried a sawed-off shotgun inside my jacket. I'd fought creatures and aliens and robots big and small over the centuries and lived to tell about it. An impolite receptionist with a speech impediment was not a frightening adversary to me.

"Just call him," I strongly suggested.

Even with her knees pinned under the desk, she didn't drop her snooty demeanor.

"Not without an appointment."

"Hank?" Cliston called, walking to the front of the office. "I *thought* I heard a table break."

"Cliston. You got a minute?"

"Only a minute. Come on back," he said.

Cliston was a robot. A Dredel Led species. He looked like a jowly, fat man made out of polished bronze, wearing a metal tuxedo. The PCC, the Post-Colmarian Confederation Colmarian Confederation, was at war with his people. But that didn't stop Cliston from being the best talent agent around.

When he wasn't running this agency, Cliston also had the odd distinction of being my household butler. This was a peculiar ability he possessed. Cliston could embody multiple personalities without the hassle of schizophrenia. He could hop between his personas at will—and seemed to do so whenever it suited him.

Past the lobby, the Artistry Agency was filled with enclosed offices. Young Damakan hopefuls paced the halls with anxious looks on their faces, dreaming of that coveted recommendation to a Guild. Despite the temperature in here, a number of them wore thick coats.

Cliston's office was in the front corner. It was so cavernous you could probably schedule two simultaneous, full-contact glocken matches with room to spare. Cliston sat down behind his imposing desk, which was gothic and flanked with snarling gargoyles. His executive chair was equally frightening and looked decidedly uncomfortable. But who knew what a metal man found relaxing.

"Make it quick," Cliston said impatiently.

I never could quite get used to Cliston's ability to switch personalities. As a talent agent, he was a go-getting hustler. As my butler, he was a model of propriety and manners, always addressing me as 'sir.' I considered Cliston one of my closest friends, but only when he was my butler.

"Weelon Poshor has been murdered," I said.

"Are you certain?" he asked.

"Pretty sure."

"He's a dramatic actor. He may have been rehearsing a role and you didn't realize it. Damakans can be very convincing."

"I know that. But I also know a corpse when I see one. He was shot and stabbed."

"Has his Guild been contacted yet?" Cliston asked.

"No. I came here first. MTB is investigating with his forensics people."

"He has forensics people?"

"No," I said.

"Hell. This is going to throw a wet blanket on his show," Cliston said, putting his metal finger to his metal lips as if he were thinking. "Do you have any details of the killing?"

"Gruesome details, but nothing helpful if that's what you mean."

"I hired you to safeguard him. How did this happen?" Cliston asked.

"I wasn't sleeping," I replied.

"Alright, so we know what you *weren't* doing. What were you doing?"

"I was at the house, but I didn't see the killer. I didn't hear it happen. He, or she, or they, got in and out without me knowing."

Cliston swiveled back and forth in his ugly chair, mimicking a Colmarian fidgeting.

"If you hadn't told me otherwise, I might believe you were asleep on the job."

"Just my bad luck," I said.

"More than bad luck. That's a primetime show in jeopardy. And I was grooming Weelon Poshor. Another 392 or so days in the serials and he would have been a star. Feature films. This costs me a lot of money, Hank."

"I don't mean to try and tell you your business, Cliston, but this city is filled with Damakan actors. Just grab a replacement."

Cliston stared at me with his robotic mouth drooping open. It was his only facial feature that could truly move.

"Do you understand Damakans?" he asked.

"Sure. They're a race of actors."

"There are 50,000 species in the Post-Colmarian Confederation Colmarian Confederation. Most of them can act. Pretend they're something else. I'm a Dredel Led robot. Even I can act. Damakans have an ability to make us *feel* a certain way. 'Broadcast empathy' is what I call it. It even works over transmissions. They can manipulate us into feeling whatever they want us to feel. No other species can do that."

"Yeah. About five years ago, I saw my first Damakan perform. It was a one-man play. Just a guy on a stage with no props or costumes or anything. At one point, he acted like he was in a burning building. The next thing I knew, a bunch of us in the audience screamed, 'Get out of there, you fool!' I'd never seen anything like it," I said.

"Sure. What regular actors can compete with that? None," Cliston said. "The dramatic industry is going to be huge. And they're all here on Belvaille! It was a miracle when we discovered Damakans."

"It's weird we're still finding new species and civilizations after all this time," I said.

"You don't get out much, Hank. The galaxy is a *big* place. And the rewards for exploration aren't nearly as great as they once were. History books aren't exactly going to record the names of the intrepid heroes who found the 52,324th species in the PCC. Damakans never developed space travel. It was purely coincidence they were found at all."

"I always wondered, Cliston. Do Damakans affect you like they do us? Do you fall in love or get angry when you watch a show?"

"I can *sense* it, but it doesn't jerk me around like it does Colmarians. That's why the Guilds need me. You asked why I don't snap up some replacement for Weelon Poshor. Only a small number of Damakans are really talented. Most Damakans can only affect a small group of people. Like their immediate family and friends. That's no good for tele programs."

"So maybe this is a bad time, but do you think you could get me another job? You know, as security," I asked.

"Because you did such a bang-up job on Weelon Poshor?"

"Word hasn't gotten out about that yet."

"It's gotten to me!"

"But you're my...I mean, I don't know how all this works, Cliston. When you come home, you'll be my butler. You'll take 15% of my money and bake me food and tuck me in at night. We'll talk about this and you'll tell me that, 'Everything will work out, sir.' Let me talk to *that* Cliston."

"That other Cliston doesn't give you assignments. I do. You know that, Hank."

"I suppose. But I still need a job. I can't keep borrowing money from my butler or things will get awkward."

"Your butler sounds like he has a screw loose if he's loaning *you* money."

I frowned. Was that a robot joke? Cliston never joked. At least butler Cliston didn't.

"No work, then?" I asked.

"I'm not going to deny that your carelessness has set me back a lot," he said.

"Sorry."

"This is a dirty city full of dangerous people. The Damakans can't navigate it. They only know about things like homicides and double-crosses through stories. That's how they learned our language and culture. They studied Colmarian mythology and folk tales."

"Why not our history?"

Cliston waved his shiny hands around.

"Eh, they're artsy. Boring history isn't going to mean anything to them. They need emotions."

"Colmarian history isn't boring. Awful lot of wars," I said.

"In between the dull stuff, sure. But they want to learn about colorful people. Outlaws. Damakans don't have those."

"That's not true. I asked my fiancée Laesa and she said her people have crooks just like we do."

"Every species has bad guys. Hell, even Dredel Led specifically manufacture robots who are criminals."

"Why?" I asked.

"So the rest of us Dredel Led have experience dealing with lowlifes like you," he replied. "But Colmarians turned being crummy into a science. And Belvaille is where they go to get their doctorate degrees. This city manufactures crime like other cities make widgets. I need someone who knows this town to guard my clients. A thug to fight off the thugs."

"That's me!" I said.

"You do have credentials, despite what Scanhand says. You're a wanted felon and you've been doing this ever since someone got the bright idea that they could *steal* what they wanted instead of earning it."

"Technically, stealing *is* earning. Just after the fact," I said.

"There's plenty of muscle for rent on this station. But half the time I'd worry that I was handing my clients over to someone who'd rob them. Or worse. Still, having Weelon Poshor killed makes me question your abilities."

"How do you want me to prove myself? I could beat up your receptionist."

"I'm thinking an arena match in Cheat Hall. If you win the next fight, I'll hire you."

"I'm not a big fan of the arena. Can I do something else?" I asked.

"It took me a long while to get Weelon Poshor to the point where I was about to start making hard currency off him. I lost all of that effort. I'll be able to recoup some of my losses by organizing an arena match."

"And when will I have to do this?"

"How about tonight?"

"That's not a lot of notice."

"You don't have anything else to do. The guy you were *supposed* to be working for is dead. I'll get with the other fight promoters and put together a ticket."

"Will I get paid for this?"

"You just murdered my actor and now you want money? This will be a last-minute deal on a weekday. Still, I'll give you 1% of the purse."

I knew better than to enter negotiations with Cliston. Butler or agent. He always won. Cliston was something like 15,000 years old. He was a great butler, maybe the best in the galaxy. But sometimes—many times—I wished he wasn't so good at everything else.

"Alright, I guess. Hey, have you had a chance to see Laesa's play yet?" I asked.

Cliston stood up, seemingly done with our conversation.

"What? No. No, I haven't," he said, walking to his office door.

"I can get you tickets. I heard it's getting great reviews. I really enjoyed it."

"Busy. Busy. I'll try and get around to it."

"Okay. Can I...can I talk to butler Cliston for a second? I need to know what time dinner will be. And he has to change the menu to heavy carbs so I have energy for the fight later."

Cliston's whole posture changed. He dropped his arms to his sides and stood up straighter. He became his butler persona.

"The first course should be served by 6 pm provided I do not have to stay later at my other job, sir."

"You know, Cliston, one of the requirements of you working as a talent agent is that it doesn't interfere with you being my butler," I said. I felt the need to hassle him after his alter ego just chewed me out.

"Sir, are your finances in order?" he asked.

"In order? I'm poor, if that's what you're getting at."

"Precisely. Perhaps it would be beneficial if at least *one* of us was earning as much as possible," he said.

"So, 6 pm?"

"Yes, sir. Will anyone else be joining you?"

"No, Laesa's got her acting class. You really should see her play."

"I'm sure it's splendid, sir."

"Tell the other Cliston to see her play," I said, walking to the door.

"You need to notify the Drama Guild about Weelon Poshor," Cliston said. He had reverted to talent agent again.

"I'll get with them later. I want to rest up for this evening," I said, leaving the office.

"There are some pastries in the top cupboard if you get hungry, sir," he called after me.

CHAPTER 3

I went down and showered in my apartment and ate some pastries from the cupboard. I actually owned a suite of apartments whose layout and furnishings changed at Cliston's pleasure. All of City Hall used to be business offices, so the fact my home was not only comfortable but tasteful, was a reflection on my butler.

In contrast to the rest of the city, my apartment was kept cold. Cliston turned up the heat when Laesa came over, but not very much. She was always shivering, poor girl.

Since Cliston had talked me into an arena match in exchange for more employment, I wanted to be rested for the fight. I puttered and watched a few soap operas and got some sleep.

That evening, Cliston was his usual endearing and conscientious butler self. Between serving my dinner and cleaning up the place, he was on the tele setting up the arena bout. It was disconcerting to overhear him planning how I would get beat up.

Of course, gambling was what made the arena possible and profitable. No one wanted to see a fight that was 40:1 odds—they had to make it as close as possible so people would bet on either side.

I was a mutant who healed rapidly, was heavy, strong, and bulletproof. Normal brawls weren't a concern to me. But Cliston used to be my general manager when I played for the Super Class Belvaille Glocken Team. He knew my abilities better than anyone. Maybe even more than I did. Therefore, I was justifiably worried what Cliston was putting together to ensure gambling participation.

He switched to his talent agent self while scheduling the fight. I'm not sure what criteria Cliston used to determine when he needed a new identity, but the skills and personality used by a talent manager and arena hustler were roughly identical.

I got a massage and rubdown from Cliston after dinner. We didn't talk for the rest of the evening. I was trying to mentally prepare for what I had to do, and Cliston was perceptive enough that he didn't distract me. A few hours later, he drove me to Cheat Hall.

The structure had various names. Cheater's Hall. Cheater's Palace. The Cheat. It was the last remaining sports stadium located on Belvaille. It was constructed *above* a huge section of buildings. Therefore, it was not only out of the way, but too complicated to tear down without endangering a lot of buildings underneath.

The stadium had hosted Belvaille's only Championship glocken match. It earned its current nickname from the small fact that I had murdered all the referees during that game to try and stop an economic catastrophe. I succeeded, but failed to prevent another calamity: the entire Belvaille System was mutated by a scientist working for the mad immortal, Thad Elon.

Some years later, the arena fights started innocuously. Newly created mutants, with nothing better to do, began dueling in the arena to test out their abilities. Soon enough, spectators showed up to watch. Then they began wagering on the outcomes. What had started as random, infrequent activities, morphed into nightly, organized events. They had become quite popular and I heard there was talk of broadcasting them in pay-per-view.

Belvaille was *the* central hub in the Post-Colmarian Confederation Colmarian Confederation. Because of the Portals. Belvaille had the most Portals of any System in the galaxy. They allowed spaceships to travel vast distances. Without them, interstellar trade, and the whole PCC empire, wouldn't exist.

Countless ships passed through this System every day. Most never stopped, but simply went on through to deliver their goods across the empire. Some ships came to Belvaille to refuel, repair, or refresh their crews. People came off those long-haul transports looking for distraction. Belvaille had it. Food. Hotels. Liquor. Drugs. Prostitution. Casinos. And yes, our custom, homegrown, arena battles in a comfortable, modern stadium.

Our fights even spawned a bush league of underground arena tournaments that crisscrossed the PCC. The transport haulers, which had to make regular tours of the galaxy, would also ferry along the professional fighters who competed in the territories. Some gladiators might specialize with weapons, others were mutants created in Belvaille, and some were strange aliens that were naturally good at blood sports. Fans got bored of seeing the same matches every night, so the transports were key to keeping the fight circuit lively by regularly shuffling the contenders across the empire.

I had participated in some of Belvaille's early brawls, but I felt it was a bum deal. The gamblers and odds-makers made all the money and I ended up in the hospital. But if you wanted to tour the galaxy, and you could take a lot of abuse, being an arena fighter was a ticket out of whatever mundane existence you might have otherwise faced.

Cliston and I parked his car in the stadium's vast lot. We were early and there were only a small number of cars. Although Belvaille didn't orbit a star, we still had a day and night to maintain our sanity. The city dimmed the latticework lights at night. More than a few times, we had completely changed our clocks to match some major trade routes. Whatever the time was, the criminals would sleep during the day and wake up at night. There was just something about darkness that made doing illicit activities more comfortable.

Cliston met up with the other promoters and bookies. Off to the side stood the prospective fighters, looking to earn a payday. They were a sad lot. Some had their suitcases on the ground next to them, having just come from a transport or not possessing enough money to afford a hotel. Some even had their families with them. Snot-nosed little kids too tired to frolic and worried spouses straightening synth battle gear.

The combatants provided their arena records to the bookies. Wins, losses, ties, concussions, broken bones, and whatever else they thought was pertinent. Sometimes, they would have video displays to show how good, and entertaining, they were. The people without past records made do by looking tough to try and impress the promoters enough to get on the ticket for tonight's event.

Some of the more talented warriors had agents—the ability to negotiate wasn't the same as the ability to take a punch.

There were even a handful of Ontakians milling around, hoping for a match. The new Belvaille economy had not been kind to the Ontakian species and they had fallen on hard times. I was technically an Ontakian—a mutant Ontakian. Still, I didn't have much in common with members of my species and didn't care for them as a whole. My uncle Frank was also on Belvaille and he personified our race by being brutal, stoic, and more dangerous—and less sentimental—than ass cancer.

The Cheat arena operated under gladiator rules. You could have weapons, but no guns. Most of the bush-league fights were illegal and took place in small venues. You couldn't tote around weapons that might be confiscated by the police or might inadvertently kill members of the audience. The best fighters used only their bodies.

Cliston returned, accompanied by the biggest—literally—fight promoter in the city. I had worked with him before in another capacity. His name was Procon Hobb.

Procon Hobb was a cross between a frog, a lizard, and a nightmare. He stood about ten feet tall, and with his black eyes and clawed hands, looked absolutely terrifying even when he was absently munching some vegetarian foliage. He had two small, bipedal lizard attendants spritzing him with water. While Belvaille was far too hot for me, it was too dry for Procon Hobb.

He was some kind of religious figure to his strange, amphibian species. Procon Hobb was a mutant. He could mentally speak to you using your own inner voice as his own. He was also very wealthy. Last I heard he possessed numerous solar systems. Procon Hobb as a monstrous creature frightened me. But Procon Hobb as a walking tower of money enticed me.

"Hank," Procon Hobb said to me in my head. "It was my understanding that you retired from the arena."

It was disconcerting having your brain speak to you against your will, but I was somewhat used to it. I answered by talking, even though Procon Hobb could hear my thoughts.

"I wouldn't say retired. A man has to eat. And I have a big stomach."

"Hank, we've decided you're going to be the headliner for tonight," Cliston said. "We have a suitable title match for you."

"Yeah? Who will I fight?" I asked.

Hobb and Cliston looked to the side and I followed their gaze. Away from the crowd stood the Rough Boys. Actually, I don't know if it was spelled ruff, like the sound a dog makes, or rough as in tough. The three Rough Boys looked like enormous white wolves that had taken absurd amounts of performance-enhancing drugs, learned how to stand on two feet, and wear dirty clothes.

Normally, mutations were completely random and individual. Even ones that were sort of similar had unique side effects. When Belvaille had been systematically mutated during the glocken championship, there were some cases of duplicate mutations. No one could figure out why. It didn't happen to siblings or people in the same areas or anything easy to explain like that.

The Rough Boys had all been normal Colmarians at one point who had nothing in common and didn't even know one another. When they were mutated, they quit whatever they once did, and became hired enforcers working for criminal gangs. They were good at it. Super strong, fast, resilient. And mean as hell. Every time they ripped someone apart, or turned over a car, someone told me about it. For years, there had been a not-so-subtle push to see who was the toughest mutant on Belvaille, me or them. I never took the bait. I was long past the age where I needed to get in dangerous pissing contests.

The leader of the Rough Boys was named Kaxle. He was two feet taller than me and significantly wider. He snarled in my direction when I looked at him, but maybe that was his way of smiling.

"Uh, how much are you paying?" I asked.

"We've already worked out our agreement," Cliston reminded me.

"I'll pay you 50,000 credits directly to take on Kaxle in single combat," Procon Hobb thought at me.

I didn't even hesitate.

"No way," I said. "Not remotely interested."

"It is the best ticket we can organize," Cliston explained.

"I wouldn't fight him for ten times that amount," I said.

"May I ask why?" Hobb thought.

"Because it will be a good fight. A *great* fight. And you want to schedule it tonight, with no advertisement, on three hours' notice. What you're offering won't cover my hospital bills—assuming I survive. A fight between me and Kaxle could make a fortune if you prepare it months in advance. You'll pack this stadium and all of us will make a lot more."

Procon Hobb languidly blinked his enormous eyes.

"Very well. We have another event but it will require you to fight three opponents at once. And you won't receive any additional payment."

"That's okay with me," I said.

"I shall make the arrangements," Hobb thought. Then he touched his head and telepathically contacted whoever needed to be contacted. When he was done, he turned and waddled slowly away.

"Kaxle is eager to fight you," Cliston said, when Hobb had left.

"Sure he is. He's got everything to gain. If he beats me, he'll be able to charge a lot more as a professional head-cracker."

Cliston sighed. The action seemed perfectly appropriate except he was a mechanical construct that didn't breathe.

"Let me finish the details with Procon Hobb," he said.

"When will I be fighting?" I asked.

"Not until we get a bigger audience. We'll put out a tele alert and start taking wagers online. But it might not be for three or four hours. Go to one of the sky boxes and make yourself comfortable. I'll bring you up some food in a while."

"Alright," I said.

I waved goodbye to the Rough Boys and took an elevator up to what had once been a restricted area of the arena. Inside one of the VIP boxes I spread out on the couches.

Cliston woke me up some time later. Not sure how he found which box I was in, maybe he could smell me.

"I prepared you some food, sir," Cliston the butler said.

"Thanks," I answered, rubbing my eyes.

"What do you think of the matches so far?"

"How could I see them? The field is a million miles away. My eyesight isn't *that* good."

"The windows have integrated zoom controls. You can pan around to any of the camera feeds as well."

"Oh. No, I just napped."

Cliston sat down on a nearby chair. His splayed-leg stance told me he was no longer in butler mode. Also, the fact that he sat down. I'm not sure if butler Cliston *ever* sat.

"So you're going to be fighting two scrubs from the bush leagues and one mutant," he said.

"What mutant level is he?" I asked.

"How should I know?" he replied.

The original Colmarian Confederation had assigned mutant levels to its citizens to classify us. On a scale to ten, I had been designated a level-four mutant. I had only met one level ten, and he was basically a god. Of course, the Colmarian Confederation no longer existed, so there wasn't an official body to categorize us.

"Well, what can the mutant do?" I asked, shoveling food into my mouth. The good thing about talking to talent agent Cliston was that I could eat as sloppily as I wanted without getting a reprimand from my stuffy butler.

"They call him The Wall," Cliston answered.

I stopped eating a moment.

"Is he that big?"

"Somewhat. But his mutation is that he can solidify himself into a wall."

"A wall?" I asked, confused.

"Yes."

"Like that?" I said, pointing to the rear of the box.

"I suppose. Or some other wall."

I laughed.

"What a terrible mutation. How is that going to help him?"

"I don't know. The two other men have decent records, but mostly in tiny arenas. This is their first trip to Belvaille."

"Trying to make it in the big time? What weapons will they have?"

"I didn't ask," he said.

"What if they have anti-Hank missiles?"

"They aren't allowed to use accelerated projectiles."

"Anti-Hank grenades?"

"They aren't allowed to use explosives."

"You know what I mean."

"When I arranged this, I figured you could handle some Colmarian gladiators. If I was wrong, maybe you're not the best person to be providing protection for my actors."

"Okay, okay," I said.

"Let's go over strategy," Cliston said.

"Wait. Are you talking to me as a butler or talent agent?" I asked suspiciously.

"Why do you care?"

He was clearly talking as talent agent. Butler Cliston would never be that rude.

"Because I don't trust talent agent Cliston," I said.

"I'm promoting you. I make 1200% more if you win than if you lose."

"Oh. Okay. Strategy."

"Yeah. During your bout, the stadium will flip the gravity back and forth. From low to normal and back."

"Why?" I asked.

"Because that will play to your strengths."

"How so? I don't have a spacesuit."

"It won't be a vacuum. The stadium is capable of manipulating the artificial gravity on the playing field. Everything else will remain the same, such as the air you breathe."

"Well isn't that nice? What am I supposed to do in low gravity?"

"Fly, stupid. You can fly, remember?" Cliston said.

Actually, I kind of *had* forgotten. When Belvaille was mutated, I received an entirely new ability. I could fly! The problem was, I didn't have enough thrust to actually move. I was simply too heavy. But if I was in outer space, I could soar like a fleshy rocket ship.

"I can't stop once I get going," I complained. "I'm not exactly maneuverable."

"This isn't the void of space, there is still wind resistance. You won't go as fast. But it's also why the gravity will oscillate. So you can fly in low gravity, and then clobber them in normal gravity."

I thought it over.

"How did you swing this with Procon Hobb?"

"He doesn't know you can fly."

He was right. Only a few people had ever seen me fly. I couldn't do it on Belvaille, I had to be in space. And most people didn't regularly hang out in space.

"Alright, this sounds good. How much will I make if I win?"

"As we agreed, 1%. But wagers are still coming in through bookies so I don't know the total yet. We're going to schedule you as the last contest of the night. We sent out word you were fighting and people are making their way here to buy tickets."

"Glad to know there's still interest in me."

"It should be another few hours. I'll call you when you need to come down," he said.

"Where are you going? I thought we were talking strategy."

"We just did: fly and beat them. I need to work out concession stand details."

"Okay. Bring me some more food while you're there," I said.

"You've eaten enough. I don't want you to be bloated," he replied.

I was too excited to sleep and I was out of food. I tried to watch the fights, using the telescoping windows, but they weren't very entertaining. Watching regular people fight was like watching children play sports. Sure, they had a lot of enthusiasm, but they were so bad at it.

The time finally came and Cliston called me to get ready.

My opponents were the under-ticket, so they went out onto the field first. Belvaille wasn't a city that believed in polite applause. The three guys facing me were greeted by catcalls and hurled garbage.

My turn came and I got a nice Cheat Hall introduction. They dimmed the lights and set a few barrels of oil on fire to get everyone's attention.

"And now, coming out of years and years of retirement," the announcer blared. "Your hometown favorite. The man. The legend. Hank, the Hard Luck Hero!"

There were only about a thousand people in the stands in a stadium that seated approximately one bazillion. Still, I got a fair number of cheers. It felt good.

I jogged out onto the field and held up my arms to the crowd. Then I got tired and put my arms down and walked the rest of the way to stand near my opponents.

Out in the center of the field, this was the showing-off period. We were supposed to swagger, flex, and jump around so the spectators could get a good look at us. Last-minute wagers were being placed. People were allowed to keep making bets right up until someone was declared the winner. Of course, the odds would change as the fight went on.

One of the guys on the other team was wearing green armor and twirling around an electronic rod. It was maybe two inches in diameter, four feet long, and crackled and fizzed in the air. He handled the weapon expertly.

His companion wore dark-gray armor and had thick, metallic gloves that connected to a power supply on his back. I couldn't figure out what his weapon was until he picked up some balls and began juggling. Juggling! The audience seemed amused.

The mutant from the other team, The Wall, stood a few feet away from me. He posed like a professional bodybuilder, sticking his arms and legs out and flexing obscure muscles. He was a big guy, about my size, and wore a t-shirt and pants. He met and held my gaze.

"You're supposed to display for the audience," he told me in mid-flex.

"They know who I am," I replied coolly.

"Your Dredel Led promoter tried to scam us," he said.

"That so?" I answered. This was gamesmanship. Part of the job.

"Yeah, he figured you were a scaled-up mutant and we were nobody pit fighters from the outer rim. Not exactly fair," he said.

"If I had a credit for every time life wasn't fair to me, I wouldn't need to be fighting in the arena," I said.

"Too bad Procon Hobb didn't tell your metal friend that we're a regular team. We have been fighting *together* for five years. Undefeated. They call us *Vicious Blood*. We're going to wreck you." The Wall smiled.

"Wow. In those five years in the arenas, did you learn to give your secrets to your opponents before a match? Is there anything else you want to tell me?"

The Wall scowled.

"Is that your mutation?" I asked, pointing at his head. "Making a disappointed stinkface?"

"You'll see my mutation, buddy."

"I'm sure I will. But unless your mutation is the ability to change probability, the bookies have given me 3:1 odds. That means if I hop around on one foot with an arm behind my back, it will be close to an even fight. Too bad I'm not going to do that."

"Keep talking. You're going to *eat* those words," he sneered.

"Eat. Words. Huh. I bet that is a quality insult where you come from. When you're 3,000 light-years from civilization, fighting a rabid mud monkey for a hot meal, people are thrilled to have *any* entertainment. But you're on Belvaille now. I have murdered, quite literally, hundreds of people just like you."

"Yeah? Well you ain't murdered us," he said.

I laughed.

"Yes. You are correct. I have not, in fact, murdered you. I have to think you would remember something like that."

"Shut up," he said.

"Hey, you were the one who started jawing. I'm content to stand here quietly. *Remembering...*"

I turned away and smiled. It took him five seconds, but he finally couldn't help himself.

"Remembering what?"

I faced him, feigning surprise.

"Oh, the last time I was in this arena. You see, I was the 10-lane Weight in the Super Class glocken Championship. Belvaille's home team. I'm the one who killed the referees and got the game cancelled. And that robot you think Procon Hobb tricked, he was our General Manager, Cliston. And your promoter, Procon Hobb, he was our team *owner*. Belvaille is really a tight-knit community in some ways."

The Wall appeared stunned. Anyone who wasn't in suspended animation for the last few decades had heard of Belvaille's championship game. Even if they weren't glocken fans. It was a galactic-wide scandal and topic of conversation. Now he was trying to figure out if I was lying. He moved over to his friends and began whispering to them. I nonchalantly fussed with my hair.

We stood around for another ten minutes while people got refreshments and placed bets. Vicious Blood stood off by themselves, glancing furtively in my direction. I had clearly stirred up some doubt.

The match was about to start and I kept trying to walk closer to my opponents. Vicious Blood kept walking away. This went on and on until we were at the far end of the field and the announcer told us to move back to the center because no one could see us.

There wasn't any kind of official signal that indicated the start of the fight. I knew it had begun when the juggler with the metal gloves threw a ball at me from forty feet away. It hit me square in the chest and I was no longer laughing about the weapon. The ball travelled incredibly fast, not nearly the velocity of a bullet, but it had much more mass. It would have been devastating to a normal person. The ball bounced away and was attracted back to the gloves of the thrower. The weapon seemed to be a sneaky way to get around the prohibition of guns.

"Okay, so you want to play like that?" I yelled.

I began to run toward the gloved thrower. Well, fast-walked. I was not a quick man. Although strong, I was not proportionately strong compared to my weight. This created very real limitations when it came to my fighting prowess. I could not punch or kick very well because I couldn't accelerate my limbs fast enough. I was a bulletproof wrestler. Which wasn't a bad thing to be, but out here on a wide-open field versus three opponents, it wasn't the best.

The thrower kept throwing. I got hit in the leg. The arm. The nose. The impacts stung, but didn't have enough power to do any serious harm. Getting hit in the face, however, was very disorienting and a few dozen of those and I might get concussed. I figured that Ball Boy was my primary target.

I got within about ten feet of Ball Boy and the man with the electric staff stepped forward. A white-blue bolt of electricity arced out and connected with me. I was momentarily blinded. The artificial grass around my feet melted and caught on fire. But other than that, there was no effect. I had once dated a mutant who could throw lightning bolts. Compared to her, this was nothing.

"That won't work on me," I yelled to Staff Guy.

"It only works on *muscles*," he replied. "You must be made out of blubber."

I ignored him and moved again to intercept Ball Boy when he stepped behind his mutant friend, The Wall.

It was at this point I understood where he got his name. The mutant instantly expanded. From my view, there was now an eight-foot-high wall that was fifteen feet wide! It was not thin, either. Maybe a foot thick. I'm not sure where all that mass came from, but it seemed to defy physics. The wall wasn't even the color of the man's original skin, it was kind of a dark brown and had no features like a face, arms, legs or anything. It was a real wall. Both Ball Boy and Staff Guy were hiding behind him.

"Am I supposed to chase you? I thought you were warriors, not sprinters," I taunted.

"You can always give up," Ball Boy yelled.

I resigned myself to this nonsense and approached the mutant wall, who was exactly as intimidating as any non-mutant wall.

However, they either pushed him over or The Wall himself tumbled. I was hit first in the head, and his enormous size had enough leverage that I fell backwards, with The Wall resting on top of me. He was heavy! Easily over a thousand pounds. Not nearly as much as me, but it could have crushed a normal person. No wonder these guys were undefeated.

So now I was trapped under a wall. I felt more weight added on top as the other two guys climbed on. Then they began to jump up and down while laughing.

I was pinned. I could lift The Wall in ordinary circumstances, but not with my arms by my sides and only a few inches of movement. I couldn't even wiggle my toes.

"Do you surrender?" Ball Boy challenged.

"Gno," I said. I was going to say more, but that was about all I could articulate.

They could probably keep me here forever, but I was relying on the Belvaille audience to save me—they didn't have the patience for this kind of strategy. Their combined weight wasn't enough to squish me and they couldn't attack with their weapons while I was under here.

It took at least three minutes, but I began to hear jeers and catcalls from the crowd. They paid for excitement, as well as a speedy resolution to their gambling. This was neither.

The weight suddenly vanished and I picked myself up from the ground with as much grace as possible.

Ball Boy and Staff Guy had moved to either side of the field—they were going to use their range advantage. The Wall stood ten feet in front of me.

Okay, so I needed a plan. I probably should have thought of one before I began. I was lazy and underestimated them. The fans rescued me, but I couldn't bank on that again. Belvaille was fickle and they might turn on me if I get trapped again. Even if I didn't die, it wouldn't do my reputation any good to know I couldn't match the combat skills of a barricade.

The Wall was a wall. If I kept my arms apart and braced myself, I felt I could prevent him from falling on me, or at least get out of the way. Staff Guy's electricity wasn't a threat. Ball Boy wasn't *immediately* deadly, but he was annoying.

As if on cue, I got smacked on the chin with another high-velocity ball. Keeping my left hand in front of my face, I began to slowly walk toward Ball Boy. I did my best to keep The Wall in front of me. If I didn't want to get pinned again, I had to watch what that mutant was doing. My fear was that he would rush at me and transform, which would be enough momentum to knock me over. I didn't care what Staff Guy did.

Another streak of electricity arced toward me and scorched the grass. The groundskeeper of this field was going to have a word with these guys when we were done.

The Vicious Blood team was well coordinated. You could see they had been working as a unit for years. As I moved toward Ball Boy, he backed away and the others rotated in unison. They kept Staff Guy on my blind side at all times while The Wall tried to press in closer.

The Wall was smart enough to recognize that I was braced for another building attack, so he held off. But he kept trying to get behind me and I kept turning. Of course, I was getting smacked with ball after ball while I was doing this.

After a few minutes of us jockeying for position, it was clear I was not going to reach Ball Boy without leaving myself open for The Wall to pin me.

The audience was not happy. We were the last bout of the night and people wanted to collect their winnings, if any, and go home.

Although their mutant seemed to be more of a defensive player, he was the fulcrum that the others pivoted around. If I could take him out, or at least slow him down, then I could go after the other two unhindered.

I purposely eased up to let The Wall push closer. His goal was to be near enough that he could catch me unprepared. I waited until he was about a step away from being directly behind me. Then I turned, put my arms wide, and rushed at him.

It all happened so quick that I'm not sure what went first. At some point I hit the mutant, tripped, and then I was facedown on top of a wall.

Okay.

I tried to punch The Wall. My fist bonked his façade and he remained annoyingly wall-like.

A ball hit me on the back of the head. Then another. But I noticed Staff Guy held off firing any bolts. I wondered if that meant the electricity could hurt The Wall, who was currently underneath me.

I wasn't sure what to do next. I squatted on The Wall and covered myself up. I was too heavy for the mutant to budge, and he was a wall, he didn't have any arms or legs even if he *could* budge me. I had effectively neutralized him for the moment.

Only Ball Boy was moving around, chucking sphere after sphere, looking for a weak spot. The audience was fed up. They began yelling at me to get going. "Coward" and "idiot" were the nicest things I was called.

I took the abuse, both verbal and physical. In my patience, I learned that Ball Boy simply wasn't that accurate. I could tell he was trying to hit my head, but I was hunched over. He kept nailing my forearms and shoulders. That little bit of information gave me a plan.

As my attackers shifted positions, and the chorus of agitated gamblers grew louder, I finally stood up and rushed at Staff Guy. It was such a contrary move that no one was ready for it, least of all Staff Guy.

He zapped me once before I swallowed him in a bear hug. He was a strong Colmarian, heavy of build, but to me he was practically a stuffed animal. I picked him up and turned around, my arms still wrapped around him.

Now I had a shield. I hoped that Ball Boy would cease fire, not wanting to jeopardize hitting his teammate. While the missiles were irksome to me, a missed shot might do serious damage to his teammate. Not only that, but my shield was holding a dangerous cattle prod. The weapon might be enough to keep The Wall, who had reverted to normal form, away from me.

It's not as if I was suddenly in a position of strength. It's more that I was no longer in a position of weakness. They couldn't attack me, but I couldn't strike them either. My hands were full.

And then I threw up.

Being suddenly flung into zero gravity when you're full of adrenaline was about the most disorienting thing possible. Cliston had said they would switch to *low* gravity, but it was completely off. The bit of momentum I had possessed when it deactivated was enough to send me floating across the field, a few inches in the air and rising.

Despite puking, I somehow kept a loose grip on Staff Guy. When I had recovered somewhat, I noticed The Wall and Ball Boy were almost as inconvenienced as I was. Ball Boy tried to hurl a projectile at me, but his wind-up caused him to go tumbling instead.

The field was completely empty except for artificial turf. There were no obstacles or railings or anything to grab onto. It was preposterous to expect us to do battle on a massive field in zero gravity. We couldn't reach each other even if we wanted to, and the smallest collision would send us flying away again.

Oh, that's right. I could fly.

Holding onto Staff Guy's shoulders, I pushed him upward as hard as I could. He immediately went soaring, and screaming, toward the sky. I lightly touched down to the field.

The Wall saw his compatriot sailing away and he promptly transformed himself into a wall. The change was physical. That meant it imparted some motion, however slight. In zero gravity, it left an eight-foot wall slowly spinning above the field.

I wasn't sure how much time I had in reduced gravity. I had to make the most of it. My idea was to fly at Ball Boy, hit him, and use my tremendous weight to grapple. Once I was in melee distance, I could pull him apart if I had to.

I concentrated to activate my flying mutation. It wasn't spectacular. No flames shot out of my butt or anything. I merely looked like I was lying facedown in the air and skimming along the ground at a very slow walking pace.

Cliston was right. There was still wind resistance and I didn't fly as fast as I did in space. It was taking me a lot longer to pick up speed.

But I had underestimated these guys yet again. Ball Boy, who had been twisting in the air, reached down and steadied himself by grabbing a handful of grass. While hanging upside down with one arm extended, he threw another ball and hit me right in the forehead!

It was an amazing shot and it disrupted my trajectory. I barely prevented myself from crash-landing into the turf. The fact he struck me with the same force as when he was standing upright in normal gravity told me that those gloves were doing the hard work. There's simply no way he could generate that kind of power, upside down, using one arm.

I had no experience avoiding anti-aircraft fire or taking evasive actions. But I realized I had to avoid getting hit if I wanted to fly straight. I didn't have a lot of thrust and the ball collisions were enough to completely halt my progress. And when gravity turned back on, I would lose my advantage again.

I decided to fly away from Ball Boy. I could avoid the projectiles and pick up speed. If I could ram him at even twenty-five miles an hour, I wouldn't need to worry about fighting him, he'd be a wet smear.

I changed course and flew almost straight up. Several balls passed underneath me as I climbed out of his range and gathered speed. Up above, Staff Guy was still climbing from when I shoved him earlier.

It was difficult for me to turn while flying so I borrowed Staff Guy. I simply crashed into him. The impact allowed me to re-angle back toward the field below. It had the side effect of pushing Staff Guy upward at a faster clip. He was screaming, spinning, and heading up toward the latticework where the space station lights and ventilation were.

I was now on a collision course with Ball Boy and accelerating again. I was at such a high angle that he couldn't throw at me. He also couldn't dodge me since the only leverage he had was a fistful of grass.

I was going faster. I was probably up to eight miles an hour, which isn't exactly speedy, but it didn't need to be. I was really heavy. Besides, my goal wasn't to kill Ball Boy, just take him out of the fight.

And then I was in freefall.

It was clear that the stadium's artificial gravity had been turned back on and my feeble flight mutation could no longer support me. I was like a bottle rocket trying to fly against a hurricane.

Ball Boy gently landed on the ground and looked up at me in horror. I made a perfect impression of a meteor as I streaked toward the field at terminal velocity. I overshot Ball Boy and hit the turf just before the edge of the field.

Fake grass, fake soil, padding, tubing, electronics—all exploded as I dug a crater about six feet long and two feet deep. I had seen monsters, tens of thousands of pounds in weight, go thrashing down this field and not cause as much damage as my splashdown made.

I was on my back, my arms askew. My right shoulder, neck, and the right side of my face felt like they were part of someone else's body. Specifically, someone who had decided to take a belly flop into a bed of lava-coated razor blades.

The fight wasn't over, but at least half my body was voting that it should be.

High above the stands, I saw some movement It took me a moment to realize it was Staff Guy. He wasn't in the stands, of course, he was still falling. He had been going straight up this whole time.

The poor guy hit the ground seconds after I did. It was a fatal fall. Not only was there an erupting mist of blood, but I could hear bones shattering even above the stadium noise.

It had not been my intention to kill him, of course. I had only been trying to push Staff Guy out of the way and change my heading. Apparently, I had forgotten how gravity worked—my own landing was testament to that.

The Wall and Ball Boy inspected their departed friend while I took my sweet time regaining my senses. Not only was I in tremendous pain, but what was left of my brain had slammed into one side of my skull. If my body had a manufacturer's warranty, it would be forfeit.

The crowd was screaming. The announcer was yelling. I even heard Cliston, somehow, above the din. He must have his own frequency. Even more annoying, I realized that Procon Hobb had borrowed my inner voice and was trying to speak to me. Unfortunately for him, my inner voice, outer voice, and sideways voice, were all on the fritz right now. So I only heard nonsense:

"Hankle. Rob the tankle. Flank the spankle with your cankle," he said to me.

I slowly got up. It felt like I had a stroke. My whole right side was malfunctioning.

Ball Boy turned toward me, furious. He threw a ball. Another ball. Another. *Wham! Wham! Wham!* They just kept coming.

I didn't even bother to try and block them. The jolts were quaint and comforting distractions from the massive trauma the rest of me had sustained.

The Wall took off toward the sideline as I continued to get pelted. I dragged myself over to where Staff Guy landed. Ball Boy didn't let up. He was so frothing enraged that even as I stood partially paralyzed at point-blank range, he missed a number of throws.

There wasn't much left of Staff Guy. I had never seen anyone fall from that height before. I always heard that bodies stayed relatively intact. But not Staff Guy. I could see what happened. His own armor had squashed him when it compressed from the impact. That's what had caused the shower of blood. It was like stomping on a tin can that had some tomato juice in it.

"Hank!" I heard The Wall yell at me from the side of the field.

I looked over dimly. He was holding a rocket launcher of some kind. A very modern design. Small and portable. Someone must have smuggled it on to the field for him.

"No, don't," I managed to say.

"You're trying to *beg* for mercy?" The Wall asked incredulously.

I slowly looked up at the audience. My neck squealing in pain.

"Not begging. Warning," I said.

"Save it!" He replied. "I said you'd eat your words."

He put his head to the sights and readied the weapon.

"Well...Eat suck, suckface," I whispered.

There were maybe a thousand or fifteen hundred people in the stands at this point. That's fifteen hundred crooks and gangsters and smugglers. They had come to gamble.

Maybe half those people bet on me. Half on the Vicious Blood team. But *everyone* had something to lose.

Fighters weren't allowed to use guns in arena matches. That was true across the galaxy in even the lowliest gladiator battle. The rules weren't enforced by referees or adjudicators or penalty boxes. We didn't need them.

We had the crowd.

About fifteen hundred people opened fire on the field simultaneously.

They weren't *all* shooting at The Wall for his rule violation. The citizens of Belvaille were more self-interested than that. Some people shot at me. Some shot at The Wall and Ball Boy. And some people were just shooting because they didn't want to be left out.

Fifteen hundred guns is an incredible amount of firepower. Most everyone used small caliber pistols, had been drinking, were not trained marksmen, and were trying to hit targets standing in the middle of a stadium. Still, the air was *filled* with bullets. Maybe only 10% actually struck anyone. But that was 150 impacts between the three of us.

The Wall was cut down instantly, his rocket launcher never having a chance to be used. Ball Boy staggered a moment, his armor protecting him briefly, before the sheer number of rounds made their way through gaps and unprotected areas.

I was pelted in my head, my chest, my legs, my arms, and one bullet even wedged in my ear.

After a few volleys, I was the only one still standing. The guns didn't immediately fall silent, however. Some people were poor losers or they didn't know I was bulletproof. Others were having too much fun to let up so soon.

After a few minutes, the firing slowed and eventually died off. The announcer, not remotely fazed by the turn of events, enthusiastically declared me the winner. As if this had been a typical arena bout.

I got shot a few more times for good measure.

I sat down on the field. Because I was tired and severely hurt from my nosedive. Cliston came out thirty minutes later when the stands began to clear and the threat of gunfire was over.

He handed me some food. My mutation would heal my injuries, but I needed sustenance. A *lot*. The next week or so would be a blur of eating and sleeping in equal portions as my body attempted to repair the damage.

"You fought well," Cliston said.

"How much...did I make?" I asked weakly.

"1%. Minus my 15% promoter's fee, 15% to your butler. Minus cleanup costs. Vendor fees. Concession fees. Parking fees. Field maintenance. Announcer fees. Staff salaries—" he began.

"Just give me the end result," I said.

"398 credits."

I took the money offered.

"This is why I don't trust talent agent Cliston."

CHAPTER 4

It didn't take me as long to recover as I had anticipated. I didn't even have to check myself into the hospital. That said, I was bedridden for more than two weeks and ate enough food to feed a small planet. My mutation could heal nearly any injury if given enough rest, time, and calories. I have regrown teeth, cured diseases, and unbroken every bone in my body at least three times over.

The plummet I took at the stadium was tremendous. But compared to some of the mishaps I've had, it wasn't all that noteworthy.

I think I used the bathroom only once during my convalescence, my body converting every molecule of food into Hank Version 5,389—or whatever number I was currently at.

When I was finally repaired enough to ambulate and string together coherent sentences, I reluctantly got back to work. Putting on some dry, loose-fitting clothes, I headed out to the Drama Guild.

The actor Weelon Poshor had been murdered, and I needed to give his Guild an explanation. I hoped that while I was incapacitated, Cliston or MTB might have done it, but they both said they were leaving it to me. Thanks, guys.

The Guild looked like a massive upside down funnel. It was painted gleaming white and had no windows. The base was little more than a set of elevators that took you up the funnel. It was an attractive building, but a colossal waste of real estate.

A lone security guard stood outside the Guild. He was a plump Colmarian sweating in his fancy uniform. He smiled as I approached.

"Hey Hank, how's life treating you?"

"Like I slept with his wife and gave her herpes. How about you, Miles?"

"I'd complain about the weather, but what's the point? You going inside?"

"Yeah," I said.

"I need your gun."

I handed over my shotgun. He didn't bother frisking me or even asking if I had more weapons. For such an important building, it was not very well defended.

I continued to the front door but Miles stopped me.

"Hey. It's hot in there," he said.

"I'm sure. It's a nest of Damakans."

"No, it's *really* hot in there. I don't go inside unless they pay me," he said seriously.

Inside was unbelievable. I had no idea what the temperature was, but I was barely functioning. They couldn't have carpet in here because it would probably catch on fire. I could see heat waves radiating off some metal surfaces.

I plopped down in a chair and practically burned my hands on the armrests. I had brought two chillwipes with me, anticipating it would be uncomfortable, but not this bad. I put one wipe on my groin and another on top of my head. I didn't care if it looked unprofessional.

A whole cottage industry had sprung up trying to keep Colmarians cool on Belvaille. For instance, my coat, despite being an opaque navy blue, was so thin and permeable that it didn't trap air. If I sneezed, I would probably shred it into a thousand pieces. My necktie also contained a small device that blew cool air against the center of my torso.

"Who are you here to see?" the young receptionist asked me in a thick accent. She had platinum blonde hair and lips so thin it looked like her mouth had been created with a single slash of a knife.

"I don't know. I'm here to tell someone that actor Weelon Poshor was murdered," I said. Normally, that wasn't something I would tell a receptionist, but my brain was melting and I wanted to get out of there as soon as possible.

The receptionist didn't react in the slightest. She couldn't, she was a Damakan and I wasn't. Which meant I couldn't provoke an emotional response in her even if I put a gun directly to her forehead.

While I waited, I slumped in my seat with my mouth open and my eyes glazed. An older gentleman approached after some time and bent over me. Probably to see if I was still alive.

"I understand you have some information about Weelon Poshor?" he asked.

I nodded.

"I am Raym Chaddle, President of the Guild." He put his hand out to shake, but I just stared at it, not wanting to make contact with another warm body. "Please, come with me."

Raym Chaddle looked exactly like the President of a Guild should look. He wore a beautiful suit, had white, thinning hair, and strong features just starting to get droopy from age.

I reluctantly got up and plodded after him, pressing both chillwipes to my face.

We walked through the Guild, which was bustling with Damakans, and into a side conference room. I felt a blast of cold air hit me as soon as I entered.

Raym Chaddle turned on the lights and closed the door behind us.

"We keep some rooms specifically for meeting with Colmarians. I hope this is more comfortable to you," he said, and he rubbed his elbows from the "cold." It was still probably 80 degrees in here.

"Much better, thanks," I said.

"Can you explain things to me? One of our actors is missing. I've heard rumors that he was identified at the morgue, but I can't confirm it."

"Yeah. I was working as Weelon Poshor's bodyguard. I found him dead about two weeks ago. Shot and stabbed. I notified the police."

"Two weeks? Why are you just informing us now?"

"I was very sick."

"This is frightening news. A Damakan has never been murdered in this city. You could have at least sent a tele warning us."

"I was unconscious."

"Were you injured protecting Weelon Poshor?"

"No. Belvaille is a dangerous space station," I said, not elaborating.

"Indeed. Did Mr. Poshor hire you?"

"No, the Artistry Agency. Cliston."

Raym Chaddle began pacing around, deep in thought. He was probably moving to try and stay warm.

"I was afraid this was going to happen sooner or later. We learned all about Colmarian folktales before our people joined the PCC. You have an incredibly violent history. Damakans are not capable of defending ourselves from your kind," he pleaded. "My entire life on our home planet I had never heard of a murder. In my handful of years on Belvaille, there have been dozens."

"A lot more than dozens. I know this must be difficult for you. Cliston said he was working to find you a replacement actor," I said.

"That's imperative. The show will lose ratings if we go on hiatus. I'm sorry, I didn't catch your name."

"Hank," I said.

"Hank? Are you named after *the* Hank?"

"After him? No. I wasn't named after anyone. But I'm sure there are other Hanks in the galaxy," I said.

"Hank the Fat Mutant of Belvaille?" he clarified.

"Well...I'm not sure I would approve of that description. But I am a mutant. And I'm on Belvaille."

"You fought Thad Elon! You started the Colmarian Civil War! You fought the Dredel Led and Boranjame and Therezian giants!"

"I sort of did those things. Where did you hear that?"

"I've read about you. All Damakans have. You're part of the Colmarian legends. You're a mass murderer! Are you going to kill me? Or my office? Are you going to eat me?"

"What? No. It's not...that doesn't happen. I mean, I wouldn't wait in your lobby for hours and then kill you," I said, confused. "I don't even know you."

"Oh. Forgive me. Violence is very foreign to us. It makes for great movies, but we don't understand it very well."

"Yeah, I know. I'm dating a Damakan and she tells me the same," I said.

"You're *dating* a Damakan? You? A Colmarian?"

"Uh, yeah. Why?" Not many people knew I was an Ontakian. I tried to keep it secret.

"We've written some famous tragic scenes with that same plotline: Damakan and alien love affair," he said.

"Tragedy, huh?"

"I doubt even the Romance Guild could create a happy ending to such a story."

"Why is that?" I asked, a bit offended.

"You have to understand what we are." Raym Chaddle swept his arms around and took two quick hops, as if he were suddenly on a stage. "We are not a young race. But we only discovered the wider galaxy a short while ago. We did not spend our time building spaceships or learning advanced mathematics. We evolved as performers."

This wasn't a conversation, it was a dramatization. I stood motionless, taking in the show.

"You Colmarians experience the emotions that are already *inside* you. You can sit in a corner all alone and weep at the loneliness of your corner. But we Damakans feel emotions because another Damakan *helped* us to feel them. Our society is an audience and we are all players."

He stepped close and took hold of my lower jaw with his fingertips.

"So you see, a Damakan who is paired with a foreigner can never experience her full emotions. It would be as if she were living in a frozen world, devoid of colors and sensations."

My heart sank.

"That's not true," I blurted. "We're happy."

"I'm sure *you* are," he said matter-of-factly. "Colmarian emotions bubble and flow with even the gentlest of Damakan tugs. But you cannot provide the same to your lover."

I thought of Laesa. Happy Laesa. Laughing. Joking. Fun. But I wasn't here for relationship advice.

"I'm not here for relationship advice," I said.

* 33 *

"No. What can be done to ensure the rest of our Guild members' safety?" Raym Chaddle asked, standing proper and dignified again.

"You can start by having more than one security guard outside."

"Are you available for hire? Your murderous, eating talents would lend themselves to such a role, correct?" he asked.

I didn't relish the idea of standing outside all day in a silly uniform. At least as a bodyguard I got to move around and talk to people. The reason there were so many "inside jobs" involving security guards wasn't just because security was underpaid, it was because they were bored and had nothing better to do than daydream about ripping off what they were guarding.

"I get my assignments through Cliston," I replied diplomatically.

"Cliston. I need to contact him and see how far he's gotten on new actors. We can't afford to let Open Heart's ratings slip just because we lost Weelon Poshor."

"Cliston only learned about it a short while ago," I said.

"How did he find out before me?"

"Cliston is also my butler," I said.

Raym Chaddle's brow furrowed and he contemplated that news.

"I see. I see. He is forced to be your butler because Hank the Fat Mutant of Belvaille would otherwise murder him?"

"What? No. He's a Dredel Led."

"Yes. A mechanical being. So he is incapable of being murdered?"

I didn't feel like explaining the galaxy to him. But maybe I could get Laesa a job.

"You know, the Damakan I'm dating, my fiancée, is a great actor. Maybe you could use her on the show."

"Is she a member of the Drama Guild?" he asked.

"I don't think so."

"I'm afraid we can only put on productions using our own members. That is strict policy for all the Guilds."

Raym Chaddle opened the door to the conference room and I was assaulted by the heat.

"I want to thank you for coming and bringing this to our attention," he said. His eyes were distant, his thoughts already on other Guild issues.

"Sure. The police will be in contact if they get any suspects or leads in the case," I said.

"This is my first exposure to such things. What would you say the chances are of the police getting any such suspects?" he asked.

"On Belvaille? Almost zero." I looked at my tele. "There's probably been two more murders in the city just in the time we've been talking."

"It is truly frightening what a savage empire this is," he said, though he didn't look frightened.

"Is it true I'm in your history books?" I asked.

"Not *our* history. It was provided by the PCC. It's your history."

"Am I really called Hank the Fat Mutant of Belvaille?"

"That was your official name. The individual characters would often insult you," he said. "It is truly an honor to meet you and not die at your hands."

CHAPTER 5

Raym Chaddle was right about one thing. I *was* happy. I was unabashedly joyous and I had my Laesa to thank for it.

The following afternoon I went to visit her at work.

She was doing a small play in a diner on the Westside. Just about every restaurant, bar, and store had performances now because of the influx of Damakans. They were cheap entertainment and far better than what Belvaille was used to.

"Hi, Hank," the restaurant hostess said to me in a sour voice.

They were kind of tired of seeing me, I think. At first I hadn't really understood the concept of lunch theater and I had bullied everyone into being quiet while the actors performed. But the players themselves had let me know it was supposed to be a kind of pleasant background noise that you could take or leave while you ate.

I sat in my usual booth near the front and ordered a beer and some food. There were only four actors on the tiny stage. They took turns handling sound effects and switching into different characters. The story was about a crooked small-town politician who witnessed a miracle and then tried to help everyone.

Laesa was up there performing and I leaned over to the table next to me, interrupting a couple in their conversation.

"That's my girl," I said proudly.

The couple took a look at me and felt it prudent to offer congratulations.

Laesa was totally different from anyone I had ever been romantically involved with. There weren't many types of people to date on Belvaille. I had gone out with a lot of cocktail waitresses, exotic dancers, smugglers, strippers, and a few assassins. But Laesa was the first person who actually taught me new things on a daily basis.

She could *read* people. In my business, knowing what someone was thinking was often a matter of life or death—or at least wealth and poverty. She gave me pointers. How to find the clues in their reactions, their mannerisms, their inflections. To shut my yapper for a minute and observe.

A small group entered the diner and was standing and talking by the front table. They were blocking my view of the stage.

"Hey, sit down before I drag you outside and break your legs," I called out. "Please," I added, as the hostess frowned.

The people moved immediately. I wasn't *really* going to hurt them, but a simple threat saved a whole lot of unnecessary conversation.

I leaned over to the table next to me again.

"Watch how he reaches for the glass of water," I whispered excitedly.

The actor pantomimed being in an office and pouring himself water. I must have seen him do that a dozen times but every time he did, I had to drink something. It was so convincing, so authentic, it made me thirsty.

I took a swig of beer.

The Damakan actors were not only performing for the audience, us unsophisticated Colmarians, they were acting for each other—helping one another *feel* emotions. Something they had difficulty with on their own. This wasn't merely amusement, it was part of their normal, biological interactions.

When the show was over, I stood up and applauded with vigor. No one else in the diner gave more than a casual glance.

"Great work, everyone," I said, walking over as they packed up. "Police Officer #2, excellent as always."

Laesa wrapped me in a hug and planted a kiss on my lips.

"Hey, doll," I said.

Laesa had a young face. A fresh face. She had more dimples than a tin can put in a clothes dryer. Her skin was pale. She had wide, brown eyes, baby-thin brown hair that was often tangled or blown into a maelstrom, and a perfect smile that almost never went away. She was what they called an ingénue. When she was a kid, she could probably have coerced you into buying so many cookies or lemonade that you'd go bankrupt.

My face was old. Not quite ancient, but it had scars and bumps and cracks and crevasses and warts and moles and tags and wrinkles and everything skin had in its huge assortment of flaws. I wasn't just *physically* ugly. I had seen, and created, enough misery over the centuries that I half believed it was the normal state of things. I wasn't totally a cynic. I was wise—in a cynical sort of way.

Laesa didn't think like me. She was too young. She was knee deep in optimism and passed it around for free. I was more than happy to accept.

"Hank," she said. "You can't threaten the audience. It's bad for the restaurant."

"I said please."

"Did you notice how I flubbed my lines in the second act?"

"No. But you dropped your jacket. That was new."

"It slipped when he handed it to me. He's such a pro that he went with it and made up that joke on the spot. Goodnight, Trevis," Laesa said to one of the other actors, but he didn't hear her.

"Your speech sounded great," I said.

"I'm still working on it. Colmarian isn't a difficult language, but the pronunciations can be tricky," she said.

I shook my head in wonderment.

"It's so crazy that every Damakan speaks Colmarian as a second language. It's been the standard galactic tongue for, I don't know, 100,000 years."

"We're new to this party." She smiled. "Our language doesn't even have a name, because we never knew there were other languages. Let alone other species."

"I was thinking, maybe your play could have a fight scene. After the grandmother comes back home. It would be exciting," I said.

Laesa laughed. She had a jolly laugh. The kind you could hear from across the street and grow jealous at not knowing what was so funny.

"Hank, this is a restaurant. Why do you think the play has us eating and drinking so many times? We're trying to get the audience to buy food. We don't want to incite a riot. People might clobber the waiters. Pow!" She said, flexing her bicep.

"Just an idea. I really wish Cliston would come to see you."

"Oh, no, don't have him come here. He should see my other play. This is just lunch theater. I'd be embarrassed if he saw this."

We walked out of the diner.

"Why? You're really good."

"No, I'm not. I only have small roles. And my performance has to compete with a lot of belching and clinking silverware from the audience."

"I didn't hear anything."

"How's work?" she asked, changing the subject.

"Bad. I had to talk to the Guild about their dead actor today."

"Did you ever figure out who did it?"

"No. I doubt we'll ever know. Maybe some kidnapping that didn't pan out. The police will have their forensics check."

"What do you mean by forensics?"

"Nothing. It's just a figure of speech. The Guild president wasn't happy."

"You personally spoke with him?" she asked, amazed. "What was he like?"

"That building has to be the hottest place I've ever been in my life. I could barely move. I asked if he could use you as a replacement."

"Me? A replacement what?"

"Actor. For Weelon Poshor who was killed while I was asleep—but seriously, don't tell anyone that."

"Hank, Damakans don't sit around talking about murders and bodyguards. The city I grew up in went for generations without anyone ever *fighting*. We only heard of those things because of the PCC."

"Because of our folk stuff?" I asked.

"Your fiction. Much more exciting than native Damakan drama. And it's a lot of fun acting in it," she said.

"Did you read about me?"

"You? When?"

"When you were learning about Colmarians. Learning our language. Was there a character based on me?"

Laesa laughed.

"Hank, why would it be about you? This was official Post-Colmarian Confederation Colmarian Confederation orientation material."

"There wasn't a guy named Hank of Belvaille?" I asked.

Laesa was packing up her things and removing her stage make-up. She paused and looked up at me curiously.

"There was a character who was in a number of stories I read. But he was called Hank the Fat Mutant of Belvaille."

"That's me," I sighed.

"No, Hank. This character was really different. He was incredibly violent. He caused a whole civil war. And he was fat. It's right there in his name."

"That's me, Laesa. I'm not exactly thin—I wouldn't go so far as to say I was fat. How many Hanks on Belvaille did you think there were?"

"I figured it was a common name. I didn't know it was *this* space station. That's really you? Wow! I...I never imagined I'd meet people from those stories. We thought it was mythology. Did you really do all those things?"

"I don't know. Probably not. They exaggerate," I said.

"Is there really a Thad Elon?"

"Oh, yeah. I fought him a few times. He's a jerk."

Laesa's jaw dropped.

"Did you really *eat* a Therezian?" she asked.

"That's absurd. They're too big. And their skin is too hard."

"You didn't crash a battleship into Belvaille?"

"No. It was a dreadnaught. And I didn't *crash* it. I wasn't even piloting it. Not really," I said. I could see from Laesa's dazed look that I needed to move on. "So why can't you work on Weelon Poshor's show?"

She shook her head at the abrupt change. Her thin hair looked like a mist around her.

"I would need to get sponsored by the Guild first. Which means I need a talent agent. Which means I need to get some real gigs instead of acting for people with indigestion."

"All you need is a little luck. Which is what I need," I said.

"You got me," she said, planting a kiss on my mouth, which I gladly returned.

"Everyone needs luck," I said.

"Did you kill a Boranjame?"

"How would I do that? They're practically gods. Though I kind of *got* one killed. Not on purpose."

"Are you famous, Hank? Or is it infamous? I don't know the right word."

"Not really. The only people who know me are dead. They should have given your people history books. Educational stories."

"It *was* educational. You have no idea."

"Yeah, but I'm not fat. Not that fat," I sulked.

We got into my beat-up car and I pulled away. I wasn't a very good driver, which accounted for all the dents and dings in my vehicle, but my butler was too busy to chauffeur me around.

"I need to score a quick job. I'm months behind on my rent," I said.

"Can you talk to your landlord?"

"I'm already on Cliston's bad side."

"Cliston owns City Hall? Is there anything he doesn't do?" Laesa asked, surprised.

"He leases a bunch of floors and I rent from him. But yeah, he does a lot. Did you read about him? He's way older than me."

"I don't think so. Most of the Dredel Led were bad guys," she said.

"From the sounds of it, I was a bad guy."

"But they're really bad. Like monsters," she said.

"We've been at war with them off and on for thousands of years."

"War. It's such a strange concept," Laesa said, confused. "Pedestrian!" she said suddenly, bracing her arm against the dashboard.

I swerved. I was as lazy driving as I was at anything else, so I tended to do things like cut corners and drive on the sidewalk. Belvaille was practically a lawless city, but for some reason everyone was uptight about traffic regulations.

"What will you do for your next job?" Laesa asked, her voice still elevated from our near miss.

"Hopefully Cliston will come through. I fought at the Cheat Hall for him, but he said he doesn't have anything yet. I think he might be mad I let his client die."

"Do a character study on the actor who died," Laesa said.

"Why?"

"To try and learn why he was killed."

"I didn't know him that well."

"You know *nothing* about him?" she coaxed.

"He always wanted the temperature exactly 101."

"Good. So what does that mean?"

"He was a Damakan."

"But what else?"

"I don't know. Is it a number thing?"

"Maybe he was picky? A little bossy?"

"Yeah, I guess he was kind of bossy."

"And what happens to picky, bossy Damakan actors?"

"They end up stabbed and shot?"

"They make enemies?" Laesa prompted. "Who would want him dead? Come on, think."

"An actor!" I said, suddenly enlightened.

"An actor? Why would you think that?"

"Because, with Weelon Poshor dead, another actor could take his place!"

"Take his place?"

"Sure. Cliston and Raym Chaddle were talking about finding a replacement on the show."

"But how could any actor possibly know *they* would be chosen as a replacement?" Laesa asked, puzzled.

"Because they looked like Weelon Poshor. Maybe it was one of the actors who missed out on the role."

"No, Hank. They don't mean they are going to find someone else to play Cousin Randolph. They will retire that character. They simply want enough main characters to write episodes about. That's all."

"Oh. So they could be looking for any actor?"

"Sure. Or two actors. But they would have to be part of the Drama Guild because the show is dramatic."

"Then I don't know," I said. "But I got into working for the dramatic industry because it was supposed to be easy. If there's going to be shootings and stabbings, I might as well go back to working for criminals."

CHAPTER 6

"I need a job," I said to the crime boss Ulteem. He had once been an important employer, but fortunes come and go. And his had mostly gone.

I didn't feel like waiting for Cliston's benediction. Besides, if I kept relying on him for everything, pretty soon I was going to end up as *his* butler.

Ulteem's dance club looked like it had been decorated by an interior designer who was color blind and hated everyone who wasn't. I found myself squinting to try and block out the retina assault

Ulteem wore a white toga. It looked as if he just stepped out of bed and dragged his sheets with him. His most obvious feature, though, was that he didn't have a head. Normally he wore a prosthetic head on top of his shoulders, but he either lost them or got tired of making other people comfortable. All he had now was a yellow rubber ball sitting where his skull should be. It didn't have features drawn on it. It was simply a ball that looked in danger of being kicked by children at any moment.

"I thought you were working in the dramatic industry," Ulteem shouted to me over the music.

"I was doing security for them. But not right now."

"Didn't some guy you were working for get murdered?" he asked.

"Not that I'm aware of," I lied, not wanting to advertise my failures.

"Well, you're just in time. Come to my office. I'm putting something together right now."

We walked down a dimly lit hallway and I absently wondered how Ulteem could see without a head. But then he turned a few steps early and ran into the wall, cursing.

In the back room, two men were waiting.

One man had four eyes situated at the corners of his face in a diamond pattern. His skull was decorated with little wisps of red hair sticking up like a baby doll's.

The other man was thin and wiry, and definitely had a fear of grooming. He was unshaven, his clothes were tatty, and I think he had mustard on his nose.

"Hank, this is Borgin Two-Eyes and that's Perkle Dolabin. Guys, this is Hank," Ulteem said.

The two men tilted their heads at me which was the universal greeting among unskilled thugs such as myself.

"Hank, huh? I heard you were dating a Damakan," Perkle Dolabin said with a curled-lip sneer, which showed off his decaying teeth.

"That so? I heard if I punched you in the face, you'd look like one of those serving dishes they put finger sandwiches on," I replied.

"I could go for some sandwiches. Is there any food here?" Borgin Two-Eyes asked.

"This ain't a damn cafeteria. Eat on your own time," Ulteem barked.

Perkle was staring me down and I was staring back. There was a whole secret language among criminals that was developed over countless millennia. Every move and countermove was an attempt to determine who could urinate the farthest.

Gang boss Ulteem dropped into a little chair at the back of the room and his rubber ball head wobbled and fell off his body.

"Dammit," Ulteem said. He put out his arms and tried to connect with the ball, but it rolled out of his way. It was one of the oddest things I've ever seen, and I've had the misfortune of watching interspecies pornography.

The rubber ball came to a rest by Two-Eyes and he looked at us with his four eyes as if to ask whether he should pick it up. There was no established social protocol for picking up your boss's head.

"Forget it," Ulteem said, and he sat back down. "So I got a job for you all. There is a movie set in the northeast. I want you to go there and steal some lights."

"Lights?" I asked.

"Yeah, lights. You know, the things that make light," he snapped.

"What do they use the lights for?" Perkle asked.

"For light! They're movie lights," Ulteem yelled.

"I don't know anything about movie lights," Two-Eyes said.

"What is this, a moron convention? You don't have to know anything about them. You have to steal them," he said.

"Are they valuable?" I asked.

"They're insured," Ulteem said.

Us thugs all exchanged glances. None of us wanted to ask what that meant and annoy Ulteem further. But he apparently saw our reactions.

"The Guilds hire insurance companies to cover their property. In case of fire or accident or in this case, theft. You steal the lights and I'll sell them back to the insurance company at a discount," he said.

"How much does the job pay?" I asked.

"Hank gets 5,000 and you two get 4,000," Ulteem said.

"Why does he get five?" Perkle asked angrily. "You paying by the pound?"

That was a mistake. You negotiated with your hired muscle in private. That way no one got sore. Now the guys making less had to step up or they'd lose face. I sighed with exasperation. It would take hours to settle this.

"I say he gets five and if you don't like it you can go panhandle on a street corner," Ulteem shouted.

Everyone was quiet. I guess it wouldn't take hours after all.

"Which one of you is going to drive?" Ulteem asked.

"I can drive," I volunteered.

"I've seen you drive, Hank. You all won't make it there in one piece. Can anyone else drive?"

"My car is in the shop," Perkle said.

"They won't give me a driver's license because of these," Two-Eyes said, pointing to his eyes.

"What's a driver's license?" I asked.

"You're kidding. From the Motor Vehicle Administration," Perkle said.

"Never heard of it," I said, shrugging. "I've run into plenty of cars."

"It's not a damn hunting license," Perkle sputtered, looking around for some confirmation. But no one cared.

"Okay. Hank, you drive. Here are the directions," Ulteem said, and he passed me a message by tele. "I'm told they put up a fence at night."

"Around the lights?" I asked.

"Yes! The lights! Why would you care if they put a fence around their toilets?" he asked.

"How do we get in?" Perkle asked.

"Cut the fence. Or jump over it. Or tunnel under it. I don't care," Ulteem said.

"You guys got any wire cutters?" Perkle asked us.

"No," we both replied.

Ulteem stood up from his chair, stomped across the room, picked up his yellow ball, and stuffed it inside the neck of his shirt angrily.

"You all are worthless. I'll get you some damn wire cutters."

"Are there any guards at the site? I used to work security on productions," I said.

"Did it pay?" Two-Eyes asked me.

"Yeah. It's a sweet gig if you can get it. And they usually leave out the craft services tables so you can eat the leftovers."

"Good food?" Perkle asked.

"Not bad. But Damakans have strange diets. Lots of fruit."

"Gross," Two-Eyes said.

"If there's security, I'm expecting you three robbers to handle it," Ulteem interrupted.

"We should wear masks," I said.

"Why? You afraid you'll ruin your movie career?" Perkle taunted.

"Yes. And you should be worried too. Won't be able to work security for the Guilds if they know we robbed them," I said.

"I don't have a mask," Two-Eyes said.

"We'll stop by my place. I can get some stockings," I said, thinking that Laesa had left a box of pantyhose.

"Great. Excellent. Can this brain trust get a move on? They begin production in the morning, which is fast approaching," Ulteem said.

I got the pantyhose from my place and we resumed driving across the city. There wasn't much traffic at this time of night. Belvaille was normally quite easy to navigate. It was a square space station, fifteen miles on each side. You couldn't get too lost, because cars couldn't drive into outer space.

Even though Belvaille was a city that didn't orbit a star, the latticework lights went dim at night. We had sixteen hours of daylight and then, poof, instant darkness, no setting sun or gradual transition. It could be quite jarring if you weren't ready for it. The dimmest the lights went was about 5% power, so you could still get around without breaking your neck.

"Thad Elon's Nutsack," Perkle swore at me from the passenger seat of my car. "Watch the curb!"

"Hey, Borgin. Why do they call you Two-Eyes? You have four eyes, right?" I asked. I couldn't figure that out.

"Yeah. But I got *two* more eyes than usual," he said.

We parked a few blocks away from the movie set and put on our stockings. Our features smushed all around. But Borgin still had four eyes so it wasn't much of a disguise for him.

Exiting the car, we snuck over to the streets where they would be filming. We could see all the equipment set up in the distance.

"That's a big fence," Perkle said.

It was. I hadn't been worried about the idea of a fence, my weight being sufficient to push past any chain links, but this was a heavy-duty job suitable for riot control or stopping runaway cars. We hurried over to the edge of the fence and Two-Eyes took out the wire cutters and began to work.

"Ai!" he screamed. "It's electric." He hopped around and shook his hands furiously.

"Wrap the handles in something," I said.

"You got some rubber underwear we can borrow?" Perkle sneered. He was getting on my nerves.

I took off my jacket. It was synth, so it would help.

Two-Eyes gingerly started cutting again. The fence was quite thick and it was slow going. When he had finally created a hole at the bottom, the guys went prone and carefully climbed under.

It was my turn and I was having problems.

"Hurry up," Perkle whispered urgently.

"I'm stuck," I said.

"Come on," Two-Eyes called, as if saying that would magically free me.

"You cut the hole too small," I said.

"You're too fat," Perkle hissed.

I twisted around under the fence, not caring if I touched the metal. My thick skin could protect me from bullets, so I wasn't tremendously concerned about a little electricity. But then my stocking mask burst into flames.

"Crap!" I yelled.

The guys began slapping at my face. They were more concerned about the sudden bright light than the fact I was burning. Someone threw my jacket over my head and that smothered the flames. Then they both hauled on my arms and helped drag me from under the fence.

I stood up, my face sooty and hair smoldering.

"Let's go," I said, trying to recover my dignity.

There were piles of movie equipment stacked everywhere, and more cables than you could possibly imagine. It was like the city's whole electrical grid was flowing through here.

"Are those it?" Two-Eyes asked, pointing.

They were lights all right. But they were huge. There was a section of the street with dozens of them. They had blinders and baffles and rested on ten-foot poles with tripods.

We stared up at them.

"Those aren't going to fit in my car," I said.

"Your car? How are we even going to get them past the fence?" Perkle asked.

"Maybe they disassemble," Two-Eyes said. He began monkeying around with one of the lights. The pole suddenly collapsed and the whole thing fell over with a tremendous crash. You could have probably heard the noise three light-years away.

We froze.

A few moments later, a flashlight was shined on us. We all instinctively put up our hands.

"Hank?" an old man's voice asked. I was the only one not wearing a stocking after it caught on fire.

The security guard walked cautiously closer. It was obvious we had woken him up. His clothes were wrinkled, his hat was on crooked, and his eyes looked bleary.

"Hi, Micka," I said.

Micka was an old-timer. Had a pot belly and white hair. He was a retiree and now did odd jobs for money to gamble away on the weekends. I had worked with him a few times.

"What are you doing here?" he asked.

I glanced at my compatriots, who looked like they had been *born* guilty, the pantyhose on their faces not exactly helping.

"Well, we're here to steal some lights," I said. I put my hands down, but Two-Eyes and Perkle kept theirs raised.

"Lights? Why?" Micka asked.

"Insurance, I guess," I said.

"The lights aren't insured," Micka said, confused.

"How do you know?" Perkle asked, putting down his hands.

"Because they told me. Only things insured are the generators and the fence."

"Are those the lights?" I asked.

"Yeah. That thing you pushed over is one," Micka said.

"We didn't push it over, it fell," Two-Eyes replied. He finally put his hands down.

"It fell all by itself, did it?" Micka asked.

"Where are the generators?" Perkle asked.

"I think you all should be leaving," Micka replied cautiously.

"Take out your guns," Perkle whispered to us. "I don't have one."

"I don't have one either," Two-Eyes whispered back.

"Oh, come on," I said. I removed my sawed-off double-barreled shotgun from its holster under my left arm.

Micka dropped his flashlight and raised his arms so straight you'd think he was about to fly away. I was struck by how bad my night vision was after having a light shined in my eyes.

"Grab the flashlight," I said.

Two-Eyes picked it up.

"Now where are the generators?" Perkle repeated.

"Over there," Micka said, pointing his fingers without lowering his arms.

"Show us," Perkle said.

A minute later, we stood quietly around two brand-new generators. Each had a pair of car tires on them and hitches for transport. They were massive. Like perfectly rectangular automobiles.

"Well?" Perkle asked me.

"My car doesn't have a winch or hook to tow that," I said. "Nothing else is insured?"

"No. Like I said, just the fence and those generators," Micka replied.

The guys started fumbling with one of the generators. Perkle removed the blocks from the tires and Two-Eyes lifted the trailer arm. He could roll the generator, but just barely.

While I kept Micka covered with my shotgun, I figured I would do a character study on the security guard using the skills Laesa had taught me.

Even with me pointing a gun at him, his eyes were friendly. He wasn't concerned about protecting this stuff. It's not like it was his. He seemed to think we were rash and foolish young men. He was concerned. Concerned for *us*. Micka was like a kindly grandfather.

"Hank?" Micka said.

"Yeah?"

"You going to shoot me?" he asked quietly.

I laughed at the concept of blasting kindly old Micka.

"No, don't sweat it, pal," I replied.

"Then screw this," he yelled.

Micka put down his arms, turned, and sprinted away, moving far faster than his age would have indicated possible. We three robbers watched him go until his footsteps echoed from the darkness.

I guessed I needed to work on my character-study abilities.

"Why did you say you weren't going to shoot him?" Perkle demanded.

"If I said I was, you think he would have *not* run away?" I replied.

"Hank, help me out," Two-Eyes said.

I pushed Two-Eyes out of the way and grabbed hold of the trailer arm. This was practically what I was designed to do. I was all low-end torque. I couldn't do a cartwheel. I couldn't touch my toes—or even see them. But I could push things. If there was ever a pushing-things competition, I would be the galaxy champ.

Two-Eyes walked ahead of me with the flashlight. Perkle was behind, covering us with my shotgun. I was wheezing along trying not to break my back while I pretended to be a tractor.

We came back to the electric fence and stopped cold.

"Can you ram it through?" Perkle asked me.

"No. Look at that fence," I said.

"Yeah. No wonder they insured it," he replied.

Two-Eyes shined the light to the side.

"There's the gate," he said.

I pivoted the generator and rolled it to the gate. It was secured with a thick chain, too beefy for the wire cutters.

"Shoot the lock," I said to Perkle.

Perkle hesitated for a moment, then raised the shotgun and fired. The wiry man was almost knocked down from the recoil. But he must have been standing twenty feet away from the fence. Nothing happened of course, except a lot of noise.

"That's a sawed-off shotgun, not a sniper rifle. You have to put the barrel right up next to the lock. You only have one shot left," I said.

"What kind of stupid gun is this?" he asked.

"At least he *has* a gun," Two-Eyes said.

"You don't have a gun either," Perkle replied.

"I was told it was a burglary, not a military assault. If I want to join the Navy, I'll join the Navy," he said.

"Shoot again. Closer," I said.

Perkle walked so close to the gate that sparks leapt between the barrel of the gun and the electric fence. They sure were pumping a lot of juice through that gate.

Boom! The shotgun fired.

"Dammit!" Perkle cursed, dropping my gun and hopping around in pain. Some shrapnel must have hit him. But the chain was broken and the gate unlocked.

I pushed the generator against the fence and it scraped open. As I walked past, I picked up the gun and put it back in my holster.

"Take off those stockings and give me a hand," I said.

When we reached my car, we were struck by the impossibility of it all. The generator was about half the size of my car.

"Where the hell are we going to put that? It's not like it's going to fit in the back seat," Perkle said.

"Can you drive?" I asked him.

The towing arm of the generator was shaped like a wishbone. I put the narrow end up on the rear bumper. I popped the trunk, and then I climbed in back. I had special suspension on my car on account of my weight, but even still, the fenders were pressed against the tires.

I sat in the trunk and dangled my legs out. My calves hooked inside the wishbone of the towing arm.

"Can you hold that?" Two-Eyes asked skeptically.

"Just keep it under five miles an hour," I said.

"It will take us forever to get across town," Perkle complained, as if he was an important business executive instead of a meathead who just stole a generator after shooting himself in the hand.

"It's either that or we drag it. I'm not leaving here with nothing. Ulteem won't pay us," I said.

The guys got in the car and started it up. Perkle put it in gear and almost took off my legs as he pulled away. I banged on the open trunk to let him know he was going too fast.

After a while, it wasn't so bad. At stops, I let the car's bumper slow down the generator. It was only speeding up that was painful. Once we were rolling, it wasn't difficult to hold at all. The generator coasted on its wheels just fine.

But then I looked up and noticed flashing lights behind us. Couldn't be cops. MTB wasn't stupid enough to advertise he was police by displaying colored lights.

There were three private security vehicles gaining on us.

"Rental cops. They won't do anything," I said to the generator, since no one else could hear me.

Gunfire erupted from the cars.

Perkle stepped on the gas, my legs stretched out, and I felt the generator slipping. I couldn't figure out why the security guards were shooting. That was a lousy way to protect your property. But as their cars pulled up closer, I noticed they were firing their weapons into the air. As if they believed loud noises were going to frighten us into giving back their generator.

Perkle was clearly a frustrated race car driver, because he kept speeding up and weaving back and forth in the road. I was now halfway out of the trunk and only my stubbornness and fat ankles were keeping the generator from flying away. I screamed as loud as I could for Perkle to slow down.

My car made a razor-sharp turn up a side street and that was it.

I slid along the trunk and then flipped out the back. It happened almost leisurely. A scoot. A plop. And a roll.

I tumbled on the street and splatted against the door of a dry cleaners. I watched the generator sail past in a straight line and the pursuing security cars all make the turn and continue chasing my car.

My hands and knees and face were scraped up and most of my clothes had been road-burned away. The metal streets on Belvaille were sprayed with a tacky, rubberized substance to help traction. The road had gripped my clothes and erased them like turpentine on cheap spray paint. One of my shoes was also missing.

The generator had coasted a hundred feet away and come to a pleasant stop. I blinked in confusion. I had just fallen out of a moving car and I was slightly disoriented.

I peeked through the window of the dry cleaners to check if there were any clothes that fit me but it was too dark to tell. My measurements weren't exactly typical anyway.

I kicked off my other shoe and walked to the generator. I stood around for about ten minutes in my underwear, waiting for...something. Either the security guards to return, or the guys with my car. But the street was silent.

I lifted the towing arm of the generator and began pushing.

CHAPTER 7

"Here's next month's rent and all the money I owe you," I said proudly, slapping the cash down on Cliston's desk like I was an influential man of means.

Ulteem had given me half of what he received from the insurance company. It was a painless, fifteen-minute transaction after I had pushed the generator across the city for five hours. The same security guards who chased us came and towed the generator away. Just to reinforce how wrong my character profile was, old Micka spat in my face as they were leaving.

Two-Eyes and Perkle never showed up so they didn't get paid. That could become bad blood later, but I didn't care because they still had my car.

Cliston nodded absently at the money, but otherwise ignored me and kept talking on his tele.

I fidgeted.

"So that's *this* month's rent, next month's, and what I owed you," I repeated.

Cliston covered up the tele.

"Hank, this is an important call. I'll speak with you another time," he said.

I had made a big show of giving Cliston all the money I possessed. It was a significant gesture to me and I assumed it would be significant to him. But compared to what Cliston made as a talent agent, my rent payment was likely inconsequential.

Downstairs in my apartment, I moped around feeling sorry for myself. Being in debt made me very uneasy. It was a constant shadow that sapped the joy out of whatever I did. I thought erasing my debt to Cliston would be a great relief. But being broke felt pretty much the same.

At this point, I'd been alive for hundreds of years and had positively nothing to show for it in terms of assets. I was living paycheck to paycheck.

I *did* own a spaceship. It was an old Colmarian Navy corvette. But now that Belvaille was thriving again, I didn't need a spaceship. What's worse, I wasn't sure I could even sell it. The ship was complicated, cramped, and had almost no cargo room. No one in this System would ever buy it—except maybe the PCC Navy. But I was a fugitive from justice according to the Navy, so dropping by and seeing if they wanted to purchase my junk seemed like a bad move.

I also owned a broken Rettosian pistol. The pistol used to have artificial intelligence. It could talk. It could shoot invisible energy and never missed. But it didn't work anymore and it looked like a toy. Explaining to people it *used* to be a self-aware ray gun made me sound like a feeble con man.

I really had nothing. My list of experiences was quite impressive, but that's not the same as having bankable assets. I should get royalties for the PCC educating the Damakans about Hank the Fat Mutant of Belvaille. But I wasn't sure I wanted to claim that title and how does one go about getting royalties for unflattering folktales?

I needed a job. I went outside to pound the pavement and drum up some work. I hadn't gone five blocks when I saw someone loading empty plastic bottles into the back of his truck.

"Paggo-Nosa?" I asked.

The man in question turned around.

"Hank. What do you know?"

"A little less every day—I think I have slow-onset dementia. What are you doing?"

"Working."

"Hauling garbage?" I asked uncertainly.

"I go to all the bars and restaurants and collect for recycling," he said.

Theoretically, I knew that the space station took care of our trash. I mean, someone did. It didn't just magically disappear. But I hadn't really thought about the specifics.

"You're not gambling anymore?" I asked. Paggo-Nosa used to be a stylish regular in the casinos.

"Nah. Get a knife in the guts doing that. Too risky."

Paggo-Nosa's clothes were stained, his hair was disheveled. His truck was a mess. I think he noticed my expression as I scrutinized his new profession.

"Feel this: I cleared ten grand last week. Almost the same the week before."

"Credits?" I asked, shocked. I wondered if he was speaking in some strange unit of measurement. Like ten thousand used napkins. I couldn't believe he was pulling in that kind of scratch moving trash.

"City needs this hauled. Can't throw it out the window. Got to keep the space lanes clear."

"And all you need is a truck?" I asked. "I'm looking for a new career."

Paggo-Nosa just realized he had instructed a desperate and destitute person how to compete in the recycling business and he quickly sought to correct his mistake.

"Feel it: it's all about relationships and seniority. I've been doing this a while now. Aren't you working on the Skim?" he asked nervously.

The Skim was Belvaille's main source of revenue. Because this System had a huge number of Portals, lots of cargo shipped through here. There was a massive criminal enterprise built around taking a few percent off each transport and selling it on the side.

"I can't. I'm a wanted felon."

"Oh."

"Yeah. The whole point of the Skim is to sneak past the Navy regulations. Everyone is afraid I'll attract too much attention. Like there's an army out hunting for me," I said, irritated.

"If you need work, my cousin can help. He wants people like you," Paggo-Nosa suggested.

Since I lost my car, I had to hire a cab. I relied on my usual driver, Zzzho.

Zzzho was a Keilvin Kamigan, a gaseous lifeform. He looked like a reddish cloud punctuated with little lightning bolts. He drove his vehicle by plugging directly into the electronics. Zzzho was also the pilot for my spaceship, the Suckface. But I wasn't doing a lot of spaceship flying nowadays, so Zzzho bought himself a cab to make some extra money. Though what Zzzho needed with money was anyone's guess. He didn't sleep, didn't live anywhere, and he "ate" radiation. My guess is was he simply enjoyed talking to people. He didn't have a mouth, or nose, or anything, so he communicated via speakers.

"You ever worried about anyone running out on a fare?" I asked Zzzho, when I closed the cab door.

"Nah. Once you warned people that I could shove myself into their lungs and fry them, everyone became much more respectful."

"Glad I could be of help," I said. I had been given a mild zap from Zzzho before and that was more than enough for me.

"You're lucky you caught me. Cab business has picked up recently."

"Because of the Damakans?" I asked.

"Yeah. They don't know how to drive. They never invented cars."

"They're such a backwards species," I said.

"Yeah, but they're great actors. One fare sat where you are now and he did a warm-up where he pretended to be a dinosaur. I almost crashed into a pole I was so scared."

"You're a puff of smoke. What's a dinosaur going to do to you?"

"Nothing. But don't tell me you wouldn't be startled if a dinosaur suddenly appeared in your rearview mirror."

When Zzzho dropped me off, I was dismayed to find out Paggo-Nosa's cousin had his office in his apartment. Specifically, in his dingy living room.

"I *do* need people," the cousin confirmed. "I'm not sure if I need people like you, though. You hear me?"

The man's girlfriend was preparing dinner in the kitchen noisily. I knew she was his girlfriend because you didn't marry women like her.

"What's wrong with me?" I asked.

"Nothing, Hank, you got great skills," he said. "But you're overkill for this assignment. This is what I call 'statue work.' You just got to stand around."

"I can stand around," I said. "What is the job, exactly? I drove over here, might as well hear it."

"The gangs are chiseling into the dramatic industry."

"Gangs are making movies now?"

"Hah, no. I got word that yesterday some guys made off with power generators, studio lights, and a whole damn electrified fence!"

Typical Belvaille. If you stole a handful of dirty gravel, two weeks later people were talking like it was the largest diamond heist in history.

"That's a shame," I said. "So the job is security? I've already been doing security work for the dramatic industry. I have experience."

"It's not *real* security. They just want choppers to stand around and look scary. It makes the Damakans feel better. You wouldn't even get a gun."

"I can provide my own guns. But I'm not a very good shot," I said.

"Is your little buddy staying for dinner?" the woman screeched from the kitchen.

"Close your trap and cook the food!" The cousin yelled at her. "He's a client."

"Oh, a *client*. Excuse me, Mr. Senior Vice President. I'll go wait in the lobby," she replied. There followed a series of smashing dishes and stomping feet.

We waited a moment until things were quiet.

"No guns. No shooting. All you do is wear a black t-shirt and cross your arms. But none of the shirts I have will fit you. And I can't pay much."

"I'm just looking for grocery money. I can hold up the shirt if it helps," I said.

"That might work. I don't want you to, you know, think this is a *good* job. If half the stuff I've read about you in Scanhand is true... You're a mutant, right?"

"Yeah, I'm a mutant. I got thick skin and I heal. I can also fly, but not really."

"I should probably be working for you," he laughed.

"What's it take to start a business like this?" I asked.

"You need to work with the guys in charge," he said.

"Do insurance companies pay you?"

"No, the producers." I nodded like I knew what that was, but it was clear from my blank look that he should continue. "You know what producers are?"

"Yeah. They're the people that like...*produce* the money to pay you, right?"

"Hah. I got to remember that. Lots of stuff goes into making dramatic programs."

"I know they use actors. And talent agents. And they have lights and generators," I said, shrugging.

"Producers *pay* for all that."

"Oh! So they're like gang bosses?" I asked, thinking I finally understood the dramatic industry.

"No, the Guilds are the real bosses. *Anyone* can invest money. Only Damakans can act. Damakans call the shots. But the producers kick in the coin and make big decisions."

"And these same producers are paying for guys to stand around in black t-shirts?" I asked.

"Exactly. And cross your arms. But if you're holding up the t-shirt, just stand there and look mean."

"I can do that," I said.

"Great. Let me get you a shirt."

"Hey, that robbery you heard about. With the generators and the fence. Would I be working there? With those security guards?"

"No, that's just something I heard about. Why?"

"Because I stole that generator."

The movie set wasn't the same one we robbed. Belvaille had hundreds of shows and movies being made at any one time. I was getting paid just enough that I could afford a small meal and the cab rides to and from the set.

In exchange, I stood off to the side with a black t-shirt that had "security" written on the front. The shirt was much too small for my ample proportions, so I merely held it up like a sign. I tried to look mean but I think I looked philosophical: questioning how my life had become so pathetic.

Lots of people were running around the set yelling at each other and using power tools. I never thought they could use so many big lights and generators, but there they were. That one patch of scenery had enough illumination it seemed like three stars were in close orbit. How could anyone see under all that sunshine?

A woman in a dark suit and skirt walked by me. She did a double take on seeing me and stopped.

"Thad Elon's Double Chin," she exclaimed, staring.

My arms had gone limp holding the t-shirt, but I snapped to and held the garment up straight and tried to appear unfriendly.

"What's your name?" she asked.

"Hank," I said, wondering how bad my life could get if I was fired from this job.

"What's your surname?" she asked.

"No one calls me 'sir' except butlers."

"Oh my," she exclaimed. "Don't move. Don't go anywhere."

She hustled away and with the combination of tight skirt and six-inch heels I thought she would plaster herself all over the road, but she hopped over cables and dodged between workers like she was born in that outfit.

She returned a few moments later dragging a lanky man with greasy hair and a goatee. He carried himself like he was important even though he was dressed like a bum. I pointed my security t-shirt at them to prove I was working and shouldn't be fired.

"Look at him. What does he remind you of?" the woman asked.

The goatee grimaced. I could tell both of them were Damakans. They were wearing too many layers of clothes for this heat.

"What are you doing on set?" the goatee asked me.

"Just this," I said weakly.

At this point, I felt foolish. I hadn't really before because no one had been scrutinizing me. But now I realized I was earning subsistence wages to hold a piece of clothing. I wasn't even instructed to stop any thieves or abductors. I was furniture.

"How much do you weigh?" the man asked me.

"Like a couple hundred pounds," I said.

"Huh?"

"A couple thousand, I mean."

"Okay, you're coming with me," he said, and he grabbed my hand to pull me away like I hadn't just told him I was fifteen times heavier than he was.

"I'm supposed to stand here," I said weakly. My only thought was that they were going to parade me around, making fun of me in ways I didn't understand, before they fired me.

"Forget that. You're an actor now," he said.

"Are you the producer?" I asked.

"That clueless simpleton?" the woman sneered.

"No, I'm the director," the goatee said.

CHAPTER 8

So now I was an actor instead of a security guard? But I wasn't a Damakan.

The director and his female assistant I spoke with earlier left to do other things. I wasn't sure what I was supposed to be doing so I held up my security t-shirt now and then just to be safe.

Was I supposed to act? I didn't know how to act. Laesa had tried to explain it countless times, but it was nonsense to me. I thought about calling her and asking for help, but I didn't want to attract any attention. I was hoping they would forget about me.

Finally, the director, his assistant, and another woman came over to me. The second woman started dabbing at my face with some crap.

"Knock it off," I said.

"Hank, she's putting make-up on you," the director said.

I was still concerned they were going to make fun of me, and painting me like a clown would definitely be one way to do it.

"I don't need make-up," I said.

"You need a *lot* of make-up," she countered.

I relented, and she powdered, outlined, and smeared stuff on me.

"Have you ever acted before?" the assistant asked.

"No."

"It's just pretending. It's simple. Your job is to walk through that door holding a gun and ask where your drug money is," the director said.

He pointed to a door under all the lights, attached to a disembodied wall standing in the middle of the street. I was already lost.

"Drug money?" I asked.

"He wants his backstory I think," the female assistant said.

"Okay, good. Your brother, Mart Nuzzle, made a deal with those two gentlemen and now he's missing. You suspect foul play. Understand?"

"I'm a security guard," I said dumbly.

"How much are you being paid as a security guard?" the assistant asked.

"A hundred," I said.

"Credits?" the director asked, confused.

"Yeah."

The director started digging through his wallet and the assistant went to her purse.

"Here's about...a thousand credits. You're now an actor, okay?" he said.

"Can I also eat at the food services table?" I asked.

"Sure. Eat as much as you like. Take some home with you," the assistant said.

"Wait. All I can eat?" I tried to confirm. That alone would be worth a lot.

"Absolutely," the director said. "Now go over there."

A jacket was put on me by someone and I was handed a gun.

I stopped walking.

"What's wrong, Hank?" the director asked.

"This isn't a real gun," I said.

"This is pretend, remember?"

"Oh."

"Go out that door and knock when you hear the word 'action.'"

I walked around the flimsy wall and saw it was only decorated and painted on one side. I stood by the fake door.

A bunch of people were talking and then suddenly everyone was dead silent. A hundred people all held their breaths. I couldn't see them but it was eerie how quiet it had become.

"Action, Hank!" The director called.

"Knock, knock," I said.

"Cut! Hank, what are you doing?" he called over the wall.

"You said to knock on the door."

"But you didn't knock. You *said* knock."

"I thought I was pretending."

"No, it's okay to actually knock on the door. Okay?"

"Okay."

"Action, Hank!" The director said again.

My fist went through the cheap fake door.

"Knock, knock," I said.

"Cut!"

There was a lot of talking and the director and assistant walked around the wall. Carpenters began to repair the door.

"Hank," the director said, pulling at his goatee and stretching his lower lip. "This is a set. It's not very sturdy."

"It's just supposed to *look* like a real wall," the assistant added, like she was speaking to a particularly feeble-minded deaf person.

"So just pretend to knock?" I asked.

"No, you really knock, but don't knock hard," the director said.

"And don't say, 'knock, knock.' You don't speak when you're walking inside."

"Inside what?" I asked, looking around.

"The other side of the wall. That's inside," she said.

"Okay?" the director said with a big smile, patting my shoulder.

"Alright."

I knocked on the door gingerly.

"No, no, wait until we're over there and I say action," the director said.

"I was just practicing," I replied, though I hadn't been.

"That was good. Perfect," the assistant said.

They hustled around the fake wall as I waited.

"Action, Hank."

I tapped on the door.

"Come in," someone called from the other side.

I wasn't sure what to do. This was as far as I'd gotten. I knocked again.

"Come in," the voice replied louder.

"Do I open the door?" I yelled.

"Yes, Hank," the director said.

I turned the handle carefully and opened the door. The wall was very thin and I turned sideways as I walked past the fake threshold.

There were two Damakan thespians dressed in ridiculous "gang" attire standing on the other side of the fake door. They looked particularly irritated at me, but who could tell with Damakans? Maybe they were acting.

"Cut!"

The director and assistant were next to me again. "Hank, just walk inside," the director said, his voice filled with puzzlement.

"Like you walk into any building," the assistant added.

"After I knock, right?"

"Yes. You knock first, wait for their response, then walk in."

"Got it."

I stood there as the director and assistant moved away.

"Hank, go back on the other side," he said.

"Okay."

"Action, Hank."

I knocked on the door.

"Come in," the actor said.

I walked forward, bumped into the side of the wall and the whole façade broke its mooring and began to lean.

"Move!" someone yelled.

There was panic and screaming and the wall tilted over and slammed to the ground. No one was hit, as it wasn't that tall and the actors had scampered to safety.

While they put the wall back into place, the director and assistant returned.

"He seems to have trouble entering. Maybe we can start with him standing there. We can cut it together. We have enough shots of the knock and them saying come in," the assistant said.

"Let's do that. Hank, you're going to start here this time," the director said.

"Inside?" I asked.

"Exactly. Inside. And you ask where your drug money is while pointing the gun," he continued.

"The fake gun, right?"

"Yes," the assistant said.

"Does it matter where I point it?" I asked.

"No. No, doesn't matter at all. But point it at those two guys. You should probably not have it directly pointed at either one since you're trying to cover them both. And you know the one on the right is Fasty Loose Fingers who is a hired killer. But you don't know if either, or both, of them are armed," the director said.

It sounded like it mattered where I pointed it, but I didn't reply.

I went and stood in front of the fake door by the two actors who were giving me dirty looks. They definitely had the gang expression down. They looked really angry. I tried to look angry as well.

"Action," the director said.

I pointed the gun between the two actors. It was so hot over here because of the lights. I had been protected earlier when I was behind the wall. I felt like a bug under a magnifying glass.

There were literally a hundred people staring at me.

"Hank, say your line," the director added.

I had no idea what my line was. I searched my mind frantically. This was a lot of pressure. It felt like hours passed in the dead silence of infinite light.

"Brother, what's the cheese?" I asked finally.

"Cut!"

The director and assistant walked over along with the make-up lady, who began trying to repair the damage my sweat was causing to her efforts.

People didn't seem upset anymore. They were regarding me as if I was some fantastical creature they had never encountered.

"So, Hank. What you do is ask where your drug money is. Remember?" the director said patiently.

"Maybe you should give him exact words. He's not a Damakan," the assistant suggested.

"Right. Say, 'where is my drug money?'"

"Where is my drug money," I said.

"Perfect! Except say it to them. And ask it like a question. Like, 'hey, where is it? I am very concerned.'"

"Okay."

Everyone retreated and I was back in position.

"Action, Hank!"

I paused. I looked over and saw all the people staring. Some were opening and closing their mouths as if they could force me to talk like a puppet. But I couldn't read their lips because of the light.

"I'm concerned…. brother, where is my cheese?" I asked, confused.

"Cut!"

They were back in front of me, gawking. The make-up lady was toweling me off.

"Why are you saying cheese?" the director asked. "And brother. There's no brother."

"He has a brother, Mart Nuzzle. I think that's conflicting him," the assistant said.

I felt a lot less stupid when I was holding the t-shirt as a security guard. I had no clue what was happening. It was like I was dreaming. Not a nightmare. Just one of those dreams where you're trying to run but you don't go anywhere.

"I can't work with this. He's pouring buckets," the make-up lady complained.

"It's fine. He's a sweaty gangster," the director said.

"It's smearing his make-up and catching the light," the assistant said.

"Do you have a pan of ice water I can stand in?" I asked.

They regarded me as if I had just barfed up an acoustic guitar.

"It will help with my sweating," I added.

"Sure. Get him a bucket of ice water," the director shrugged.

Not sure where it came from, but a few moments later a large pan of ice water was placed at my feet. I took off my shoes and socks and stood in it. The chilly water on my feet helped me forget I was standing under a solar flare of light.

"No brother." The director pointed to me.

"No brother," I repeated.

"Okay, let's try this," he said, and everyone returned to their positions.

"Action, Hank."

All I could remember was, "no brother." I was thinking, "no brother," over and over like a mantra. As soon as the commotion of the set stopped and all attention shifted to me, it was nerve-racking. I knew I was screwing up, but I only had the vaguest idea how or why.

"Where is my drug money?" one of the actors said to me.

"I don't know. Maybe your brother has it," I replied.

"Cut!"

The director dragged himself over like his legs were broken.

"Why did you say that?" he asked me.

"I thought we were switching," I said.

"I was just telling him the line," the actor explained.

"Don't help him! It's not working. Hank, say, 'where is my drug money?'" the director said.

"Now? Don't I wait for you to say 'action?'"

"Action."

"Where is my drug money?"

"Again. Action."

"Where is my drug money?"

"Action."

"Where is my drug money?"

The director held up his palms toward me with his eyes bulging.

"No one move! Say that when I call action."

The director ran back to his chair and before he sat down he called out.

"Action!"

"Where is my drug money?" I asked.

"Louder!"

"Where is my drug money?"

"Angrier!"

"Where is my drug money?"

Each time I said it, the pair of Damakan actors reacted like I had just walked in a real door, I was a real gangster, with a real gun, saying real words. It was insanity.

"Now *shoot* them!" The director screamed.

My heart was beating a thousand times a minute. I felt like it was one second to Doomsday and I had my hand on the plunger. The tension was unbelievable. People were standing on their tippy toes, leaning forward. But my gun was fake. How do I shoot them?

"I'm shooting you! Both of you," I said, waving my arms in what I felt was a dramatic fashion. I had seen an actor do that once in a play. "Bzow! Bzow!" I added, unsure if my fake gun was supposed to be an Ontakian plasma pistol, but it would be cool if it was.

I expected both of the actors to pretend like they were shot. Or dodging. Or shooting back. Or something. But they just stood there with their mouths open.

"Cut," the director said.

A small group of people formed around the director and the assistant and I could hear them talking but not what they were saying.

"Is that how you do it?" I asked one of the actors.

"You need to confirm with the director," he replied, and his face was a perfect mask which gave no hint of expression.

The assistant walked over a few minutes later. People removed my jacket and took my toy gun.

"We're done here now, Hank. You did great," she said. Her voice and manner were pleasant. Congratulatory.

"Thanks. Can I get some food from craft services?" I asked.

"You can. You can get food now. Yes," she replied.

I didn't bother putting on my shoes and socks. People whispered and pointed as they watched me walk away, but I didn't care.

I kept eating until about half the table was clear and I made a take-home bag using my security t-shirt.

I was pretty certain my acting career was over. I couldn't say I was sorry.

CHAPTER 9

Laesa and I were on the couch watching my large-screen tele.

Cliston was busying himself as my butler. He unobtrusively handed us drinks, snacks, cleaned my apartment, balanced our household finances, and in between he was writing a pamphlet on caring for exotic fish that came from a planet he had never visited. I think Cliston liked showing off. Nah, that's not fair. Cliston was okay. He was just an overachiever.

We were watching a dramatic show about a woman born without hands who struggled to master a complicated musical instrument called a zitheraphone. Everyone told her she could never use the instrument because she lacked fingers. She dared to prove them wrong and attempted to play the zitheraphone using her *face*. It was brutal. After an hour, Laesa and I were both crying, and Cliston brought us tissues.

I was witnessing the full power of Damakan acting. It didn't even matter it was over the tele and not in person. My logical mind *knew* this was a maudlin fantasy. But we sat there blubbering at the woman's futile efforts to make music by bashing her head on the instrument.

When it was over, the character had successfully become a virtuoso and we were giddy with delight.

"That's what I want to do!" Laesa declared, pointing at the screen.

"Okay," I said, wiping my nose. "I'll go shopping for a zitheraphone tomorrow."

"No, Hank, the acting. Did you see how good she was? Didn't you *feel* it?"

Of course I had. A pile of used tissues next to me was testament to what I had experienced. But now the program was over and I was released from the Damakan spell. It was so fleeting. So false.

"We got to stop doing this," I said, rising from the couch.

Cliston swooped in and removed all our dirty dishes and trash. He was so fast that if you blinked you would miss him. The perfect butler.

"Stop doing what?" Laesa asked.

"These shows. We're always watching the tele. I'm drained. I was yelling at an electronic device on my wall. At people who don't exist. At a character who could, I don't know, could try using her feet instead of her forehead," I said, recalling, in retrospect, how ludicrous it was.

"But you were also laughing. And excited. It doesn't have to make sense," Laesa objected.

"I know acting is your thing. But I feel cheated. I poured out all these feelings and in the end they pull back the sheet and go, 'Haha, we tricked you.'"

"You don't *lose* those sentiments. It's not like they were taken from you."

"I'm not a Damakan. I don't need every day to be a rollercoaster of emotions. I get enough sensations emptying the trash."

"Cliston empties the trash," she said, confused.

"You know what I mean. I feel raw. I'm perfectly content to be...content."

Laesa snuck in and cuddled with me. I immediately settled down. Cliston walked over and stood to the side.

"Yes, Cliston?" I asked, knowing he wanted to speak.

"Sir, MTB called while you were watching the program. He said he would like to talk with you at the crotch tomorrow at 7 am."

"Why does he wake up so early? What policing can he possibly do when 90% of the station is asleep?" I complained.

"Can I come with you?" Laesa asked.

I stared down at her, where she clung to my chest. Her arms were not long enough to reach my broad sides. Or maybe my gut was in the way.

"Don't give me that sour face. You're not going to fight MTB, are you?" she asked.

"Of course not. He wants to talk about gangsters."

"Exactly. That will be exciting for me. And I've never met MTB. I'd like to meet your friends. He'd be a perfect person for a character study," she said.

I shrugged.

"Fine, you can wake me up tomorrow," I said.

"Cliston, what did you honestly think of the tele program?" Laesa asked.

"I can't say I was paying much attention," Cliston replied delicately.

"That's butler Cliston, not talent agent Cliston," I told her.

"I wish I could talk with talent agent Cliston," she said.

"Perhaps you should try making an appointment at his office," Cliston said, as he walked away.

"I have!" Laesa called after him. "The jerk never takes my calls." She smiled at me and laughed. Then she left to use the bathroom.

I knew Cliston didn't care for Laesa. I wasn't entirely sure why. He always treated her with courtesy and charm of course, but I knew him well enough that I could spot the slight infractions.

Cliston was a robot, tens of thousands of years old, and could occupy multiple personalities with no effort. It was an understatement to say he was a complex person. But he was also a good friend. I dearly wanted him to warm to Laesa as much as I had.

It was probably a big concept for Cliston to think about me getting married. He would have to butler for a family instead of a slobby bachelor. It wasn't something I had discussed with him and I wasn't sure how to broach the subject.

That's another reason I had been so keen to pay back the money I owed Cliston. Here I was thinking about marriage when I was in debt to my butler. No wonder he disapproved.

Laesa spent the night, and the next morning, after Cliston dressed me and served us breakfast, Laesa suggested we walk across the city to meet MTB.

"Let's take a cab. It will take too long and MTB will be crankier than usual for making him wait," I said.

"I thought you wanted to save money," she said.

"I've got some cash."

"Does your new security assignment pay that much?"

It was an innocent question. I hadn't told Laesa about my brief acting work. Not for any nefarious reasons, I was simply embarrassed. But I finally had to come clean and I gave her the details.

"You were a paid actor on a movie set?" she asked, her jaw hanging open so wide a team of spelunkers were preparing to explore her esophagus.

"I don't know if it was a movie. I don't know what it was," I said.

"What was the program about?"

"I think it maybe cheese."

"Cheese?"

"And drugs. And brothers. They had a fake wall with a door. It was super confusing."

Laesa's eyes flickered rapidly as she guessed which production it might have been.

"Do you remember who hired you?"

"He had a goatee. And looked like a hobo. He was the director. A Damakan."

"Of course he was a Damakan," she said absently, as she looked through her tele. She finally held up a picture of a man. He was smiling and wearing a suit. "Was that him?"

"He didn't look that good, but yeah, I think that was the guy."

"I can't believe it. That's Reenos Ovush! He's one of the hottest young directors in the Horror Guild."

"Horror? I didn't see anything gross," I said.

"Horror encompasses a lot. Hank, you've got to be the luckiest person I've ever met. Zero experience and Reenos Ovush picks you for his next project."

"I'm not going to be in it. I was horrible."

"Why didn't you tele me?" she asked, hurt.

"What for? It was a security job that switched under my feet. I didn't understand what was happening."

"I would have loved to watch. Or even talked to anyone. That could have been a real break for me."

"I'm sorry. I was flailing about as soon as it began," I said.

"I could have helped you if nothing else," she said.

"He got mad when other actors tried to give me pointers."

"Who else was there?"

"I don't know. I got free food. That was the best part."

"You and your food," she said.

We decided to walk so Laesa could ask me a million questions about my acting job that I wasn't able to answer. I gave MTB a tele to say I would be late.

I knew how much Laesa was interested in acting. I had basically been doing her dream job and I didn't drop her a quick line. She was even excited when I'd told her about us stealing a generator from a movie set and wanted to know everything I saw.

This was a tough lesson for me. It was a real transition to suddenly have someone else around and consider their wants and needs. I was so used to being on my own. Even less than that, really. I was used to having Cliston take care of most things while I negotiated with scumbags. And I never had to worry about Cliston's feelings, I just had to stand up straight and use the proper silverware. If I wanted to take this relationship seriously, I had to stop being selfish and do better about keeping Laesa in my thoughts.

After hiking for some hours, we came to my old street.

"That's where I used to live," I said, pointing.

"There's nothing there."

"Yeah, the Navy got mad at me and vaporized my building from space. I guess no one bothered to rebuild."

"The Navy does law enforcement on Belvaille?" she asked. "I thought this station was outside the PCC and that's why you have police like MTB."

"It's complicated. We rent parts of the station to the Navy. But really, they could take control whenever they wanted. What are we going to do? We're in the exact center of the PCC empire. It works out fine for the most part. They don't bother us—except when they get really mad. Then they blow up buildings."

"Were you in it when it was destroyed?" she asked.

"I'm bulletproof, not death-ray-proof."

"What is *that*?" Laesa asked, pointing.

"You've never seen Wallow?"

She shook her head in disbelief.

"That is Wallow the Therezian," I said, indicating the reclining form of the giant that blocked the street ahead of us. "We think he had a heart attack or something and fell over dead, smashing those buildings and cutting off this whole road."

"How long ago did he die?"

"Like a decade or so."

"Why don't they move him?"

"Move him? How? We tried burning him, cutting him, shooting him. Nothing can penetrate his skin. He's not even decomposing. I think he'll be here forever," I said.

"Is that what MTB meant by 'meet at the crotch?' He wants to talk by a dead giant's groin?" she asked.

"Yeah. Our private spot is...Wallow's privates. Everyone is scared to come by here so it's very secluded."

"What are they scared of?"

"I don't know. Therezian diseases. Or that he might wake up."

"He's dead, isn't he?" she asked, not walking any further.

"I hope so. He hasn't eaten anything in a decade. If he wakes up, he's going to be awful hungry."

Laesa took her time following me as I headed past Wallow's feet and into the darker recesses of his upper legs.

MTB was waiting.

"You're even late when you say you're going to be late," MTB scowled.

"Hi, chum. This is Laesa. My almost-fiancée."

MTB nodded his head. It was clear he didn't approve of me bringing her, but I just trekked a quarter of the way across the city, so I didn't care.

"Did you rob the Alowaxy movie set some time ago?" MTB began.

"I'm fine. How are you doing?" I asked, rolling my eyes.

"Micka made a police report that you hijacked him."

"Man, I was so wrong about that guy. What kind of Belvaille security guard would actually call the cops on someone?" I said, shaking my head at the concept. "Would you arrest me if I said I had robbed him?"

"We don't arrest people," MTB replied.

"Not to be a prick, but what exactly do you do, MTB?"

"We don't arrest anyone because we don't have the resources to be watching and feeding prisoners. We fine people, confiscate property, or if the crime is bad enough, we rough them up or even shoot them," he said.

"MTB kind of makes up the laws," I explained to Laesa as she listened attentively, standing some distance away.

"I do not. However, I know you don't have any money, so I can't fine you; you have nothing to confiscate; and you're bulletproof," he continued.

"Woo! You hear that? I'm officially above the law!" I said, smiling at Laesa.

"More like below the law. Besides, sometimes you and I go bowling."

"Oh, man, they're closing down the bowling alley," I said sadly.

"No. When?"

"A few weeks. We'll have to get some lane time before then," I said.

"Is that what we played?" Laesa asked me.

"No, we played chorball. That place is closing too," I told her.

"What a shame. You think the city's demographic changes are making the rent too high for a bowling alley to survive?" MTB asked me.

"No. I've seen Belvaille rich and I've seen it poor. It's somewhere in between right now. The bowling alley is closing because we were the only two people who ever used it."

"So did you rob that movie set?" he asked again.

"Yeah. It was a simple job."

Laesa looked back and forth between me and MTB. She seemed to be enjoying herself.

"Micka said you sexually abused him while he was captive," MTB said.

"*What?* I need to stop doing character studies," I muttered. "No one so much as gave him a dirty look. We snatched a generator and sold it back to them within six hours."

MTB nodded.

"It *sounded* pretty far-fetched. I was mostly telling you so you'd know what he's been saying."

"Great. Now people will think I'm a molester."

"I got more information on Weelon Poshor's murder," MTB said.

I leaned against Wallow's left thigh.

"Okay. Let's hear it."

"The stab wounds were definitely after he was already dead. Or at least when he was on the ground and not moving. They all have the same angle. They also didn't penetrate very far. Seem pretty haphazard."

"Jittery knife-killer?" I asked.

"I thought you said he was shot," Laesa cut in.

"He was shot *and* stabbed," MTB replied.

"So then you know it was at least two different attackers, right?" she asked.

"No, it's..." MTB started, but then he looked at me. I could see he didn't feel like answering her questions.

"Not necessarily," I said for him. "The shooter may also have used a knife. Just because there were two weapons doesn't mean there were two people."

"Oh."

"Pretty sure the gun had a heavy suppressor. The shots were close enough that some powder marks were on the clothes. At that range, more of the bullets should have penetrated the body completely. Only one did," MTB said.

"You think a silencer made the gun lose muzzle velocity?" I asked.

"Exactly. And it would be easier for you to keep sleeping on the couch," MTB said. "I also analyzed the sweat that we found at the scene."

"I thought you said you couldn't. You made fun of me when I suggested it."

"This was simple."

"Analyzing sweat is simple? You know, for a guy without a crime lab or forensics team, you got an awful lot of results," I said.

"It wasn't sweat. It was Belvaille tap water," he said.

"So Weelon Poshor was shot, stabbed, and hit with water balloons? Talk about ruthless."

"I don't know why the water was there. What do you think?"

"I'd say maybe question the pool boy or the gardener to see if they killed him and dropped their wet tools. But he didn't have a pool or a garden, so they have solid alibis."

"This is serious, Hank. A Damakan was murdered," he said, looking briefly at Laesa.

"I know, I'm being serious. But what you told me aren't really clues. Everyone I know that has a silenced gun knows how to stab people. Hell, everyone I know has a silenced gun."

"Maybe someone wanted us to *think* it was sweat," MTB said.

I laughed.

"So a snowman could get away with murder?" I asked.

"No, because maybe it was someone who doesn't normally sweat in a house that's a constant 101 degrees. A Gandrine rock creature. A Qwintine insectoid. Or a Damakan, for instance."

I was taken aback.

"You're kind of reaching. That wasn't exactly a tidy murder. I was asleep in the next room. Yet they go to the trouble of sprinkling water everywhere to make us think someone was sweating? Maybe it was a Dredel Led?"

"Cliston is the only Dredel Led in the city and he would have tidied up the place after he killed someone."

"That's true. No way he would have left water on the floor. Someone could slip and fall," I agreed. "But a Gandrine probably couldn't *hold* a gun, let alone a knife."

"It doesn't make sense it was a Damakan," Laesa interrupted.

"Why?" MTB asked.

She smiled like it was obvious.

"Because Weelon Poshor was a famous actor. He was extremely talented."

"That doesn't mean he can dodge bullets," I said.

"No, but the way Damakan culture works is we cherish people like that. They can pass emotions to huge groups. They've reached the pinnacle of our society."

"He was only Cousin Randolph," MTB said, shrugging.

"He was broadcasting to billions of people across the galaxy—even other Damakans back on our home world. That's an incredible accomplishment," she said.

"Weelon Poshor was untouchable because he was on a weekly program?" I asked.

"No, because he was *helping* people. Damakans get our emotional release from other Damakans. Those might be simple tele programs to you, but we *need* them. Besides, Damakans don't really kill people," she said.

"Belvaille isn't a great place for pacifists," MTB said.

"We're not pacifists. Not exactly. We're just not good at killing people. And it's out of the question we'd attack someone like Weelon Poshor. At least knowingly," she explained.

"We all agree the killer knew him. This wasn't random," MTB said.

"What she's saying matches what the head of the Drama Guild told me," I confirmed.

"Listen to this guy. He hangs out with the President of the Drama Guild," Laesa teased.

"I guess I'm going to have to learn about this Damakan stuff," MTB sighed.

"I can help if you like," Laesa offered.

MTB nodded grimly.

"I asked you about the robbery earlier because I've noticed an increase in attacks against productions. I was wondering if you heard anything or were involved," MTB said.

"I just did the one job, but someone else said the same thing. I guess the gangs are finally realizing there's money to be made from the dramatic industry after all," I said.

"I don't buy that," he said.

"Don't buy what?"

"Last six months there were maybe...two dozen thefts that got reported. This last month there's been twice that many."

"Maybe it's just one or two gangs ratcheting up," I said.

"It's not. The few leads I have point to different organizations. Why would this suddenly happen?"

I thought about it.

"Well, there are a lot of criminals in this city," I started.

"Yeah. And?"

"And let's be honest, most criminals become criminals because they can't do much else. It's not like you give up your doctor's practice or lawyer gig to pursue your dream of stealing hubcaps," I said.

"You saying that the gangs started hitting the movie industry because they're stupid and didn't realize the potential?" he asked.

"I guess."

"That doesn't scan. These crooks may suck at algebra and art appreciation, but they can smell money a light-year away. The thing is, what I'm seeing in many cases doesn't have much payoff."

"I made decent coin stealing that generator. Though I'm not sure it was worth the hours I put in."

"I'm seeing arson, theft, and plain old destruction of property. There's no money in those except stealing. And Belvaille is a small community. We black-market to other people, not to ourselves. If someone steals your gun, you're not going to buy it back, you're going to beat up the guy who stole it, because you know who it was."

"Good point. But the dramatic industry is different. We stole the generator because it was insured," I said.

"Insured?" he asked. "What's that entail?"

"I don't have the specifics. But it paid. I guess they knew enough about Belvaille that they laid down some money ahead of time to protect their operations. It worked in my case."

"Okay. Good to know. I figured it was some crazy scheme I didn't understand."

"Yeah. But you say it's happening a lot now?"

"I'm using all my people to try and contain it and we can't keep up," MTB replied.

"What do you think, Hank?" Laesa asked me.

"I think it sounds like there is a lot of work to be had either providing protection for the productions or attacking them," I said. "And I'm looking for a job."

"What side are you going to choose?" MTB asked.

"Come on. You should know me better than that. I'm going to be on the side that pays the most money for the least amount of work. If I learn anything more, I *might* tell you about it. But not if you're going to arrest me."

"I already said I won't arrest you. It's not just me that's interested in this. Those dramatic broadcasts go out across the galaxy. They're a big deal. You know who runs the movie industry?" MTB asked.

"The Guilds," I said.

"No. They run the productions. Every program is sent out using Belvaille's telescopes. The Post-Colmarian Confederation Colmarian Confederation owns those telescopes."

I squinted in frustration.

"And Garm controls the telescopes," I sighed.

"Right. And if Garm has her income disrupted, she's going to call all her Navy friends or Quadrad assassin friends or whatever friends to come fix it in the most head-pounding way possible. You won't have to worry about being arrested, you'll have to worry about a battlecruiser erasing your house from orbit," he said.

"Had that happen once. Not looking for a repeat. I miss my old carpets," I said. On a hunch, I pulled out my tele and flipped through my latest messages. "Hey, guess who got a call from Garm last night at three in the morning?"

Laesa and I were walking back to my place as I kicked this around in my head.

"What's your plan?" Laesa asked me.

"Go home and eat and take a nap."

"After that?"

"I'll make a plan after I eat and sleep. What's your personality profile of MTB?" I asked.

"It's not very thorough. One conversation isn't much," she said.

"Come on. Give it a shot. I want to hear your take on him."

"He's tough, but it's largely a façade. It's one he's maintained for so long that it has become the truth, even to himself. I think something happened in his youth. Something bad. He doesn't trust many people. He keeps his word—probably to a fault, and it frustrates him that other people aren't as predictable. He's desperately lonely. I expect you're one of his only friends. He covers up that deficiency by throwing himself into his work. If he's always working, he doesn't have to worry about being normal. He's been doing it so long that he missed out on the social training and indoctrination that we all go through, and, consequently, he's uncomfortable in informal situations. If crime suddenly stopped on Belvaille, if there was nothing but peace and love here, I expect MTB would relocate to some terrible place so he could start it all over again. He doesn't truly want order. He would be hopeless and lost in a peaceful setting. MTB wants to fight something. He needs it to give his vacant life meaning. Right now he fights crime. If there was no crime he would find it, or search for something else to fight."

I stood there blinking.

"How does that sound?" she asked.

"Damn, woman."

CHAPTER 10

Garm. Good old Garm. She'd left a curt tele message asking me to meet at her office.

Garm was an Adjunct Overwatch, which meant she was the senior-ranking Navy official on the space station. She was smart, sexy, lethal, and corrupt beyond belief. I had grown up around crooks, but Garm could pull off things that ordinary gang bosses couldn't dream of. She extracted her cut from nearly every dirty deal and scam that went on in Belvaille.

I got ulcers simply from owing people money. I couldn't imagine the stress of being the top police officer in the System while simultaneously being its biggest criminal. She had a lot of guts. We also dated at one point, which was something she perpetually tried to forget.

I was an escaped convict according to the PCC Navy, so Garm normally didn't like associating with me in public. It was unusual she wanted to speak at her office.

Garm worked at the far north side of the space station. That's where the giant telescopes were and the buildings that controlled them. Even when Belvaille was a deserted city at the ass end of the galaxy, it still had value because of those telescopes. They not only helped coordinate shipping traffic along the entire Post-Colmarian Confederation Colmarian Confederation, they also broadcast the station's dramatic programs. Apparently, they were technological marvels of the old empire and were beyond valuable.

I took a cab ride north, with the driver yelling at me the whole way because my weight was messing up the car's suspension. I didn't give him a tip. If you weren't a people person, then don't get a job where you worked with people—that included overweight people.

Walking to Garm's administration building, I noticed the security guards outside. To be clear, these weren't rental cops. They weren't Belvaille thugs. They were polished Navy soldiers. They had big guns, body armor, and marched around like they went to Marching School and majored in March. There weren't many of them, but enough that you would think twice before littering. Not sure how they could handle wearing body armor in this heat. Maybe they had air conditioning.

I put my head down and scratched my nose with the palm of my hand to obscure my face. I felt keenly aware that there was an outstanding warrant for my arrest and I was surrounded by arresters.

Entering the administration building, I was immediately confronted with some kind of electronic security kiosk I had to get past. An employee in front of me presented a badge and went on through. I had no such credentials, so I figured I would just walk around it.

Three Navy guards came out of nowhere, guns ready.

"Get on the ground! Stop him! Stop him! There he is!" They yelled.

I *knew* I shouldn't have come here. They must have recognized me. What kind of idiot walked into a Navy facility when they were being hunted by the Navy?

But I wasn't going quietly.

The first guard put his rifle muzzle practically in my face. Bad move. At that close, even my slow reflexes were able to deal with it. I took a step to the side, blocking the angle of fire of one of his partners. I took hold of the gun barrel and pulled the guard closer toward me.

I headbutted him right in the faceplate of his helmet, bending the metal. He dropped like a sack of dead hamsters.

I stiff-armed his partner who rushed me. He was going so fast that he practically did a backflip when we connected.

The third guard now had an open shot at me. But I had just dispatched two of his buddies in a few seconds. He took the opportunity to back up cautiously.

That was all the hesitation I needed. I made a feint as if I was going to charge him, and instead I hightailed it out the exit. I wasn't so cocky that I believed I could fight my way past the Navy. My only hope was to run and hide. Retreat into obscurity and never come to this area again.

Outside, I hopped over a small railing and down some steps, which was the first time I jumped over anything larger than a drop of water in about 75 years. Fear does that. My mind was a blur of activity. I calculated how long it would take me to reach the closest friendly location where I could lay low. Seven minutes if I cut corners and wasn't followed. It would be close.

I looked up and counted about thirty guns pointed at me. There had been only a handful of guards outside when I arrived, but it had suddenly morphed into a soldier assembly plant.

Yes, I was bulletproof. But these guys had more than bullets. Besides, I couldn't outrun a battalion. I couldn't even outrun *one* soldier unless he was easily distracted and had two hip replacements.

I stopped and put my hands up. They frisked me. No talk. No rough stuff. They were pure business. They even removed some lint from the inside of my pocket. Seriously. As if they were concerned it might be armor-piercing lint.

We then paraded back inside the building I just vacated. They didn't hold me at gunpoint, but it was obvious that if I made any sudden moves, I'd be wearing a lot of bullets for jewelry.

I begrudgingly had to admire these soldiers. They were classy. This was like a real career for them. The Belvaille crooks were crooks because they couldn't *get* real careers. These people were actual professionals.

"My name is Korpitan Hash-Gull. What are you doing here?" a man asked. He had gray hair, some wrinkles, and his uniform boasted more stripes and buttons than the others.

"I was sightseeing and got lost," I said sarcastically.

"What's your name?" Hash-Gull asked.

"Aynold Butt-Licker," I taunted.

"Is this how you spell Butt-Licker?" he continued. He was keying it into the security kiosk.

"Sure," I sneered.

When they frisked me earlier, they had taken my shotgun. Now, one of the soldiers held the gun toward me.

"What are you trying to do?" I asked.

He jiggled the gun around, as if he wanted me to take it. Did they think I was going to try and arm myself in front of this firing squad? That would give them all the alibi they needed to blast me in self-defense. No, thanks.

"Here's your gun, tele, and wallet. We had to unload the firearm. You can't have a loaded gun inside. We'll return the ammunition when you leave," the guard explained.

It was slowly occurring to me that I might not be destroyed. I might not even be arrested.

The guards I fought with a few moments ago were scowling and looked ready to escalate things, but the others were completely businesslike. I had assumed the guards recognized me and that's why they attacked, but now it didn't seem like it.

I cautiously took the items offered and put the shotgun away immediately.

"Why did you bypass the security terminal and resist?" Hash-Gull asked.

"They came at me with their guns out!" I said. "I panicked."

Korpitan Hash-Gull gave a withering look at the other soldiers but I wanted this dropped immediately.

"It's okay," I said. "I overreacted. I apologize. I am sorry. It's my fault."

People make a huge deal about saying sorry, but I find it's the easiest thing in the world. I'm perfectly happy to take the blame for something if it prevents getting my ass beat.

"Would you like to register a complaint?" Hash-Gull asked.

"Absolutely not. You all are just doing your jobs." I smiled, trying to project sincerity.

"You mentioned you were sightseeing?" he asked.

"Yes. I mean, no. I'm here to see Garm," I said.

"Who?"

"Garm. The Adjunct Overwatch. I think that's her title."

"Let me confirm that," he replied.

Once I apologized, everyone seemed to relax. Most of the soldiers returned outside when it was clear there would be no more excitement. Even the man whose helmet I bent didn't seem put out, though he was currently trying to bang it back into shape with a wrench.

"Okay. You'll need to be escorted. Please wait here," Hash-Gull said.

"Sure. Sorry again about the misunderstanding earlier."

"Everyone needs to sign in to the building. Even if they have an appointment," he said, indicating the security kiosk I had tried to walk around. "We realize it's inconvenient, but it's procedure."

"Perfectly understandable. I was simply startled by the guards and their weapons. I didn't know what was going on," I said, pretending I was an innocent religious salesman.

"We aren't supposed to react like that, I can assure you," Hash-Gull replied. "What, may I ask, is your business with the Adjunct Overwatch?"

"She sent for me," I said, raising my hands to indicate it wasn't my fault.

"You have met with her before?" he asked.

"Oh, sure. I've known Garm since she was a young girl. Back in the original Colmarian Confederation."

"Interesting. What was her occupation then?" he asked.

"Heh, she was Adjunct Overwatch."

"I don't understand," he said.

"The Post-Colmarian Confederation Colmarian Confederation isn't *that* different from the original Colmarian Confederation. She was in charge of Belvaille back then on behalf of the Navy. Same as she is now."

"But this space station was in a completely different area of the galaxy under the Colmarian Confederation. It was tasked with different objectives and strategic values," he said, confused.

"Yeah, Belvaille was so far away from civilization it was kind of a criminal waystation."

"I heard rumors of that. Was the Navy not aware of the situation?" he asked.

"They knew. It was like a prison without walls. If the outlaws were at the edge of the galaxy, they couldn't bother any of the nice people in the more inhabited areas," I said.

"I see, and it was the Adjunct Overwatch's responsibility to punish these criminals?"

"Punish? Why would she punish anyone? We were already stuck on Belvaille."

"Forgive me for prying, but might I inquire if you were one of those criminals?" Hash-Gull asked politely.

"Me? Nah. I worked in the sewers. I was an upstanding, law-abiding citizen," I coughed.

"I also understand that Garm was a member of the Quadrad assassins," Hash-Gull hinted.

"Quad-what? Never heard of them," I said.

Two guards marched up from deeper inside the building and came to a rest in front of me.

"They'll take you to the Adjunct Overwatch," Hash-Gull said.

"Okay. Thanks."

"And thank you for enlightening us about this space station's intriguing past."

I had never been so happy to be escorted away by soldiers. We walked through the building and I was deposited in front of Garm's office door. I knocked gently.

"Come in," Garm called.

Inside the office I was immediately confronted with the torso of a mannequin, dressed up in a military uniform, covered in medals and citations. Garm herself sat behind her ugly, stamped-metal desk. It was typical Navy. A puke green-blue color and probably created shortly after the universe was formed. The office carpet was only slightly newer and had likely been bright red in some mist-shrouded past. It was now a deep burgundy, pockmarked with black stains. It was a strange set of furnishings for her. Garm had an appreciation for the finer things and was not shy about showing them off.

Garm herself was a short woman, with cropped black hair, and angular features. She was a mutant. Her ability was that she didn't need to sleep. Despite a lifetime devoid of naps, she looked fantastic.

Garm wore a uniform which matched what was draped over the mannequin. Except Garm's wardrobe was saturated with every kind of military award you could imagine. Like they had shoved citations into a cannon with the intent of decorating an entire army at once, and Garm had stepped in front of it. All you could see was her head and the top of her neck. The rest was swallowed in silver, gold, ribbons, and badges.

"What the hell happened out there?" Garm said, dispensing with the niceties.

"Happened where?"

"At the front door!"

I was now a little embarrassed about my confrontation with the soldiers.

"Nothing," I said.

"Really?" She looked at her tele. "So you know nothing about the fact that Aynold Butt-Licker is a potential security risk?"

"I guess there was a bit of confusion. But it got sorted."

"Confusion? We had a Stage Three alarm. We nearly evacuated the building."

"Your security is obscene. Why did you invite me here? I'm a wanted criminal."

"You still worried about that? No one cares about you," she said.

"Did you remove the warrant for my arrest?"

"You can't erase paperwork in the PCC. It floats around forever. But I requested some beans."

"Beans?" I asked.

"The stuff you eat. Then I denied it. Then forwarded the request. Then attached it to a maintenance log. I did this and similar things about a hundred times. If you dig into the middle of a fifty-page record you'll find a rap sheet that shows you assassinated a Wardian, escaped from a maximum-security prison, you're a Dredel Led sympathizer, and all your other crimes. Even if someone was *looking* for your record, which they wouldn't, because who cares about Hanks on Belvaille, they couldn't find it. Unless they also happen to be cross-referencing bean requisitions," she explained.

"So I'm safe?" I tried to confirm.

"Just don't go around bragging you're Hank the Wardian Killer and you should be fine."

"Okay. But why all the guards around here? It's like...I don't know, a *real* base."

"Tell me about it," she sighed. "I used to have a great system for running this place: hire incompetent fools."

"Why?"

"Because, Hank, I'm breaking the rules. Terrible workers are usually too terrible to notice what I'm doing. And they're so thankful to have a job, they don't cause trouble."

"What changed?" I was tired of standing. But Garm wasn't about to offer me a seat, so I stepped over to the couch by the wall. I had to walk past the mannequin. "And what's with this dummy?"

"That was my mistake. I have too many medals to put on my uniform. But regulations require that I display them at all times. Therefore, I have that stupid thing. When I give formal speeches, it has to stand next to me. So people can see I was awarded the Distinguished Badge of Delegation."

"Awarded them to yourself," I said, sitting down. Garm found a loophole where she could give herself commendations.

"I increased my salary so much that I make more than most admirals."

"Nice. I think I met a budding admiral on the way in here. Korpitone Hash-Gull."

"Korpitan. Yeah, he's the worst of them. This station was a dead end as far as career opportunities went. But now young go-getters are actually looking to *transfer* here. It's annoying as hell."

"I bet. Competent people can be tiresome. Um, he asked me a bunch of questions about you."

"What did you tell him?" she asked, alarmed.

"Nothing. Nothing much. Just chit-chat."

"Don't tell him anything. He's my biggest troublemaker. If he asks you something, just stay quiet."

"Alright."

"So we have a problem," Garm started.

"*You* have a problem. And now you're going to try and make it mine."

"No, this affects everyone. The gangs are interfering with the station's dramatic productions and it has to stop," Garm said.

I laughed.

"How is that *everyone's* problem?"

"It's causing shows to be delayed and costs to overrun."

"Okay. Why would anyone outside of the industry care?"

"The Navy might get involved."

"*You're* the Navy. You're the living, breathing, representative of the Navy on this station. You control those telescopes and you pocket *all* the money from the broadcasts. Look, if you want my help on something, just make me an offer. But don't pretend I should be concerned about the fate of some tele programs. I hardly watch them."

Garm stared at me blankly for a moment.

"I guess we haven't talked in a while," she began. "Back when there were only a handful of Damakans here and I first started airing shows, I made money. Must have been about four years ago, the Grand Auditor General came to visit and looked through all my accounting and operations. I barely survived. Do you have any idea how much revenue the telescopes generate from the dramatic industry?"

"Three, four million?" I guessed.

"*Billions*, Hank. A *lot* of billions. An insane amount. The Navy considers us a sizeable revenue center. We're paying for the construction of a brand-new cruiser."

"Wow."

"All the money is transferred directly to the Navy. I'm lucky if I can embezzle a coffee mug now. We've had something like fifteen consecutive quarters of increasing profits. Now I have to tell them we got our first decline. You need to rein in your gang buddies before 75,000 armed accountants descend and try and figure out why our budget is short. They will uncover the Skim, not to mention everything else that's going on."

"Okay, you convinced me. But I don't speak for all the gangs. MTB told me there has been a rise in activity against productions, but what do you want me to do about it?"

"You have to let them know that it might seem easy to stick up Damakans on the front end, but they're going to bring a lot of heat on this station if they keep it up," she said.

"I can try. But criminals don't often look at consequences very closely. That's why they're criminals. How much will you pay me for my time?"

"I can hire you as a security consultant. We have a standard rate for that, which I can't deviate from, so don't bother haggling for a better price. It's a solid, middle-class salary."

"Great. I always wanted to be a low-grade civil servant."

"Just keep me posted on what's going on. Already some of my staff, like Hash-Gull, are eager to take this on themselves."

"What a kiss-ass."

"It's been really hard keeping all of Belvaille's extracurricular activities in the dark. And managing the dramatic industry is becoming a fulltime job," she said.

"I bet, if it's worth billions. Hey, I was wondering. How do you pick which shows to put on?"

"Void, that's one of my biggest headaches. It used to be the Guilds would send me the shows and I'd put up anything they paid for. There weren't that many. But I can't deal with five Guilds, each one with hundreds of programs vying for the same distribution slots. I told them they need to create *one* point of contact and *one* schedule they all agree on. It will be fixed later this year, but right now it's a complete mess."

"So you don't get to decide who is an actor or anything?" I asked.

"Is this because of your Damakan girlfriend?"

"Laesa. She's kind of my pre-fiancée. How do you know about her?"

"I met her. I was curious what kind of woman could put up with you for an extended period of time."

"Hey, thanks. She didn't mention talking to you."

"I didn't tell her who I was. I was spying, not making a social call. Be sure she's what you want, Hank. Marriage isn't easy."

"Didn't you *murder* your ex-husband?" I asked.

"Yes. So I know what I'm talking about."

CHAPTER 11

Despite making fun of Garm's offer to be a security consultant, it's exactly what I was looking for.

Her employees filled out the paperwork and sent me a tele message within an hour of leaving her office. Certified message. I didn't even know there was such a thing. At the end of the following day, I received my first official paycheck. It was prorated to reflect my short time on the job.

The PCC was known for its backwardness and bureaucracy. It was a running joke across the galaxy. But Garm's people seemed tremendously competent. No wonder she was stressed. Garm normally working with Belvaille regulars: a bunch of half-assed morons who didn't care if she was a crook. Now she was surrounded by the ambitious elite who were watching her every move.

I headed to The Club to earn my new pay. I had to figure out why the gangs were attacking so many productions all of a sudden. Once I knew why they were doing it, maybe I could work on redirecting their efforts. Laesa wanted to tag along and watch. I explained it wouldn't be very exciting, just a lot of drinking and body odor.

"I've grown used to that," she told me.

"If you think *I* smell bad, you might want to stay home. The Club is known as the place where noses go to die."

The Club was an ancient establishment that bustled every day of the week and all hours of the night. I particularly liked the place because I got a half-off discount on food and drink after helping the management get rid of an unruly demigod some time ago.

Laesa was bundled up like she was about to invade an arctic planet. The Club catered to Colmarians. Specifically, scumbag Colmarians. The climate in here wasn't conducive to Laesa's Damakan physiology.

"Hank! It's been a while," a bouncer said, as soon as we stepped inside. I nodded my salutations and then explained to Laesa.

"Everyone knows me here." Since it was her first time visiting I felt I should act like a tour guide.

"I heard you robbed Micka and tried to take off his clothes," the bouncer said nervously.

"He's a saggy old man. Why would I, or anyone, want to see him nude? I don't even want to see myself naked."

"I'm only repeating what's going around," the bouncer replied.

"This is my fiancée," I said, trying to change the subject.

"Nice to take up your face," he said. While Colmarian was the standard tongue across the galaxy, there were idioms particular to each region. Planets without water aren't going to say the same stuff as planets covered with snow, even if they know the same words. "So why would Micka lie about you molesting him?" the bouncer persisted.

I frowned and drew Laesa along. I wasn't going to debate that nonsense.

"How often do you come here?" she asked, after we had walked deeper inside the building.

The Club had gone through a lot of iterations in terms of décor. Right now, space was at a premium so there were only tables and chairs and some makeshift dividers set down between them. There was no artwork, or plants, or decorations of any kind. As soon as anything was put up, it was stolen by the clientele, so they stopped buying it.

Nearly every species that called the PCC home was represented inside The Club. There were aliens with orange skin; some with three arms; others were covered in scales; some glowed in the dark; and they came in every imaginable size and shape. Evolution was a harsh taskmaster.

"Not so much anymore," I told Laesa. "But nearly every illegal deal worth mentioning gets its start here. He was joking about that Micka stuff. Just razzing me."

"He seemed fairly concerned about your sexual conduct with geriatric men," Laesa countered.

"Don't even tease about it. Reputation is a big deal on Belvaille. Especially in this circle of miscreants."

"Reputation is important everywhere. But if you want to be intimidating, having guys worried that you might beat them up *or* strip them naked would make you a double threat."

"Shush," I said, smiling.

We went up to the third floor of the ten-story building and found a seat in a less rowdy section.

"You were right about the stench," Laesa said.

I thought she was making another joke, but I looked over and her eyes were watering and she was slightly crouched, as if she could duck underneath the odor.

"Criminals aren't known for their personal hygiene," I explained.

"Where do you begin in a place like this? Is your process simply to walk up to members and ask why they're attacking the dramatic industry?" she asked, staring around like she was at a zoo.

"No. I start with food and drink."

"What's the significance of that?"

"I'm hungry and thirsty."

"Where is the menu?"

"Menu? They have sausages."

"Is that a criminal thing?"

"They aren't *that* bad. But The Club has about every kind of alcohol available in the galaxy. If you have gills and five livers, you could still get drunk here."

"I guess that's something to brag about," she said, laughing.

When she laughed, I laughed. Roughnecks nearby who had been on the verge of punching someone, heard Laesa, promptly stopped what they were doing and smiled. You couldn't help it. I don't know if it was because she was a Damakan or she simply had an infectious laugh.

I had never proposed marriage to a woman before Laesa. She was the kind of gal you spotted walking on the street one day, and you spent a lifetime thinking about. She was special.

Someone like me ended up with a dame like her maybe once every thousand years and then people couldn't stop talking about it. Our relationship would probably become a fairy tale: The Monster and the Maiden. I knew I was lucky to have her for as long as I could. Every day I expected her to dump me. To realize what a cold, stupid, selfish oaf I was.

But thankfully, she didn't leave. So I asked her to marry me. She said she wanted to be more secure in her career before we took that step. I told her it didn't matter, since I wasn't exactly on firm footing in my own employment. But she was adamant. She said she wanted to bring as much to the marriage as I did. She didn't want to be the weak link.

Laesa made me happy. It's a corny thing to say, but she gave me joy. I'm not normally a jolly person. Not that I'm a sad person, either. I'm just me. But around her, I felt like something more. Part of me knew it was because of her species. But what did it matter? *How* you got to heaven didn't make a damn difference once you were there, right?

I was busy eating my sausages. Laesa barely touched hers, so I ate them as well.

"Hank, how do you go about beating someone up?" she asked.

"I don't know. Usually there's a lot of name calling. Maybe some pushing and shoving," I said.

"I don't mean physically. How do you process it emotionally? Most people, don't get in a lot of fights. How do you justify it?"

I took a swig of beer and mulled that over.

"I've lived on Belvaille nearly my whole life. There have always been criminals here. Crime. I don't go looking for people to beat up just to beat them up. I always try and find a *real* solution. Because fighting someone almost always causes more problems than it solves. At least in the long run."

"But you do it. You've fought people. You've killed people. Right?"

Laesa knew about my past in broad terms, but I hadn't gone into details. The stuff she read about me when she was learning Colmarian was tall tales. Eighth-hand allegorical sagas that also taught proper sentence structure. I told her to forget all that junk.

"Yeah. I've killed people. Again, it's not something I like doing. It's a last resort."

"But how do you reconcile that behavior? How do you live with the...guilt?"

"The guys I've killed wouldn't listen to reason. Or they were trying to kill me or someone I was protecting," I explained.

"Come on. Sometimes you're a bodyguard for other criminals. It's not like you were saving a martyr."

"I guess that's true. I always try and not take sides, but if you get caught in a tornado, you're going to get blown around whether you like it or not."

"Right. So how do you rationalize killing one criminal over another criminal? How do you measure the value of lives?"

I sat there a long while.

"I guess this is just the world I'm in. It's what I've always known. Despite trying to negotiate terms so that everyone is happy, some instances are zero sum games. One person *has* to lose. The galaxy has winners and losers. That's an irrefutable, immutable truth. In those situations where I have control, I'm going to try and make sure that *I'm* a winner. When the stakes are life and death, you can't afford to be in second place."

She stared at me and I wondered what was going through her head. But then she grinned.

"You're saying it's okay to bury someone else if it means securing your future. Protecting your dreams," she said.

"Look, I'm not a brilliant scientist or doctor or economist. There's not a lot I'm good at. I'm bulletproof and I'm strong. That lets me be a good negotiator among people who value strength and bullets. My career *can* be violent. I try and avoid it when possible, but it's always there. So, yes, to get ahead, sometimes I have to choose someone who gets left behind."

"Left behind? That's being polite. You mean killed. But how do you think about it? Do you remember their faces? Does it haunt you?" she asked, her eyes intent.

I wanted to say yes. To pretend it was traumatic. That the countless jerks I busted up made me cry into my pillow at night. Shake my fists at the latticework and curse the unforgiving nature of fate.

"It doesn't bother me much. Maybe it should. But like you said, it's not as if I'm fighting saints or Great Men. Either I gave them a chance to take the easy way out and they refused, or I didn't have a choice because it was him or me."

"Or they were standing in the way of your goals? Win at any cost?" Laesa asked.

"I suppose."

She bent over the table and kissed my nose. It was a small gesture, but it felt great. I laid out some pretty stark details of my life and she still accepted me. It felt like forgiveness.

"I know all this sounds bad," I said. "It's weird, I haven't actually talked like this to anyone before. I've been doing this for so long it's just become...I don't want to say routine. But it's a part of the landscape."

"I think I understand," she replied. "I'm not judging you. I haven't lived the same life you have. Like you haven't lived my life."

"Yeah. I tried acting and failed miserably," I said.

I sat there, basking in the warmth of her charity, when the air got extra stinky and a shadow passed over the table. Three large figures towered over me. It was the Rough Boys. Kaxle was in front. His fur smelled like mildewed blood.

"Hello," I said.

"What gang you run with?" Kaxle growled from deep in his chest. Man, he had some big, sharp teeth.

"What did you say?" I asked.

"Your gang," he repeated.

"I'm not in a gang," I stated.

"You mutant. We mutants," he said.

"Um. That's true," I answered, not sure what else to say.

"Just savvy that you got no ties to us. You dance with the enemy, we drop you like wet dirt," he sneered.

"Wet dirt? You mean mud? Uh, okay," I replied.

The three men squinted their feral eyes and moved their heads about, as if they were contemplating the deeper meaning of my reply. Finally, Kaxle made a quick hiss and they stalked away.

"That was unusual," Laesa said.

"He asked my gang, didn't he?"

"I think so. What does it mean?" she asked.

"I have no idea."

I didn't have long to think over that encounter before Roll Bungalow walked up with a full entourage.

Roll looked like a toy action figure that had been stripped of his clothes. He only wore tight shorts and shoes. His impeccable, muscled body was shaved and oiled. He had fabulous blond hair that he must have spent hours every day maintaining.

"Stank Delicious," he said to me, on approaching.

"What?" Laesa asked.

"Stank Delicious. That was my old moniker when I played Super Class glocken with Roll Bungalow," I explained. "By the way, I used to play Super Class glocken. Roll, this is my fiancée, Laesa."

He walked over and kissed her hand. Then he sat down at our table, unasked.

"We need to talk, Hank," he said.

"Why are you stomping heavy?" I inquired. He had four guards with him and they were openly carrying submachine guns.

"It's dangerous times. Not everyone respects the sanctity of The Club," he said.

"I've been coming here for hundreds of years and never seen a gun go off in anger. This is where you put differences aside so you can get drunk in peace. You're going to lose your membership if you walk around with that pocket army," I warned.

"Never mind that. I need to know who you're with," he said, leaning in so close that I could practically see myself reflected in his perfect, shiny teeth.

"You don't have to interview anyone," Laesa laughed. "They're all coming to you."

"I don't know what's going on. The Rough Boys just asked me about my gang not a minute ago."

"Rough Boys are here?" Roll asked, alarmed.

"Yeah. I didn't even know they came to The Club."

"I'll pay you twice what they offered," Roll said urgently.

"They didn't offer me anything. Slow down and explain what's going on."

"I can't go into details," he said, looking around to see if anyone was listening.

"I have a job. I'm working as a security consultant," I said.

"Hank, you and I go back a long way. And you have to fight with someone," Roll said.

"Fight who? What are you trying to say?" I asked.

"You joshing me? You haven't heard?"

"I'm on the edge of my seat. Spill."

"It's a gang war," Roll said.

I snorted at the idea.

"There hasn't been a gang war in ages. Sure, people get murdered all the time, but that's life in the big city. A gang war is when there is gunfire on every street and coming from every doorway. Those days are over."

"You're out of the loop, Hank. It's going down," he said.

"What for? The Skim is working like clockwork. The dramatic industry is only getting bigger. There's work for everyone. We might have turf skirmishes, but those get settled by talking a lot easier than with firepower."

"Boss!" One of Roll Bungalow's men yelled.

I looked over casually and saw the whole population of The Club seemed to suddenly sprout weapons and adopt bad attitudes. I couldn't tell who were the offended parties, but it seemed like everyone was against everyone.

My mind couldn't grasp it. Was this a gag? There were *never* any hostilities here beyond drunken brawls.

The first gunshot went off from somewhere and it was followed by what sounded like a hundred replies. Bullets ricocheted off the thick steel walls. Tables were flipped over to provide cover as armed men jockeyed for position. If someone was playing a practical joke, they had tremendous attention to detail.

"Hank," a tiny voice cried.

Laesa! She was huddled down in her chair. Her eyes conveyed abject terror.

I was bulletproof. Gun battles were a mere irritation to me. Like a debilitating case of the hiccups. I had been shot on thousands of occasions and had never gotten much more than a bruise or ear infection.

But Laesa *wasn't* a mutant Ontakian. She could die any moment. I was overcome with such a sensation of dread that I momentarily froze.

Roll dropped to the ground and began barking commands to his men. That brought me back to reality.

I grabbed hold of Laesa, shielding her as best I could with my body. She was a small woman and I was a large man, so it wasn't difficult. But the air itself seemed like it had been replaced with lead projectiles as The Club exploded into the biggest indoor firefight I had ever experienced.

There was no escape. I couldn't use any of my usual tactics because of the danger to Laesa. I couldn't wait them out. I couldn't join in the conflict. I couldn't try and negotiate a ceasefire, as I had no idea who was fighting or why. I didn't dare take out my shotgun, because then I'd just be another armed idiot begging to be shot at.

The elevator!

I maneuvered Laesa back against the far wall, all the while covering her with my body. This location cut down on the directions bullets were coming from. I got shot in my rear thigh with what must have been a small caliber pistol. If I hadn't been here, that could have easily hit Laesa and done serious damage. I had to get her to safety.

We didn't run. In a firefight, people panic and shoot at anything that attracts the eye. We gently slid along the wall, trying to look as unthreatening as possible. I had my back to the combat and my arms wrapped around a woman. I couldn't look any less dangerous unless I put a diaper on my head—and I didn't have one handy.

It felt like ages for us to make it to the elevator. Every bullet that whizzed by or hit the wall made my heart skip a beat. It was pure luck that Laesa hadn't been clipped by an errant round. There seemed to be at least three firing guns for every one person on the floor. I'm not sure *anyone* knew what was happening. It was complete madness.

The elevator doors opened and there were two men inside. I didn't check if they were armed, angry, surprised, or what. In one fluid motion, I pushed Laesa past them, where she immediately dropped and huddled in the corner. I grabbed both men by the front of their clothes and threw them behind me. I stepped into the elevator and punched the buttons.

Three bullets panged against the back of the elevator before the doors closed. If Laesa had been standing instead of shielding herself on the floor, she would have been hit.

The elevator car began descending. I waited a few seconds and then punched the emergency stop.

"What are you doing?" Laesa asked.

"This whole club could be a war zone," I said. "In between floors of an original Belvaille building is the most secure spot on this space station. We got at least two feet of industrial carbon steel protecting us on all sides."

"Are we going to *wait* in here?"

"Yes. Stay down and keep your head covered. I'm going to make some calls."

I said it with confidence. Like I did this all the time. But I was honestly terrified. Not for myself, for Laesa. Why did I bring her to an underworld club? What was I thinking?

I couldn't call MTB. He was beyond trustworthy, but he didn't have the manpower to put down a battle of this magnitude. His police were in the business of arriving after the dust settled and handing out warped justice in hindsight.

Garm was also out of the question. This was outside her jurisdiction and outside her very narrow set of concerns. I was also afraid what would happen if her overeager Navy soldiers, not known for their restraint, came face to face with a gangland conflict.

I called Cliston and my scientist friend Delovoa. Cliston was at work and Delovoa at home. Even in the best-case scenario it would be thirty minutes before they could get here. I explained what to do. Explained it again. I had to scream at them so they could hear me. A few times I had to type things out.

"You're going to be fine," I said to Laesa, when I got off the tele. "No one is shooting at you. Besides, this kind of thing is rarely fatal. Just a lot of commotion."

Laesa looked bad. She wasn't injured, but she was shell-shocked and scared. Just about everyone I dealt with in the last half-millennia had been some kind of crook, noble, fixer, or vagrant. They were not normal people. You started to take it for granted that everyone was like that. I was not *remotely* a normal person. But Laesa was. She was not prepared for this. She didn't deserve it.

"Are we going to be okay?" she asked pitifully.

"The Club is an original Belvaille structure. A laser torch would take ten hours to reach us. If the whole space station spiraled into a star it might get a little warm, but we'd be fine," I said, trying to brighten her spirits. "You'd probably enjoy the heat."

"Are we going to starve to death?" she asked, as if the elevator might be our new home.

This was so beyond her experiences she didn't have a clue. It would be like if I started deep-sea diving. I'd barely even *seen* water larger than a glassful. If some ocean creature came up to me, I wouldn't have the faintest idea what to do.

"We'll stay until we don't hear shooting," I said. "It shouldn't take long. Bullets are expensive."

Despite being deep inside a metal coffin, it was not the least bit quiet. Seeing guns on tele shows could make someone underestimate how loud the weapons were in real life. It wasn't just the sheer volume, which was greater than anything short of a spaceship engine. Guns accelerated a chunk of metal past the speed of sound. Physics protested loudly at the disturbance and firearms tended to be in the 150-decibel range. Anything above 90 would make you deaf after a while.

The rapid-fire shots echoing through The Club made it feel like an unruly adolescent was beating on my brain with a mallet. Even if you covered your ears, the sound waves traveled through your bones.

"It's unbearable," she moaned.

I was already half-deaf and The Club was incredibly loud to me. Laesa's virgin ears probably hadn't dealt with anything more thundering than actual thunder.

"Why is this happening?" Laesa asked.

"I don't know."

I could glean *some* information from the noise. The number of different weapons firing had increased, but they were shooting less frequently. That told me the sides were hunkering down and squaring off. The battle lines were becoming entrenched. I could also hear shooting on all sides and altitudes. The fighting was now on the floors above *and* below us. It was good I stopped the elevator. We might not have reached the street.

I just realized that when I dashed from our table, I stuffed a sausage in my jacket pocket. Even my subconscious was a glutton. I took out the sausage and began nibbling on it.

"Can I have some?" Laesa asked.

I tore it in half and handed her a piece. She held it in front of her face like a protective talisman, but didn't eat. She was just searching for a distraction. Greasy, processed meat was all we had at the moment.

After a while, the firing grew more sporadic, but it was still coming from all angles. Our adrenaline rush had worn off and even Laesa was growing restless.

"Should we try and sneak out?" she asked.

"Our elevator is in the center of the building. We can't sneak from here. It's too risky. Just wait for Cliston and Delovoa."

"What will they do?"

"I gave them instructions," I said.

I knew I could depend on Cliston. He was the most competent *entity* I had ever encountered in my life. Delovoa was another story.

Ten minutes later, the shooting completely stopped.

"Listen," I said.

A loudspeaker outside The Club was pitched to truly mindboggling levels. We could hear it as if someone was shouting right next to us.

"I repeat, this is the PCC Navy," Delovoa said. "You are all under arrest! You are to be henceforth interred in a forced labor prison camp. There you will manufacture senior citizen undergarments while serving as sexual playthings for the Navy's legion of rabid attack dogs."

I chuckled at the description. It made sense that Delovoa was doing the talking and not Cliston. Cliston's voice and manner were too recognizable. And he wasn't a good liar.

"Is the Navy here?" Laesa asked hopefully.

"No. It's the guys."

"They're making it up? What if they look outside and sees it's a trick?"

I chuckled.

"This club is for *career criminals*. The only thing that scares them more than honest work is incarceration. They're probably jumping out the windows right now."

But my gleefulness was interrupted by several tremendous booms that shook the entire building.

"What was that?" Laesa asked.

"Not sure. Maybe someone had grenades?" I said, knowing that grenades couldn't possibly cause the reinforced building to shudder.

"This is the PCC Navy," Delovoa blared again. "You are in violation of Section 1-2-3 of the 4-5-6 Protocol. Those found on the premises will be castrated using wooden forks. Then you will be fed a steady diet of alkaline hydration so that your piss burns where your dingalings used to be."

"I don't understand," Laesa said.

"Just wait."

We sat for another thirty minutes. Delovoa belted out a series of gruesome tortures that only someone with experience torturing people could dream up. I finally received a tele from Cliston. He was inside The Club and said it appeared to be empty.

I released the emergency stop and we descended to the first floor. When the doors opened, Cliston and Delovoa were waiting for us.

"My throat hurts," Delovoa complained, rubbing his neck.

Laesa had met Delovoa before, but she never got used to him and always stared. It was understandable.

Delovoa had constructed his body using "parts" he scavenged from various unlucky citizens. He was covered in gashes, knobs, stitches, plates, and puss-like ooze. He had a snot-covered pig nose, a gaping jaw filled with metal teeth, and three eyeballs that blinked and gazed out of sequence.

Cliston walked forward with a blanket and gently wrapped it around Laesa. Damn was he the perfect butler.

"I think perhaps we should be retiring home," Cliston stated.

"An excellent idea," I agreed. "Thank you both for rescuing us."

"What happened? I thought there was never shooting at The Club," Delovoa asked.

"Let's talk on the way. People might be pissed off when they learn you're the sole member of the PCC Navy."

"I fired a couple missiles at the building just to make it convincing," Delovoa replied.

"You could have killed us!" I said.

"They were small missiles." He shrugged. "Sort of small."

CHAPTER 12

I didn't want to risk running into any more inexplicable bloodbaths like what happened at The Club, so the next day I decided to visit an old colleague to try and make sense of what was going on in the city.

Rendrae was a journalist. He was the absolute best journalist I knew. I suppose that wasn't saying a lot since he was the only journalist I knew.

There had been a persistent rumor that Rendrae had died. I hadn't seen him in ages, but his name was still listed on the masthead of the local tele publication, *The News*. Besides, Rendrae was such an insatiable reporter there was no way he would allow himself to die without writing about it first. *The News* used to be a must-read publication, but a handful of years ago it changed formats and become a tabloid rag that reported primarily about the personal lives of famous Damakan actors.

I expected the headquarters of *The News* to be a dilapidated flophouse filled with degenerate journalists. But it was sleek, modern, staffed with bright young things, and the office thermostat was set to approximately a zillion degrees. Everyone inside was a Damakan.

"Can I help you?" the receptionist asked with a thick accent.

"Is there someone who works here named Rendrae?" I replied.

"Not that I'm familiar with."

"He's kind of fat and green," I said.

"Do you have the correct office? Oh, I see his name in the directory. My apologies. He's in room 24A. That's way in back."

"Okay. Thanks."

I took off my jacket and dragged it behind me on the carpet. I was too hot to lift my arm. These Damakans were going to be the death of me.

It felt like I walked halfway across the city. Behind a stack of spare office chairs, broken computer equipment, and piles of boxes, I found office 24A. It was practically walled off it was so out of the way. Through the open door, I spotted a thin man on the floor doing what looked like push-ups. Either that or he was trying, and failing, to get up from the carpet over and over again.

"Excuse me," I said, "I'm looking for a man named Rendrae."

The exerciser ignored me and pumped out thirty more push-ups before I even had time to get annoyed. When he was done, he hopped up and faced me. The man's skin was a bit droopy around the eyes and chin, but otherwise he appeared youthful. He had what looked like a dinner plate on his head. I suppose it was a hat. His skin tone was such a dark shade of green it was almost black.

"Hank!" the man exclaimed.

"Do I know you?" I asked.

"It's me, Rendrae," he said, smiling brightly.

"Um. No, it's not."

"It is. I had corrective surgery," he said, hurrying over and holding out his arms like he was expecting a hug.

"Corrected what? You don't look anything like Rendrae."

"I know I lost some weight—" he began.

"You're a twig. Rendrae is fat. Huge."

"You're one to talk," he replied, annoyed. "I was sick. I didn't know I was, but I had my entire circulatory system overhauled."

I was still skeptical. I'd seen diets before, but nothing this extreme. He didn't even *sound* particularly like Rendrae.

"You're a darker shade of green," I said.

"That's because my whole body was out of whack. I almost died."

I gingerly gave the thin man a hug.

"There you go. How's it hanging?" Rendrae asked.

"I'd like to say 'below my knees,' but that only applies to my scrotum. Old age and gravity did a tag team on me. How are *you* doing?" I asked.

"Great! Fantastic. I got a new heart. New veins. The works."

"I didn't know they could do that here. They can't even check my temperature when *I* go into the hospital."

"I had to travel to a whole other quadrant for specialists. Twenty-four separate operations. I technically died three times on the table. I've been recovering this whole while. I was gone for years. Didn't you notice?" he asked in a hurt tone.

"I hadn't seen you around. But I guess I lost track. I haven't been as connected with things as I used to be. I got engaged to be married."

"You? Unbelievable."

"Did *The News* change because you went away for surgery?" I asked.

"That is correct. I knew I had to turn over operations to keep it going. I'm still the publisher, but I haven't taken over all the editorial duties until I can get back to full strength."

"You look pretty strong. Were you just doing push-ups?"

"I'm all about fitness now. I won't make the mistake of falling back into my old habits. I got a second chance at life."

"Is everyone at *The News* a Damakan?" I asked, not sure where to begin.

"Come inside," he said.

I walked into Rendrae's office and immediately felt better. Every wall had an air conditioner blowing full blast. Rendrae closed the door behind us.

"Wow, this is like old times," he said joyfully. "Except you're married and I'm skinny."

"I'm only engaged. Engaged to be engaged."

"Is it to Garm?"

"Garm? No. You don't know her. Her name is Laesa," I said.

"I can't comprehend you agreeing to marriage. But Belvaille always was a city in a constant state of flux. That's what makes reporting here so rewarding," he said.

"Were there Damakans on Belvaille when you left for surgery?" I asked.

"Some, but not like now. If you told either of us thirty years ago that this space station would become a televised entertainment capital, we would have laughed at you."

"And then beaten you up and stolen your wallet."

"Precisely," he agreed. "Oh, Hank, it's fantastic to see your ugly face. I was concerned all the truly old, old-timers had left or died."

"Delovoa is still around."

"That maniac? He's hardly worth speaking about."

"He's not so bad. Just misunderstood," I said.

"Delovoa conducted secret, dangerous experiments on our population for years!"

"Yeah, but—" I started, but I didn't have anything to add. "So did *The News* change because of all the Damakans that arrived while you were gone?"

"Yes. In a way. My beloved paper has become garbage. It runs stories of the lowest sort. Gossip. Tabloid. That's not the stuff I'm interested in."

"It really has taken a bad turn," I said.

"You don't have to tell me. I read copies of it while I was recuperating and I think it slowed down my healing process. I have to try and get this city interested in reading hard news again."

"How do you do that? The only thing people care about is the Skim and the dramatic industry. And it's hard to write about the Skim without attracting attention."

"I need an exposé. Something that will blow this city up!"

"Don't do that. I live here," I said.

"I don't mean literally. I need a series of stories that will make people take notice. Like the old days. It will be my entry back into the reporting world. It will also give me the ability to change the format of *The News*. A return to hard journalism. You remember what *The News* was like, don't you?"

"Sure. I thought it was tops. I'd read it every day on the toilet. Or taking a bath. You always got to the bottom of things. No matter who you pissed off."

"Thank you for that, Hank. Listen, I have a few ideas I'm kicking around for my breakout piece. How about this. *Boranjame: Myth or Mythology?*"

"Are you trying to say the Boranjame aren't real? I've personally had my brain fried by two of them."

"I wasn't aware of that," he said.

"There's a Boranjame sitting in this System right now in his very own spaceship. The Marquor of Lunacy, Gax, the Unfathomable and Disreputable."

"Yes, but have you actually *seen* him?"

"Yeah, he fried my brain."

"Okay. How about this story? *The Great Ank Monetary Scheme: How Your Credits Aren't Worth What You Think They Are.*"

"What does that mean? Are the Ank up to something again?" I asked worriedly.

"I don't know. I've gotten a few Ank spokespeople to talk to me, but I couldn't understand anything they were saying. Not that they speak a different language, it's all obfuscation. Overnight leveraged discount rates, float currency exchanges, volatility inversion."

I relaxed.

"That's just the way they talk. I don't trust the Ank, but they know money. The problem with doing an article on them is that regular people won't understand it."

"That's what I feared. I wrote four pages so far and had six pages of footnotes and appendices."

The reporter slumped, defeated.

"Something happened to you, Rendrae," I said.

"I replaced my entire vascular system."

"Where is that pudgy old newshound? I came here looking for information and you seem to know less than I do."

"What information were you looking for?" he asked, intrigued.

"Alright. There seems to be a gang war brewing and I can't figure out how, why, or what."

"That doesn't particularly sound like a gang war. They're usually straightforward. Side A. Side B. Fight until someone wins. The *reason* they start can be obscure and pedantic, however. Like someone made a frowny face at someone else and two months later a hundred people are dead. But the war itself is often self-explanatory. Who have you spoken with?"

"I've called a ton of insiders. Most of them say they don't know what's happening or think I'm exaggerating. But there was a full-blown firefight at The

Club. And when I called around to find out what started it, no one knew. I've never seen anything like it. It's like a top-secret gang war."

"That's a contradiction. Tell me everything you know," Rendrae said, excited.

I did. Weelon Poshor's murder. Stealing the generator for Ulteem. What MTB told me. Garm told me. What happened at The Club. The Rough Boys. The Guilds. The productions. My acting career. Cliston's Artistry Agency. And everything in between.

It took several hours of talking. Rendrae took copious notes and rarely interrupted me. When I was finally done, I was sitting on the floor, my mouth was dry, and I was exhausted.

Rendrae stood there with his eyes glinting like fire.

"This is it!" He said.

"Is what?"

"My exposé. A gang war. A *covert* gang war! Hank, this comes at a perfect time."

"How can a gang war be perfect?"

He sighed.

"I wasn't completely forthcoming about my position here at *The News*. My surgeries were expensive. Extremely. Out of necessity, I now have another investor in this company. He hired an editor to run the paper while I was away. The editor says my reporting style is too archaic and doesn't fit the new format. *That's* why I need a killer story. Something I can leverage to regain ownership of the paper. You've handed it to me."

"I have?"

"Sure. A gang war has broad appeal. Even beyond the station. This is excitement on an intergalactic level."

"How can you be sure? You just heard about it."

"I can *smell* it, Hank. I can *feel* it! This is what I was looking for."

"Okay. But full disclosure: I was hired as a security consultant by Garm to find out the cause of these attacks and put an end to them."

"Because they're interrupting our dear Adjunct Overwatch's profits?"

I snorted at the idea.

"You obviously don't understand the dramatic industry," I said with authority.

"Go on. Explain it to me. You're always taking up for Garm when she screws us over."

"Okay. The Belvaille dramatic industry has grown beyond her control. The revenue is booked under the PCC Navy. She said it was *billions* of credits."

"Hank, you're gullible. You could buy a planet for a billion credits. Maybe not a great planet, but one certainly more valuable than some boring soap operas. There is no way the button-down Navy is going to concern itself with that foolishness."

"Rendrae, the Supreme Super Accountant Vice-General came here and audited her when the movies weren't doing well. He was like, 'hey, where's our money?'"

"That does not remotely sound like language a military accountant would employ."

"I'm paraphrasing. We're used to thinking of Belvaille being local. It's not. Garm uses those telescopes to broadcast the shows. They reach every corner of the empire. Your newspaper is a gossip sheet devoted to their actors. That has to tell you something."

Rendrae mulled this over.

"You know, perhaps it's true. I was halfway across the galaxy and I watched Belvaille shows in the hospital. I hadn't made the connection because I was busy fighting for my life."

"Damakan actors are pretty amazing, right?"

"Frankly, I don't see it. Everyone in my ward went on and on about the programs, but I thought they were cheap melodrama."

"Huh. Maybe they don't work on you. But they work on everyone else. Hell, they work on me, and I'm not exactly the king of sentimental. Getting back to my original issue, though, what should I do as far as the gang war?"

"What should we do. This is my story now. Let me clear out my schedule. Come back in a few days and we'll go snooping around."

"What do you have to clear out? It didn't sound like you were working. The receptionist didn't even know you."

Rendrae appeared embarrassed, his dark green cheeks blushing.

"I was going to interview some actors. Try and *ease* myself back into reporting. But your story is much better. Especially if what you say about their revenue is true. Money and violence. All we need is some romance and it would be a Damakan drama."

"Alright. I'll be in touch," I said.

"It's great seeing you, Hank. Just like old times. Thanks for stopping by. Don't talk to any other reporters," he said.

"There aren't any."

I was walking out of *The News* building, trying to reach the door before I melted from the heat, when I saw all the Damakan employees staring at me. They peeked over cubicle walls, around corners, and stood in the hallway. Something was clearly up.

"Is your name Hank?" one of them asked.

"Yeah. Why?"

"Are you in any way related to Hank the Fat Mutant of Belvaille?" another one asked.

"I'm not entirely comfortable with that name. But yeah, I suppose that's me," I replied.

The Damakans erupted with joy. They were squealing and cheering and otherwise celebrating in exaggerated fashion. They were passing those emotions back and forth between themselves. I wanted to leave, but they were blocking the hall.

"Do you have a second to speak with us?" one asked.

"What do you want to know?" I asked.

They all drew near and had their teles out to record me. I felt strangely important and stood up straighter.

"How did you manage to eat a Therezian?" a lady asked. Her hair was bright red and she had puffy lips and high cheekbones. She seemed to be the designated spokesperson of the bunch.

"I didn't. The reading materials you Damakans were provided weren't actual history. It was all make-believe."

"But you're here on Belvaille. And you're Hank," she said.

"And he's fat," another pointed out, and they all nodded.

"You tell stories. You're Damakans. Those stories aren't true, right? You make it entertaining," I said.

"Our theater is nothing compared to Colmarian history. You have murders every single day," she exclaimed breathlessly.

"Belvaille is risky, but I'm not sure about murders *every* day," I replied.

"On our home planet, someone might be slain every four or five years," she said. "But I was referring to the whole PCC. You don't think someone is murdered every day somewhere?"

They all stared at me for an answer.

"The whole empire?" I asked, shocked. "Probably thousands, or tens of thousands of people are murdered every day."

The Damakans couldn't comprehend that. They spoke, and acted, to one another to try and process what I was saying.

"The galaxy is huge," I continued. "We have 50,000 species in the PCC. Just think about all the times someone is cheating on their wife, or ripping off their neighbors, or up to their throats in gambling debts."

I blew their minds.

"You're just like you are in the stories," the lady said breathlessly. "Gambling debts..."

"I never *ate* a Therezian. You want to see a real Therezian you can go out and stand on his corpse. Then you'll understand how it's completely impossible for anyone my size to eat something *that* size," I said.

"Did you kill Wallow?" she asked.

"No. He beat me up a bunch of times. No one *killed* Wallow. No one kills Therezians without strategic weapons. We think he died of a heart attack" I said.

"Wallow is in the stories as well," she said.

"What did he do?"

"You ate him," she replied.

"See, that's just bad reporting. You all are journalists. You need to concentrate on facts. Not that crazy fiction. Go back there and talk to Rendrae. He can teach you true journalism."

"Who are you dating?" she asked, apparently not interested in true journalism.

"I'm kind of engaged. Pre-engaged. Sort of. She's a Damakan like you guys," I said.

That got the biggest reaction yet.

"How did you meet your Damakan wife?" the woman asked.

"She was at the Artistry Agency trying to get in to see Cliston. I was also trying to see him. We got to talking while we waited and we hit it off."

"She's an actor?" she asked.

"Yes. A great actor," I confirmed.

"What's her name?"

"Laesa Swavort."

"What kind of ring did you get her?" she asked.

"Ring of what?"

"Engagement ring," she said.

"What's that?"

"You need a ring," she explained. "It's standard in any Damakan engagement."

"I'm not a Damakan," I shrugged.

"We know that, Hank the Fat Mutant of Belvaille. But you still need a ring. What is your marriage like? Do you act for her?" she asked.

"We talk a lot. And go to shows. And we watch the tele."

"What are your favorite programs?" the woman inquired.

I was drawing a blank. The questions were coming so fast.

"I don't know. We watch everything. What about this ring again? What's it supposed to be made out of?"

"Gold. Platinum. And delfiblinium," she stated.

Delfiblinium was not only a super-rare substance, it was explosive. Though only in large quantities.

"And diamonds," she added.

"What the hell?" I complained. "Do only wealthy Damakans get married? How do you even know about delfiblinium? I thought you all weren't advanced technologically."

"We never developed space travel but we were still modern. We used delfiblinium. The raw materials are plentiful on our home world. I'm describing a traditional ring. You can have other designs, but it's supposed to have those in some quantities for good luck," she said. Then she held up her own hand to show off a ring. It was smaller than I thought. I had to squint to see the delfiblinium.

"Just one diamond?" I asked.

"One for each year you want to be married," she replied.

"So like, a hundred diamonds? She'd have to carry it around in a wheelbarrow!"

"They don't need to be large," the woman clarified.

I took out my own tele and began writing this down. This was the first I ever heard about a ring.

"If you're engaged, where will the ceremony take place?" she asked.

"Ceremony?" I repeated.

"What kind of facility is it going to be in? How many guests? What kind of food will you serve? Will there be dancing? Will you send out invitations? How about her relatives? Will you pay for their travel expenses? What about her wedding gown?" they took turns asking.

I stopped writing.

"Is all this traditional too?" I asked skeptically.

"How do Colmarians normally get married?" she asked, confused.

"I just thought people kind of agreed on it. I've never been married before," I said.

They kept asking me questions and I answered numbly. I realized that I probably couldn't afford to get married. Not the way they were describing it. Where was I going to get a delfiblinium and diamond ring?

After an hour of answering questions on my love life, and what kind of aliens I'd eaten over the decades, I'd had enough. They followed me out to the street, making inquiries and taking pictures the whole way.

If anything, it was a learning experience. From now on if someone asked if I was Hank the Fat Mutant of Belvaille, I was going to categorically say no.

CHAPTER 13

"I don't really understand why he's your friend," Laesa said to me the next day.

"There are some people you've been friends with for so long, you stop questioning why," I replied.

"You said yourself that he's strange. Why do you want to be associated with him?"

"I've known him longer than I've known anyone alive. The fact he's eccentric is part of his charm."

"And you're going to visit him for breakfast?" Laesa asked incredulously.

"He *said* breakfast, but knowing Delovoa it won't be simple biscuits and juice."

"I still don't understand why he's your best friend."

"When you live your whole life on a *criminal* space station, it's to be expected that a lot of your friends will be criminals. He and I have been through a lot together. We've seen the galaxy turn itself inside out. That kind of history weaves people together no matter how different they started out. He's saved my life a number of times. That's not something I can forget."

Laesa saw it was futile trying to apply logic to the relationship and simply gave me a kiss.

Delovoa lived some floors above me at City Hall. For whatever reason, he told me to meet him on the ground floor and bring some walking clothes. When I went outside, Delovoa was waiting.

"I said walking-around clothes, not a bathing suit," Delovoa snorted.

I had on shorts and a t-shirt. It was an outfit I would have never worn in the past. Not because I was a fancy dresser or anything. Summer clothes hadn't existed on Belvaille before the Damakans came and messed with our climate control. Now it was permanently beach weather.

Delovoa was standing in front of a large white vehicle.

"Is this your ride?" I asked.

"Yes."

"You own a dodgy-looking van covered in graffiti with tinted windows?"

"It's more presentable than you in shorts. No one should be forced to look at your knees," he countered.

"No one's *forcing* you."

"I can't look away. I thought your face was bad. It looks like a train ran over your kneecaps."

"A train *did* run over my kneecaps. Back when the city had trains. I miss them. It was so easy to get around," I said wistfully.

"Yeah, and no one had to fear you driving. Okay, now that we've settled that, get in. I need your help," he said.

I got in the passenger side and Delovoa drove. There was a partition between the front cab and the cargo so I couldn't see if anything was back there. We began driving west. The air conditioning was cranked to max.

"This van is slow," I observed.

"Belvaille isn't a racetrack. The reason you don't have a car is because you kept crashing yours."

"No. My car was stolen. I haven't saved enough money for a new one. I'm not sure if I need one."

"Walking is for peasants," he said.

"I am a peasant. Besides, you said to bring walking clothes."

"I would have told you to wear a tuxedo if I knew I was going to be presented with your deformed knees. They're even worse with your legs bent."

"Have you looked in the mirror...like, ever? You have metal teeth. You have fifty different skin types stitched together and secured with zippers and staples. Your nose is leaking snot all over your shirt!"

"A lot of people find me enticing," Delovoa said, unconcerned.

"No one in the history of the universe has referred to you as enticing."

"Jealous?" Delovoa smirked, his sharp metal teeth catching the light.

"Forget it. You're incapable of taking criticism. Which somehow reminds me: I need you to be the Alternate Man at my wedding."

"Alternate Man? What does that entail? Do I have to marry her if you get cold feet?"

"I'm still getting the details. The Damakan nuptials are kind of confusing. I think you're supposed to stand there and smile."

"Stand *and* smile? You ask too much, my friend."

"I know. But I'm trying to get everything ready for the wedding," I sighed.

"Do you have a date planned? That happened fast."

"No. She hasn't said yes, officially. But I want to be prepared."

"Brilliant. I'm doing something similar. I'm making arrangements for when they elect me King of the Galaxy."

"I think my wedding is a bit more likely than that. Laesa just wants to have a better career first. It will happen. But man, I had no idea that a wedding was such a *gigantic* event. So complicated," I said.

"Really? I thought two people simply agreed they were married and that was it."

"That's what I thought! But not for Damakans. I got to find some delfiblinium for a ring. Can you believe it?"

"No. I figured you would want Cliston to be your Alternate Man. He's great at ceremonial nonsense."

"Cliston is going to be my wedding planner, wedding arranger, decorator, and he's going to perform the service. Did you know he's registered to conduct weddings in forty-three different Systems?"

"Doesn't surprise me. How much is all this going to cost?"

"Lots! I haven't been able to get my head around it yet, but I would guess hundreds of thousands of credits," I said.

"What a scam. Why don't you get your new bride to pay for the wedding?"

"Laesa can't afford it. She has even less money than me."

"You ever wonder if maybe you're getting the short end of this union?" Delovoa asked.

"You think she's marrying me for my money? I can't afford a car, remember?"

"Women can be crafty. Far more devious than men. Look at Garm."

"You irradiated thousands of innocent people in the past."

"That wasn't being crafty. That was screwing up. If I was crafty, no one would have learned about it. Women, the galaxy over, are a lot more subtle than men. You can never be sure of their motives. That might include your Damakan bride-to-be."

"Don't stereotype. All women aren't the same, just like all men aren't the same. You and I aren't anything alike. The PCC has 50,000 different species. Men and women only exist in like a third of those races. There are all kinds of strange genders we never even dreamed of."

"I'm just trying to give you a friendly warning is all. I don't need a genetics lesson. I know more about biology than you ever will," he said.

"Laesa's great. She's turning my life around."

Delovoa stared at me with two of his three eyes, keeping one looking at the road. I had to admit, Delovoa was a pretty good driver. He managed the van's blinky-light things, turning, and could talk to me, all while staying in the proper lanes.

"I didn't want to do this, but it looks like I have no choice," Delovoa began.

"Please don't make this awkward by declaring your love for me."

"Is it possible that maybe your girl is only using you?" he asked.

"My *girl?* You've met Laesa like a dozen times. You can say her name."

"Okay. Is Laesa using you?"

"How could she possibly be using me? I just got out of debt to my butler."

"Belvaille is a challenging place to live. You probably don't realize that, because you're one of the people that makes it challenging."

"You do worse things than me. Why doesn't Laesa marry you?"

"She's not my type," Delovoa said, drawing his hand over his misshapen skull in an effort to slick back his imaginary hair.

"You think she's with me for safety?"

"She needed your help to escape The Club," he said.

"She wouldn't have been there if it wasn't for me. I'm the one who got her in trouble. Besides, Laesa is a tough gal."

"No Damakan is tough. Not by Belvaille standards. You have more contacts and connections than nearly anyone on this space station. You probably robbed, saved, or blackmailed every living soul here at one point or another."

"How would that help Laesa? She's not a bookie. She's an actor," I said.

"A *starving* actor. And you're the boss of the hottest talent agent in the city."

"Cliston? More like he's my boss."

"Whatever. Most Damakans would kill for a meeting with Cliston and she gets to eat dinner with him every night."

"He's only a butler when he's serving dinner. You know that," I replied.

"I do. But she doesn't. Cliston isn't easy to understand for normal people."

"Okay, but she doesn't need to marry me for that."

"But she hasn't married you. You're the one talking marriage. But how often do you pay her bills? Her rent? Her food? Her clothing?"

"I'm hardly rich. Kicking in something now and then is just what couples do for each other," I said.

"You're not rich *now*. But despite your best efforts, you've managed to become fantastically wealthy on a number of occasions. If she asked around she would know that. She could be biding her time until you're wealthy again."

I shook my head.

"You don't understand Laesa at all. You haven't given her a chance."

"Maybe *you* don't understand her, Hank. Seriously, ask yourself why a woman like her, a species like hers, would be with a guy like you. A Damakan and an Ontakian? Does that make any sense? You're a mutant, a test-tube soldier who has spent a thousand years beating up people and getting beaten up. And she's an actor. Do those things really go together?"

"You don't get to choose who you like. I think *you're* just miserable and upset that you don't have me to wallow alongside you as usual."

"That's it, Hank. I'm sobbing into my pillow every night. When have you ever seen me depressed?" he asked.

He had a point. Delovoa was a patchwork mess of leaking body parts and he didn't care. He was cheerful—in a morbid sort of way.

"She can get any man she wants and she chose you?" he continued.

"I think Laesa is beautiful, but it's far-fetched to say she could have *anyone*."

"She's a Damakan. She can *force* men to fall in love with her and then use them."

I laughed.

"You're making her out to be some evil genius. Don't assume other people share *your* personality traits. You're one of a kind, Delovoa."

"That's true," he admitted.

"Look, I know you guys don't care for each other. She thinks you're a disgusting weirdo who is putting me in jeopardy—and she has a point. You think she's a boring 'normal' who doesn't know martial arts, is unable to bench-press a car, and isn't running a major criminal enterprise. She's not like anyone I've ever dated. Laesa is a simple woman."

"She's a Damakan. She's not so simple as all that."

"Maybe not. But she's a sweetheart. She's what I need in my life. I have enough excitement in my day that I don't want to come home to a fistfight every night. Why can't you wish me well?"

"Fine. Fine. But in a moment, you'll get to see how hard this city can be on people."

"That doesn't sound promising," I said.

After another ten minutes driving, we found ourselves in the far southwest. This area was a bit seedy and trash littered the streets. Delovoa stuck his head out the window and sniffed the air. Because of his giant, wet nose, he had an excellent sense of smell.

"There's one," Delovoa said.

"One what?"

But he didn't answer. Instead, he pulled over and got out. I followed him around to the back of the van where he opened the doors. Inside, it looked like a fully stocked hospital.

"Grab that cart," Delovoa said.

He activated a hydraulic lift. I rode it up and walked into the back of the van to retrieve the cart.

"What is this thing?" I asked.

"One of my inventions," he answered vaguely.

I took my hands off.

"One of your inventions that will kill *me* or one of your inventions that will kill others?" I asked. Delovoa only seemed to make two types of things.

"Others, you big baby. Now hurry up."

"You're awfully pushy for someone who isn't paying me."

"Consider it compensation for my efforts as Alternate Man at your wedding."

"*Efforts.* As if standing and smiling is such a chore."

"Come on before he gets away," Delovoa said.

"Who? Damn, this thing is heavy."

I had to put my back into it to move the cart. I pushed it after Delovoa, who was moving down the sidewalk. He stopped beside what was obviously a homeless man sitting against a nearby building. Delovoa crouched down.

"Hey, you want to make 500 credits?" Delovoa said.

The homeless man was startled. He must have felt he was in the grips of some horrible hallucination. The three-eyed, snot-nosed Delovoa was leaning over and grinning, showing rows of teeth that looked straight from a junkyard.

"Huh?" the man asked.

"Five hundred. You want it?"

The homeless man looked at me for some confirmation. I shrugged.

"Sure," he said, not even caring what was involved.

"Let me see your left arm," Delovoa said.

The man dutifully held out his arm. Delovoa took it and rolled up the sleeve. He examined it like he was admiring a piece of artwork that he picked out at a flea market.

"How's your right arm?" Delovoa asked.

"Good."

Delovoa checked it.

"Both of these are pretty lousy, but looking at your shoes, I can't imagine your feet are any better."

"What are you going to do?" the homeless man asked.

"Cut off your arm."

"What?" the man said, shocked.

"And give you 500 credits."

"No way," the man said.

"Oh, come on. How many arms do you need? Think about it. Most stuff you do with just one hand. Lift a glass. Scratch your head. Wipe your butt. It's a lot of money."

"I'll die!" The man pleaded.

"No, you won't. Hank, bring that over here."

I pushed the cart closer and Delovoa activated some controls. A huge assortment of robotic surgical tools swiveled up and out of the thick cart. There was every type of saw, syringe, scalpel, and suture that existed.

"You'll be numbed, sterilized, and stitched. You won't feel a thing—except the wad of cash in your pocket," Delovoa said.

The homeless man looked back at me again.

"Yeah," I admitted weakly, "he's good at this stuff."

"Let me see the money," the man said, his eyes squinting with mistrust.

Delovoa fished in his pockets and threw a bundle of plastic credits down. The man counted them and seemed amazed at the sum. It looked like a sale.

"What do I have to do?" he asked.

Delovoa stuck out his hand and sprayed the man in the face with a small canister. The homeless man slumped to the side, unconscious.

"Hank, pick him up and put him on top of the cart, please."

I sighed and did so, as Delovoa retracted all the devices that weren't going to be used.

"Is he going to be okay?" I asked, before setting the man down.

"Of course. I make my money off repeat business and word of mouth— unless I take their mouths. I can't go around murdering people," he scoffed. "I'll never get another volunteer."

"Is the arm for you?"

"No. I sell them to plastic surgeons. Belvaille doesn't have a donor system in place. If you lose a hand, you have to make do with a cheap prosthetic. But no one wants a mechanical limb, they want the real deal."

"Seems pretty sleazy," I said.

"It is. But what job on Belvaille *isn't* sleazy? By the way, keep your eyeballs out for some good eyeballs. Blue especially. Those are worth a lot."

Delovoa began his efforts and I turned my head away. Not that I was squeamish, but seeing Delovoa work reminded me just how dark life could be at times.

Besides, if I didn't look, I could technically say that I had never *seen* the Alternate Man of my wedding chop off the arm of someone in the middle of the street so he could sell it as an aftermarket replacement.

CHAPTER 14

Later that night, Laesa and I were dining in my apartment. Cliston buzzed around in the background, quietly doing chores.

"Do you think Rendrae will help you try and figure out your little thing?" Laesa asked me.

"You mean the gang war?"

"No, the person killing Damakans."

"It's the same thing. I think it's a gang war and maybe the productions and actors are just collateral damage."

"That doesn't sound good."

"You're safe. As long as you aren't involved with gangs or famous shows."

"Then that's definitely not me," she smiled.

"Rendrae seemed excited to help. And it's better than working alone."

"I thought you liked working by yourself. Other people get in your way."

"When did I say that? I was probably annoyed at someone at the time," I replied.

"You made it seem very important."

"Don't pay too much attention to the stuff I say. I'm not exactly the Lord of Wisdom. Sometimes I'm just complaining. Oh, I remember. I said that after we took a generator and I was left naked in the street and they stole my car. Yeah, they weren't very good co-workers."

"It's weird you call them co-workers. Like you're working at an office."

"It *is* work. Hard work. I had to push that generator across town in my underwear." I said.

"I just remembered, I have some fees for my acting class due tomorrow. Hank, is it okay if I borrow some money?" she asked.

"I told you a million times, you can live here if you want. That would save you a ton of cash."

"I can't do that. It wouldn't be proper," she said.

"We've already done everything that would get us kicked out of church. I don't see what the difference is."

"Maybe it's cultural. What do Ontakians feel about cohabiting?"

"I don't know. Considering our home world was destroyed, it's pretty surprising when I meet other Ontakians."

"How does your uncle feel about it?"

My dirtbag uncle Frank lived on Belvaille, but we didn't talk much. Every time I saw him, he tried to screw me over.

"I don't care what he thinks. Cultural or not, living together would save money. I've been reading about what it takes to get married. You didn't tell me about the ring. And the ceremony. And all the other stuff."

"I didn't want to scare you. I know finances are tight right now."

"My underwear is *tight*. Money, on the other hand, is welded onto a black hole at the bottom of an ocean."

"Sir, do you require new undergarments?" Cliston asked, appearing out of nowhere.

"I was joking, Cliston. With Garm's job, I'm getting a regular paycheck. Not a lot, but it's a welcome change. I can give you whatever you need for acting class. Though I wish you'd reconsider moving in. It wouldn't be too much trouble. Right, Cliston?"

He pretended not to hear me. Even though Cliston's robotic ears could register the sound a speck of dust made as it fell onto a pillow in another room.

I reached into my pocket and handed Laesa all the money I had on me.

"Thanks. This course I'm taking is on Empathic Resonance," she said.

"Great."

"Sir, might I have a private word with you in the arboretum?"

"The what?"

"The arboretum, sir."

"I don't know what that is," I said.

"I am growing fruit trees to cut down on expenses and add a bit more variety to your meals."

"You're growing trees in the apartment?" Laesa asked.

"Yes," he said.

"We can talk here," I replied.

Cliston looked briefly at Laesa.

"Will you permit me to speak as a talent agent? I know I haven't cleared the dishes yet, but it may be important."

"Oh, boy," Laesa said, smiling.

"Sure, Cliston. But don't get too excited, Laesa. He's probably going to yell at me."

"What the hell is going on!" Cliston yelled.

"Told you," I said. "What's up?"

"How about three of my clients murdered in the last week. People are too scared to go to rehearsals."

"Are they all actors killed?" I asked.

"I only represent actors. What do I know about set design?" he asked.

"I don't know. You do interior decorating. I told the other Cliston about this, but I'm working on it. For Garm. Rendrae is assisting me. I'm going to get to the bottom of it."

"How will that protect my clients? They are scared to death," he said.

"Well, not to be an ass, but at this moment I'm not working for you or your clients. I'm working for Garm," I said.

"Would you like your rent raised?" he asked.

"Not really. What do you expect me to do?"

"You said you wanted bodyguard work. That you were dying to get more assignments."

"I can only protect one actor at a time. You got dozens of clients."

"Hundreds," he corrected.

"Exactly. If I can stop the gang war, it will help them all."

"How about this: you protect a different one each night. That will reassure everyone and make it more likely you run into whatever groups are responsible."

"I'm already a consultant for Garm. I can't pull down another fulltime job."

"I'll pay you 5,000 credits a week," he said.

"Now that you mention it," I said, persuaded by the huge sum of money, "Garm is fairly understanding. And this is *kind of* working on the same thing. I can do her stuff during the day and babysit your actors at night."

"Then it's a deal?"

"7,000 a week," I countered.

"3,000 and I cut your rent by 25%."

"That's less than your original offer," I said.

"Yes, but I was going to raise your utilities. I heard you've got a bunch of fruit trees growing in your apartment now."

"Okay, okay," I said, agreeing before Cliston inevitably negotiated me down to nothing. "Just make up a schedule and let them know I'm coming. And give me all the information on the people who were killed."

"MTB has that. I made a full report. Coordinate with him. You should be working with the police, not Rendrae."

"I can do both. I'll talk to MTB."

Laesa suddenly jumped up from her chair.

"Cliston! Can I give you my headshots and work history? I'm an actor!"

Cliston's posture changed immediately.

"Would either of you care for dessert? I have chocolate pie and a custard," he said.

Laesa sat back down, defeated. But she couldn't help chuckling at Cliston's slipperiness.

"None for me. Thank you, butler Cliston," Laesa said.

"I'll take both," I said.

Laesa spent the night. The next morning, we were sitting in my kitchen, trying to wake up. When she stayed over, we compromised on the room temperature. It was too hot for me to sleep well and still too cold for her. So both of us were still sleepy.

"Here's coffee and some muffins. I'm afraid I don't have time to do more. I'm in a rush," Cliston said.

I grumbled and ate.

"Your first appointment is an actor named Gordle Maytop. He lives at 2834 Blood River Lane. I've arranged for security at the set and on the ride home, but you need to cover him all night," Cliston said.

"What's a talent agent doing in my kitchen?" I asked Cliston.

"Sir, I'm trying to save you time. If you wish, I can require you to come up to my office when speaking in my capacity as agent."

"Nah, I'm just busting your balls, Cliston. I forgot they were metal. Is your actor some weirdo I'm going to have to tiptoe around?" I asked. I wasn't a morning person.

"He's a tremendously successful thespian with fans across the galaxy. Yes, he's a weirdo," Cliston said.

"What Guild is he with?" I asked.

"Romance."

"Great. He's going to be gushing poetry or trying to seduce me," I said.

"The Guilds aren't that narrow," Laesa offered, stifling a yawn. "Gordle Maytop is a song-and-dance man. He acts in musicals."

"Just make him feel safe, Hank. Belvaille is turning ugly for my clients and that's bad for everyone," Cliston said.

"Okay. I'll go over tonight."

"You have the address?" Cliston asked.

"Let me write it down," I said, taking out my tele.

"2834 Blood River Lane."

"This city has such strange street names. They're either numbers, letters, a rich person, or about violence," Laesa said.

"They're named after things that happened here. My street used to be called Hank Block. Then a Therezian fell over dead. Now it's North and South Wallow. Do I need a passkey for the entrance?"

"No. He'll be expecting you. Goodbye, sir, miss," Cliston said on his way out.

"Bye, Cliston," Laesa called. I could tell she was tired because she didn't make an attempt to talk to agent Cliston.

"You going to eat your muffin?" I asked Laesa.

"No," she said, fiddling with her tele.

I took her food. Ate it. Drank my coffee. Got up and poured some more. Laesa seemed distant. Wasn't like her.

"Something wrong?" I asked, blundering right into it.

"You said you would go see *The Power* tonight," she accused.

"The power what?"

"It's a play. They offered me a part."

"Oh. Congratulations."

"I'm not sure I'll take the offer. I would have to leave the play I'm already in. *That's* why I wanted you to see it and let me know. You don't remember?" she asked, hurt.

"Yeah, I do. I remember. Sort of."

"You never listen when I'm talking about my acting. I asked if you'd watch the show and let me know if it was any good."

"Me? What do I know about acting? I can't even bluff at cards," I said.

"You and I watch the tele all the time. You've gotten good at spotting things I miss. We said we were going to help each other in our careers."

"We did? Are you going to load my guns?" I joked.

"No. But I did a profile on MTB. I can do things like that. Why is it you can remember Lester Big Face, the safe-cracker from a hundred years ago, and every credit you ever earned or spent, but you can't remember important things?"

"I'm old. I've got an old brain. I don't forget on purpose. Why can't you go see the show? You know what you like better than I do," I said.

"I'm acting across town at the same time. That's why I asked you about this last week."

"I have to help Cliston. I can see the play another night."

"What if they withdraw their offer? I'm not exactly a top-tier actor who can brush off casting directors," she said.

"It's not that," I began, but then I clamped my mouth shut. I could see she was upset. Like I wasn't taking her career seriously. "What time does *The Power* end? Do you know?"

"I think eight or nine. But if it's terrible, you don't have to stay for the whole thing," she said.

"I guess I can do that. If I go over to that guy's house too early, he might be eating. I hate watching other people eat because it makes me hungry. Do you know him?"

"Gordle Maytop?" she asked.

"Yeah."

"I don't *personally* know him. He's a very good dancer."

"What's *The Power* about?" I asked.

"I don't want to spoil it. You should see it unfiltered," she said.

"I'll feel dumb going all by myself."

"Why? It's a mid-matinee on a weekday. There won't be many people there. But tell me if there are. I could use the exposure."

"What should I look for specifically? What part would you be playing?"

"They didn't say. Just look at the overall play. Is it tasteful? Exciting? Funny? Does the audience enjoy it? And most importantly, does it seem like the play will have a long run?"

"I don't know if I'm cut out for this."

Laesa snuggled close.

"Thank you. I know I'm asking a lot."

"It's not a lot," I said. "You're right. It will be good if we can help each other."

"I'm ready to back *you* up. Hah!" She said, kicking her leg out at an invisible attacker. "But seriously, I can do things for you. Run errands. I could be your secretary."

"You could be my receptionist when you're not acting. Can you talk with an accent?"

"Hello, welcome to Hank Enterprises," she said with an accent.

"That's perfect."

"I could even change my accent. And wear costumes. People would think you have a dozen secretaries," she laughed.

"Either that or they keep quitting because I'm a lecherous slob."

"That's high praise in your line of work, right? Do you need me to do anything for you now? I still have a few hours before I need to leave."

"Yeah. Can you get me some information on—" I looked at my tele again. "Gordle Maytop?"

"Sure. I'll search through the trades."

"Check *The News*, too."

"The gossip paper? You want to know who he's dating and his favorite foods?"

"Why not? Let me be professional for once and come prepared."

"Nice. I'll do it and send you the information by tele," she said.

I bummed around the house for a while and watched some Legend Class glocken. Then I went out and ate brunch. Enjoyed some sparkling wine and lots of salty meat, cheeses, and crackers. All synthetic, of course. The real stuff cost too much.

Laesa sent me a lengthy tele report a few hours later. She had been busy.

Gordle Maytop was married, but apparently estranged from his wife. At least *this* week he was. It seemed they had a big knockdown fight every other week. They had two grown children who lived in some other solar system.

Gordle Maytop's dancing style had been called everything from masculine, to feminine, to refined, to haphazard. He headlined a major movie every four or five months. He was one of the highest-billed actors in the entire Romance Guild. No wonder Cliston wanted him guarded.

As for his personality, Laesa said it was hard to know what was real and what were planted stories by his public relations people—which probably meant Cliston. I had a lot to learn about this business. Laesa found one interview in *The News*, where Gordle Maytop had made an obscure hint that he was gay.

Laesa ended the report by saying she had to go to work and hoped she had given me enough information. She also reminded me that I had to watch *The Power*. I read her letter several times. She was pretty good at this. I could totally see her being the research division of Hank Services, Enterprises, Limited, Incorporated. Of course, I'd need to get some more assignments so I could afford paying her, but one step at a time.

The Power was running at a small venue. It was a dance club on the weekends, but I guess they rented it out for theater during the day. The seating was terrible but there was a lot of alcohol to drink. There were thirty of us in the audience. Most of them were Damakans come to get their daily dose of emotions.

I tried to take notes on the scenery, parking, ambiance, and whatever else I could think of, but once the play began, I was under the actors' spell.

The play was a sordid, erotic thriller.

About half the show I was sitting there, so turned on I could barely see straight, the rest of the time I was horrified at the plot. Every damn character died in some gruesome, sexually explicit manner. One person was slowly impaled on an electric spike and spent five minutes screaming in agony and ecstasy. That was considered a good death compared to everyone else.

At the end of it all, I was excited, but also traumatized. I wanted to cuddle with Laesa—and then have her rub vinegar in my eyes. It was a twisted kind of entertainment.

This was not a good play for Laesa. Not because of the nudity or even the cruelty. It was a show you could only watch once. It was too exhausting and disturbing. I couldn't see the play lasting more than a few weeks. It wasn't a career opportunity for Laesa, in my opinion.

The best, most concise description I could give was that Delovoa would love it. I'd tell Laesa that and she'd understand perfectly.

I tried to clear my head as I took a cab over to Gordle Maytop's home.

It was a nice building. There was an actual line of small bushes on each side of the walkway to the door. Growing, green bushes. A very rare sight on a space station.

I put my head over one of the nearest bushes and inhaled its fragrance. I sneezed for about two minutes. Figured. I'd had almost no exposure to living vegetation my entire life. Who knew what kind of weird pollen or spores or fungus that thing had?

I finally recovered enough to ring the doorbell. Knocked. Rang the bell again. And again. And again. I wasn't *that* late, was I? It was 9:30. Maybe he was fighting with his wife and didn't want to be disturbed.

I sat down and rang the bell every minute or so. After an hour, I knew I had to take desperate actions. I took out my tele.

"Hi, Cliston. Tomorrow, is it possible you prepare pancakes for me?"

"Of course, sir. Do you know what time you'll return?" he answered.

"Not sure. Not sure. Oh! While I have you on the line, I'm sitting outside of Gordle Maytop's house. He's not answering the door."

"Sir, you realize this is the tele number for your *butler*. You should contact his agent if you're having difficulties."

"I know, Cliston. But his agent never picks up my calls and I can't get past the switchboard."

"Just this once, sir."

"Okay. Thanks."

"What's the problem?" Cliston the agent asked.

"Gordle Maytop isn't answering the door."

"Did you *just* get there?"

"No. I've been here for like, hours. And hours," I lied.

"Did you knock?"

"Yes, I knocked, Cliston. If his door wasn't reinforced steel I would have caved it in by now. My finger is sore from punching the bell."

"Did you check if the door was locked?" he asked.

"Yes, Cliston," I said, annoyed.

I turned the handle and the door opened.

"Hold on. I got it. Don't forget the pancakes tomorrow."

Inside, the home was dark. I fumbled around for the lights and found them on the other side of the door.

A dead man was lying on his back not five feet from me. He had what looked like multiple gunshot wounds on his chest.

"Oh, come on!" I complained.

CHAPTER 15

I felt pretty certain the killer was no longer in the house. Not based on any clues I saw, but because I had been standing outside knocking and ringing the doorbell for an hour. Stuff like that tended to shoo murderers away from the scene.

Based on the wounds, condition of the body, and blood on the floor, I would say Gordle Maytop hadn't been killed very long ago. I doubt it was while I was outside creating a disturbance, but maybe within a handful of hours.

I *assumed* that was Gordle Maytop lying dead. Not only was this his home, and the man appeared as if he could have been a charming Romance star, but my luck demanded that the deceased be the one guy in the entire galaxy I was hired to keep alive.

I reached down and felt the man's legs. They were well shaped and muscular. He was wearing shoes that probably cost more than my last car. Even in death, he looked like he was ready to waltz away at any moment. There was little doubt in my mind that this was a professional dancer.

"Anyone here?" I bellowed. "Hello?"

No answer. Not that I expected the murderer to suddenly introduce himself.

I picked up the dead actor and walked outside. Rigor mortis hadn't had time to set in yet so the body was still pliable.

I moved down the dark, adjoining street, being careful to look out for any spectators. Fortunately, there were none. I placed the body in the center of the road and adjusted his limbs. Then I hurried back to the sidewalk and waited.

And waited.

It was nighttime, but it wasn't *that* late. Where were all the cars? Finally, I saw a couple walking up the sidewalk a few blocks away. Excellent.

I rushed over to Gordle Maytop's body in the road and knelt down next to him.

"Oh, no!" I yelled, cradling the dead man in my arms.

The people saw me, hesitated, then turned around and ran the opposite direction.

I sighed and went back to my position on the sidewalk. It was another fifteen minutes before someone approached in the distance. I ran back to the corpse in the street. I had time to mentally work on my dialogue.

"Oh, no! There has been a grievous automobile accident," I said woodenly. "You. Bystander. Call for an emergency ambulance!"

It was a man on the sidewalk. He kept walking toward me but didn't seem to be in a tremendous hurry. I knelt there in the road, wondering what was taking him so long.

"Hey, Hank," he said, as he drew near.

"Hi, Gaggle," I replied. Gaggle was a brawny tough guy. A bouncer and sometime trigger man.

"You kill that guy?" he asked.

"Me? No. He was hit by a reckless automobile. A car," I said.

Gaggle took a step closer to look things over.

"Did the car have a gun mounted on it? Because that guy was shot," he said.

I stood up.

"Just blow off, alright?" I replied angrily.

"Okay, okay. Take it easy."

Gaggle walked away, not sparing a glance back and probably wiping his memory clean of the incident. It figured the first person I encountered would be an authority on gun injuries.

I went back to my spot and waited. An old lady came into view on the sidewalk ahead. Perfect. I couldn't ask for a better witness.

"Curse the heavens!" I shouted, my arms raised in frustration. "Gordle Maytop, the dancing sensation, is no more. His life hath been snuffed by that most insidious Colmarian invention: the speeding automobile. Our lust for efficient transportation will be our doom. Doom, I say!"

The little lady hustled over at my cries. When she arrived, we both stood on the curb looking at the sad remains of the dead actor.

"My word, what happened?" she asked, handkerchief over her mouth.

"I barely turned my head and the next thing I knew this big green car came around the corner. Careening. I held up my hands, and said, 'Stop! Driver! There is someone in the road! You need to turn or slow down!' But I'm afraid he didn't hear me or couldn't react in time. One of the car's lights was out, which might account for his lack of visibility. The car *hit* that man straight on, killing him instantly. The driver left the scene without stopping—a horrible act of cowardice. I just checked the fallen man's identification. He is none other than Gordle Maytop, the renowned actor."

The old woman was silent for a long while. It was probably quite a shock to see a dead body in the street. She might even have been a fan of the actor. That would work out well for me.

"I don't know," she said finally. "Those wounds look like they came from a firearm. Small caliber pistol at close range, if I had to guess."

"What is wrong with you people?" I exclaimed.

"How do you mean?"

"Get out of here, lady!"

The woman straightened with umbrage and resumed her walk.

I suppose I didn't need witnesses. The only person who could really contradict my version of events was the murderer, and that seemed unlikely.

I hefted the body and carried it back to the house. When I set him down on the floor, I searched him thoroughly. When opening his coat and shirt, I noticed he had stab wounds on his chest. I hadn't seen them before because I was too busy trying to make myself an alibi for why this wasn't my fault. The stabs weren't very deep, but there they were. Shot and stabbed. This was the second one after Weelon Poshor.

I called up my favorite cabbie and waited. I needed someone who could keep his mouth shut.

In the meantime, I searched Gordle Maytop's house. I found a money clip with several hundred credits and pocketed that. There was actually quite a lot of valuable things to steal but my conscience was poking me repeatedly in the ribs. I wasn't burglarizing for my own benefit—not exactly. But I knew I had a few payoffs to make tonight. Besides, Gordle Maytop was dead. His need for worldly goods was at an end. I couldn't say the same for myself.

I put a pillowcase over the actor's head in an effort to mask his identity from any casual observation. But no one was around. Casual or otherwise. By the time the cab arrived, the corpse was fairly stiff.

"Hiya, Zzzho," I said. I called Zzzho because I was sure he could keep his mouth shut. Especially since he didn't have a mouth. The gaseous Keilvin Kamigan was perpetually helpful.

I tried to fit the body in the back seat lengthwise.

"Does that body stink? Just because I don't have a nose doesn't mean my fares want to smell a corpse," Zzzho said.

"No, not yet," I assured him.

"Where we going?"

"The morgue," I said.

"Okay. Did you kill that guy?" he asked, driving us away.

"No. He was hit by a car."

"Hank, I don't have eyes but even I can see he was shot."

"I got an extra hundred credits here that says he was hit by a car."

"That's pretty terrible, Hank," Zzzho replied. "The car that killed that guy almost ran into me! A blue truck as I recall."

"It was a big green sedan."

"Yeah, that's what I said."

I gave Zzzho a nice tip for the ride and hauled out the body.

There was an actual line at the morgue, so I had to stand there holding the well-dressed, brutally murdered corpse of Gordle Maytop. With a pillowcase over his head. The fact no one gawked was a testament to life on Belvaille.

When my turn came up, I asked specifically for Muck-Mock, the Chief Coroner. I had to wait another thirty minutes. I set the corpse down against the wall and took a seat. The morgue had coffee, but it was old and weak. The nice thing, at least, was the morgue was cold. No Damakan temperatures in here.

Space stations lived in perpetual fear of diseases. Belvaille had absolutely top-notch life support. Corpses on Belvaille were skillfully disposed of. Everyone was sterilized, incinerated, and sterilized again. You were pure, industrial-grade carbon when they were done with you. If you were some weirdo species that couldn't be cooked, they had other methods ranging from acids, bacterial decomposition, friction erosion, and if all else failed, they could squish you into a sheet of near-nothingness with an atomic press. The only corpse they failed to process was the Therezian giant Wallow—though they sure as hell tried.

There was a debate about what they would do to me when I croaked. My mutations made me a difficult case. I never much liked coming to the morgue because all the coroners acted like they couldn't wait to try out their toys on me.

Muck-Mock came out to meet me and shook my hand. I had been carrying around a dead guy for a couple hours, but I still felt like my hand was suddenly coated with nastiness.

Muck-Mock was a huge man. He stood a foot taller than me and was almost twice as wide. He had an enormous pot belly and wore white coveralls that were smeared with things that I'm sure I didn't want to know. His most interesting feature was that he had two heads. The heads were small, but mounted on long, sinewy necks. One head held nothing but his mouth, while the other had his ears, nose, eyes. It was a good design that allowed his species to be eating while keeping a lookout for predators. Whatever was big enough to eat Muck-Mock deserved keeping an eye on.

"Hello, Hank, how you feeling?" the coroner asked.

"Like I got third-degree burns on my hands and feet and the world is covered in sandpaper. How are you?"

He saw the corpse on the ground and understood immediately.

"Come into my office."

I picked up the body and carried it past the furnace rooms. Muck-Mock's office was filled with ghastly devices and posters showing the anatomy of bizarre aliens. I leaned the corpse against the wall and closed the door.

"Who's the stiff?" he asked.

I took off the pillowcase to show him.

"Hey, that's an actor. Um, the dancey guy."

"Gordle Maytop," I said. "He got hit by a car. Or I need you to report that."

Muck-Mock scratched the chin on his mouth-head.

"Hank, I can sell pictures of that corpse for a small fortune. Actors are a hot commodity."

"Come on, Muck-Mock. What about the sanctity of death?"

"What about it?"

"Who's going to care if you report it was a car accident?"

"Reporters will. They can write fifty stories about an actor having the flu. One getting shot is big news."

"I got...250 credits," I said, counting the money I borrowed from Gordle Maytop's house.

"We still have to document it. Autopsy. Photos. Death report."

"This isn't my first trip to the morgue, you know," I said.

"I know. But this isn't some gang thug you iced, neither."

"I didn't kill him."

"I don't care."

"Alright," I sighed, and shifted through the other items I took. "I got this: gold and sapphire pendant-necklace-thing."

"I don't go much for jewelry. That would look stupid on me."

"You can sell it."

"Too much hassle. Besides, I might get in trouble if anyone comes asking."

"Who's gonna ask?"

"MTB. You know that guy can *smell* if something isn't regulation. I want to be on your good side, Hank. But I can't operate if I get on MTB's bad side."

"Don't worry, I'll talk to MTB."

"Nah," he said.

"Okay, I saved the best for last." I rummaged around my coat and pulled out a sock. I rolled it down and held up a shimmering gold statuette.

"Is that a GuildAR?" he asked.

"It is. A Guild Acting Reward." I read the inscription. "Best Dance Routine."

"What am I going to do with that?"

"Pawn it. Melt it down in your furnace. This is probably solid gold."

"Yeah, right. It would have melted in the Damakan weather outside," he said.

"No kidding. Used to be you only had to worry about getting shot walking around Belvaille. Now I'm scared of heat stroke. So maybe it's not solid gold. But it's still valuable. People kill for these, right?"

"Only actors."

"Sell it to an actor."

His mouth-head was grimacing and his eye-head was squinting. It was hard to cobble together what Muck-Mock was thinking because his heads were so far apart.

"Let me see it," he said after a moment.

I handed it to him and he wiped his hands clean on his pants before taking hold of it. The award seemed tiny in his meaty paws.

"Alright," he sighed. "Car accident."

"What will you do about the pictures for the official record?" I asked.

"I can use images of people you ran into with *your* car. Got a bunch of those."

"I hit *one* person. And I paid his nephew a fortune to make things right."

"Aren't you a sweetheart? You may have only *killed* one person with your car, but you ran into a lot. I sometimes eat lunch with technicians from the hospital. Between your driving, your grunt work, and your own hospital stays, you supply half the business for the hospital."

"You'll be happy to learn I'm no longer driving. Someone stole my damn car."

"No wonder things have been slow around here. I may have to lay people off until you can get your wheels back."

"Funny stuff. Hey, have there been other actors in here recently?"

"Not that I've seen," he replied.

"Really? I heard a number of actors were killed."

"Damakans? No. Not everybody comes to the morgue, though. Sometimes families ship them back home. Though it's damn expensive. We call it C&C. Cemeteries and ceremonies."

"Alright, I'm off. Thanks for the help."

"No problem. Be sure to keep MTB away."

"Will do."

"What the hell happened?" MTB asked me when I met him the next night at the bowling alley.

"Can you be more specific?" I replied.

"Here." He held out his arms toward the interior of the building. "There must be two hundred people bowling. I thought you said the lanes were going out of business."

"They *were* closing as of last week. But they started offering pitchers of beer for one credit and they have naked go-go dancers. I don't think anyone here even knows *how* to bowl."

"How long you been waiting?" he asked, seeing the five empty beer pitchers on my table.

"Not long. I reserved us a lane."

"Good. I'm not sitting around all night," MTB glared. He was always glaring.

I picked up my bowling bag and we headed to our lane. Bowling was a relatively new sport on Belvaille. It had originally been modified from a carnival game. Each player got three balls of increasing size and weight. You had to knock over pins at the end of the lane that were beyond some obstacles. You could also try and prevent your opponent from knocking them over.

MTB was a finesse player. He could curve the balls and make complicated bounce shots off the obstacles. I was a brute player. I simply threw every ball as hard as I could.

We pushed our way through a throng of drunken men ogling the dancers.

"I'm surprised there isn't any fighting," MTB said.

"Night is still early. Uh-oh."

"What?" he asked.

"Hey, guys, this is our lane. We have it reserved," I said. Six young punks were trying to bowl while apparently setting a drinking record. The floor was saturated with beer. At one credit a pitcher, people were practically taking showers in it.

"How about you push off to your retirement homes and let us play?" one of the drunken punks said.

The guys laughed, though one of them seemed more than concerned.

"Hi. This is MTB, the Chief of Police," I said, motioning to him.

"And that's Hank. He's a mutant who used to play Super Class glocken on the 10-lane. You might remember him from the Championship some years ago."

You could see the punks trying to mentally recalculate their odds. The one who had been silent and concerned decided to speak up.

"Oh, you had this *reserved*. I told you guys we were supposed to be down there. This is our first time playing. We got the lane numbers wrong."

"Yeah, probably," I said.

The punks all muttered and mumbled. They had been given a face-saving way to back off by their designated driver. But one guy couldn't resist.

"We didn't know this lane was set aside for senior citizens," the guy said.

Immediately after he spoke, his body slid across the bowling alley and spun to a stop. MTB had pulled out his gun and pistol-whipped the fool before I even had a chance to open my mouth.

There were lots of apologies and excuses as the punks picked up their unconscious friend and backed away. The entire bowling alley seemed to quiet down a bit, which was fine by me.

"Always has to be one big mouth in any group of people on Belvaille," MTB said.

"At *least* one," I replied. "But I thought you were the good guys. Why're you smacking around someone for giving you lip?"

"I learned that from you. You always said don't let anyone get away with talking trash or they'll lose respect and make your job harder."

"I said don't let anyone get away with *shooting* you."

"That works for you. I'm not bulletproof. I have to draw the line a lot sooner."

We cleaned up our lane a bit and got ready to play. MTB led off and already I was bowling from a deficit. He was a more skilled player than I was, but I hadn't gotten this far in life relying on skill. I made use of my natural talents.

I flung the heavy ball down the lane and one of the pins actually shattered.

"Wow. Is that legal?" MTB asked.

"I don't know. Never done it before. How about I get an extra point?"

"How about no."

We got some pitchers of cheap beer in us and started to play better. Normally when we came here, our voices would echo because we were the only ones around. Now we were trying to drown out the commotion.

"Okay," I said. "So tell me about Cliston's dead actors."

"What do you want to know?"

"Were they from the same Guild?"

"Nope. All different."

"Huh. Three dead actors?"

"Four dead actors. One dead director. One dead key grip."

"What's a key grip? Does he carry the keys?"

"I don't know."

"Cliston said it was only three."

"Probably only three were his clients."

"That makes sense. I talked to Muck-Mock and he said no Damakan actors had come in lately."

"I don't trust that guy. I've caught him cooking the books a few times," MTB said, eyes squinted.

"Cooking the books? He's not an accountant."

"No, he's a crooked coroner. Besides, maybe he was lying to you."

"Maybe. But he doesn't seem like a liar."

"Everyone lies," MTB said.

"Muck-Mock spends most of his time talking to dead people. I don't think he has the most advanced social skills in the galaxy." I picked up my next ball and hurled it. I battered everything around but didn't score any points. "So. MTB."

"Okay. Here it comes," he said.

"There's another dead actor I know about."

"I was wondering why you said you talked to Muck-Mock. You dump a body on him?"

"Yeah."

"Who?

"Gordle Maytop," I said.

"The dancer?"

"Yup. He got hit by a car."

"You expect me to believe that?" MTB laughed.

"Sure. Why wouldn't you?"

"Do you know anything about Gordle Maytop?"

"Laesa gave me a little research on him before I took the job," I said.

"What job? You hired to kill him?"

"No. I was hired to protect him."

MTB laughed again.

"You have the worst luck ever. I would say someone is trying to frame you for the murders if there was any reason to frame you."

"That's why I'm saying he was hit by a car. I'm trying to save money for a wedding and for sure no one is going to hire me if they learn the last two people I was guarding ended up dead."

"You're going to lie to Cliston and the Guild?" he asked.

"I'll lie to *agent* Cliston. I'll tell my butler the truth."

MTB shook his head at that.

"You need to come up with something better than a car accident. That won't sell," MTB said.

"Why not?"

"Gordle Maytop won a GuildAR. Best Dancing."

"Best Dance Routine. So?" I asked.

"Yeah. He got it for a scene where he danced *through* traffic. Moving cars everywhere. He's probably the least likely person to die from a car crash in the galaxy. It's like saying you died from losing too much weight."

"Funny stuff. How do you know so much about his career? You watching romance movies?"

"I got a lot of downtime as a cop. On one stakeout I can go through maybe a dozen tele programs," he said.

"Muck-Mock already made the report or I'd change it to something that doesn't involve cars."

"You should have called me when it happened."

"I was trying to avoid making a scene."

"Yeah, wouldn't want the murder of a high-profile actor to cause a fuss," he grumbled.

"I know, I know. But I need to keep my name out of it."

"What are the details of the death? Did you clean up or is the crime scene intact?"

"I didn't touch nothing. He was shot. Six times in the chest. Close range. Just inside his door. Not very accurate. There were also knife wounds. Not deep. Must have been later. No signs of a struggle or fight."

"That sounds a lot like the other murder, Weelon Poshor."

"But no water this time."

"Your murders are different than the other actors. And key grip," MTB said, thinking.

"They aren't *my* murders."

"You know what I mean. The others seemed like standard gang hits. A drive-by. A break-in. A mugging. And a few innocent bystanders."

"You think they're different people doing them?"

"The ones you found seemed like they knew the victims. Have you heard anything on the street?" he asked.

"No. But I'm going to get with Rendrae and start canvasing the city."

"Rendrae is still alive?"

"Yeah. He's skinny now," I said.

"Rendrae?"

"Yup. He talked to me for like five minutes before I finally believed it was him. You wouldn't recognize him."

"Huh." MTB took out his tele and started taking notes. "Gordle Maytop. Anything else unusual?"

"It was all kind of unusual. But the stabbing is what I don't understand. They weren't even deep wounds."

"Were they from a knife?" MTB asked.

"What else do you get stabbed with?"

"Spoons. Mops. Pork chops. I don't know. You were there, not me."

"I'd guess it was a knife."

"Hmm. Did he have any family?"

"Wife. Maybe split. Kids are in some other System," I said.

"Wife still on Belvaille?"

"I think so."

"After I check out his house, I want you to come with me to speak with her."

"Why?" I asked.

"Because I'll feel stupid trying to explain he got hit by a car. That's your lie, so you tell it. But she also might have some clues. And you can charm them out of her."

"Charm? I'm not charming," I said.

"More than me."

"Genital warts are more charming than you, MTB."

We got tired of the noise at the bowling alley and I got tired of MTB beating me.

"You've been practicing, haven't you?" I accused him.

"I only come here with you."

I didn't have a car, of course, so we had to take MTB's police vehicle.

"What the hell is this?"

"I got Delovoa to make some modifications," he said casually.

The only reason you couldn't call it a tank was because it didn't have a cannon or treads, and it seated two comfortably.

"Where do you put prisoners in this?" I asked him.

"I told you, we don't have a jail. I don't take prisoners."

"Seems odd having a two-seat cop car. This thing has got so much armor it must burn fuel like crazy."

"Yeah, she's thirsty. So we going to see Gordle Maytop's wife?"

"Now?" I asked.

"I'm still drunk. I figure now is the best time. Telling someone their husband is dead is never easy," he said. MTB's eyes were glassy and he was sweating booze.

"If you weren't the top cop in the city, and your car wasn't a tank, I'd say you were too drunk to drive."

I sat in the passenger seat and looked up the wife's info on my tele. Even intoxicated, and driving this wrecking ball he called a car, MTB was still an excellent driver.

I wasn't sure why I was so bad at driving. I wondered if it had to do with my Ontakian species, but my uncle Frank drove fine. He even stole cars now and then. Only way I could reliably be a car thief is if I pushed them away.

"What's this lady's name?" MTB asked.

"Syla Mour," I said.

"She an actor?"

"I don't know," I mumbled. I was a bit nauseous. That cheap beer was doing a number on my head.

"You got your tele open. Check," MTB said.

I flipped through it begrudgingly.

"Yeah, she's an actor. Romance. Don't see anything recent."

We reached her home. I staggered out of the tank and MTB fell out. Wow, he was more wasted than I thought.

"You're some inspirational model: drunk driving cop," I said.

"Drunk driving isn't illegal on Belvaille."

"It isn't? How come your flunkies always try and ticket me?"

"Because you hit people with your car! *That's* illegal. And you never pay the tickets anyway."

"Because it's a stupid rule," I said.

"Okay, how are we going to do this?"

"Let's ask her some questions first. You tell her she's a widow and she'll fall to pieces and then we won't get anything out of her."

"Good idea," he said.

We asked the doorman which condo Syla Mour was in and he told us after a bit of haggling. I offered him ten credits. MTB offered to arrest him.

I rang the doorbell and leaned against the wall, my head drooping. MTB slouched against the far wall. His locked knees were the only thing preventing him from becoming a puddle on the floor. It was steaming hot in here.

The door opened and I did a double-take.

"Wow," MTB slurred.

A woman was standing there in a slinky red dress, crisscrossed with stylish holes and slits. But the most striking aspect of the woman was her chest. She had the largest bosom I had ever seen. I mean it was about five seconds after she opened the door that I managed to even look up at her face. Not because I was staring, it took that long for the rest of her to appear.

"Uh. Syla Mour?" I asked her breasts.

"Yes. Who are you?"

"I'm MTB. Chief of Police," MTB said, hurrying forward and almost decapitating himself on her cleavage.

"What do you want?" she asked.

"Your husband is dead," MTB said. "I mean, do you know anything about your husband?"

"Dead?" she asked, alarmed.

"What, um. My friend here means..." I trailed off.

I want to be clear, we weren't total creeps. Her chest was simply that large. I've been alive for a long, long time. I've seen people from thousands of different species. We were looking at not only a miracle of biology, but physics itself. It's like our eyeballs were stuck in orbit around her bust. And her dress was cut in such a way that very little was left to the imagination.

Syla Mour gripped a walking stick in each hand. She was not an old woman. She needed the canes to keep from falling on her face. Her spine must have been reinforced with steel.

"Can we come in?" I asked.

"I don't understand what's going on," she said.

"Are you the wife of Gordle Maytop?" MTB asked.

"I am."

"I'm afraid we have bad news. He was hit by a car. A green car," I said.

"That's absurd. Let me see some identification," she demanded.

I didn't have any. Nothing that would matter. MTB stood there swaying, eyes fixed, mouth open. He was mesmerized.

"Let me just, uh..." I frisked the unresponsive MTB. "See? He's got a gun. And...handcuffs. Police have those things. This is a magnifying glass. That's for like, looking at fingerprints I guess. Ah, *here's* his badge."

I held it up.

Syla Mour had to squint at it. Her chest made it difficult to get any closer.

"Come inside," she said. She had to back in and turn around.

MTB stared at me.

"Pull it together, man," I hissed at him.

"Shut up. You're married."

The inside of the condo was hip. Sexy. Punctuated with lots of reds, whites, and fuzzy carpeting.

Syla Mour fell into a chair that seemed specifically designed for her. It had supports that held her up under her arms. She began drinking a cocktail.

MTB and I moved near a white couch.

"May we sit?" I asked.

"No."

MTB had been in mid-sit and had to jerk himself to the side to miss the couch. He landed on the floor.

"Is he drunk or stoned?" Syla Mour asked.

"Neither. He's got muscle disease. But he's a great cop."

"Everything still works," MTB blurted.

"So Gordy is dead?" Syla Mour asked. Not a bit emotional. But that was to be expected. We weren't Damakans, so we couldn't trigger a profound response. She would have to wait for a Damakan to help her feel sorrow.

"Yes. Um. Car."

"Were you there?" she asked skeptically.

"Yeah. He was trying out a new dance number. He danced in front of a car."

"That sounds like Gordy," she sniffed, then gulped down her drink.

MTB had finally gotten back to his feet.

"Miss Gordy, you don't sound very heartbroken," MTB said.

"I can say it now that he's dead. Gordy was gay. Didn't like women at all," she replied.

MTB and I shared a confused look.

"Uh. So?" I asked.

"You guys new at this? Gordy's movies are romantic. Not just the story, the idea that he might come and dance with *you*: lonesome housewives. Sweep you off your feet. Dance through moving cars. So we pretended to be married."

"Just to...what? I don't understand," I said.

"The audiences have to believe that Gordy was a hot-blooded heterosexual. You can't sell romance without that. Don't you Colmarians know anything?" she asked.

"I can't speak for the entire PCC empire. But Belvaille has long catered to whatever sexual tastes people are into. If we can make money off it, we don't care," I explained.

"Aren't you an enlightened bunch? I don't think the rest of the galaxy is as metropolitan as Belvaille," she replied.

"What did you get out of this arrangement?" MTB asked.

"Money. And he helped my career," she said.

"Was the marriage your idea?" I asked.

"His agent suggested it," she said.

"Cliston?" I asked.

"I don't remember his name."

"Was he a Dredel Led?" I added.

"Might have been. Who can remember?"

"How many robot talent agents do you know?" I asked.

"Gordy did all that. We barely ever saw one another. We would get photographed now and then, have some screaming fight—all acting—and then we'd live our separate lives."

"Did that fool anyone?" I asked.

"Fooled you, didn't it?" she replied.

"He have any enemies?" MTB asked.

"Gordy? Why?"

"These are standard police questions when someone is hit by a car," I said. We hadn't even hinted foul play was involved, so I wanted to keep it broad.

"Oh, probably. Actors can sometimes be jealous."

"He have anything valuable?" MTB asked.

"He was rich. The only thing he really treasured was his GuildAR for Best Dance Routine. I'll have to stop by and pick that up," she said.

"Yeah, about that. We think there was also a robbery at his home," I said.

"A robbery? *And* he was hit by a car?"

"Bad, bad luck," MTB said solemnly.

"Right. But if you want the GuildAR, we already have a lead on it. If you go to the morgue and ask around, you might be able to buy it," I said.

"*Buy* it? But you told me it was stolen," she said.

"You know how these things are," I stated with finality.

"No, I don't. You're suggesting he was dancing in the street and then burglarized. Who are you, exactly? I know who he is," she said, pointing at MTB.

"I'm a security consultant for the Navy," I replied.

"What's the Navy have to do with this? Was Gordy dating a sailor again?" she asked.

"Look, did Gordy ever say he was in danger? Or do you know anyone who might want to rob him. Or even kill him?" I asked.

She thought that over, downing another drink.

"He said something big was happening."

"Big? Like how? When?" MTB asked.

"It was vague. He almost never called me, but he gave me a tele last week. Really late at night. He had been out whoring around and was high. He said something important was going on and he was a part of it."

"What exactly?" I said, stepping closer.

"I didn't care. I hung up. Do I have to examine the body?" she asked.

"Nah, it's carbon by now. We can't have decaying bodies on a space station," MTB explained.

"What about his possessions? His money?" she asked.

"Did he have a will? You have children, right?" I asked.

"No, they were hired actors. I guess I'll talk to his lawyer. You're sure he's dead?"

"Oh, yeah. That car really got him," I said.

"The *green* car?" she added. It was clear she didn't believe everything we said, but she also didn't seem to be upset that she might be in for some inheritance.

"If you think of anything else, can you give us a call?" I asked her.

"Sure. Do I call..."

"Me! MTB. Just ask for me. I'm in the directory," he blurted.

"Okay," she sighed.

"Well, thank you for your time. And I'm very sorry about—"

MTB rushed in and gave her a hug. He couldn't get his arms all the way around her, but he tried. She was apparently used to this kind of attention because she merely rolled her eyes.

"Sorry about Gordle," I finished.

"He's dancing in a better place," she said.

CHAPTER 16

It was the next afternoon and I was sitting in the lobby of the Artistry Agency.

The receptionist blabbered something at me in a thick accent, but I just bellowed for Cliston until the walls shook. Of course, he wouldn't respond immediately to my yelling, no self-respecting talent agent would come when beckoned. But he also didn't want to scare off his prospective clients by leaving a rowdy Ontakian in his waiting room. Besides, it was Cliston who scheduled this appointment, and I'd be damned if I was going to wait around.

"New canst poking me towels," the receptionist said.

"Huh?" I asked.

She repeated it.

"I'm going to throw your desk if you don't talk normal," I warned her.

"You can go see him now," she said in perfect Colmarian.

I *knew* that accent was a put-on. I got up and dragged myself over to Cliston's office.

The Dredel Led in question sat barricaded behind his throne of power. The gargoyles which decorated his desk looked even more unfriendly than ever—I think they somehow reacted to Cliston's mood. My face was sweaty, and my clothes soaked through, so I knelt down and wiped my face on Cliston's sumptuous carpet. It was his fault for keeping the temperature so high.

"I got a call from the talentless Syla Mour. She wanted to know about her husband's insurance policies. She wouldn't say why. Any time I get a call from Gordle Maytop's balloon-chested, fictitious wife, I know it's trouble. Usually she's short on cash and wants me to pay her. But this felt different. Especially since she mentioned speaking to you. Care to explain what's going on?" he asked.

It was hard to tell Cliston's emotions. Because he was a robot and all. But he sure sounded mad. His body language looked mad. His red, glowing eyes seemed especially red and glowing.

"Can I talk to my butler for a second?"

"No! This is not your home. You don't make the rules here. You're talking to me. Now answer, you mutant moron."

"Good one. But it's urgent I speak to my butler. Please? Then I'll talk to you right after. I swear."

"Fat lot of good your promises are worth."

"Please? Butler Cliston?"

Cliston was so upset he almost seemed relieved to switch personas. As if he needed to give his reactor a break before he had a meltdown.

"Sir. How may I assist you?"

"Cliston," I said, relieved. "Gordle Maytop was murdered. I got there too late to save him."

"That's terrible, sir. But you should have told his agent when it happened."

"I know. Been avoiding it."

"Do you have the identity or motive of the killer?"

"I don't. I feel like I'm juggling knives in the dark."

"Why would you do that, sir?"

"I wouldn't. Gordle told his wife something big was happening. I have a hunch the murders are connected. At least the bodies I found."

"What about the others? I heard a number of actors have been killed. Though some were merely injured."

"Not sure about those. I need to get out in the city and poke around. Pull the roots and see what color the bulb is," I said.

"I'm confused as to the meaning of your metaphor, sir."

"Roots have bulbs, right? Or do they have buds? I'm not a farmer, I don't know."

"I believe roots are merely roots in most cases, sir. What is your next step, and do you require my assistance?"

Talking to somber, capable, butler Cliston was making me more comfortable. He was a buzzkill, but in a good way.

"I *do* need your help. Can you please talk to agent Cliston and tell him about the murder?" I began.

"Of course, sir."

I was about to say, "tell him tomorrow," but I didn't get a chance to finish.

"What do you *mean* Gordle Maytop was murdered? What was I paying you for?" agent Cliston blared at me.

"Oh. So you heard?"

"Yes, I heard. I heard you failed to do a simple task. I heard I might as well hire you to *kill* my clients because at least then you'd follow through!"

"Sorry. I'm heading out now to find the perpetrators," I said, moving to exit the office.

A chair flew at me with such force and precision, it shattered against my back and knocked me down. I was about three thousand pounds. For a piece of furniture to flip me over like a doll it must have been travelling at about Mach 2.

"I was insane to think you could actually protect anyone. You're bankrupting me. I should have believed your Scanhand profile. When have you shown even the slightest hint of aptitude or competence?" Cliston bellowed.

I covered myself up as Cliston lifted his massive desk over his head and hurled it. Fortunately, the desk was so long it banged into the wall before it reached me and spun to the side. But the wall itself cracked and the desk broke in half. A gargoyle rested on the carpet, six inches from my face. It promised pain and ruin if I hung around waiting for Cliston to find more throwing weapons. I scrambled to my feet and out Cliston's office.

"You'll never work in this town again!" he shouted after me.

Fear and adrenaline overpowered my clumsiness and I hurried, past the stunned looks of Damakan talent agents, toward the exit.

But I was humiliated. I just let my butler beat me up. In a moment of passive aggressive angst, I stopped at the receptionist. I tipped her desk over, scattering papers and headshots everywhere.

"Hah," I said triumphantly.

Cliston surged out of his office a moment later with an ornate lamp in his hand. The lamp was metal and seemed tailor made to be thrown by an angry Dredel Led.

I dashed to the front door, but before I could reach it, the lamp smacked into the back of my skull. I crawled the rest of the way out of the Artistry Agency.

So now I lost a job and talent agent Cliston was pissed off.

Cliston had never been this mad at me before. I never knew he could throw that well. He probably invented throwing and wrote a manual on the best ways to kill mutant Ontakians using furniture.

I couldn't think of a worse person to be on the outs with. With my luck, Cliston would create ten more personas, corner every employment market on Belvaille, and make sure I couldn't get work.

I would have to start fighting in Cheat Hall just to get my finances in order. I still had Garm's pay, but that wasn't enough to marry a Damakan.

My problem, one of my *many* problems, was that I had morals. Maybe not a lot, but on Belvaille, even one small moral could really trip you up, since no one else had any.

Case in point, I felt I needed to go to the Romance Guild. I had to explain that their top star, Gordle Maytop, was dead. Because of me. I didn't want to. Technically, I didn't *have* to. I wasn't being paid by anyone. But my morals were beginning to nag at me. It was a persistent sting like when you didn't wipe your butt perfectly and then your crack started to itch.

I didn't kill Gordle Maytop directly, but if I had been better, or at least arrived earlier, he might have lived. Of course, that was a big maybe. I might have also been killed. Or I might have gone to sleep on the job again. Or gone out for food. Or been too slow or too stupid to save him.

But I couldn't deny I had been hired to protect him and I failed. I at least owed his Guild an explanation.

This might sound weird, but I got a ride to the Romance Guild later in the day from Cliston. Butler Cliston, who wasn't mad at me at all and was even sympathetic that talent agent Cliston was so furious.

The Romance Guild was a monolithic building that took up half a block. It looked like a lot of squares of decreasing size piled on top of each other. Very rigid and cold. The building was constructed decades before by a nobleman who made his fortune selling military hardware. He wanted the building to reflect that. And it did. The building loudly proclaimed it was a modern-day fortress.

To soften up the image, the Romance Guild painted the entire structure bright pink. I suppose that was a romantic color, but it still couldn't subdue the imposing building. It was like putting a fake mustache on a shark.

I had never been to the Romance Guild before and I actually looked around to see if anyone was watching me enter. My reputation didn't need people knowing I hung out with a bunch of romance actors.

The building was way more space than they needed. I could tell because the lobby was completely empty. They must have run out of paint coating the outside, because inside it looked like a high-tech industrial complex. Black marble, gray steel, and white concrete. Hard edges everywhere. If you tripped and fell in here, it seemed certain that you would not only suffer a bruise on these unforgiving surfaces, but the building itself would kick you while you were down.

I took the elevator to the top floor. I was trying to get straight what I would say when I realized I still had a gun in my jacket. It was simply habit to grab a gun when I left the house. I couldn't throw desks and chairs like Cliston.

There wasn't much I could do to make my gun less conspicuous, but I decided to remove the ammunition. If I was frisked, they would see the gun was unloaded.

The elevator door opened and someone grabbed my gun and wrenched it from my hands.

"Hey," I said dumbly.

The gun was thrown backwards, sending it skidding across the black marble floor. A strong hand then grabbed hold of me by the neck, pulled me out of the elevator, and turned me around.

"Frank?" I asked, startled.

It was my uncle. He was also an Ontakian. But not a mutant. What was really startling though, besides *all* of this, was he didn't have on his breathing mask. He always wore that.

"Hey, kiddo," he said.

Frank removed his hand from my neck and then roundhouse punched me in the right ear. It didn't hurt tremendously, but it dazed me. Frank was super strong, but I was super-duper dense. I was pretty sure I could beat him in a fight. I just wasn't sure why we were fighting.

Frank took hold of my arm, swiveled around close to me, and then began roaring with exertion. One moment I was looking at the far wall. Then I was looking at the floor. And now I was looking at the ceiling.

Somehow he had flipped me up and over and now I was lying on my back on the floor. He kept hold of my arm and wrenched it while he stood on top of my face.

"Why are you here?" he yelled at me.

I tried to talk past his foot but failed.

"Who are you working for?" he asked.

I pulled my arm, but that just ground his boot harder into my face. I *needed* my face. I used it to eat. Finally, Frank turned his boot so he was only pressing against my forehead and my mouth was free.

"Well?" he asked.

"I guess I'm working for Garm."

On further reflection, maybe I couldn't beat Frank in a fight. In my defense, he had surprised me at the elevator, so I wasn't ready. But Frank was also a lot faster than me.

Despite spending much of my life fighting, I had never really gotten *good* at it. I wasn't a skilled fighter. I wasn't exactly a skilled fighter. Most of the people I went up against were a tenth my size. You rose to the level of your competition and I never had any worth mentioning. Instead of developing combat ability, I worked on my people skills.

"Cut the crap. Garm? What's she have to do with this?" Frank snorted. His people skills were terrible.

"Do with what? You standing on me?"

"Who are you here to kill?" Frank demanded, spraining my wrist and digging his heel between my eyes.

"No one. Here to talk. Courtesy call," I stammered.

"You swear?" he asked skeptically.

"Yes," I squeaked.

"Okay," Frank said. He hopped off my face, let go of my arm, and casually walked over to stand next to the elevator.

I turned over on my side and looked at Frank, who was now busy fiddling with his tele.

"Hey," I demanded.

"What?" he asked, seemingly surprised I was still here.

"You're...you're just going to take my word for it? What if I was here to kill someone?" I asked.

"You swore. And you take that crap seriously."

"Right. And you don't," I said.

"Nope."

I felt I should be indignant. More than that.

"Hey, kick me my gun," I demanded. It was resting ten feet past Frank.

"Get it yourself," he replied, not looking up from his tele. "I'm trying to sell some cars."

"Are they stolen?"

"Barely," he said.

I got to my feet, feeling light-headed from my skirmish.

"You got any cars that could fit me?"

He finally looked up. Eyeing me as if it was the first time we had met.

"Can you drive a triple-stick Urelian truck?" he asked.

"Probably as good as I can drive anything else." I walked over and picked up my gun. I purposely moved closer to Frank, hinting that I might attack him in retribution. He kept his eyes on his tele, not even registering me. "So, what's going on here?" I asked.

"This is the Romance Guild," he said conversationally. Like he *hadn't* just socked me in the ear and stuck his foot in my mouth a moment ago. The likelihood of Frank ever apologizing was about the same as my chances of becoming a synchronized swimmer.

"How much does that truck cost?" I asked.

"Twenty grand."

"What the hell? Why does it cost so much?"

"It's an industrial vehicle."

"I'm not in the mining business. Why would I want that?" I asked.

"To haul around your fat ass. You think a unicycle is going to carry you?"

"Forget it," I sneered. The act of refusing my uncle's truck made me feel I had somewhat atoned for being manhandled.

I headed to the front door of the Romance Guild and Frank fell in line behind me.

"Where are you going?" I asked him.

"With you."

"Why?"

"I work as security here."

"No kidding? You don't attack people inside random buildings? I figured this was just an unusual hobby."

"You're a known reprobate, with criminal contacts, carrying a gun. I have to be cautious," he said.

"If I'm a reprobate, what are you?" I asked, annoyed.

"A security guard at the Romance Guild."

"*You're* one of my criminal contacts."

"Exactly," he replied.

"I said I wasn't here to kill anyone. Or do anything bad."

"Then as a law-abiding citizen, you shouldn't be concerned about added protection." I was about to say more, but Frank spoke first. "I'm paid by the hour."

I walked inside the hot office and stomped over to the receptionist's desk. She was currently talking on the tele in a thick accent, so I stood waiting.

"How you been?" Frank asked me.

"Okay, I guess. Just got attacked by a relative."

"You probably deserved it."

"Can I help you?" the receptionist finally asked.

"Hi. I need to speak to someone about one of your members. Gordle Maytop," I said pleasantly.

"Oh, we haven't been able to get in touch with him."

"I have some information that I'd like to pass on. I'm not sure who would be appropriate. I'm just an innocent bystander."

Frank snorted. The receptionist spoke on the tele, relaying my message up the food chain.

"Someone will be with you shortly," she said.

I loosened the collar of my shirt and leaned against the nearest wall.

"I hope they have an air-conditioned room to talk in," I said to Frank.

A somewhat past middle-aged man strolled out to meet me. His black hair was oiled and streaked with white. He was tall and springy, and his arms swung elegantly as he moved. He wore a black suit that looked like it would be perfect for a funeral *or* a wedding. The man kept his head perpetually tilted upward, and in consequence, would look down at you with his eyes. This made him seem even taller than he was. He sported a meticulous, pencil-thin mustache. If this wasn't the Romance Guild President then I was a baby Dredel Led in a tinfoil diaper.

"Greetings. I'm Mancel MaGove, President of the Guild. I understand you have a message from Gordle Maytop?"

"Sort of. Could we speak somewhere privately? Maybe a room that's a little cooler? I'm not a Damakan."

"Of course. This way," he said.

The President walked with his back forward and his nose pointed up. His arms swung and wrists snapped with every stride. It was a strange effect, but he pulled it off with grace and confidence. If I tried that, I'd fall down the first flight of stairs I came to.

Frank followed close behind me and I got the sense he didn't entirely believe I was here out of politeness.

They had a room similar to the Drama Guild's air-conditioned paradise. The problem was, we had to go down two flights in the elevator and walk halfway across the building to get to it. It entirely defeated the purpose of having a climate-controlled room if you had to run a marathon to reach it. By the time I got inside, I was winded and dripping sweat.

"Thad Elon," Frank exclaimed at my condition. "You been popping amphetamines?"

"Aren't you hot?" I asked him.

"Yeah, but I'm not about to evaporate."

"Please," the President said, "tell me what you know."

"Well, sir, here's the deal. I was minding my own business—" I started.

"Sure you were," Frank muttered.

"Hey. I'm trying to relate the events. Why are you even here?"

"Don't concern yourself with Frank," the President said, waving his long fingers. "Go on."

"Right. So I was in the street. Ass-More Avenue—"

"Well-known hangout for prostitutes and gigolos," Frank translated.

"Not on the north end of it. That's where I was. Between Radiation Lane and Blowhole Alley."

I waited for Frank to interrupt again, but he was silent.

"So I see this guy. You know, I could tell he was different. Not like, you know, bad. But he was someone I should be watching. Next thing, he hops off the sidewalk right in front of an oncoming car. I said, 'Get out of there, you madman!' But this car comes and, *woop-twist,* he dances out of the way like it was nothing. A car comes from the other way and I'm all like, 'Hey, man, you're going to get killed!' But he's enjoying himself. At the last minute he goes, *flip-hop,* off to the side. No one can dance like that. No one! But he just keeps going. Car after car. It was amazing. It was inspirational. I felt like I was watching—and I use this word very reluctantly—I felt like I was watching *magic.* So he's dancing back and forth across the street. Cars honking, cars swerving, the drivers screaming. And it's the most beautiful thing you can imagine."

"Then what happened?" Mancel MaGove asked.

"The *unthinkable.* It felt like I had been watching him for hours. No, days. I could have watched him my whole life, I think. Now, when cars approached him, I no longer cried out with concern. I got excited to see how he was going to dance past it. But somehow, he didn't see there was a big pothole in the road. Who knows how they blew a crater in a steel road, but there it was. A big green car was driving along and the dancer's foot caught in that pothole. I saw his ankle twist and he went down. I thought for sure this was part of the routine. You know, to pump audience excitement. But that green car came up and, *whamo*, it hit him and took off around the corner."

"Which corner?" Frank asked.

"Radiation Lane. Going west. I'm not sure if the driver saw him or what. But he must have known he ran into someone. He didn't stop or come back. It just goes to show the lack of sensitivity in this city," I said, shaking my head.

"You're saying a car killed Gordle Maytop?" the President asked.

"I didn't know who it was. I ran over to help him, of course. I crouched down next to him and could see he was terribly hurt. Just...well, I won't describe it out of respect. One eye fluttered open and he said very weakly, 'Tell the Guild I was working on a new routine. And I love them.' He didn't speak fast. Or all at once. You know, because his face was smashed and bones were sticking through his skin and he must have swallowed half his teeth. But I'm *sure* that's what he said. When I checked his identification, that's when I learned it was Gordle Maytop."

Frank looked over to the President, who stood there impassively looking down his nose at me.

"I heard you killed him," Mancel MaGove said.

"You don't even know me," I said.

"Your name is Hank, correct?" Mancel MaGove asked.

I looked at Frank, but there was no way he could have told him who I was. He was with me the whole time.

"That's him," Frank said.

"Yeah, so?" I asked. I was extremely irritated that he doubted my depiction of events. I spent a lot of time on that speech.

"Cliston called me, earlier. He explained that you killed Gordle Maytop and would be coming by at some point to confess," the President said.

Frank promptly put me in an armlock. I was like three times stronger than Frank yet I couldn't escape from this stupid hold. As we jockeyed for position, I finally picked my uncle off his feet, no matter how much it hurt my shoulder.

But then I realized this wasn't how I wanted to proceed. It wouldn't solve anything. I put Frank down and he promptly put me back in an armlock.

"Dammit, Frank," I said.

"Do you two know each other?" the President asked.

"He's my nephew. He's murdered about half as many people as I have in a third of the time. He was also a Super Class glocken player."

"Fascinating," Mancel MaGove stated. "What's a Super Class glocken?"

"A blood sport. I bet he killed your actor guy and he's here to kill you," Frank said.

"I promised. And you said you believed me," I complained.

"I lied."

"I'm not here to hurt anyone. Stop breaking my arm and I'll explain," I said.

The President pursed his mustache a moment and then nodded. Frank let go.

"Okay. So Cliston is mad at me," I began.

"Cliston's his butler," Frank explained.

"Cliston of the Artistry Agency?" the President asked.

"Don't confuse him. Cliston is upset. He hired me to protect some actors but they got killed. I felt you guys should know the situation. You're owed that, right? Sorry I made up the story. But I didn't want the consequences after I told you," I said.

"Let me see if I understand correctly. You had been enlisted to *guard* Gordle Maytop?" the President asked.

"Yes. But he was murdered before I showed up. I didn't even *see* him."

"Then how do you know he's dead?" Frank asked.

"I mean, I *saw* him, obviously. Just not alive. Doesn't count if someone is dead."

"Who was the trigger man?" Frank asked suspiciously.

"I don't know. A bunch of actors have been killed lately. We think the incidents may be related."

"Who is we?" Mancel MaGove asked.

"Me, Cliston, the Police Chief, and a reporter named Rendrae."

"From *The News*? I owe them a list of my favorite songs," the President said.

"He's not that kind of reporter. He's a vegetarian journalist," I said.

The Guild President appeared deep in thought. Frank stood close, his body poised for combat.

"Frank," the President began, "would you say your nephew is a dangerous man?"

"Absolutely. He's been running dirty deals on this space station longer than anyone alive."

"That's not fair," I said.

"Then how would you like a job, young man?" Mancel MaGove asked jovially.

Both Frank and I turned toward him, puzzled. Not only was I probably centuries older than Mancel MaGove, and thus, hardly a "young man," but he apparently didn't have a good grasp of the Colmarian language.

"Um," I began, "a job doing what?"

"Protecting our Guild. Like your uncle here."

"He just admitted that the actors he tried to protect got mulched," Frank said.

"I believe in second chances," the President beamed.

"He's married to a Damakan," Frank said, as if it was the worst thing ever.

"Really?" Mancel MaGove asked, startled.

"Well, we're anticipating engagement. Yes," I said.

"Amazing. What Guild does your wife belong to?" he asked.

"She's kind of working freelance right now. I think she wants to be solo for the time being so she can really get the feel for which Guild suits her best," I replied.

"That's admirable. Many actors select a Guild prematurely. Guilds are a very new concept for us," the President said.

"Exactly," I nodded.

"Hank's not a good fit for this place. I don't recommend hiring him," Frank said, crossing his arms defiantly. Ever the supportive uncle.

"Why not? With his domestic arrangement, he may well understand us better than most Colmarians," Mancel MaGove said.

"We're not Colmar—" Frank began.

"Frank's right," I interrupted. "I'm working for someone else at the moment. Security consultant for the Navy. But maybe you could help. Gordle Maytop's wife said that he mentioned something big was going on. Or about to happen. Would you know anything about that?"

"Nothing comes to mind," he said simply.

I studied his face. It seemed like he was telling the truth. But he was a Damakan. A *Guild President*. If he had answered, "blueberry tacos," I would have also believed him.

"Okay," I said. "That's all I wanted to tell you, I suppose."

"I do thank you for coming by. And please pass along my sympathies to his wife; give my regards to Cliston; enjoy your wedding; and if you should reconsider employment, don't hesitate to contact me."

Mancel MaGove twirled and walked out the door of the air-conditioned meeting room.

"He didn't take the news very hard," I said to Frank.

"He's a Damakan and you're not," Frank shrugged.

"I'm tempted to stay in here a while. It's an oven out there."

"Because you're fat."

"No, I'm not. And why aren't you wearing a breathing mask? You said this air was poisonous to us Ontakians."

"I ran out of my mixture and the mask was too stuffy with the climate changes. I tried going without it for a month and found I had more stamina. So I decided to ditch it."

"You were breathing fluorine gas! That had to be eating away your body from the inside. I told you it was crazy."

"No, you didn't," he said.

"I must have said it a hundred times."

"I don't remember that."

I shook my head in disbelief. I think Frank was physically unable to admit I was right and he was wrong.

"Why didn't you back me up with the President? You're supposed to be my blood relative. I feel like I get better treatment from my enemies."

"Do you ever do anything except complain?" he asked.

"Yes. I've murdered four-tenths as many people as you in eight-elevenths the time, remember?"

"I said that so Mancel MaGove would take you seriously. You haven't done *anything* compared to me," Frank said.

"That so? Your boss just offered me a job."

"Only because he learned you're my nephew. He probably figured you share my work ethic."

"You don't have any ethics," I said.

"I have a great work ethic. I *always* get the job done! Unless there's a better job. Your attitude is why you're graded so low on Scanhand."

"Low on Scanhand?" I asked.

"Yeah."

I shook my head.

"Are you kidding?"

"No. What's Scanhand?" I asked.

"That wife of yours has really screwed your head. She's another reason why no one wants to hire you."

"We're not married yet," I said angrily.

"Fine, but don't ask me to give you away at the wedding. I don't approve of the union."

"You're not 'giving me away.' You and I barely talk. And you just attacked me—twice."

"Well, I'm not giving her away either."

"You're not *in* the wedding, Frank!"

"I know. Because I'm not going to be a part of it," he said defiantly.

"What is Scanhand?"

"It's a way to rate employees."

"Employees of what?"

"Like document forgers, hitmen, collection agents, bookmakers, the normal jobs around Belvaille. There's a profile on everyone."

"All that is in a database? They'll arrest the whole station," I said, alarmed.

"Who will? This isn't PCC territory. How do you think I got this job?"

"Cliston *mentioned* something about Scanhand a while ago. I figured it was some robot thing. Did you make this yourself?"

"Don't be stupid. No one knows who made it. Some group of eggheads. You post anonymously. That way no one gets pissed off and starts a bloodbath."

"That will never work. Everyone hates everyone on Belvaille. Gangs are always fighting. We might be in a gang war at this very moment. Why is it called Scanhand? Does it scan your hand?"

"They probably called it that because 'Gang Database' sounded lame. You should check it out. You need to work on your reputation."

"And what do you mean about Laesa?"

"Who?"

"My fiancée."

"I don't know anything about her. Except she's a Damakan. And she's got you spinning around."

"No, she hasn't."

"So you're saying your clients *usually* get killed?" he asked.

"Actually, yeah."

"That's why your Trouble rating is bad," he said.

"Trouble? Is that another Scanhand thing?"

"It has everything. Like you don't hire a drug dealer who's a junkie, or a pit boss who's a gambler. All that's in there."

"How do I find it?" I asked.

"Your tele, stupid."

"Is Garm on it? She'll kill you guys if she is."

"She is. But it's blank."

I pulled out my tele and started browsing around.

"This ain't your living room. Get out of here so I can go back to patrolling," Frank said.

"Fine. Nice seeing you, Uncle."

"Don't expect some fancy gift for your wedding," he said.

"You're not *coming* to my wedding," I replied.

"So that floozy is trying to keep me from watching my own nephew get hitched? Who does that bitch think she is?"

I wound up and took a swing at Frank. He sidestepped me like I was a boulder attempting to roll uphill against a stiff breeze. He then socked me in my left ear.

"That woman has made you flabby. Better watch out she doesn't get you killed."

CHAPTER 17

I should have questioned my slimeball uncle Frank. Maybe he had information about the gang war. But I was too busy storming out the door of the Romance Guild after he insulted Laesa. Also, I wanted to check on this so-called Scanhand database. My curiosity was boiling over.

As soon as I was in the street, I took out my tele and looked it up. It wasn't hard to find. To log in and confirm you were a citizen of Belvaille, they asked a few questions about the station and its underworld. Some of the questions were pretty obscure, but for me, it was easy stuff. I answered and created an account.

When I put in Hank for my name, it asked if I wanted to link up with my current profile. Sure.

There I was.

It had my name and a lot of categories underneath it. Like in a category for known aliases, there were pages and pages of names I had used in the past. Some of them went back half a thousand years. How did they have all this stuff?

I couldn't make sense of the profile at first. There were lots of numbers and colored bars. But then I figured out it was an attribute list.

My "Toughness" was a red ten. I assumed that was good. Linked to it, there was a separate area for comments. Most were short, with lots of typos. They were anonymous, so I couldn't see who wrote them. There were things like:

Don't try and fight him. You lose.

If you shoot Hank he gets mad.

Hank a stoopid lazee bulldozer.

There were hundreds more like that. The next attribute was called "Smarts." I got a blue eight. Not sure what the color meant, but eight was surprisingly high, assuming it went up to ten. I wondered what they would label a genius like Delovoa. I read the comments.

Gives gud advice.

Can't con him. He know every angle.

Great broker. Market savvy.

Hank has been doing this crap longer than anyone. He setup or worked on just about every scam we got in the city.

Those remarks were pretty gratifying. There were tons more. The last attribute was called "Trouble." I got a black zero on that. I read the associated comments.

Hank has worst luck of anyone I ever met!

I bought a tool from Hank once. Flaze Torch with Zenodrine attachment. Don't make them no more. Patch welding. Or circular rebar inversion fit. Not sure where he got it. Next day a Therezian stepped on my car. Torch was inside.

If you work with Hank someone you know will die in a few days. Happens every time. Not saying Hank kill them. But someone near Hank or don't like Hank or something about Hank. Then your friend gets shot and his sister blown up.

Hank knows more gods and Boranjame and Dredel Led and mutants than anyone should. They always hanging around him. They always pissed off.

I hired Hank to deliver some product. I don't need to say what kind of product. Don't matter what kind. Drugs. But specifics no your concern. Was a night job. New suppliers. Risky. Worried double-cross. I made a profit, but eight people went to hospital. Me too. Fractured kidney. But not Hank. Hank always fine. Everyone else get hurt.

You haveta understand. Hank bulletproof. Don't stand close to him! I see Hank in a room I walk the other side. Safer go to other bar. Don't even finish drink. Close tab. Get out.

I sees Hank shot by missile. Rocket. What difference? Didn't do nothing. Blew out windows of my restaurant. Four grand repairs. Four grand! Not include estimate. Estimate was wrong. Don't trust Malley. Bad estimates. He like, this has missile damage, why you no say that? I like, this was rocket, not missile, and you do estimate, not me. What matter if missile or spill food? He say blah blah blah. Don't trust Malley. Three customer hurt and I lose four grand. Hank bad for business.

Hank is wanted by the Navy. He ATE entire crew of a battlecruiser. Every last one! Kids. Women. Pets. He destroyed the Colmarian empire by accident. Didn't even try to do it! We all know what he did in Super Class Championship. He murders all the refs and coaches and players and gets league and city banned. Every time I say we should get rid of Hank, people tell me be quiet. Cuz you even to say his name it bad luck. And we don't know how to get rid of him.

I don't know what everyone's problem is. I never had the slightest issue with Hank. Just give him food and have pretty women around. He's easy.

Can't bribe Hank. What you going to do with that?

Other guy is wrong. I bribed Hank. But my friend still got broken arm. Avoid Hank. Unless you got to. But don't send him near aux storage containers in southwest on weekdays. I work there. Weekend is okay.

It went on and on. It was so unfair that there were no signatures. I tried to guess who had written each entry. Maybe this was all done by one person with a lot of free time.

I looked around the database for MTB but couldn't find him at first. Then I saw there were entirely different sections of profiles. I was listed on the criminal side. MTB was in a Notable Peoples section. That's where they had Delovoa, MTB, and Garm.

For Garm, comments were disabled. All it said was, "Incorruptible Adjunct Overwatch of Belvaille." That was clever. She would crack down on anything that even hinted she wasn't on the level.

I went back to my profile as I walked home.

They listed *thousands* of stories from my past, but a lot of the details were wrong. I was reading my history a few sentences at a time and it was all left-handed compliments or straight-up insults.

I looked up Frank's profile and he had eight Toughness, eight Smarts, and ten Trouble. Ten! That was good. The opposite of me. I read the comments and there was nothing but praise for how well Frank handled himself. I couldn't believe it. Was my uncle a scumbag only toward me?

Scanhand was comprehensive. At first glance it seemed as if a lot of stuff was missing, but you just had to hunt around for it. It was clunky to use. It was misspelled, misattributed, and filled with profanity. But if you took all the profiles and rearranged everything perfectly you could read Belvaille's entire background in minute detail.

I was the only person listed who had a ten in Toughness or a zero in Trouble. You could sort on each attribute, which sucked. Because no one was going to be *searching* for the most troublesome person in the city to hire. I tried to put in some nice comments about myself, but it wouldn't let me.

I was tempted to go through all the people I knew and leave pissy remarks about all the screw-ups I'd seen them do over the years. But I thought better of it. Just because I had a bad profile didn't mean I had to wreck everyone else's.

I'd have to really sit down and decide how I should approach Scanhand. It seemed to me the application was very useful. If Frank was right, I might have a difficult time getting work while my profile had so many bad marks. So far there was no reference to my actors getting murdered while I was protecting them. But I couldn't get any lower in Trouble than I already had. Thank goodness I still had Garm's job.

At home, I was surprised to see Cliston back early.

"Hey, Cliston."

"Good evening, sir. What would you care for dinner?"

"Is it dinner time already? Wow, I lost track. Sure. Something yummy."

"Will Laesa be joining you?"

"No, she left a message and said she was working as an understudy tonight. Cliston, do you know about Scanhand?"

"No, sir."

"I was just wondering if you might be putting bad reviews on my profile."

"I'm not sure what a profile is, sir. But talent agent Cliston might be entering information into the database."

"Hey. How do you know it's a database? You just said you never heard of it," I asked.

"I spoke with talent agent Cliston some nanoseconds ago and he mentioned it."

"Then ask him if he's writing bad stuff about me."

"He's not available now. You might call him tomorrow."

"Cliston. You can be really annoying sometimes."

"I'm sorry, sir. That is not my intention. What is Scanhand, exactly?"

"It's like a big electronic thing of just about everyone and everything on the station. You're listed as a Notable Person, but there isn't much about you. You're probably too complicated. When will dinner be ready?"

"Are you going to shower first? I detect large amounts of dried saline on your skin, sir."

"Yeah, I walked halfway across the station. I'm pretty crusty."

"Dinner should be ready in 42 minutes."

"Great. Thanks. You *sure* you aren't putting any comments on my profile? Some of this stuff is pretty detailed and only someone like you would know it."

"I am certain that I am not manipulating anything that I have never seen or heard of before now, sir."

"But talent agent Cliston might?"

"Yes, sir. But I suspect he does not know you as well as I do."

"Suspect? You're guessing what's in the other half of your computer brain?"

"It is not half my brain and it is not a computer. But I am guessing, sir."

"Okay. 42 minutes for dinner?"

"I'm afraid it's 44 minutes now, sir."

"Are you punishing me for asking you questions?"

"No, sir. I am not starting dinner while I answer them."

"Right. I'm going to shower."

"Very good, sir."

CHAPTER 18

The next morning, I was resting my eyes while soaking in the tub. I liked taking baths. Normally I took showers, but Cliston had recently installed a spa with an attached aircraft engine. The engine powered turbines that rubbed me down—or could even be used to remove paint from metal surfaces. It wasn't as good as a patented Cliston massage session, but he didn't have much time for those nowadays. The tub wasn't very deep, because I couldn't swim, and it would be just my luck to drown in the bath.

"Get up," a woman barked at me.

I had been hovering halfway between dreaming and waking. But I retained enough brain power to realize the only woman who was comfortable yelling at me in my own home was Garm. I cracked open one eyelid.

Garm was indeed standing at the entrance to my master bathroom. She wasn't wearing her military outfit. Probably because the weight of all her medals and citations hurt her spine.

"How did you get in here? Cliston should have kicked your ass," I said.

"He left for work hours ago. Get up."

"You've been watching my apartment for hours?"

"No, I have people do that for me."

"Military people or Quadrad people?" I asked nervously.

"There's no Quadrad within five Systems of Portal Depot #4382 other than me. This is *my* territory."

Portal Depot #4382 was the official name of our System, according to the PCC. But no one ever called it that. Even on most official shipping forms it was simply referred to as Belvaille. Though they would sometimes put it in quotes.

"What do you want?" I said, closing my eyes again.

"I want an update on your assignment," she answered, walking closer. "You're taking a *bubble bath?*"

"A guy can't relax now and then?"

"So then you've made progress in stopping attacks on the dramatic industry?" she demanded.

"I'm sleeping at the moment," I dodged.

"Get up!"

I ignored her. Garm was an expert at all forms of combat. She could murder people a block away using a single strand of hair—probably. But I wasn't a person. A whole *headful* of her hair wouldn't do anything to me except make her scalp drafty.

"Come back later. As you can see, I'm trying to wash myself," I said.

"Anyone past infancy doesn't 'try' to wash themselves, they just do it. You handle bathing like you handle every responsibility: by being lazy and hoping it works out. As if the dirt is going to get tired and find other toenails to hide under."

"First off, for all you know this is how every Ontakian bathes. Second, I don't have dirt under my toenails."

"When's the last time you *saw* your toenails, let alone your feet? That's not a bathtub, it's a swimming pool. Did Cliston empty out a transport freighter to build this? Attention!" She barked.

"Garm, I'm not one of your soldiers you can yell at. I'm not even in the PCC."

"No, but they pay you. You are officially on the payroll of the PCC Navy. Specifically, the Security Detail of the Thirty-Eighth Stellar Conglomeration of the Auxiliary Communications and Transportation Framework under the General Subdivision of Chairs, Sofas, and Upholstery," she said.

"Did you say chairs? What do I have to do with chairs?" I asked.

"That's how budgeting works. You take money from whatever department has resources to spare. But the point is, you work for the Grand Auditor General. He doesn't care if you're a PCC citizen or a PCC terrorist. I can file a claim against you."

"Claim of what?"

"Malfeasance."

"Claim of what using simple words?"

"Misconduct. Impropriety. Treason!" She yelled.

"Oh, come on. I'm working. Just not this very second. Even the Navy won't think I'm doing bad."

"There's all kinds of things you can do wrong according to the Navy. You're the walking embodiment of Misappropriation of Funds and Dereliction of Duty."

"You're bluffing. There's no way the Supreme Bookkeeper Lord is going to notice my little salary in missing chairs for Belvaille."

"He will if I tell him," she said.

"And that's the bluff. Because you want him down here looking at your records even less than I do."

Garm cooled off and took a different approach.

"Hank, I'm getting a lot of pushback. I've gotten a dozen calls from senior administrators asking where their favorite shows are. I had to tell a *Senator* of the PCC that he missed his program because it is currently doing double-reshoot-callback rehearsals."

"Is that a thing?" I asked.

"How should I know? I'm not a Damakan. But we need to get these actors back on schedule. I'm running out of excuses. If a bunch of admirals can't find things to do on the weekend, they're liable to start another war to pass the time."

"The PCC never wins wars."

"So? Do you want a billion people to die because you're taking a bubble bath?"

"It's not that simple. It's a gang war. But like secret," I said.

"I don't care about the inner workings of Fat Man Sheezer's criminal operations and who he's currently arguing with. I take my cut and deal with the Navy. That's our arrangement. That's how Belvaille continues to exist. You all aren't holding up your end of the agreement. You're pissing off the Navy. And while we might be horrendous at fighting wars with real empires, Belvaille isn't a real empire. It isn't even a fake one. The Navy can roll over this station any time it wants. Before they put me up in front of a firing squad, I'll make sure they take care of every last one of you."

"You guys still use firing squads?" I asked.

"Whatever is cheapest. I read about one Adjunct Overwatch who was court-martialed and buried in algae because they wanted to save bullets."

"Come on. The PCC isn't that bloodthirsty. If you got in trouble you could fight it in court. That would take years," I said. "Which would be a speedy trial according to the PCC bureaucracy."

"That kind of delay only happens for big shots. Which I am not," she said.

"You run this entire city. Twenty thousand spaceships a day pass through this System."

"I don't *run* the station. I *can't* run it. I'm a liaison to you freaks. And while the Portals are important and fleet is important and the telescopes are important, I am not."

"Oh."

"You have to speed this up. If not for me, for you. If not for you, the city. If not for the city, the entire galaxy," she said.

"That's heavy. But can you sweeten the deal? I hardly know anyone in this galaxy so I'm not terribly concerned if it gets destroyed."

Garm stewed, her fists clenched. Which was fine. I only worried when Garm looked happy.

"I can't pay you more. I literally can't. You're on the official payroll. What else do you want?" she asked.

"Get Laesa in the movies," I said.

"Exactly how can I do that?"

"You transmit them. You're the gatekeeper."

"I don't control content. They give us files. I don't even look at them. I wouldn't know the first thing about a tele program."

"Talk to the Guilds," I said.

"And tell them what? I'm the Navy Adjunct Overwatch. What the hell do I know about actors?"

"Talk to Cliston," I said.

"Your *butler?*"

"No, *talent agent* Cliston. She needs an agent."

"I'm not going to get into a haggling session with Cliston. Even as a butler he always wins. His talent agent persona is cutthroat."

"His agency must use some services from the city. From the Navy."

"Like our refueling depot? Or weapons cache? He's got a big office, but it's not that big."

"He uses electricity, right? Water, right? Essential city services are under your authority," I said.

"Not my *authority*. Guidance."

I was getting a headache. Garm usually wasn't this hard to deal with. She wasn't easy, but she mostly dealt fair with me, and then screwed everyone else.

"Garm, I'm giving you a break," I said. "I don't want more money. But I'm trying to get married and Laesa said she wants to wait until her career improves. This will help. Talk to Cliston about representing her."

"Why can't you talk to him? You live together."

"I'm lucky he still *occasionally* works as my butler. I have nothing Cliston needs or wants."

"And you assume I have something a Dredel Led needs or wants?" she asked.

"If anyone has leverage over Cliston, it's you. Whatever the Skim is skimming, you're skimming off the Skim. You can turn off the telescopes tomorrow. You can crank up the city's air conditioning and freeze all his actors. You can create import taxes on robot grease and have his joints rust. Something."

Garm looked around my bathroom warily. As if I had hidden microphones.

"I can ask him. It's not like I can threaten Cliston," she said finally.

"Sure you can. He's a Dredel Led. You could shoot him."

"I'm not shooting Cliston. I can't promise anything. You know how Cliston is. I'll try. But I need your gangs to get back in line so productions can resume."

"You're not going to let me enjoy this bath, are you?"

She dipped her hand in the water.

"It's cold. And the bubbles are almost gone. Your knees look horrible. What did you do, have a Therezian step on them?"

"Yes, that's exactly what happened," I got out of the bathtub. Garm wasn't squeamish and didn't seem impressed by my nakedness.

"While I'm here, you have anything to eat? I want some Cliston food," now that we had finished negotiating, Garm was relaxed and friendly. Or at least as friendly as she ever got.

"Let me get dressed and we can look around. But we might have to go to a restaurant," I said.

I went into my bedroom and started sorting through my clothes.

"Thad Elon's Blue Balls, you take longer to get ready than I do," Garm said after waiting a while.

"Not when you put on all your medallions. Besides, I'm a bigger person, it only makes sense it would take me longer to look beautiful."

"If you had a thousand years to prepare, Hank, you'd still be dumpy."

"You're awful catty for someone who's begging for my help."

"I'm not *begging* for anything. I'm bartering for your services. Colmarians have had this kind of regular interaction for hundreds of thousands of years. Though I'm not sure she's worth it."

"Who's not worth it?"

"Laesa. You think maybe if Cliston hasn't offered to represent her there's a reason?"

"He's jealous."

"How could Cliston be jealous of anyone? Let alone your wife-to-be?"

"He's jealous that I'm not spending as much time with him as I used to. He's worried we're drifting apart."

Garm began sputtering and blinking her eyes trying to digest what I said.

"Ease up or you'll swallow your tongue. Where do you want to get lunch?" I asked.

"I'm not going out in public with you. I said I want Cliston food. Don't you have anything here? Cliston prepares enormous, fantastical meals all the time."

I timidly stepped into my spacious kitchen. This was Cliston's kingdom. He could probably sense I was invading.

"Everything is all Dredel Led organized. I think it's binary or something," I said.

Garm stormed past me and went to an overhead cabinet and threw it open. A dozen containers spilled out onto the floor.

"Put that back how you found it! If Cliston sees that, I'll have to tell him it was your fault."

"I'm not worried about your damn food arrangement," she said.

"Alright. Help me look around. Cliston said I had some vegetables growing in here someplace. But seriously, put that stuff back."

Garm tried to pick up the spilled containers, but they wouldn't fit and I was hungry.

Garm and I walked through my apartment. I wasn't entirely familiar with this building even though I had lived here for years. City Hall had primarily been offices and Cliston seemed to randomly expand and contract my apartment suites. Over the course of living here, walls, rooms, and doors appeared and vanished with no discernible pattern or purpose—other than to keep me confused.

"I miss my old house," I said, as I tried another door.

"Well, don't piss off the Navy and they won't vaporize it from outer space," she said. "What are we looking for?"

"Something to eat."

"Does he have storehouses back here? Should the Navy designate this a shelter?" she asked.

"The Navy better leave me alone." I opened another door and: "Wow."

"What?" Garm asked, walking up behind me.

It was a huge room. About five times the size of most of the common areas and two stories tall. Inside there were rows and rows of *trees* bearing all kinds of strange and colorful fruits.

"How the hell did Cliston manage this?" Garm asked, amazed. "You're on the 46th floor of a space station skyrise. And there's another 50 or so floors above you. How do they grow? Where did it come from? This stuff should be quarantined."

I went over to one of the trees that was adorned with luscious purple fruit. I was about to take one.

"Wait. Do you know what that is?"

"No," I said.

"What if it's poison?"

"Cliston could drown me in my bathtub if he wanted to. He doesn't need to go to the trouble of growing a forest to poison me."

"It might not be poison once he prepares it. Maybe he uses it for decoration. Or dye for your clothes."

I paused with my hand outstretched. It would be just like Cliston to cultivate some crazy fruit you weren't supposed to eat. He probably didn't expect me to come back here poking around his jungle.

"I need food. You know how I get when I don't eat."

"You probably ate two hours ago."

"I don't care if I ate two seconds ago. I'm hungry," I said.

"Cliston is upstirs in his office. Do you think you can convince him to come down and make a special meal? I was really looking forward to it."

"No. Talent agent Cliston is mad at me."

"I thought you said he was jealous."

"My butler is jealous. And when he sees the mess you made in his kitchen, he'll be mad as well."

"Fine, let's get take-out. You're buying," she said.

"You have like a trillion times more money than I do. I'm saving up for a wedding."

"You can expense it since you're eating with me and we're talking security."

"What's that mean?"

"You can bill the cost of lunch to the Navy."

"Wait. Wait. Wait," I said. "The Navy pays for my food? Since when?"

"Just this lunch."

"Why can't I do it for every meal? The Navy can't expect me to work on an empty stomach."

"Because no accountant is going to believe you eat as much as you do. They'll think you're falsifying invoices. Then they'll come investigate and I'll have to kill you."

"What else can I expense?" I asked.

"Nothing. In fact, forget it. I'll pay. Cheap bastard."

Garm took out her wallet and she had so much cash she had to hold it with both hands.

"Do you think they'll have change for a thousand? I need to break some of these large bills," she said.

"You got enough scratch there to choke a toilet. Are you going to refinance a planet?"

"I'm buying a new car later."

"Most businesses take electronic payment through teles. Maybe you've heard of them."

"Frank doesn't," she said.

"Frank? My uncle? His cars are stolen."

"Barely."

"What's that even *mean*? Something is stolen or it's not."

"What does choke a toilet mean?"

"It's an expression," I said.

"No, it isn't. And what I do with my money is none of your concern."

"Buy me a car. I've been without one for weeks."

"You know, I just read a report that the Navy's intra-city transportation costs had gone down 23% this month. I couldn't figure out why. It was probably because you weren't out there causing traffic jams," she said seriously.

"You shouldn't carry that much cash. What if someone robs you?"

"Who's going to rob me?" she asked.

"I might."

I'm not sure how she did it, but next thing I knew, Garm's pointer and middle fingers were up my nostrils. *All* the way up. I could feel her nails scraping the bottom of my brain.

"Are your insides as bulletproof as your outside?" she threatened.

"Nyeah. Dey are," I said nasally.

She pulled out her fingers and wiped them on my shirt.

"Figures."

"Wow," I said, sniffing. "I didn't realize how congested I was until now. I think you doubled my airflow."

"Don't get used to it. I'm not your mother. Clean out your own sinuses."

"Speaking of mothers, how's your granddaughter doing?"

"You won't believe it," she said.

"Probably. But go on."

"Malla has quit the Quadrad."

"No way. I thought it was, by death, by design."

"By birth, by death. It is. But she's rich now. Super rich. She donated like...a hundred million credits to the Quadrad and they let her out. There's only been a couple instances of that in Quadrad history. I couldn't believe it. She just *paid* them," Garm seemed disgusted and disappointed that her granddaughter was no longer an assassin.

"Huh. So you're like, considered a bad parent by the Quadrad?"

"Grandparent. No. They took the money. All our traditions, honor, and values and they were like, 'Pfft, thanks for the check!'"

"Who pays by check? I wouldn't accept a check. Only the Ank use those."

"When was the last time you bought something for a hundred million?" she asked.

"Not today. So are you ordering food or what? Get something that smells good. Now that my nose is working, I want to savor the aroma."

CHAPTER 19

The next day, I got a message from Rendrae reminding me we had work to do. I called up Zzzho to get a cab ride to Rendrae's office. He arrived promptly as usual.

"Hey, Hank," Zzzho said through his electronic speaker. "How's it going?"

"Going? It's gone. I need you to drive me to *The News* headquarters."

"Is it possible I can speak to you first? It's important."

"Can it wait? I have a meeting."

"It's important to me. It will only take about fifteen minutes."

"Did something happen? I just spoke to you a few days ago."

"Actually, you didn't. But that's kind of what I want to talk about."

"You want to tell me my memory is getting even worse? Alright. Let me just send Rendrae a quick note."

"It will help if I can show you. Let's go for a drive."

He took me to the southwest of the city. This was close to the area where Delovoa had paid a guy for his body parts.

Zzzho parked the car and I noticed two identical taxi cabs on the same street.

"We're here. You'll need to come with me," Zzzho said.

"You're...getting out?" I asked, surprised. I rarely saw Zzzho outside the cockpit of a spaceship or car. He was perpetually driving *something*.

I was sitting in the back and suddenly Zzzho's reddish cloud was on the sidewalk next to the car. He didn't have to open the door or window or anything.

I got out and followed. Zzzho kind of drifted along the sidewalk at a slow pace. Without his speaker system, he couldn't talk. Not sure if he could even hear me.

I looked around somewhat anxiously to see if anyone noticed us. For the longest time, Keilvin Kamigans weren't allowed on Belvaille. I guess we had to draw the line somewhere. Sentient, colored, lightning clouds was apparently where we drew it.

Zzzho floated over to the wall of a building and then slowly disappeared. I stood there blinking my eyes, wondering if Zzzho had changed colors or something. But I finally got the idea he went inside.

"I can't walk through walls, Zzzho," I said to nothing.

After searching a bit, I found a doorway around the corner. It was blocked with garbage and obviously hadn't been opened in years. I forced my way inside the dark building.

I wasn't worried about getting mugged because I was a bulletproof mutant, and I didn't have any money worth mugging.

"Hello?" I called out.

I wandered around a bit, and after tripping over junk and bumping into walls, I finally took out my tele and used its light to help me see.

This was an odd building. It had lots of piping and exposed, heavy-duty wiring. It was obviously some kind of maintenance building. It made me slightly nervous that anything that might be connected to Belvaille's operation seemed to be in such a state of disuse.

I kept wandering around until up ahead I saw a reddish light in the distance. I hadn't thought about it, but Zzzho probably glowed in the dark. I headed that way.

I came into a large room that was *filled* with Zzzho. Other than that, the room appeared heavily industrial, the same as the rest of the building.

"Is this where you live?" I asked.

"Yes," Zzzho said. He had a small speaker in the room.

"Well, it's lovely," I said.

"This is an auxiliary transmission station. It's not used much. But a lot of radiation comes through here and we absorb it."

"Am I going to get nuked?" I asked, alarmed.

"No, you should be fine. Just stay over there."

"You said 'we' absorb it?" I asked.

"Yeah. That's what I wanted to talk to you about. I have some friends here with me. They've also been driving cabs. You met them a few times and assumed it was me."

I stared at the big room brimming with cloudy lightning bolts.

"Uh, you guys aren't planning on taking over the space station are you?"

"No. How would we even accomplish that?"

"I don't know. How could *we* fight off gas clouds?"

"You could use fans," he said.

"Fans of what?"

"No, fans. Things that push air. You can literally blow us away."

"How many of your friends are here?" I asked, still not convinced. Pretty much every alien species I ever ran into started trouble. I was rightfully cautious.

"There's three of us."

"Oh. I thought there might be a hundred or something. It's a big room. When did the others come?"

"A few months ago."

"How did you contact them? Was it like...a brain thing? Dredel Led can kind of communicate through brains and electricity. They have a whole city of computers."

"I called them on the tele."

"Oh," I said, disappointed. "So what's the problem?"

"Well, it's kind of your initial reaction that worries us. Everyone seems scared at first. I don't know why. As far as I know the Keilvin Kamigans have never been at war with another species. We take all the planets that no one else wants."

"I don't know why either, I guess. You guys are strange. Boranjame are super strange and they wipe out solar systems when they're bored."

"Keilvin Kamigans like driving cars and trucks and spaceships. We're not exactly on the same level as Boranjame."

"I guess not. So what do you need?"

"The others have been pretending they're me. It's not very hard because we look similar and no one really pays much attention."

"Are they your relatives or something?" I asked.

"No. We don't have that kind of distinction."

"Fair enough. Which...one of you is which?" I asked, pointing at the big cloud.

"There's a number of concepts we don't share with Colmarians. Keilvin Kamigans can occupy the same spaces with each other. The notion of *travel* is relatively new to us. Maybe that's why we enjoy doing it."

"I thought you guys were super fast," I said.

"Not at all. We're quite slow compared to Colmarians."

"So what do you want me to do?"

"We'd like you to be our corporeal interface with the rest of the city."

"What's that mean?"

"We can't really *do* anything physically."

"Oh. I can like lift stuff for you. You need some furniture moved?"

"All kinds of things, actually. We'd like to stop pretending to be me and let everyone know there are more of us. And maybe buy some things. Rent a real apartment."

"Sure. What are the names of the other guys? Or gals? Or gasses?" I asked.

"Hi," Zzzho said.

"Um. Hi, Zzzho."

"I'm not him. My name is..." And a high-pitched blast of static and feedback assaulted me.

"Ow. You might want to work on that name. You sound just like Zzzho."

"Of course. We're using the same speaker. I'm plugged in now."

It hadn't occurred to me that the speaker wasn't actually *amplifying* his voice but *was* his voice. They had no vocal sounds of their own.

"Nice to meet you," I said.

"Thank you. Zzzho has told us a lot about you. We hope you can be our proxy here."

"I'm not sure I like that word, but I understand what you mean."

"What name do you recommend I adopt for Colmarian-speak?"

"I'm not sure. Usually nicknames are based on your personality or appearance or some notable event from your past."

"I once had a vacation on the polar end of a pulsar and absorbed some of its transmitted radiation," the static name said.

"Okay. How about calling yourself, Red Sparkles?"

"I don't understand how that applies to my experience," he said.

"It doesn't. But you're red and you kind of sparkle."

"Hank?"

"Um. Yes?"

"This is Zzzho again."

"Great. I think the first thing you need to do is get yourself some different speakers. Maybe you could also form yourself into distinct shapes so people could tell you apart," I suggested.

"Do you think you could get everyone on Belvaille to wear gamma-releasing necklaces so we could identify each of you better?" Zzzho asked.

"What? No. People aren't going to wear radiation!"

"Then why do you expect us to shape ourselves like your species?"

"It was just an idea. Are more of your people coming to Belvaille?"

"Not at the moment. I want to see what the employment situation is like. In exchange for your help, we can do things for you in return."

"I can definitely use some cab rides until I get my wheels. And you already pilot my ship."

"We also see and hear a lot of things."

"Like through the gaseous ether?" I asked.

"No. We drive cabs, Hank."

"Oh, yeah. So have you seen anything different lately?"

"Can you be more specific? Each of us works about 24 hours a day. We see a lot."

"Have you ever given any rides to the Rough Boys?"

"Sure. They don't tip. Ever. Kaxle chewed one of my seats but I made him pay for it," he said.

"How did you *make* him pay?" I asked, eager to learn any weaknesses.

"I said I would never give him another ride if he didn't. They drive worse than you."

"Hmm. Do you shuttle around other gang members?"

"All the time. But they don't usually tell us their plans, if that's what you're going to ask."

"Can you start checking which gang they're with and keeping track of where they're going?"

"How can we do that?" Zzzho asked.

"Simple. Ask them if they are running with Roll Bungalow. Or *any* name. Hoodlums are quick to correct being labeled in the wrong gang."

"We can try, but I *have* noticed that guys are talking less than usual. And it's not like people spoke with us much to begin with."

"Yeah, I think they're uncomfortable around you."

"But why? That's what we don't understand."

"You look like bad weather. You're the only species in the entire galaxy like that."

"So? The Dredel Led are at war with your species and people still talk to Cliston without a problem."

"No one can be upset at Cliston. Just try and keep track of things if you can. And pay attention to anything out of the ordinary. Is there something I can do for you in the meantime?"

"Can you get us a few more sets of speakers? And we need to get some parts for our cabs. We can order them, but the mechanics around here aren't very good, or they're spaceship jockeys and too expensive."

"Delovoa can do anything for you. Just make sure he doesn't add on a missile launcher when you aren't looking."

"He can't tell when we're looking," he said.

"Good point. I personally use Delovoa for anything technical. He can be kind of dangerous to normal people, but you guys are at least as bulletproof as I am. You shouldn't have any problems."

"Hank?" he asked.

"Uh, yes?"

"This is" —a blare of static and feedback erupted— "talking."

"Ow. Okay."

"Can you think of some Colmarian-friendly names we might use? Something easy like Zzzho."

"Zzzho isn't actually that easy."

"What? Why didn't you tell me?" he said.

"A lot of alien names are difficult. We just muddle through as best we can. That's the Colmarian way."

"We aren't Colmarians."

"Neither am I, but we're speaking Colmarian, and we're dealing with Colmarians. This language can't process static, however," I said.

"Alright. When do you think you can get the speakers?"

"I'll shop around later tonight. Can one of you give me a ride to Rendrae now?"

"Sure. I can," one of the Keilvin Kamigans said. I didn't ask which one.

I walked through the stifling offices of *The News* to reach Rendrae.

"What have you learned?" I asked the skinny reporter, closing the door and soaking up the air conditioning.

"Learned about what?" he replied, looking up from his salad.

"I thought you would be combing the streets, trying to find out about the gang war."

"No, I've been fighting with my editors, trying to get control of my newspaper. What have *you* learned?"

"Not much. There's a bunch of Keilvin Kamigans here now."

"Really? Are they going to attack?"

"With what? They can't even hold weapons. I think they just want to drive taxis. The gang thing seems to be involved with the dramatic business."

"Maybe they're fighting over who will get the right to extort them."

"Maybe. Hey, have you heard of Scanhand?"

"No. Who is that?"

"It's not a who. It's a database on the tele. It's got just about everyone in it."

"Will that help us figure out the gang war?"

"It might."

I took out my tele and called it up. I then handed it to Rendrae. He spent some quiet minutes flipping through.

"This is impressive," he said finally.

"No. It's really shoddy reporting work. It's all hearsay."

"Well, that's all reporting is unless you record an actual event. You collect hearsay and weed out the truth."

"Exactly. It's all weeds. I think it might even be slanderous," I said.

"Slander? Are you going to file criminal charges? Is this because you got a low score on your Trouble rating?"

"Not just that. Other stuff is wrong. You aren't even in the system."

"I was gone for years and just got back. I guess someone created this application to fill the news gap once this paper stopped reporting properly."

"I can't believe you've never heard of Scanhand," I accused, even though I had only learned about it recently. I was still kind of iffy on Rendrae. I had wanted to use his reporter's knowledge, but he seemed to be more out of touch than me.

"Who are the editors you're fighting with?" I asked.

"I'm mostly trying to work against the other owner."

"Does he live on the station or is it some far-flung investor?"

"He's here. It's Hobb," Rendrae said, still reading Scanhand.

"Procon Hobb?" I asked, surprised.

"He's not a Procon any longer. That was a noble title that doesn't exist now."

"The big lizard guy? Who owned the Belvaille Glocken Team?"

"Yes," Rendrae answered, annoyed.

"What the hell does he want with a broken newspaper? The guy owns planets."

"And he has a church on Belvaille devoted to him."

"Wow. Who goes to it?"

"How should I know? Hobb worshippers, I suppose. But he also owns half The News."

I still couldn't believe it. Then again, Procon Hobb was as weird as weird got. He took a personal hand in running arena fights at Cheat Hall. If that wasn't beneath him, I guess owning a gossip rag wasn't either.

"Does Procon Hobb actually edit the newspaper?"

"He's not a Procon. No, he doesn't edit it. But he hired, or someone in his organization hired, all the editors here now. I have to get my paper back."

"Have you tried talking to him?"

"I've never even seen him in person. Only pictures. He spoke to me telepathically when I was in the hospital. I thought it was the drugs at first. But he paid for my operations in exchange for half ownership of The News."

"He spoke to you across the galaxy?" I asked, amazed.

"I don't know where he was. If he was on Belvaille, then yes."

"Wow, again."

"You used to work for him. If I can show that I can take The News in a viable other direction, do you think he'll let me? Or sell back his share of the paper?" Rendrae asked.

"I don't know much about Procon Hobb. But if his servants pissed him off, he used them to feed a gigantic lizard."

"They had to feed the lizard?"

"No. I mean he *fed* them to the lizard. You know, it ate them."

* 169 *

Rendrae blinked several times.

"Does he still do that?"

"No. I killed the lizard."

"Why?"

"It's a long story."

"Is it listed in Scanhand?"

"No one knows about it except Delovoa. And you. Don't tell Procon Hobb. I don't want him mad at me."

"You don't think you could beat him in a fight?" Rendrae asked, even more worried.

"I doubt it. He's a really big mutant with his own religion. If nothing else, he could talk in my head all day and night and drive me insane. Maybe you should start a new paper," I said.

"*The News* is all I've done for centuries," Rendrae said defiantly. "It's *my* paper."

"Half yours," I corrected.

"Let's go break this story. At least it will give me a bargaining chip with Hobb."

"I don't think it will matter, honestly," I said.

The more I thought about it, the less sure I was about having Rendrae along.

"I want to do hard news. A gang war that everyone is keeping secret is exactly that. Trust me, Hank, I'm still a 'Force for Facts.'"

That had been Rendrae's tagline when he did a station-wide news broadcast. It brought back a lot of memories. Particularly, just how long Rendrae had been involved with news in one form or another. As long as I had been involved in crime. Experience had to count for something.

"Besides, I have a car," he added.

"Oh," I said, brightening. "Alright. I think I have an idea who we should interview first."

"Hobb?"

"Forget Procon Hobb."

"He's not a Procon..."

"Anyone who owns planets and can talk to people across the galaxy using their mind is allowed to call himself whatever he wants. No. We're going to visit a trash man."

CHAPTER 20

It wasn't easy finding Paggo-Nosa, the trash recycler. Every restaurant we went to said we had just missed him.

Rendrae was driving, and getting bothered by the number of stops we were making.

"Why don't we just talk to people we meet?" he asked.

"Because I want to get an outsider's view before we jump in. I've already called a number of heavy hitters and no one would tell me anything. My uncle said it might be because I'm dating a Damakan."

"What's that have to do with it?"

"If this gang war and violence is somehow connected to the movie business, that might be a reason."

"Is your woman in the entertainment industry?"

"Dramatic industry. Her name's Laesa Swavort. And she sort of is. Not really."

We were zigzagging across the city, finding no discernable pattern to Paggo-Nosa's pickup route, when we finally ran into him. He was putting a stack of plastic bottles in the back of his stupendously overloaded truck. The mass of recyclables towered three stories high and was secured with wires, poles, and other jury-rigged solutions.

"Man, we've been looking for you all day," I called out the window of the car.

"Hank? What did I do?" he asked, somewhat alarmed.

"Nothing. This is Rendrae, a reporter with *The News*. We'd like to talk to you for a minute. Hold up, we need to park. You aren't in any trouble."

The alley was too small to pass the truck so Rendrae backed out and we parked a few blocks away. When we returned to Paggo-Nosa, he was nearly finished loading.

Rendrae began doing squat thrusts now that we were on foot. He really took his new fitness lifestyle seriously. He had even done hand exercises while we were driving.

"You're with *The News*? Feel it: I don't know nothing about actors," Paggo-Nosa explained.

"I'm not with that side of reporting," Rendrae said, stretching his arms.

"You go to nearly every bar and restaurant on Belvaille, right?" I asked.

"Some yes. Some no," Paggo-Nosa hedged uneasily. He was still unclear on our motives.

"We want to know what you've seen as far as gang activity," I said.

"Gangs? Feel it: I pick up recyclables. I don't bother no gangs."

Rendrae walked closer with his tele out so he could record the conversation.

"We're interested in your observations. Have you noticed them carrying more weapons than usual? Or have you noticed them appearing in larger numbers than they had in the past? Do they seem more concerned or suspicious?"

Paggo-Nosa thought for a moment.

"Yup. Yup to all of that."

"Do you see the same people at the same restaurants and bars?" Rendrae continued.

"In the trash?" he asked.

"I don't think he goes inside," I clarified.

"Let me rephrase it. At each of your pickups, would you say you get a wide sampling of empties or does each establishment tend to have a preponderance of individual products?" Rendrae continued.

"Huh?" Paggo-Nosa asked.

"Yeah," I echoed.

"Sorry, I haven't interviewed in a while. I have to recover the vernacular. This bar you just cleared. What brand of liquor is most common?"

"Sasheeth. Lots of Sasheeth," he said, and pointed to a case of empty bottles he hadn't put up yet. They all had the same label.

"Why do you stack your truck so tall?" I asked. "That thing is going to topple over and kill someone."

"Why don't you carry an axe instead of a gun?" he replied, pointing to where my shotgun bulged from my jacket.

"An axe? That's a terrible weapon. I don't think I've even *seen* an axe in a couple hundred years. Used to be, there was an axe by every emergency airlock. But then they figured if there's a real emergency, we probably won't have gravity and no one will be able to swing an axe. Now they have crowbars. Why would I ever use an axe?"

"Feels you: you let me do *my* business and I'll let you do yours," Paggo-Nosa said.

Rendrae turned to me.

"What those bottles indicate is a further stratification and segregation of the city's watering holes."

"And what would *that* indicate?" I asked Rendrae, not understanding.

"During gang wars in the past, each faction tried to claim territory. Once settled, they rarely strayed outside of it unless to attack. That way they could protect themselves, ensure some stability, and keep their business interests flowing. That's why they return to the same restaurants and bars and clubs."

"That's right," Paggo-Nosa agreed.

"Huh," I said. Maybe it was a good idea to work with Rendrae after all. I wouldn't have thought to ask those questions.

"Oi, yoze!" Someone yelled at us.

A half-block away stood five men who clearly looked like gang members. They all had on white synth pants and red synth jackets. Their coordinated dress code clearly hadn't kept up with the temperature and they were dabbing chillwipes all over their sweating faces. Standing with them was Perkle Dolabin. He was the jerk who drove off with my car when we robbed the movie set of its generator. But this wasn't the ideal moment to ask where my vehicle was.

"Greetings," Rendrae stated. "I'm a reporter for *The News*, looking to gather some information on the latest kerfuffle that has enveloped our luminous city."

"I don't care if you're Thad Elon's grandmother. Clear that truck out of here. You're blocking the street," one of the toughs said.

I could see that most of the men were openly carrying submachine guns and looked ready to use them. I prided myself on being plugged in to Belvaille society, but other than Perkle, I didn't know any of the men and they clearly didn't know me.

"I better move," Paggo-Nosa said.

"Oi, yoze!" Someone else called from the opposite end of the alley.

We looked back and there were four armed men a few blocks away. Their outfits were pastel jumpsuits decorated with some quasi-military insignias. Why did gangs force their members to dress so awkwardly? I guess it helped identify them at a distance, but I got itchy just looking at those clothes. They were also carrying weapons. I spotted at least two battle rifles. As I was counting their guns, I noticed among their number was Borgin Two-Eyes. He was the four-eyed man who had been with Perkle Dolabin and I when we pulled the robbery for Ulteem.

"When did 'oi, yoze' become the standard Belvaille greeting?" Rendrae whispered to me.

I shrugged.

"Do you know whose turf this is?" I asked Paggo-Nosa. He had the truck door open and his foot inside, but had paused on seeing the other group of men.

"Feels me: I think we're kind of in between turfs," he said.

"Great," I muttered.

"Hey guys," I yelled, holding both my arms up and turning back and forth between the two parties. "We're just going to get out of the way here. Picking up bottles. We'll be gone in a second."

"In the meantime," Rendrae declared, walking forward calmly, "if anyone wishes to discuss their proceedings and grievances, *The News* will gladly observe and report. Though I can't guarantee publication at this time."

"Borgin, what are you doing here?" Perkle shouted to the other gang.

"Free city," Borgin called back.

Both groups of men were slowly creeping toward each other and our truck, which stood in the way.

"It doesn't take a psychologist to see this is going tits up right soon," I said. In front of the truck was Borgin's group and four men. Behind the truck was Perkle's group and five men. But there was a connecting street to the side of the alley. It was the only gang-free route of escape. "I say we get in and go that way. We're about to get caught in a crossfire."

"We won't fit," Paggo-Nosa said, pointing.

Hanging between the buildings of the adjoining street were some makeshift steel walkways and bridges. I had seen buildings connected in a similar fashion before. Tenants created shortcuts across the street to their friends, relatives, and neighbors. The recyclables towering above the truck would run into the metal paths.

"You can lose some bottles or maybe your life," I warned.

"I think we should interview them," Rendrae stated.

"Do you want to get your brand new circulatory system shot full of holes?" I asked.

The two groups of men were talking at each other, but it was all disjointed, angry nonsense. A pretext to a fight. I'd seen the same thing a thousand times before. Unless someone had a very big bucket of very cold water, there was going to be a street fight. We could try and run for it, but if one person decided to shoot at us, they likely *all* would. While I was bulletproof, Rendrae and Paggo-Nosa weren't.

As the mood was reaching a boiling point, we suddenly heard the oddest thing: singing. Three men were skipping toward us from the side street, belting out a marvelous show tune as they went. I didn't know much about music or singing, but I believe they had a tenor, baritone, and bass. And by damn if they didn't sound like a full orchestra.

It took a few moments, but even the gangs shut up so they could hear the singers properly. They were *that* good. Nine men who had been on the verge of bloodshed a second ago, stopped their posturing so they could appreciate a song.

"They're amazing," Paggo-Nosa said, staring.

"It's just a drinking tune," Rendrae replied dismissively.

"Shush," I said, trying to hear the lyrics.

The singers walked into our alley. The three of them had their arms hooked with each other and had been high-stepping in a glorious mood. When they saw the situation, they stopped short.

"They're Damakans," I said, as the song abruptly ended.

I hadn't realized it, but I had been under a Damakan spell. I didn't know it also worked with music. I think they could have marched me and both gangs to the port and into outer space and we would have happily jumped after them.

"That's Mesto Mourvin!" Perkle yelled.

"There he is," Borgin said.

Gunfire!

Both sides started shooting. At what, or who, was anyone's guess.

The three Damakans were as quick as they were melodic. They dashed forward and scampered underneath the truck. Paggo-Nosa jumped inside the cab and hit the deck. Rendrae had reported on enough battles that he knew how to behave. He crouched against the side of a building behind some trashcans.

I stood there.

I was trying to figure out who I should be fighting, or where I should be running, or what I should be doing. A lifetime of being bulletproof had given me the luxury of taking my time during gun battles. It had gotten to the point that gunfire was practically white noise and it helped me concentrate.

People looked like they were shooting just to be shooting. The first glass bottle above me exploded and then everyone else got the bright idea that would be a fun target. Soon enough, it was a torrential downpour of glass, porcelain, and plastic. Other than behind barrels of toxic waste, I couldn't think of a worse place to look for cover.

It wasn't that the bullets were particularly dangerous to me or that I might get cut from shards, I just couldn't see what was happening. It was instinct to blink your eyes when fragments were flying through the air. And if that wasn't enough, they were colored, reflective fragments. Adding to the lack of sight was the cacophony of guns and shattering containers. I was left without my senses of sight and hearing. It was unlikely I could figure out what to do using my sense of taste.

Fortunately, I knew they didn't have infinite bullets. But as the firing went on and on, I vaguely heard Rendrae scream:

"Do they have infinite bullets?"

I wasn't sure. Maybe the types of firearms on Belvaille had changed recently as well. Some bullets hit me, but they didn't pack much punch.

I heard the Damakan with the bass voice yelling on his tele. As bewildered as I was, I took a moment to remark that I could clearly hear his voice above the mayhem. That bass frequency could probably rumble through mountains. He was calling someone for help. If it was other Damakans, I couldn't see how they would be much use.

After what felt like some minutes, people got tired of shooting me and shooting the bottles, and the gangs began shooting at each other. Without exploding bottles, I could finally see. But I was now standing in a river of broken glass, which was all that remained of Paggo-Nosa's haul.

The truck was absolutely riddled with holes, but they were very small. No wonder they had so much ammunition, their bullets were miniature.

Rendrae looked mostly okay, though he had some cuts from the splintering bottles. I couldn't see Paggo-Nosa, but the truck looked only cosmetically damaged, so I suspected he'd be safe hiding past the engine block.

I didn't know how the Damakans fared under the truck, and I couldn't check, because the vehicle was up to its floorboards in broken bottles. They would have to dig their way out.

This situation reminded me of the riot at The Club, when Laesa was with me. I was fully capable of walking out of this firefight unscathed. I could even drop my pants and moon everyone on the way out. Yeah, I might take a few bullets to the backside, but a hot bath, a good meal, and a night's rest and I'd be fine.

But Rendrae was in danger of getting murdered any second. Despite his crouching for cover, there were automatic weapons ricocheting bullets around. If nothing else, I had to get him out of here safely.

"Hey," I yelled at the gangs.

Perkle's group had mostly retreated to the front of the bar and side doorway. They were taking turns shooting and ducking back into cover.

Borgin Two-Eyes' jumpsuit-wearing group, which were further away, had headed back to the street junction they came from, poking around the corners to unload their weapons.

With the truck in the middle providing tremendous cover, and a mountain of shattered glass preventing anyone from easily crossing, this gun battle could well go on for a thousand years. There was simply no way anyone was going to get shot, except those of us stuck here in no man's land.

Even as skinny as Rendrae now was, I couldn't possibly shield him from both sides. That's assuming I could even walk across this glass without tripping and having the poor reporter get diced to pieces.

And that didn't even address the problem of getting out Paggo-Nosa or the Damakans. I certainly had to help Rendrae. And Paggo-Nosa wasn't a bad guy. But I didn't know the Damakans and they weren't my responsibility.

Instead of trying to speak to both groups, I faced Perkle's team.

"Oi, yoze!" I yelled.

I walked forward and they were trying to shoot around me, but I was still getting hit front and back. Whatever bullets they were using were indeed small. Though I took a meaty one to my right rear thigh that hurt.

"What do you want?" Perkle yelled back over the gunfire.

"Stop shooting for a second so you can hear me."

It took a while, but they finally slowed and stopped. The other side kept going. That, of course, made Perkle's goons stay in cover.

Man, walking on this glass was harder than I thought. These bottles were every kind of shape and material. From high-grade plastic cubes to crystal spheres. My ankles rolled a few times, but I didn't fall down.

Borgin's group were slowing their fire because I was in the way and Perkle's group was hidden.

"Move!" Borgin yelled at me.

"My name is Hank," I introduced myself to Perkle's hiding synth-wearers, in front of me.

I immediately got a reaction, but it wasn't one I was used to.

"That guy's Trouble rating is through the roof!" Someone whispered. He was talking about the stupid Scanhand database.

"Yeah, and he deserves it," Perkle replied. "He almost got me killed."

"You stole my car," I began, but that wasn't important right now. "Maybe we can sort this out. Who are you all shooting at?"

There was some quiet discussion among Perkle's group.

"What's going on? We fighting or what?" Borgin yelled from up the street.

"Hold up! I'll get to you in a minute," I said.

"We're after Mesto Mourvin," Perkle answered.

"That's it?" I asked.

They quietly whispered amongst themselves again.

"It's not a trick question," I added.

"There are others. But they aren't here," Perkle said.

"I'm not interested in your career objectives. I'm just trying to settle this fight in this alley at this moment," I said.

"Yeah, he's the only one. Mesto Mourvin," Perkle confirmed.

"Stay put. Don't shoot me. Or anyone," I said.

I crunched my way back to the truck. The glass was thickest here and I had to slow my movements considerably. Not that I was worried about getting hurt, I was worried that if I fell down in some comic hijinks, no one would listen to me any longer.

When I was beside the truck, I dug out a small hole under the vehicle so I could talk to the Damakans. I figured I better get their story. I probably should have talked to them first, but there was a lot of noisy gunfire.

"You guys still alive?" I asked. I must have been a sight. Here I was with my clothes shot full of holes and my shoes and socks torn to ribbons from the glass.

"We're alive," they said in perfect singing voices.

"What are your names?" I asked.

"Why should we tell you? You'll just hand us over to them," the tenor said.

Hey, they were pretty smart for Damakans.

"Well, I figure at least two of you can go free and one of you can sit here and see which group wins. *Or*, all three of you can wait here and probably get shot in the crossfire."

They talked it over in whispers, but I could plainly hear the bass vocalist murmuring his concerns. What a voice! If I sounded like that, negotiations would be so easy.

"Find out who the other people want first. Then we'll tell you," the tenor said.

"I'm not going to walk around for an hour. If you want to be stubborn, I can just pick up this truck and flip it over, exposing you," I said.

"Mesto Mourvin," the tenor whispered.

"Manso Malvouri," the baritone said.

"Malin Maridon," the bass added.

"That's a lot of M's," I said skeptically.

"Our agent assigned our professional names," Mesto Mourvin said.

I stood there for a long beat. I didn't want to ask, but I kind of had to.

"Is your agent named Cliston by any chance? He's a robot," I added to be sure.

"Yes, Cliston is our talent agent. Why?" Mesto Mourvin answered.

Well, crap. My plan was indeed to let Mesto Mourvin get caught, and the others too, if they were wanted. But if Cliston was their agent, he would take their deaths out on me. That is, if he found out. And with the damn Scanhand database, this moment was probably already being recorded.

"Wait here," I said.

"Where the hell else are we going to go?" the baritone asked.

I stumbled my way along the shattered bottles, passed the truck, and kept going. Borgin's group was peeking out from the corners but still two blocks away.

"Hank?" Rendrae asked, as I walked by. His face and arms were cut up pretty bad.

"I'll get you out of here, buddy. Just stay down."

"No. Ask them who they're working for," he said with journalistic urgency.

I grumbled and kept going.

"That's far enough," Borgin Two-Eyes said, when I was still a block away.

"Far enough for what?" I asked, and kept walking. They could already see I was bulletproof and glass-proof. Besides, I could tell they were curious about any offers I had. No one was making any headway shooting up the truck and bottles.

"You're Hank, right?" Borgin Two-Eyes asked. I suppose he wanted to confirm it for the rest of the group.

I had reached the corner and could see there were now eight guys. Some more must have joined them while they were shooting.

"Yeah, you know me," I said.

There were some mutterings. And I noticed several people were looking at my Scanhand profile.

"So who are you guys after?" I asked them.

"We're not after anyone. We're here to *protect* Malin Maridon," Borgin said.

"Then what the hell were you shooting for?" I asked.

"Because they were shooting! What are we supposed to do?"

"You idiots aren't even after the same targets! You almost killed a street full of people for nothing."

"Is Malin Maridon under that truck?" Borgin asked.

"The truck you shot full of holes? Yes, he is."

"Give him to us."

"Will you stop shooting if I get him?" I asked.

"Yeah."

"Okay. Which one was it again?"

"He's got a bad memory," one of the thugs nodded, pointing at my profile.

"Shut up," I said.

"Malin Maridon," Borgin replied.

"He's got a deep voice?"

"I've never heard him," Borgin said.

"No! He has a 'high-bass' voice," a thug with Scanhand read.

"Actors are in the system?" I asked.

"If you have authorization to view it," he said, pressing his tele flat to his chest as if it were top-secret data.

"Hmm. Alrighty. Be right back. Hold your fire," I said, turning to go. "Wait. Who are you guys working for?"

"We don't know," Borgin shrugged.

"No, I mean who's your boss?"

"We don't know. It's pretty screwed up," Borgin continued.

That begged so many follow-up questions that I stopped for a second. But I wanted to get out of this situation and go home. I could feel the bruises starting to form from the gunshots and I think I had glass in my ears.

I resumed walking, my head down, watching where I stepped as I neared the debris around the truck. Borgin called from behind me.

"It's the Rough Boys!"

"You work for the Rough Boys?" I asked, confused.

Then I saw them. The three Rough Boys were standing in the connecting street, just in front of the truck and to my left. They were hard to recognize at first.

Because instead of their normal fur and tattered clothes, they were wearing bulky, powered combat armor.

Now I knew who the Damakans called for help on their tele.

"Hank," Kaxle snarled at me.

CHAPTER 21

The three Rough Boys were all wearing powered armor, but Kaxle, their leader and the biggest of the crew, seemed to be especially well equipped.

Kaxle's left forearm was encased in a gigantic metal claw. There were three fingers and one opposing thumb. It was clear the claw was not meant for any kind of fine manipulation as the fingers were thick blades and easily five times the size of Kaxle's "normal" hand. There were pistons and cylinders all over the device and it looked capable of ripping apart steel.

Kaxle's right forearm was replaced with a three-barreled, rotating cannon. The bore of each barrel looked almost large enough for me to put my fist inside. If those guns contained nothing but water, you could extinguish a good-sized conflagration. But I suspected they didn't shoot flame retardant.

At the back of the armor were coiled electrical cables, which sparked and sizzled dangerously. Not only that, but fluids of every conceivable color seemed to be leaking from the armor. The armor itself was composed of yellow-orange metal plates that overlapped, bulged and didn't quite connect everywhere. It appeared as if it was haphazardly designed or modifications were continuously made without ever starting over. There were areas where Kaxle's fur and physique were clearly visible.

I had witnessed this style of design enough times that I immediately knew its origin. But why the hell would Delovoa build such a weapon system for the person who was probably my greatest threat on the station?

Knowing Delovoa, Kaxle's armor was almost certainly fatal—to Kaxle. At some point it would either spontaneously explode, the hydraulic engines would overextend and tear him apart, or operation of the device itself would cause some terrible disease.

But it was pretty clear from Kaxle's bloodthirsty expression that I wouldn't be able to wait for leukemia to take him.

The two other Rough Boys were wearing similar armor, but much reduced in scope and lethality. Their left hands were merely metal gloves of regular proportions. Their right hands ended in submachine gun barrels. They had protection, but it wasn't very thick and didn't look like it was enhanced with servos and pneumatics and nuclear generators like their boss's armor.

"Hi, Kaxle," I said pleasantly. "What brings you guys here? I was just hoping to settle a small disagreement that—"

Kaxle howled like a giant mutated wolf and pointed his cannon-encrusted arm in my general direction.

Kaboom!

The first barrel fired and it was like looking at a supernova! Well, I assume that's what one looked like. It was a huge flash of light and flame.

The building behind me, which was the club that Paggo-Nosa had taken bottles from, lost a quarter of its wall. It exploded in a burst of bricks and dust. The pile of bottles I had been standing in was now a pile of building. It's a good thing Kaxle had only been pointing in my *general* direction. The shockwave alone just about tore off my skin.

Kaxle looked almost as bad as I did. The recoil from the weapon had been at least somewhat absorbed by the power armor, but his upper body was twisted practically backwards. If he had spun just a little bit further, I think his torso would have torn off from his legs. From his pained and confused expression, it was clear this was the first time he had used the gun. He hadn't been prepared for Delovoa's indiscriminate engineering.

Kaxle slowly swiveled back to face me and I saw more liquids seep from the battlesuit. The barrel he had just fired was red-hot and smoking. But the big gun rotated to the second barrel, which was unharmed.

"Come on, Kaxle," I said. I *think* I said that. I couldn't hear my words. My eardrums were either ruptured or recovering from the first barrel.

Kaxle, as bestial as he was, decided to hold off on using the cannon. He raised his left arm and flexed the claw's digits, one by one. Unfortunately, everything seemed to be in working order.

He stomped toward me. I could feel his approach vibrate through the metal road. That suit must have been phenomenally heavy. It certainly moved like it was, all jerky and rigid.

I pulled out my sawed-off shotgun. The weapon had seemed lethal at one point. But that point was before I faced a mutant wearing a custom dump truck. My weapon was so laughably insufficient I might as well try and tickle him with it. But there were exposed gaps in the armor and it was already leaking, so it couldn't hurt to take a shot.

I fired twice, to no effect.

Delovoa hadn't written an instruction manual in his life and his verbal guidance tended to leave out important details because he simply didn't care. Consequently, Kaxle moved as if he had only vague familiarity with his power armor.

The armor was impressive, but it faced the same issues I had, except times ten. I was big, strong, and slow. I got around my limitations by grappling with my opponents. Wrestling. But Kaxle didn't even have a hand on his right arm and his left claw looked unsuitable for complicated fighting moves. He was just too clumsy. And coming from me, that was saying something.

Kaxle braced his legs, uncurled the claw fingers, twisted his wrist, raised his shoulder, and took a swipe at me. The motors and gears and pistons were revving and pumping the whole way. The move was so telegraphed I probably could have left the fight, gotten something to eat, and returned with just enough time to sidestep the swing. Once he was situated, his arm traveled quite fast, but the preparations leading up to it were plodding and methodical.

Kaxle was clearly struggling with the suit. His face, which was partially obscured by the armor, showed equal parts ferocious and frustrated.

The other Rough Boys were hanging back. While it might have been because Kaxle wanted to fight me one-on-one, I suspected it was simply because there wasn't enough space for us. Kaxle swinging his arm would connect with anyone unlucky enough to be within ten feet of him. Not to mention that mortar he had on his other arm.

I took a brief moment to turn my head and see what the gangs were up to. Situational awareness was important. I had to be sure they weren't setting up a heavy weapon or about to run me over with a car.

It took a moment to process what I saw as I stepped around Kaxle.

The gang members were in the middle of the street, sitting down. Some were typing on their teles. Some looked like they were placing bets. None of them seemed eager to interrupt the battle.

Glad to know I could still be entertaining.

At this point, I was simply circling around Kaxle. He was so sluggish I could probably jog away from him and he'd never catch me. But I needed to get Rendrae out of here.

"Excuse me. My name is Rendrae, I'm a reporter with *The News*. Would you be willing to answer a few inquiries regarding your occupational conditions on Belvaille?" Rendrae asked Kaxle politely.

It was such a non-sequitur that everyone paused. You had to hand it to Rendrae. He had a lot of guts asking probing questions during a high-powered street fight.

Kaxle started to say something, stopped, and then looked closer at Rendrae. I think he wondered if it was an elaborate trick.

"No, uh, no comment. Move!" Kaxle roared.

"Right. Some other time," Rendrae replied, ducking under the big armor as it headed in my direction.

Kaxle was slow. Ponderous. Made me look fast by comparison. But the damn claw was so big I had to be halfway across the street for him to miss. And I wasn't exactly an acrobat. My style of fighting didn't involve dodging or even blocking.

Of course, this wasn't *really* a fight. Kaxle had fired at me. Missed. And was scuffing up the road trying to walk after me as he periodically waved his claw around.

I was doing absolutely nothing in return. But what could I do? I didn't have any way to hurt him. Now I knew how people felt trying to deal with me.

Using my not-fancy footwork, I was trying to get behind Kaxle. The bulk of the armor's mechanics and power supply and chemicals seemed to be located back there. But Kaxle kept turning with me.

The one time I rushed behind him, the two waiting Rough Boys took shots at me with their submachine guns. They missed, but it was clear they weren't going to let me take out a screwdriver and pair of plyers and leisurely go to work on the armor.

It took most of Kaxle's efforts to keep up with me. I'm guessing he had to manually control the movement of each joint. He looked like bad stop-action animation.

By comparison, I looked like a frightened squirrel. Hopping and bouncing around the power armor.

It was conceivable that I could charge in, reach up, and grab hold of some of armor's cables. But then what? I had to hope they were *special* cables that activated the power armor's self-destruct. Otherwise, I'd merely be close enough that Kaxle could scissor me in half with his claw.

Our audience was growing restless. The thugs who were cautiously watching had started making catcalls. Nothing rude, they were calling out suggestions. But it was clear they wanted a bit more action. I guess two mutants walking in circles for five minutes wasn't very exciting.

Kaxle was either getting dizzy or got frustrated enough to take a risk. He aimed his triple cannon in my general direction again and fired.

I was prepared to take an artillery shot straight to the chest. But to my utter astonishment, a white-blue stream ejected from the barrel. The gun *did* shoot a flame retardant! Delovoa was such a goof.

The jet hit me mostly in my midsection and off to the side. I had been boiling hot during this fight because of the Damakan temperatures. But I became instantly cold. Freezing.

My jacket and shirt turned white with frost and then completely shattered like they were cheap flatware dropped on a metal floor. My stomach, chest, left shoulder, and left arm were coated in ice and felt prickly pain. My eyes and nose immediately started watering and I was blinking in the suddenly arctic air.

It wasn't merely a fire extinguisher. It was a stream of insanely cold liquid.

I tried to get out of the way and almost fell down. I had to windmill my right arm to keep my balance and step wide with my left leg. My pants broke apart after being frozen solid.

It was pure luck that my face had been spared—my chin and neck only got a slight dusting.

The weapon was clearly not meant to be used at such close range. Some of the jet had reflected back at Kaxle and his left forearm. His claw was iced, as was the whole ground behind me, which suddenly looked like a ski slope.

Both of us were disoriented.

I couldn't feel my chest and my skin was bluish-white. I began slapping my body and jumping around to try and get my blood flowing, but my upper left side was completely numb.

Kaxle's pistons and gears on his arm were squeaking and slow.

I may have looked funny hobbling around in my underwear with blue skin, but I was seriously hurt. I had suffered instant frostbite. I wasn't sure if my mutation could heal it or half my body was about to turn black and fall off.

I could no longer afford to play a waiting game and catalog the power armor's capabilities. It could freeze me and blast me with a mortar. Either one was more than enough. I had to disable Kaxle or get the hell out of here. Getting a poor Scanhand reputation was still a lot better than being dead.

With no firm strategy in my frozen head, I simply charged Kaxle. We bumped into each other and we both roared and screamed and pushed.

He bopped me on the shoulder with his cannon arm, which did nothing. And I pounded on his chest and tried to turn a thick bolt on his armor with my fingers. That also did nothing.

Kaxle's face was so close to mine that he tried to spit on me, but missed. I took several moments trying to get my cheeks and tongue unfrozen enough to generate saliva so I could spit back, but I gave up.

After a few moments of our pathetic attempts, I realized this wasn't working. He was too clumsy to fight me this close and the armor was too big for me to wrestle.

I backed up.

And that was a big mistake.

Kaxle swung his claw with tremendous force. Two industrial-steel daggers streaked across my torso and lifted me up in the air.

I landed on my back a short distance away. Looking down at my chest, I saw one of the metal fingers had broken off in my blue skin and was still embedded just short of my ribcage. The deep gashes in my body weren't the most frightening part. What concerned me more was that I couldn't feel it, and I wasn't bleeding. It looked kind of blackish-red where the slices ran up my body. Only my shoulder was dripping blood. And I could barely feel that. I definitely had a serious case of frostbite.

Okay. That settled it. Time to run.

It wasn't any logical decision on my part, it was base instinct. Fight or flight was screaming down my spine. I was possessed by the spirit of prey who had just encountered his first predator.

I rolled over on my stomach, scrambled to my knees, and jumped to my feet. I took six steps and looked over my shoulder to see if Kaxle was following.

I stopped.

When Kaxle had taken his opportunistic swing at me, he had not prepared himself for delivering such a massive blow or encountering such a massive gut. He had fallen over and was lying facedown, only moderately kicking his outsized legs and cannon arm to try and right himself.

He was on the ground and unable to stand.

My instincts did such a massive reversal I'm surprised I didn't turn into a caveman.

I dragged myself over to Kaxle's fallen form and I looked around for something to bash him with. A pickaxe. A shovel. I'd settle for a damn rock. There was debris from the exploded building, but the pieces were too small or too large. And Kaxle's head was blocked by the bulky apparatus on his back so I couldn't even punch him.

I stood on top of the armor and grabbed at the cords and gizmos and tried to do as much damage as I could. Kaxle shouted in anger as he felt my added weight.

The other two Rough Boys hurried over to help their fallen feral friend. They pushed at me and shot me and otherwise tried to remove me from the scene. I wasn't having any of it. I was frostbitten and adrenaline high and had a knife imbedded in my stomach.

I was probably about to go into shock. It wasn't unreasonable, I had just suffered massive tissue damage.

One of the armor's cords detached in my hand and it spewed a blue liquid on me. Other than emptying his windshield wiper fluid, I didn't seem to be damaging Kaxle at all.

While fending off the other two Rough Boys, I stomped my feet on Kaxle's back to try and somehow break the armor.

The other gang members began to draw closer. The battle had taken a decisive turn and they wanted to see it in more detail.

There was no way Kaxle would be able to rise with me standing on him—he couldn't get up *without* me standing on him. But I needed to get to a hospital and if I limped away now, Kaxle might regain his feet and come after me.

As I was concentrating on trying to push away the other Rough Boys, I saw Kaxle had managed to get his cannon arm free. He couldn't turn it to face me so I wasn't overly concerned. But he rotated to the last barrel.

Thump! Thump! Thump! Thump!

A bunch of colored balls of energy flew out of the barrel. They bounced off what was left of the club and arced up into the air. Everyone stopped and watched, wondering what instrument of destruction was about to befall us.

Kabooooom!

If the first barrel had been like a supernova, this one was like a *thousand* stars all exploding at once! The street was showered in fire and light. Explosions began cascading off each other and I was sure I had only moments left before I was incinerated. Maybe Belvaille itself would be destroyed.

It went on for long moments, but then I realized:

"They're fireworks. Delovoa put a damn fireworks launcher in that suit!"

I'd never been pointblank at a city-wide fireworks display. Some of the gang members were screaming because their clothes or hair had burst into flames. Even with the blinding flashes and enormous concussive booms, it was nothing compared to the abuse I'd already taken.

Kaxle himself seemed to be tiring of our fight, as he realized he couldn't remove me. I figuratively jumped at the opening.

"Kaxle. Did you specifically come here to kill me? Or are you looking for someone?" I asked, when the fireworks began to die down to a low rumble.

He sputtered and cursed for a bit, but finally answered.

"We here for... Manso Malvouri," he said.

My brain was a bit fuzzy and the lingering fireworks weren't helping. Nor were the two other Rough Boys who were still grabbing at me.

"To kill him or...? No, it doesn't matter." I said.

I looked around, stunned. That couldn't be right. Could it? We did all this for nothing? How stupid were we?

"Hey! Yoze! Everyone is here for a different Damakan. Stop!" I yelled to the street full of gangs and mutants and reporters. "Just...hey, quit it," I said to the persistent Rough Boys.

I climbed off Kaxle.

"Under there," I said, pointing to the truck. "The Damakans. Take it easy and put your guns away."

The gangs warily approached the truck from all sides.

"Help me up," Kaxle called.

The Rough Boys pulled at the massive armor to no effect.

"Hank. Give me a hand," Kaxle said.

"You kidding? You—" and I almost went off on a tirade. But I wanted this over and done with. I pushed away the Rough Boys and, with considerable difficulty, managed to get their boss standing. His armor appeared to be malfunctioning, with the left leg twitching spasmodically. Good.

Kaxle grunted at me for helping him up, but he didn't make eye contact.

The Damakans were pulled out from the wreckage and each went off with a different group. With no fighting and nothing to do, people looked at me.

I believe they wanted to hear the last word. Maybe some tough talk. A summary of what the hell just happened. A hush fell over the crowd as they waited.

A building had been destroyed. Paggo-Nosa's truck was ruined. Gang members had been set on fire, shot, and blinded. Trash was everywhere. I had been concussed, frozen, stabbed.

"Thanks for coming, everyone," I began. "I need emergency medical attention."

CHAPTER 22

I woke up in the hospital.

The hospital and I had a long history together. We had been through both bad times and terrible times. The hospital, which was technically named, "The Hospital," had a room specifically devoted to me.

I had visited enough and contributed to the coffers of this institution so often, that there was a small plaque on the door with my name on it.

It's not that the hospital was particularly skilled at taking care of me, they did almost nothing. If I stumbled in here, all they did was yank out the offending bullets or knives, have some medical technicians nod thoughtfully at one another, clean me up as best they could, and then stick in feeding tubes and let my mutation do its work.

As part of my mutation, they couldn't scan me with medical devices. So I could have a rotten liver and fifty pounds of explosives sitting in my pancreas and they would never know.

But the bed was comfortable, it supported my weight, and the food was high in nutrients and came as fast as my body could process it. Which was very fast indeed. To heal, I needed food. Lots of it. The hospital, to me, was basically a 24-hour cafeteria that reeked of disinfectant.

As I came to, remembered that I was too poor to be lounging in a hospital. I had a theory that they charged by the pound of the patient. As much as I wanted to stiff them on their outrageous bills, it was shortsighted to be a professional fighter who didn't have medical coverage. Especially when you considered how often I lost my fights.

While I slowly became aware of being aware, I noticed a man sitting in the corner of my room. I assumed he was a medical technician.

The hospital couldn't scan me. They couldn't pierce my skin with their instruments. They basically couldn't do anything *medical* to me at all. This offended some doctors and they took it as a personal challenge. Over the years I had endured a tremendous array of tests and procedures they hoped would work on me—but never did.

However, the medical technician in my room didn't resemble his profession. He had old scars marring his face and a recent black eye. He was wearing grungy synth clothes. His hair was disheveled.

"Howdy," he said, seeing my attention.

"Hello," I rasped, my mouth and nose full of tubes. "Are you a technician?"

"Naw, I'm Grassly," he said.

"What's a grassly?"

"Me!"

I lifted the sheets and looked at myself. The blade that Kaxle had embedded in me was gone and left only a faint, pink scar. My skin was not cracked and destroyed from frostbite and I didn't spot any amputations. I was healed. Presumably I had been in the hospital for some time. I didn't feel like dealing with idiots so soon after returning to consciousness. But I had nothing better to do.

"Okay. Let's start again. I'm Hank."

"I know."

"How do you know?"

"MTB told me."

"Oh, you're with the police?"

"Naw," he laughed.

Grassly tried to itch the side of his head and I saw he was double handcuffed to the chair he was sitting on.

"So you know MTB?" I asked.

"Not really."

"Alright," I concluded, not wanting to talk to the man any longer.

I reached over to the table next to me and grabbed my tele. Doing so caused a sharp pain in my side as I stretched. My mutant healing was never quite perfect.

I sent a message to MTB.

I'm awake. Who the hell is in my room?

I went back to sleep.

When I woke up, MTB was standing over my bed holding an armful of take-out from my favorite fried food restaurant. The aroma is what roused me.

Grassly was still sitting in the corner. He seemed bored.

MTB pulled a table over to my bed and dumped the food on it. The table was a sturdy hospital contraption, but it strained under the weight of the fatty morsels.

I began digging in. Most of my tubes had been removed, only a few remained in my nose.

"While you were out, we had twenty-three more homicides in show business," MTB began. "Most were actors, but we had some directors, set designers, one continuity—whatever the hell that is—and assorted others."

"Thad Elon's Busted Knapsack, we're going to run out of Damakans," I said.

"Not likely. Now that word has spread that Belvaille is *the* source of intergalactic tele programs, they're arriving by the transport-load. Their home planet must be practically deserted."

"How many are coming?" I asked.

"Tens of thousands for sure."

"Damn. It's going to be a lot harder for Laesa to get her break with all that competition. Anything consistent in the murders?"

"Yeah. They're all Damakans. I mean, there are also gang murders, but I don't count those."

"Of course, those are just *people*," I snorted sarcastically.

"Gangs kill each other all the time. I can't keep track of that," MTB said. "But even gang-on-gang fighting is way up."

"Okay. So who is that guy?" I said, pointing.

"Grassly," MTB replied.

"I got *that*. What is he doing here?"

"He's a prisoner. I captured him after his crew bumped off an assistant director working for the Fantasy Guild."

"I thought you didn't take prisoners," I said.

"We usually don't. But I've been going in circles so I thought we could question him. You said you were working with Rendrae."

"Yeah, but why did you chain him in my hospital room?"

"Cliston said I couldn't put him in your apartment."

"And why would you put him in my apartment?"

"Got to put him somewhere. We don't have a jail."

"Why not lock him to a street corner? Or put him in *your* apartment?"

"If I tied him up outside, his pals would come along and free him. And at my place, he might try and attack me while I slept."

"What about me? I'm in a hospital bed!"

"What are you worried about, Hank? Even if I gave him a chainsaw he couldn't hurt you."

"What if his friends tried to bust him out?"

"How would they know he was here? I mean, how many people came to visit you?"

"How should I know? I was unconscious. Maybe a lot of people came."

"No one did," Grassly added unhelpfully.

"I told him that if anything happened to you, he'd be responsible," MTB said.

"So I had a *criminal* protecting me?"

"Hank. You're a criminal. I'm pretty much a criminal. Who on Belvaille isn't a criminal in some way?" MTB asked.

"Whatever. So what are you going to do with him?"

"Ask him questions, I guess," he said.

"You haven't interviewed him yet?"

"I haven't had time. We've been running around like Po trying to deal with all these murders."

"Grassly," I called.

"Yup?" he answered.

"Why did you kill that guy you killed?"

"Got me," he shrugged.

"He's a bundle of help. Good thing you kept a murderer in my sickroom all this time so we could discover that information."

"Why don't you get Rendrae to talk to him?" MTB asked.

"Rendrae speaks Colmarian just like we do."

"But he's been writing a bunch of articles on the gang war. You probably haven't looked at them yet."

"Yeah, my reading goes way down when I'm comatose," I said.

"He's calling the article series, 'The Entertainment Extermination.'"

"Kind of dramatic," I sniffed.

"It's an exposé," Grassly said.

"I don't know where Rendrae is. I don't know where anyone is. I'm not even sure how long I've been out."

"When did you check in?" MTB asked.

"Can't remember, exactly. I fought with Kaxle and the Rough Boys and then—"

"That was you?" Grassly exclaimed. "Oh brother, everyone's been yapping about that! It's all over Scanhand."

"It is," MTB admitted. "I heard you took on like four gangs and Kaxle had some kind of bomb that wiped out a whole city block."

"You get around, MTB. Have you *seen* a block destroyed anywhere?" I asked.

"I don't get much chance to admire the architecture."

"But you'd *notice* if a block was straight-up missing, right?"

"Maybe."

"What was it like when you tore off Kaxle's head and spit in his dead face?" Grassly cackled, trying to mimic the act while handcuffed.

We stared at him a moment.

"What's he talking about?" MTB asked me.

"Typical Belvaille exaggerations. Kaxle is fine," I replied.

"You take Grassly." MTB tossed me the keys to the handcuffs. I tried to catch them but missed.

"Take him where? Lost and found? What am I going to do with him?"

"I thought you were investigating the murders."

"I am. But I'm not taking hostages to do it."

"You want to find out about the murders. *He's* one of the murderers. Do your Hank stuff on him."

"Hey, man, don't hurt me. I was just a driver," Grassly whimpered.

"No, he wasn't. He was a trigger man," MTB said, annoyed.

"How did you ever catch him? Were you in the neighborhood at the time?"

"No, there was another gang at the production. They fought. This guy got knocked out. I guess his pals left him."

"He doesn't sound like a valuable asset," I said.

"Then let him go," MTB shrugged.

"Aren't you supposed to punish murderers or something?" I asked.

"Fine. Break his legs before you let him go."

"I'm not the cops," I protested.

"Hank, I don't have time for this. I brought you some food and I brought you a witness. I need to go back out and stop this city from killing itself. Do what you want. If you find out anything big, let me know."

MTB started to leave, but then he backhanded Grassly across the face.

"Don't mess up his mouth. He won't be able to talk," I said.

"Hank, I swear, you complain about everything."

Grassly was handcuffed to me. We were standing outside the hospital. I was in my underwear and a courtesy gown because my clothes had been destroyed in my fight with Kaxle.

Now that he was up close, I got a better look at Grassly. He was a small man that bore the unmistakable Belvaille aura. This was not a city of winners and trust fund babies. If you voluntarily came to Belvaille it was because Life had taken a particular interest in you. And Life was a bitch.

"Where we going, pal?" he asked me. He was happy to be leaving the hospital, even if he was shackled to a fat nudist.

"You need to be quiet. I'm not in the mood for chitter-chatter."

"I thought you wanted to interrogation me."

"Not now. Did a Damakan woman come by the hospital? Brown hair. Dimples. Smiles a lot."

"Like I said, no one come by. I was alone listening to you snore."

"What about the medical technicians?"

"Sure, they was there. Change the sheets. Refill your food thingers. You eat a *lot*, man. I thought they was trying to kill you at first. You didn't even fill no bedpans. All in. No out. Ain't no wonder you're so blubbery. Can't barely fit the handcuff on you and that thang could about near fit a Therezian."

"Seriously. You need to stop talking," I said.

"You asked."

It was always weird waking up after a long hospital stay. The galaxy had gone on living without me. I wanted to fall back into my routine and get up to speed, but I had someone chained to my wrist. It was the dumbest thing. Not sure how MTB talked me into this.

I called Rendrae, but he wasn't answering. I left him a rambling message.

After a cab ride home, Cliston greeted me at the door.

"Greetings, sir. Will your guest be joining us for dinner?"

"Woo, me. Is that a Dradel Lud?" Grassly asked.

I was embarrassed. I didn't know why, exactly. Actually, I did. Cliston had worked on me for a number of years. As bad as I was, I had made tremendous improvements. I no longer threw my dirty underwear in the sink. I rarely chewed with my mouth open. I had clean sheets, a fantastic set of apartments, and I often dressed respectably, in spite of my size.

Grassly was uncultured. Uncouth. Stupid. *Gang* stupid. Which was a whole other level of dumb. Hey, not everyone could be smart. There's no shame in genetics. But gang members went out of their way to avoid learning. The best way to break up a gang fight was to throw a bar of soap at them wrapped in mathematical theorems and philosophical quotations. They'd flee instantly, lest they learn anything or wash off their musk.

"Cliston, how long was I in the hospital?" I asked.

"I didn't know you were there, sir, or I would have come to visit you."

"No one told you?"

"They did not, sir."

"They said my bill was paid. It's not like them to rent me a hospital bed for free," I said, confused. "Have you seen Laesa? Maybe she knows."

"I believe she is quite busy with work," Cliston said.

"Work? You mean acting? She was too busy to visit me in the hospital?"

"Again, sir, I'm only speculating. I'm not certain she was informed of your whereabouts."

I looked over at Grassly, expecting he might know.

"I can't get over that robot," he said. "You know if it gets hiccups?"

"May I suggest speaking to her talent agent, sir?" Cliston said.

"Laesa doesn't have an agent. She likes to stay clear of all that hassle. She gets juicier roles that way."

"Indeed, sir. But I do believe I heard her say that Cliston is now her agent."

"Cliston?"

"Yes, sir."

"Cliston, Cliston?" I asked, pointing at him.

"Yes, sir. Talent agent Cliston, to be precise."

"Uh-oh. I think he's broked," Grassly stated. "Maybe give him a kick."

"Can I talk to the other Cliston?" I asked.

"Would you like me to get you a change of clothes first? Maybe prepare dinner? Clean your guest's handcuffs?" Cliston asked.

"No, I want to hear this now."

"Very well, sir."

Cliston threw his arms wide in shock.

"Hank! It's great to see you, kid. Sorry to hear you were in the hospital," Cliston said.

"Yeah. Did you pay for that?"

"Sure did. Least I could do. You're an old friend. Who's the yokel?"

"No one," I said, suspicious of why talent agent Cliston was being so friendly.

"I'm Grassly," he beamed.

"By the way, Hank, Laesa is killing it on 'The Moon's Behind,'" Cliston said.

"What is that?"

"The movie I booked her on. Her name is above the promo. Not bad for her first feature, right?"

"She's acting in a movie?" I asked.

"Romance Guild. Pulling in big money, too. Will be nice to borrow cash from her instead of your butler, am I right?" Cliston joked.

"She's in the Romance Guild?" I asked slowly.

"Sure, sure. Called in a few favors. After Garm called me mentioning she owed you a favor. Anyway, scratching backsides is part of the game. So, Hank," Cliston said, walking over and putting his arm around me on the side Grassly wasn't shackled, "I need you to go back to doing protection work for my actors."

"But I got your actors killed."

"I know, but it's been like hunting season on Gun World since you've been in the hospital. I need the old Hank back on the job."

"I don't know, Cliston. I just got back on my feet—" I started.

Cliston dropped to his knees!

"Please! I'm begging you, guy. Half the productions have shut down and the other half are getting blasted every day. Some of my actors have guarantee clauses and I'm paying them out of my own pocket. You're the best. Everyone says so."

It was terrifying to see Cliston pleading. I knew this was talent agent Cliston—well, part of me knew that—but it was still Cliston. I was momentarily too stunned to speak.

"Everyone says I'm the best? Since when?" I asked.

"Scanhand," he said.

"Stand up. You're making me nervous. Okay, Cliston. Since you helped with my hospital bill."

"And getting Laesa a job," Grassly added.

"Yeah. And that," I said. "Is her movie finished?"

"Not yet. Maybe a few weeks for principal. Might go over. Everything is behind schedule because of the violence," Cliston said.

"Hey," I asked Grassly. "You heard about any contracts to kill Cliston?"

"*Butler* Cliston?" he asked.

"It's the same guy!" I said, unsure how he could understand Cliston so quickly.

"No way. All the gamblers will kick in your face. Cliston's the top fight promoter," Grassly said.

"Technically, I believe Procon Hobb is the top promoter," Cliston answered.

"I know I'm going to regret asking, but is fight promoter Cliston a full-fledged persona now?"

"I don't believe so," some Cliston or other replied. "Not yet."

"*Believe so.* Great."

"Since you've been away, the need for violent entertainment has risen. The gangs are flush with cash but we have to use imported fighters because all the local contenders are occupied with the gang war."

"Was I unconscious for a whole year or what?"

"No, sir. I believe I haven't spoken to you for approximately twenty-three days.," Cliston replied.

"You called it a gang war. How do you know for sure it's a war?" I asked.

"That's how Rendrae referred to Belvaille's current situation, sir."

"Alright. I'm going to shower and change. Butler Cliston, can you handcuff Grassly to something sturdy?" I said, handing over the keys.

"Is it okay if I clean him up a bit first? I don't want him to dirty the carpets," Cliston said.

"Sure. Grassly. Don't mess with Cliston. He's almost as strong as I am and ten times as fast," I warned.

"I ain't going to punch no Dradel Lud," he answered, as if I was an idiot for even suggesting it.

"We're at *war* with his species," I replied.

"Maybe you is. Not me," he said, as Cliston led him away.

I called Laesa several times, but she wasn't available. Rendrae also hadn't returned my calls.

"I need to go to work, sir," Cliston said as I was lounging on my bed. Grassly was sitting on the floor next to me.

"Which Cliston?" I asked.

"All of them. I'll be home late tonight," he said.

"Okay."

"If you go out, you need to take your guest with you, sir. Don't handcuff him to the kitchen table or something."

"I wasn't going to," I said. Though I *had* been planning on handcuffing Grassly inside my closet. There was a lock on the door and it only contained my formal wear, which I didn't use very often.

"Bye, Cliston," Grassly called.

"Good day."

When Cliston left, I wondered what I should do.

"That Cliston sure is smart. And a good cook. You got it made working for him," Grassly said.

"He works for me."

"You sure?"

"Shut up. Get your jacket and let's go," I said.

Cliston had tailored Grassly a new coat and tie. I suspect he wanted me to be handcuffed to someone who was presentable.

"We going to see Rendrae?" he asked.

"No, Laesa."

"Your financier?"

"Fiancée. Yeah. I don't like that she's acting right now. It isn't safe."

"Yup. If you hadn't abducted me, I'd probably be out shooting at some Damakans."

"Hey. Don't talk like that when you see Laesa. Don't talk at all, actually."

"Am I supposed to just stand here like a slop barrel in a nice jacket? Thad Elon gave me a mouth. It's hard not to use it," he said.

I put my beefy hand next to his face. I bent my middle finger and held it with my thumb. Then I flicked his cheek.

Grassly's head twisted like he had just been slapped hard. My finger probably weighed ten pounds. His cheek was red and starting to bruise.

"Damn! Don't bust my head off. I'll hush up."

"Do that. Laesa is a nice girl. I don't want her dealing with things she doesn't need to deal with."

"Where did you meet her?" Grassly asked. "I want a nice gal, too. You can't trust most Belvaille women. The good ones will lift your wallet, the bad ones will cut your neck. Know what I'm saying? You're always glaring at me, Hank. Big, mean, *glaring* guy like you can get a nice lady, I should have a shot, too. Right?"

Cliston had given me the location of where Laesa was shooting her project, The Moon's Behind.

"You think that means behind a moon or a moon's butt?" Grassly asked when we left the taxi.

"Be quiet or I'll gag you," I said, having endured the entire car ride with him talking non-stop. I was beginning to understand why his gang left him.

"If you gag me, you'll have to explain it to your finance-ee."

"I got to explain why you're chained to my wrist already. I'm going to tell her I'm protecting you," I said. Then I saw he was about to respond. "And that you're mute."

"If I'm mute, why would you have to gag me?"

"Just don't speak gang stuff. Laesa doesn't have anything to do with that crap."

"She's got to learn sometime if she's on Belvaille."

"If you talk about it or scare her, I'll break your arms when we get back."

"Some kind of protector you are," Grassly mumbled.

There were armed security guards at the movie set. We couldn't simply walk up. It gave me some reassurance that Laesa would be okay.

It took thirty minutes before an assistant finally came to meet me. The assistant questioned me for ten more minutes, all under the watchful security. Finally, we were escorted past the barricades and into the production.

It was chaotic and packed. There were so many people and so much valuable equipment, this movie must have cost a fortune. No wonder Cliston and Garm wanted me to sort this out. This was a real economy at play.

The assistant led us to a section of the street occupied by tents.

Tents!

I had never seen a tent on Belvaille. We had no elements. It didn't rain. There was no sunlight. It was a terrible place to go camping. But the tents were large and numerous.

The assistant motioned for me to wait. Then she walked over and knocked on a plastic panel next to a tent.

I heard Laesa's voice call out, but I didn't recognize what she said. I think she was speaking Damakan.

The assistant indicated we could enter and I fumbled with the tent flap and pulled Grassly with me. Inside, it was a dressing room. It had a bed, mirrors, lots of clothes, even a carpet. Who put a carpet inside a tent in an alley on a space station?

"Hank, my dear," Laesa said, rising from her chair by the nightstand. She was wearing a reflective blue dress that dragged on the floor and opened at her legs. But what I noticed most was the fur around the shoulders. It was Notasta ferret! That had been the most valuable fur-bearing animal in the galaxy hundreds of years ago. I hadn't seen any in ages.

"Where did you get that fur trim?" I asked, alarmed. I still had to save up for a wedding.

"This thing?" she asked, nonchalantly. "I bought it. Who is that?"

"No one. He can't talk," I said.

"I'm Grassly," he said, holding out his uncuffed hand to shake.

"He can only say his name," I amended.

"Oh. Pleasure to meet you," she said, shaking politely.

"Likewise."

"*That's* all he can say."

I jerked the handcuff, almost pulling Grassly off his feet.

"Where did you get the money for Notasta ferret? If you borrowed from a loan shark, you'll have to give it back."

"Hank, I'm working now," she smiled.

"You were working before."

"Not exactly. I'm making Guild scale. Actually more. I'm not sure. Who can keep track?" she waved casually.

"So how is the acting?" I asked.

"It's fantastic. Cliston said this role could be the start. He's trying to line up a whole string of movies for me," she said. She seemed happy, but not as ecstatic as I thought she would be.

"Are you tired?" I asked.

"A bit. Yes. It's a lot of work."

"So you're in the Romance Guild?"

"I am. I think it suits me perfectly. I don't quite have leading-lady looks. Not like a Sharail Mazlo, but I can play cute as well as the best. And there's a whole subgenre that doesn't require the heaving bosom effect," she said.

"Oh," I replied, not understanding.

"I think you're plenty pretty," Grassly oozed.

"You can talk?" Laesa asked.

"No," I said, elbowing Grassly in the head. "You're taking a break from theater? I thought you loved doing that."

"I despised it, Hank. It was so dreary and pointless. Playing to a room of five people all shoving food in their mouths. It was degrading."

I was frankly astonished. That was contrary to everything she had ever said. I had stayed awake long hours listening to her describe performances and the thrill she got from it.

"I just got out of the hospital," I said, when she didn't ask.

"Why did you visit the hospital?"

"I wasn't sightseeing. I was being treated. I was really hurt."

Laesa appeared perplexed, but she turned back and went to her chair and began putting on make-up.

"Excuse me, they're going to call for me any moment and I have to be prepared. How did you get hurt?" she asked, looking in the mirror at me.

"It was Kaxle. Mutants and machines. It doesn't matter. I was gone for a long time. Didn't you notice?"

"I've been busy acting. I thought you were off doing one of your little adventures."

"Adventures? Look, it's not safe for you to be here," I said.

"What are you talking about?"

"The gangs. There's some...I don't know, they're attacking movies— Damakans—for some reason. Killing them. No one who works in theater has been hurt. It might be better if you did that."

"Hank, I can't just quit. I'd be in breach of contract."

"Get Cliston to renegotiate. No contract can stand up to him. When he's done, they'll pay you to leave."

"Hank," she said, turning around, "I *need* to do this. This is my life. This is what Damakans dream about. This is *finally* my big break. I wouldn't leave for all the money in the galaxy."

"Well, maybe I could work here. Like as security."

Laesa went back to her make-up.

"Sure. That would be nice."

"Put in a good word for me. Ask Cliston to put in a good word for me. Both of you put in words."

"I don't want to sully my reputation with the producer. He's very prickly."

"The producer. He *produces* the money to pay for everything, right?" I laughed.

"Don't belittle his contribution," she chastised.

"No, I wasn't. I don't even understand what's going on."

"She's a movie actor," Grassly explained to me.

"Shut up."

Laesa rose from her chair and walked over. She never looked so radiant or self-confident. Grassly couldn't take his eyes off her and neither could I.

"Do you need some money, Hank?"

"I...me? Are you asking if *you* need some money? Me to give *you* money?"

"I'm billing a little over two hundred a week. Cliston has all the details. Of course, you add some from incidentals and fees and take some away for the Guild and unemployment and agency. You know how it is."

"I don't need two hundred credits. I can borrow some from Cliston if I need it," I said.

"Two hundred *thousand*," she corrected.

Grassly's jaw hit the floor. My brain practically exploded.

"A week? Two hundred? There's like...a *ton* of weeks in a year! Where are...Cliston is managing this?"

"Yes. Do you need some money? Heaven knows I've borrowed enough from you. Do you want me to pay you back?"

Grassly looked up at me with wide eyes and nodded "yes."

"I don't know if I *need*...I mean, right this moment. I think I'm okay."

"Laesa?" called a voice from outside the tent, followed by a knock on the plastic hanger. "Five minutes."

"It's been lovely seeing you, Hank, but I really must get ready or the director will scold me. This is an important scene coming up."

"Yeah," I said dumbly. "What is the movie about, anyway?"

"I only know my scenes. I'm the primary love interest who turns out to be a mistake and leads to the character finding his true love. A catalyst to transition the audience's receptive alignment without a corresponding drop in emotional resonance. Tricky to pull off accurately."

"Sounds like it," I said. "Okay. When do you want to see each other again?"

Laesa was brushing on make-up frantically.

"Can we talk later, Hank? I really have to be collected and focused."

"Oh! Sure. Absolutely. Bye."

"Bye," Grassly said, as we hurried out of the tent.

I stood there a moment. So much seemed to have shifted so quickly.

"Thad. Elon's. Bloody. Butthole," Grassly exclaimed. "You have hit the jackpot! I don't even know what to say. I'm speechless. I am standing here, completely dumbfounded. How did you ever hook up with a woman like that? You? I would give an arm, leg, and eyeball for a gal like that! Two hundred thousand a week. And those legs!"

"Just cool it, alright? And be careful saying stuff like that. I know someone who will snatch your body parts without a second thought."

As we wound our way through the tangled production, it was clear that people were gearing up for something. There was a palpable sense of excitement.

"What's going on?" Grassly asked.

"Not sure. Let's hang back and watch. Try and be inconspicuous."

"If you pull your shirt over your head, you'll look like one of those big tents."

"Shut up, Grassly."

It took another twenty minutes for anything to happen. Laesa stepped out along with some other people. They were discussing something quietly, as the cameras and lights and all sorts of things moved furiously around them. They stood in front of a large screen painted with alien scenery.

"What is that they're in front of?" Grassly asked.

"Don't you know nothing? That's a fake door. They use fake doors a lot in movies."

"But look there. They got a fake car, too. And that's a fake tree. Why not use real stuff?"

"You know what acting is, right?"

"Sure. It's like...*acting* you is something."

"Exactly. They're pretending. Think how hard it would be to pretend you're something when you're surrounded by all kinds of *real* things. So when they pretend, they're standing around pretend mountains, pretend trees, pretend cars."

"Oh, yeah. I guess that makes sense. How do you know so much about it?"

"I've acted in a movie or two before," I sniffed.

"No, way! I thought only Damakans did. Did you get two hundred large a week?"

"I got a bunch of free food."

"I woulda taken the money," he said.

"But hey, now that we got some time. Who paid you to attack that film set where you were the trigger man?" I asked.

"Don't know," he said.

"Of course you know. Don't try and insult me."

"We don't know. It's all anone-mous through Scanhand," Grassly said.

"Scanhand has job postings?"

"Sure. That where all the gangs get jobs."

"No wonder this is so confusing," I declared. "No one knows *why* they're fighting or *who* they're fighting for. You're mercenaries."

"Am not! I'm in a respectable gang."

"You don't even know who your boss is. It could be me, for all you know," I said.

"That's stupid. Couldn't be you," he snorted.

"Sure it could. You don't know who is giving you work. That's why everything is screwed up. There's no gang bosses working things out. No one to negotiate with!"

"But you ain't the boss," he declared.

"I'm saying you don't *know*, Grassly."

"If you was the boss, you wouldn't be asking all these questions. And you had feeding tubes in you for weeks," he explained triumphantly.

Suddenly the entire production went dead silent. No one moved a muscle. We looked around to see what was going on. Even Grassly was quiet.

An actor called out some words we couldn't understand. Then other actors walked back and forth. And then *boom*, the production sprang back into action and the noise level returned to normal.

"That's it?" Grassly asked.

"I don't know."

"That was like three seconds. How do they get anything done?"

"I think it's like, camera tricks. You know?"

"No. I don't think you knows, either."

We heard an explosion behind us. It was close enough that we felt a shockwave and Grassly pitched forward, though not enough that he fell down.

"Oh, they must be filming over there too. Like I said, camera tricks."

"That wasn't no trick. A chunk of metal damn near clipped my head!" Grassly shouted.

The well-disciplined production staff began to scream and run in all directions. Grassly was tugging on my handcuff, trying to join the panic.

"We got to get out of here," he said.

"I don't know," I replied warily. "I think this is part of the movie."

"Hey, man, I ain't a mutant. I can't stand around waiting for a bomb to land on my neck like you."

"I'm not going without Laesa," I said.

I began pushing through the frantic crowd, with Grassly tethered to my arm. We caught up with Laesa and some other people, who appeared legitimately frightened. But in a subdued, Damakan manner.

"Hank, what's going on?" Laesa asked.

"I don't know. I think we should—wow, how can you function under all these lights?" I said, shielding my eyes.

"Are we under attack?" Laesa asked.

"I'm not sure."

I looked around for a place to hide. But there was nothing. Despite all the equipment and fake things, this was an open area between streets. The tents were about the sturdiest construction around. At this point, a lot of automatic weapon fire sounded. It was only a few blocks away.

"Let's go through there," I said, pointing to a door.

"That's not an actual door. It doesn't go anywhere," Laesa said.

"Trust me, that's really confusing to most people. Come on," I said, pulling her along.

The rest of the Damakans followed us.

Beyond the door was the side of some buildings and nothing else. But we were obscured from view by the screen we just passed.

"We're trapped," Grassly despaired.

"We were trapped before. But now we aren't standing in the open. Where are all those security guards I saw?"

A moment later, someone knocked at the fake door, causing the screen to gently sway.

I took out my shotgun.

"Who is it?" I asked.

"Can we hide with you?" a man said.

"Alright. But hurry up."

The door opened and about a dozen people ran behind the screen with us. They were a mix of Colmarians and Damakans. Some of the Colmarians were guards carrying weapons.

"Close that door," Grassly hissed, as the last person entered.

"Hey, what are you guys doing here? Shouldn't you be out there fighting?" I asked the guards.

"We're hired to protect the director," a man said, pointing to a Damakan with a stylish beard.

"All of you are?" I asked, surprised.

"We were hired to protect the producer. But he got shot. So we're kind of done working," another security guard explained.

I looked around at these useless people. One man stood out from the rest. He was holding a black t-shirt in front of him with the word "Security" written on it.

"Why are you *holding* that? It fits you, just wear it," I said.

"This is how Hank did it. I think he knows how to run security," the man countered.

"*I'm* Hank."

The man snorted.

"No, you're not. Hank fought a Therezian and Boranjame *at the same time.* You look like a fat...fat guy."

"Alright. Is anyone here supposed to protect the actual production? The whole thing?" I asked.

The guards all looked around. Didn't appear so.

"Well, we're just going to wait here for a bit," I said.

"This is just a backdrop," the director explained.

"Yeah? Well, I say it's better we back drop here than front drop out there when we don't know what's going on," I replied.

The director blinked his eyes rapidly but didn't respond.

"We need to put some holes in this so we can look out," I said.

A guard opened fire with his submachine gun, making a half-dozen holes and considerable noise.

"Not like that! We're trying to hide," I said.

"Sorry," he answered.

The holes were low to the ground.

"Grassly. Take a peek," I said.

The small man dropped to the road, his left arm raised up behind him and still connected to my wrist.

"Don't see nothing."

Everyone was silent.

"Hank, what's going to happen to us?" Laesa asked.

"Don't believe him. That's not Hank," the man holding the t-shirt said.

Laesa didn't look scared. None of the Damakans were very frightened, but that's because they were Damakans. They had to watch a scary actor to be scared. But I was scared.

"We're going to be fine. They're probably just here to steal some lights. Or a generator," I said. "Did anyone see what was shooting?"

"I see it," Grassly said, still looking through his peepholes. "I think it's a tank."

CHAPTER 23

The Colmarian guards immediately looked through the holes in the screen when Grassly said he saw a tank. Its massive engine could be heard roaring not far away from us.

"Don't shake the screen," I said nervously.

I wasn't so much worried about our location being discovered, I was worried about it being discovered by a *tank*. I had dealt with tanks before. Or I should say they had dealt with me. I was bulletproof. I weighed thousands of pounds. I healed rapidly. All of that was worthless against an armored, mobile, artillery piece.

"It's not a tank," one of the Colmarian thugs said, and I sighed with relief. "No, it's some kind of hot rod."

"What?" I asked.

"It's an armored car," Grassly clarified. "It's got their gang logo on the side. That's Podiver Vance's Vengeance."

"It's awesome," one of the Colmarians said, deeply envious.

Podiver Vance was an old-time gang leader. He was unbelievably tall and skinny. He used to own a number of department stores. But I had sort of gotten one of them blown up and he never recovered financially.

The gang members were oohing and aahing about the armored car about to kill us. The Damakans thought we had all lost our minds.

I pulled Grassly away from the screen by tugging on the handcuff so I could take a look.

I kneeled down and peeked through a hole. It was indeed an armored car. But heavily modified. It was fire red. The roaring engine I thought belonged to a tank, was the souped-up power plant that stuck out of the hood. The air intake scoop was big enough to stick your head inside. The wheels had shiny mag rims. There was an armored turret on top that held a large machine gun barrel. The picture on the side of the vehicle was a stylized representation of Podiver Vance and what looked like some of his gang bosses.

"That's a jet engine on that thing," I said, amazed.

"Hank, can you fight it?" Grassly asked.

"He's not Hank," the jerk with the t-shirt said, still doubting my identity. As if anyone would want to impersonate me.

"I think our best bet is to stay hidden. We can't outrun that thing and it's got a machine gun," I said. I wanted to reassure Laesa and the other Damakans. Hiding wasn't much of a plan, but I didn't have any other ideas.

"We can shoot it!" a gang member said, cocking his pistol.

"You understand the concept of an *armored* car, right?" I asked. "No one here has any weapons that can take out reinforced steel. Just be quiet and hope they leave."

The engine on the vehicle was enormous. Complete overkill. We had to put our hands over our ears because the turbine screamed, even though they were only inching along. Why did people create such useless things? And where did they even get it on Belvaille?

"We got to do something," Grassly said.

"It's stopped," I said.

It was about thirty feet away from us and the bubble turret was swiveling around, looking for targets.

"This is Vance's Vengeance. The *Venomous* Vance's Vengeance," an amplified voice called out from the armored car.

What a terrible gang name.

"We aren't here to hurt you," he said, apparently forgetting they had driven in and machine-gunned a bunch of people. "Members of the Romance Guild, step forward and we will escort you to safety."

"What a stupid ploy. No one's going to fall for that," I said.

"That's us," the director replied. "Let's go."

"They're going to gun you down if you step out there," I told him.

"He just said they were going to escort us," the director replied, eager to leave.

"They're lying," Grassly said, exasperated.

None of the Colmarians were remotely fazed by the announcement, but the Damakans were ready to go. They really didn't understand criminals.

"Some others are coming out," Grassly said. He had found an empty bullet hole down by the ground to look through.

A bunch of production staff were walking out from their hidey holes and approaching the jet-powered killing machine.

"I don't believe it," I said. "What do they think is going to happen?"

"They're going to get us out of here!" The director claimed. He began to stride away from the screen but his security guards grabbed him.

"Shut him up before he gives us away," I said.

They covered the director's mouth and restrained him.

"That's it. Come on out," the amplified voice said. "You're going to be fine."

A small crowd was around the armored car.

"Man, this is too much. I can't watch," I said, standing. These were just dramatic industry people. They didn't deserve Belvaille.

Laesa was confused. But she did what I said and kept quiet and didn't move.

A moment later, the machine gun rang out. It didn't stop firing for maybe ten seconds. The director ceased struggling and his eyes went wide in shock.

"We told you," Grassly said, rising from his vantage point.

Our group didn't have a chance. The car was sent to kill everyone and these unarmed, innocent Damakans were doomed.

"Everyone stay here," I said calmly. I flashed a broad smile at Laesa, like I was merely going in the other room to trim my toenails. I wanted to kiss her farewell, but I didn't want her to suspect how bad the situation was. I absently ripped off the handcuff that connected me to Grassly. Then I stepped to the side of the screen and walked in front of the armored car.

I waited to get shot to pieces. And waited. They didn't see me. Armored cars didn't exactly have a tremendous amount of visibility.

I cleared my throat loudly. Which, over the roar of the jet engine, was not very loud.

"Hey!" I yelled.

Still nothing. Maybe we could just sneak past them.

But the turret swiveled and spotted me.

"You're not a Damakan," the voice said. "Who are you?"

"I'm Hank," I replied coolly, as if I stared down armored cars every other day.

"What?"

"I'm Hank," I replied less coolly and somewhat louder.

"I can't hear you, man," the voice said, annoyed.

I took a few steps closer.

"I'm Hank!"

"Hank? No, you're not."

I threw up my arms, exasperated.

"What do you want? To see identification?"

"Hank is a killer. You're chubby," the armored car voice said.

What was the point of being famous if no one knew it was me? Scanhand really needed to have pictures.

"I'm Hank! I'm...I don't know, ask me anything."

"Hank has a negative three Trouble rating. You look like you have *trouble* getting through doors."

"Funny stuff. Step outside and say that!"

"What are you going to do, eat me? Stop wasting our time. Where are the rest of the Damakans, fat boy?"

"*And* the Trouble rating only goes to zero, stupid!" I yelled.

"Not for Hank. He broke Scanhand."

"Hold on," I said.

I took out my tele and brought up the application. There was my profile. My attributes had changed. I now had a purple eight in Toughness. Down from a red ten. My Smarts were a blue seven, down from a blue eight. And my Trouble was a pink negative three, down from a black zero.

So I had gotten weaker, dumber, and more dangerous to be around since I last looked.

"Yeah, so I'm Hank. And you're leaving. You've done more than enough killing for one day."

"You're going to mess up your Scanhand recommendations by lying about who you are. Not to mention we'll kill you," the voice said, still not believing my identity.

"No problem. Fire away," I said.

I tilted my head down and put my hands over my groin. The machine gun was big, but it didn't appear to be high caliber, judging by the diameter of the muzzle. That was the one place they skimped on the vehicle. They probably figured they didn't *need* a huge gun—what were the chances of them encountering another armored car?

I heard a loud *Clunk* and looked up. A small porthole had opened at the upper right side of the car. A mechanical rattling came next, barely audible over the engine. Did they want to get a better look before they shot me?

A thick steel barrel inched its way out of the porthole. Another fracking cannon. I'd about had my fill of those for a while. When the barrel had locked into position, I could see it was much smaller than a true tank cannon. Maybe about the same size as the mortar Kaxle had used. And that was enough to remodel a building.

I took a big step to the left. The cannon swiveled and followed me.

I took a big step to the right. The cannon hesitated, and then rotated back.

"I thought you were Hank," the voice called on the speaker.

"I am. And despite my rating on Scanhand, I'm smart enough to avoid artillery fire."

"This is just for moving things," he said. "Watch."

Before I could respond I was hit by what sounded like a thousand explosions. I blacked out.

When I was back in the now, I felt pain.

I was used to pain. I'm not going to say I was a masochist, but pain, for me, usually meant money. I got paid to feel pain so other, wealthier people didn't have to. Pain often indicated that I was doing something right. Not *totally* right. But I wasn't dead.

"Ah," I groaned on the ground.

I was against the building. Behind the screen. The Damakans and Colmarians gawked at me. Laesa had her hands over her entire face, too afraid to look.

Whatever hit me had launched me thirty feet! That was not an easy thing to do and I couldn't say I enjoyed the experience.

I dragged myself to my feet. My bare feet. My shoes were missing. How did that happen?

I looked back to where I had been standing and there were my shoes! Just sitting there. Like they were too ignorant to know they should have moved with me. I had been hit so hard that I got knocked out of my shoes.

I hobbled weakly over to my footwear, taking my time. Trying to clear the smog from my brain.

Fortunately, I saw the screen was still intact. The hiding Colmarians and Damakans were safe for the moment. Laesa was safe.

"That *is* Hank" the guy holding the t-shirt said.

Smoke, massive amounts of smoke, were pouring out of the stubby cannon muzzle. The men inside the vehicle were wracked with coughing. They hadn't turned off the microphone.

I waited until the coughing died down. That gave me more time to compose myself and take stock of the situation. I wasn't dead, but other than that, I felt horrible. My gut was real bad and it was all I could do to stand up sort of straight.

"You weren't lying. You're Hank!" the voice cried on the speaker.

"That's right. So how about we talk this through?"

The machine gun turret kicked up and started firing. The first thirty shots missed, but it didn't take long for them to correct their aim. And it's not as if I could dodge bullets—even if I *hadn't* been gutshot by a cannon.

The machine gun felt like, I suppose, a normal person getting snapped with a very taught rubber band on their bare skin. It stung like hell. And that thing put out something like 580 rubber bands a minute. The agony from the zillion bullets was enough that I was about to shatter my teeth from clenching my jaw so tight.

I covered my face and ran. There was nowhere to take cover, so I settled for moving forward. Every step I took, no matter how slow or shoeless, the gun had to adjust. And they didn't have particularly good aim.

My insides were on fire from the mortar. My skin was beaten raw from the machine gun. It was easier to count the places that didn't hurt instead of trying to take stock of my injuries. My left earlobe seemed to be okay.

I finally reached the side of the armored car and the turret could no longer point down at me. I was too close. Moving this direction seemed to be a good decision after all.

"He's going to tip us over!" The voice on the speaker said.

Actually, I hadn't even thought of that.

The armored car was big. Boxy. Well, rectangular. I guess that's still a box, right? The idea of me tipping this thing over was preposterous.

Still, I didn't have anything better to do.

I reached down, grabbed hold of the chrome-plated running board, bent my legs, and heaved. The vehicle didn't move at all. I think I'd have an easier time pushing Belvaille.

I slapped my hand feebly against the painted side of the armored car. It really *was* a nice-looking mural. I didn't know Podiver Vance had blue eyes. Maybe that was just artistic license. He was so tall, you never looked at his eyes much, I guess.

The armored car's engine began to roar again. I could hear the men inside arguing, because they didn't switch off the speaker. They were worried I was about to lift up their ridiculous vehicle and...I don't know, squash them or something. If they knew the extent of my injuries, they wouldn't be concerned at all.

But while I was this close to the vehicle I realized something profound.

"This thing has tires," I said.

It hadn't really registered until I was right next to them. The vehicle was absolutely covered in armor from top to bottom. Sheets and sheets of plating. A turret. A mortar. A damn jet engine! But they didn't protect their wheels. It had simple rubber truck tires outfitted with fancy chrome mags.

My shotgun had remained in my holster despite my recent travels and machine gunning. The plastic handle had been pulverized by numerous bullets, but the rest of it seemed to be in working order.

I shot the front right tire of the car, flattening it. With no stock or handle, my gun flew out of my grasp. I quickly recovered it, and shot the right back tire. I lost the gun again, but it didn't matter because I was out of ammo.

The rear wheels were double tires and I had only taken out one. But the armored car was laboring with two flats. The driver probably didn't realize I had shot his tires. He could only tell the car was moving sluggishly.

In response, the driver gunned the engine—the *jet* engine. The wheels spun so fast they ripped apart the remaining tires! The rubber simply couldn't keep up with how fast the rims accelerated. The tires flexed for a second, splintered, and turned into ribbons which shot out like confetti. The whole area smelled like cannon smoke, machine gun smoke, and vulcanized rubber.

Why would anyone build such an absurd vehicle?

That said, the occupants were still safely inside an armored car. They recognized they had no tires by virtue of the vehicle dropping in height and the sound of metal wheels grinding against the road.

"Hey!" I yelled, slapping against the side of the car and hurting my hand. "You guys done?"

"Hank. Just give us the Damakans and we'll leave," the voice said.

"I don't have any Damakans. You shot them all or they ran away," I lied. "Look, what can I do to sort this out?"

This was my real talent: negotiating. Cutting through the macho crap and working out a deal. I might not have the smartest Smarts, but I had experience. More than anyone.

"There's more Damakans we're after," he said.

"You got any names or do I have to guess which ones?"

"We're supposed to kill all the Damakans here."

"If you were going to slaughter a whole movie studio why didn't you just drop a bomb?" I yelled.

"That's why we got this car. We didn't know you were going to be here. Can you round up the rest of the Damakans for us?"

"Why would I do that? I'm not some mass murderer. It's crooks like you that give the rest of us a bad image," I said.

"Your image is plenty bad. Your Trouble rating is the worstest one on the station."

"Forget Scanhand. Let's look at the situation. You got no tires. You can't get away or chase anyone down. You have to come out some time. And I can beat you silly when you do," I said. I was hurt, but I felt I could deal with whoever was inside. The fact they were here to indiscriminately kill Damakans gave me all the justification I needed to thrash them good.

"We got a bunch of weapons we haven't used. And we got food in here. You won't wait longer than us," he said.

"How do you know?"

"I'm reading your profile right now. It says you have to eat all the time. You're probably hungry right now."

Damn. He was right. My mutation was begging for sustenance, trying to rebuild. I was getting drowsy and it was unlikely I could wait them out.

"Who is paying you?" I asked.

"Podiver Vance."

"I know *that*. I'm staring at a big-ass painting of him on the side of your car."

"Hank, we've already called for backup. Bring us the last of the Damakans and I'm sure Podiver will reward you."

"I don't need a jet car. And to be honest, I'm not a very good driver."

"Yeah. A dozen people said the same thing about you in Scanhand."

"Who is writing that stuff? Bunch of cowards," I said.

"How about a hundred to walk away and leave us to our work?"

"That's an insult. First, I'm not going to let you kill a bunch of innocent people. That's not up for debate. Second, if I *did*, I would need more than a hundred credits to forget my conscience."

"No. A hundred *thousand* credits."

It was like a slap across the face. I simply couldn't comprehend movie money. Laesa was getting two hundred grand a week and these jerks were offering me a hundred thousand to limp away so they could go crazy.

It was so much money I couldn't even come up with a glib response.

"We'll take it!" Someone shouted.

It was the idiots behind the screen. The Colmarian guards pushed the scenery and it toppled over, leaving everyone completely exposed.

"What the hell? Wasn't there a mountain there just a second ago?" the man on the speaker said. "Doesn't matter. Hank, our deal is off. Fire!"

The turret began shooting even though it was still facing the wrong way. It began to swivel in the direction of the Damakans. Laesa!

Before I knew what I was doing, I had clambered up the front of the armored car. The barrel was swinging directly toward me.

I grabbed hold of it with both hands and heaved upward as hard as I could.

"Ah!" I felt tearing in my gut, and my lower back gave out.

The gun was circling toward Laesa, spitting out bullets as it went. There were only seconds to save her. I don't know where the idea came from, but I jumped straight up in the air.

I crashed, butt first, on top of the barrel with my legs splayed.

The machine gun jerked downward and began shooting directly in front of the armored car.

The turncoat Colmarian security guards took this moment to reevaluate their situation. The armored car apparently didn't care who they were firing at, Damakans or not. The guards dropped their guns and ran like hell. Grassly was the first to go.

But the gun kept shooting. I could hear the electric motors whirring, trying to raise the weapon and my bulky self. But it wasn't going anywhere as long as I sat on the barrel.

The gun started to get hot. Very hot. I began to fidget on top of the barrel as it scorched my delicates.

The center of the barrel was now glowing a pale orange. It was extremely painful. I had to keep shifting from cheek to cheek and forward and back. I might be fireproof, but this machine gun was becoming molten steel.

I was about to jump off, when the barrel sagged and exploded. Bullets flew every which way for a second until the weapon chewed itself apart. It continued firing even after most of the gun was destroyed. The bullets ricocheted inside the turret and down into the interior of the armored car. I could tell, because I heard the damage broadcast on the speaker until the entire vehicle went silent, the jet engine sputtering out.

I fell off the roof of the car and landed facedown on the metal road. I looked to see if Laesa was okay and she was. The Damakans hadn't moved the whole time I was fighting. I'm not sure they even understood the danger they were in.

The skin on the underside of my thighs, all the way to my butt, was swelled, blistered, and charred. I had first-to-third degree burns in barrel-sized patches. I could feel myself slipping into shock.

The Damakans slowly walked over to me. They were finally starting to appreciate the situation.

"Is it over?" Laesa asked.

"Yeah," I answered weakly.

"Would you...would you happen to be related to Hank the Fat Mutant of Belvaille?" the director asked me.

"That *is* him," Laesa said. "Isn't he absolutely amazing!"

CHAPTER 24

Ah, the hospital. My second home.

I came hobbling in from my injuries and requested my usual room. I had been here so recently, they were worried they hadn't had enough time to restock their food supplies.

One of the technicians took a look at my burns, which I had received from heroically sitting upon a glowing hot gun barrel. To give you an idea how incompetent the medical staff here was, he didn't even warn me, he simply poked me with his finger and asked, "Does this hurt?"

I howled in pain and reflexively pushed him away. He hit the wall and received a laceration on the back of his head. But at least he was already at the hospital.

What was really troubling me, however, was my gut. Compared to the rest of me, my stomach had no obvious wounds. So the doctors just shrugged and told the nurses to hook up my feeding tubes.

They were going to have to put this hospital visit on my already extensive tab. I doubted talent agent Cliston would foot the bill for my stay, like he did last time, considering the movie I was trying to guard had half its talent gunned down.

I woke up screaming, realized I must have had a bad dream, then saw Delovoa standing at the foot of my bed, smiling.

Delovoa's enormous nose was dripping on my sheets and his metal teeth had started to rust. He was wearing a medical gown.

"What are you doing here?" I asked, alarmed.

"I snuck in. They said you weren't supposed to have visitors yet, but I figured it couldn't hurt."

"I'm tired," I said, rubbing my burning eyes.

"Yeah, you were in a coma. I had to use this to wake you," Delovoa replied, holding up a small vial.

"What is it?"

"I'm not really sure," he said, squinting at the bottle with his three lopsided eyes.

"You injected me with an unknown substance?"

"How could I inject anything into you? No, I rubbed it on your eyeballs," he said, twiddling his fingers that were covered in medical gloves.

I tried to push aside the sheets so I could get up and throttle Delovoa. I moved my arm about six inches, felt nauseous, and began seeing spots.

"Take it easy. You have some Boranjame endocrine in your veins," Delovoa cautioned.

"What? How did you get a hold of that?"

"Wasn't easy. I had my doubts it was authentic, but it sure brought you back in a hurry."

"Boranjame are like gods. How did you know my eyes wouldn't melt?"

"I didn't."

"If I was in a coma, it's my body trying to repair the damage that your stupid vehicles did! You made the Rough Boys power armor. And you made Podiver Vance's goons a battlewagon. Don't deny it!"

"Why would I deny it?"

"Because. I almost died," I said.

"You're *always* almost dying. Honestly, I don't think Death wants you at this point."

"It's your fault I'm here."

"What do you want me to do? I build and sell weapons."

"Why would you sell to the Rough Boys?"

"Same reason you kill this person instead of that person: they paid you."

"I'm not an assassin. I'm a negotiator."

"You spend more time in the hospital than any 'negotiator' I ever heard of. I think negotiator is just another word for assassin who isn't very good at it."

"Tell me one thing. I know building those weapons takes time. A lot of work and supplies. Why do you add the most useless things to them? Is it a joke? Kaxle shot fireworks at me."

"Oh. I told him not to use that," Delovoa said.

"And Podiver's car had a mortar and a jet engine."

"And?" Delovoa asked impatiently.

"Why make all this stuff no one wants or uses?"

"I don't get paid like you, Hank. You get money for the amount of food you eat and the number of bumps you put on people's heads."

"No, I don't."

"I get paid by the invoice. I bill my clients for my work. At *each* line item, I make a bit of profit for my labors and creativity. The more lines I have, the more profit. So I keep adding and adding until they tell me to stop."

"Oh, I guess that makes sense. Why don't you do that with me?"

"Do what with you?"

"When you build me a gun, it's just a gun. Not a gun and a car and a flaming disco ball rolled together."

"Because you and I usually barter for goods. I don't give you invoices. I didn't even know you could read."

"Laugh. Laugh. Okay, well, thanks for rubbing Boranjame puss on my eyes. If I develop superpowers I'll be sure to kill you. But now I need to go back to my coma," I said.

"Wait. I heard about how you fought Kaxle."

"Yes. I already spent time in the hospital for that."

"But, do you feel...anything? Anything unusual?" he asked.

"I'm in the hospital. I was in a coma. My eyeballs feel like they're delicious berries in a dark forest. Yes. I feel extremely unusual."

"No, this is normal for you. I mean, the staff said they removed a blade from you. That must have come from Kaxle's suit. Not much could cut through your fat hide."

"It's not fat."

"Whatever. Lumpy muscle."

"In case I fight Kaxle again, are there any weaknesses to the armor? Like a hidden off switch or something?" I asked.

"Yes. I encoded a short circuit in the primary motivator circuits. You can shut down the armor if you sing a song."

"Really? What song?"

"It's one I made up. So no one can do it by accident."

"How does it go?" I asked, growing excited.

"It goes: Hank is such a moron, he's stupid all day long. He thinks I build my weapons, that turn off with a song," he hummed.

I paused, my brow furrowed.

"Can I sing that or does it have to be in your voice?"

"*Idiot!* I'm saying the armor doesn't have a weakness. Do you want me to put an off switch in the stuff I sell you?"

"All the crap you sell me blows up in my face."

"Don't blame your appearance on me. You always looked like that. So where did Kaxle stab you? And how does that area feel?" he asked.

"My stomach? It feels terrible. I don't know why. It should have mostly healed."

"Yeah. Anything else? Like, unusual bruising? Or, I don't know, throwing up pools of blood and pieces of bone?"

"No," I said, alarmed. "Though..." And I lowered my voice. "I've kind of been pooping funny for the last week or so."

"Funny how? Like haha-funny? Or something else?"

"Do you think I'm eating clowns?"

"How should I know? You brought it up," he said.

"Nah, it's just...I'm usually real regular. Cliston makes good food and I have a titanium stomach."

"Neutronium," Delovoa corrected.

"I figure it's just been stress. But, you know, diarrhea. That kind of thing."

"Any blood or tissue?"

"I don't stare at the toilet."

"Can I inspect your midsection?" Delovoa asked.

"I guess. Why, what's going on?"

Delovoa pulled over the sheets and looked at my stomach.

"Is that the scar there?" Delovoa tapped.

"That's my belly button!"

"Your what?" Delovoa asked.

"Are you kidding? You don't know what a belly button is?"

"Doesn't look like a button." Delovoa put his finger in several times. "What's it do? Is this the off switch you were talking about?"

"How many times have you operated on people? You're saying you've never seen a belly button? It's where our umbilical cords connect when we're babies."

"You think every species in the galaxy has the same gestation process? I don't have a belly button," Delovoa said. He opened his hospital gown to prove it, showing off his patchwork of different skin types and zippers and metal plates.

"That isn't even your body. Close that back up. Why are you asking me this stuff?"

"So about the invoices. The line items."

"What about them?"

"For Kaxle's armor, I added to the end of his claws some...nanobots. They're supposed to drill into the subject and rip them apart from the inside—which is of course superfluous. If you're hit by a one-foot blade swung by a mutant dog aided by pneumatic pistons, you're going to be cut in half, anyway."

"What's a nanobot?" I asked, concerned.

"Like a really small, teensy-tiny microscopic robot."

"Are you saying I have a Dredel Led in my gut?"

"No, no! Just an itty-bitty, insignificant little—"

"Robot? It's cutting my insides apart?"

"Eh. Maybe?" he hedged.

"Take it out!"

"I can't."

"Why not?"

"Same reason you're such a 'great' negotiator: no one can cut you open. I mean, if you want to let Kaxle slash at you a few dozen more times, maybe I can poke around looking for it."

"Am I going to die?"

"It should have killed you a long time ago," Delovoa muttered.

"I'm serious!"

"Me too. This is one of those extra things I made. I never worried about how effective it would be because I never thought it would matter. It just sounds cool when I describe it to someone who pays by the invoice. I figure the nanobot ran into your Hank bowels and gave a good fight, but ultimately can't do much damage."

"But it will eventually? Is it going to be grinding at me the rest of my life?"

"No, no. It has a battery. A super-small, puny, little—"

"How long does it last?"

Delovoa shrugged.

"I thought it would be dead by now. Or you would. I mean, obviously it's not going to kill *you*. But, I don't know. It's trying to chew through your gallbladder or whatever, which is presumably as strong as your hide. It wasn't designed for that."

"What was it designed *for?*"

"Overbilling clients. If you're only pooping haha-funny, get Cliston to buy more toilet paper and sleep it off."

"But it's going to stay inside me, right?"

"No, it...dissolves into an enzymatic toxin. But! If the nanobot hasn't killed you already, a mild poison isn't going to do much."

"So, you're saying I should do nothing?"

"There's not much you *can* do. Anything powerful enough to operate on you, surgically, won't exactly create a small booboo."

"Alright, I guess."

"Oh, and good news on your marriage."

"My what?"

"As your Alternate Man, Laesa came to me and asked a lot of embarrassing questions about your emotional obligations. I told her food is your only love."

I rubbed my eyes again. The Boranjame sweat must be making me hear things or the nanobot had reached my ears.

"What's this you're saying?"

"You're getting married! I still don't think she's good enough for you, but no one ever asks *my* opinion. Besides, you seem convinced, you're not getting any younger, and your intestines might slide out your backside any minute. So might as well make the most of it," he said.

"Married? I'm getting married?" I asked weakly.

"Sure are. If you don't die in this hospital, of course."

I felt myself fading back into unconsciousness.

Delovoa looked at his vial.

"I don't think this Boranjame was very fresh. I knew I should have asked for the expiration date."

I woke up drooling. Something smelled wonderful.

"Sorry to disturb you, sir," Cliston said.

My butler stood beside my hospital bed. And next to him was a huge, eleventy-course meal.

"Cliston. That looks so good. But I don't think I can eat it yet," I stated sadly.

"No, you can't. The technicians said you cannot consume solid food for another week. But I wished to discuss a few things. I hope you don't mind."

"Delovoa used Boranjame spit on my eyes to wake me up. You using food is much nicer. What can I do for you?" I asked.

"I spoke to Procon Hobb and—"

"Wait," I interrupted. "Why would my butler speak to him?"

"Forgive me, I know you're tired and I didn't want to confuse you. What I mean is that I spoke to talent agent Cliston who spoke to fight promoter Cliston who spoke to Procon Hobb."

"That's like a six-way conversation with two people and no one actually talking—since Procon Hobb uses telepathy."

"Yes, sir. He has allowed you to rent his church for your wedding ceremony."

"Oh, yeah," I said. "Delovoa told me about that. I wasn't sure if I believed him. So I'm really getting married?"

"That is my understanding, sir."

"Seems like everyone is finding out before me. What's it look like?"

"To what are you referring, sir?"

"The church. Is it pretty?" I asked.

Cliston paused. He wasn't pausing to choose his words, Cliston had a computer brain. He was pausing in imitation of polite Colmarian speech patterns.

"It is a large building. Calling it a church is perhaps a disservice. It would be a cathedral on many planets."

"But Hobb doesn't just own it, right? It's actually a church to him?" I asked.

"That is correct, sir. There are many statues and images in his honor. Your guests must be careful not to desecrate the building."

"Desecrate? You know my friends. They're kind of desecration-in-motion. What will Procon Hobb do if they spill some drinks?"

"I don't believe he will do anything—especially for so slight an infraction. But something more serious might cause his worshippers to be offended."

"Oh, yeah. Those lizard guys. I hope Laesa doesn't mind the location."

"She is very busy with work. She said she approved any of my choices, sir."

"Movie work or just work in general?"

"I'm not sure, sir."

"You're her agent!"

"Me? No, sir. I'm your butler. And the preacher for your wedding. I've done some research on Damakan culture and it seems there are eight major wedding types and three archaic subtypes. You need to decide which one you prefer. There is the Highland Sonce Primvera. The Dano-Mont Mellday. The Eastern Continent, also known as the Fiz-hallia Most. The—"

"Cliston," I interrupted. "You're speaking gibberish."

"It's Damakan-Set, actually, sir. That is the Colmarian translation of Damakan words. Would you like me to speak in native Damakan?"

"No, show off. I've never been married before and I've never been a Damakan before. I'm the least qualified person to ask about Damakan weddings."

"I can wait until you're feeling better, sir."

"Might be a long wait."

"I didn't want to put things off until the last moment. This *is* your wedding. I wanted to make sure it was to your satisfaction."

"I'm not big on ceremonies, Cliston. You know that. If you could just wave your hands around and say we're married, that would be good for me."

"One of the archaic ceremonies has some arm waving. Though I'm not sure where we could perform the ritual hunt and blood sacrifice on this space station."

"I think we should exclude any weddings that require killing or volcanoes. I know that much."

"Yes, sir. I am required...as the endowed minister, to speak on the suitability of your union."

"Am I in a union now, too? When did that happen?" I asked, confused.

"No, sir. I mean your marriage to Laesa Swavort."

"Oh. Right. Sorry. My brain is kind of mush right now."

"I understand, sir. But I am required to make sure you are entering this relationship with full knowledge, good intentions, emotional gravitas, and artistic rectitude."

"What's that last one mean?"

"It's kind of Damakan-speak, sir. I think we can ignore it. Things get a bit muddled what with her being a Damakan and you being an Ontakian. Speaking of which, I could not find any information on native Ontakian weddings. Is there anything you'd like me to add?"

"Make sure there's food. And alcohol. Wait. No alcohol. If everyone gets drunk they'll puke all over that cathedral and get the lizards mad at us," I said.

"As I was saying, I must test you on your matrimonial suitability. It is not too late to change your mind. Marriage is a big step for you. You've been, strictly speaking, single since I've known you. And for hundreds of years before that," Cliston said.

"Thanks for reminding me of my romantic shortcomings."

"Your habits are also not conducive to female sensibilities. You eat, poop, and fart more than any creature I have ever met."

"I thought you said I was about normal."

"I believe talent agent Cliston said that. I suspect he was lying."

"Laesa has been around me. She knows what I do."

"But is she comfortable with your lifestyle? Can you coexist with your very different racial and personality issues?"

"I don't know, Cliston. I hope so. That's all we can do, right? I can't see the future. She makes me happy. I don't think she'd want to marry me if I made her miserable. It's not as if she's with me for my money or my good looks."

"No, sir. I suspect not," Cliston agreed harshly. "I do need you to dwell upon this decision in all its aspects."

"Can I dwell when I get out of the hospital? I'm planning on passing out very soon."

"Of course. And I do hope you will be happy, whatever your choice. I'm more than willing to stay on as your butler, should you decide to marry—or even if you don't."

"Thanks, Cliston. Can I speak to talent agent Cliston for a moment?"

"Yes," he said.

"Yes, I can? Or yes, that's you?"

"It's me, kid. What's this I hear about you getting hitched?"

"When did you hear about that?"

"Laesa told me right after I landed her another assignment."

"Is it a movie?"

"A commercial," he said.

"Commercial? What's that?"

"It's a little movie in between other movies to advertise another movie."

"Who makes up this crap?" I asked.

"The Guilds. Damakans are naturals at this kind of thing."

"Okay, I didn't want to bring this up, but I figured I'd lay out the bad news."

"Bad news? You've been in the hospital for three weeks. How can you have any bad news?" he asked.

I was dreading this, but I felt I had to be straight with talent agent Cliston since he represented Laesa.

"You know that movie you hired me to protect?" I began.

"Yeah, it wrapped a few days ago."

"Wrapped? You mean it's done?"

"Done as dirt," he said.

"Wasn't everyone killed?" I asked.

"Not everyone. The director had scheduled reshoot after expensive reshoot, but most of the people he hired were gunned down or injured. So we got to cut a week off our production schedule. Not only that, we didn't have to pay any of the dead people."

"That's kind of deceitful. And doesn't that cut into your own profits since you represented those actors?"

"As a talent agent. But with the producer killed, I had to take over that role. I made money doing that."

"Please don't make another personality. I can't figure out what's going on as it is."

"No promises. Talent agents and producers are often working to different purposes."

"But you're saying I didn't do bad at the movie set?" I asked.

"Bad? You did terrible! If I hire you to guard a production, I expect more than half the cast and crew to survive. It was dumb luck that it ended up working."

"Will you still be Laesa's agent when she gets married?" I asked.

"Sure, sure. Though it would help if you were better looking."

"She's cute. Not a bombshell, but cute. You can't deny that."

"Not her. You."

"What's it have to do with me?"

"Reporters. They like to see glamor. You aren't glamorous. You got tubes up your nose," Cliston waved at my hospital bed.

"I'm hurt. I don't usually look like this."

"No, you usually look worse."

"I'm a professional criminal. That's got to be a bit glamorous," I said.

"Maybe I can find an angle. I've got to run." he said.

"Hey, since things worked out with the production, do you think you could see your way to paying for my hospital visit?"

"I about cut even. I lost money as a talent agent and made it back as a producer. Besides, your butler said this stay was costing a fortune. But congratulations on your wedding. My advice is, make sure she's the right dame for you."

"Are you telling me that as the preacher?"

"Preacher? Do I look like a preacher?" he asked.

"I've only met one preacher before and he looked exactly like you," I said.

"I'm just saying that I work with Damakans all the time, kid. They're screwy. No offense, but Laesa is screwier than most. I'm glad I never got married."

"You're a robot. Who are you going to marry?"

"Don't have to be a jerk about it. But I'll see you around. We'll do lunch when you get out of the sick house."

Cliston waltzed out of the room and down the hall.

"You don't eat!" I yelled after him.

Some days passed in a hospital haze and then I suddenly woke up with a start. It felt like my face was on fire!

"Laesa," I said, seeing her at the foot of the bed.

She was wearing a sporty riding outfit. Not sure what she would be riding on a space station, but she looked like a wealthy noblewoman.

"Oh, it worked," she said.

"What worked??" I asked.

"I used this liquid that Delovoa recommended would wake you up," she said.

"You put Boranjame sweat on my eyeballs?"

"He didn't say where to put it. I dripped some on your cheeks and forehead."

No wonder I felt like I was burning up.

"Is it true what everyone is saying?" I asked.

"Yes. I'm working in commercials now. But Cliston assures me it's only until a meatier role comes up. It's important to not oversaturate myself and wear out my fans."

"No, I mean are we getting married?" I asked.

"Oh, yes. Isn't it great? Cliston is making all the arrangements."

"Well, good. Because I'm mostly in a coma. But I didn't get you a ring."

"I bought one."

She held out her hand and could barely focus on it. Not because it was so bright, but because the Boranjame phlegm kept running into my eyes.

"How many diamonds does it have? Those Damakan reporters said you were supposed to have one per year you wanted to be married."

"It has a thousand," she said.

"Wow. That's a lot of anniversaries to remember. Where did you get the delfiblinium?"

"Delovoa."

"Throw that away!" I yelled.

"Why?" Laesa asked.

"If Delovoa made it, it's probably a bomb. Or cancerous. Or a cancer bomb. I'll end up in an extra-super-coma. How many line items were on the invoice?" I asked, pulling the covers up to my nose in an attempt to hide from the ring.

"What invoice?"

"For the ring."

"He didn't make the ring. He just gave me some delfiblinium."

"He *gave* it to you? Now I'm sure it's a bomb."

"I paid him."

"How much?" I asked.

"You're not supposed to talk about those things. It's bad luck. I think I got a good price."

"I doubt it. Did I tell you the time he poisoned like half the city just to see what it would do?"

"No. But I had Cliston negotiate the price."

"Oh. Oh! I guess that's okay. Cliston knows what everything is worth. And I think Delovoa is a bit scared of Cliston."

"Why? He's so nice."

"Who? Talent agent Cliston?"

"Why would my talent agent help me buy delfiblinium?" she asked as if I were a simple child.

"I don't know. Why would a butler?"

"Because he's your butler. And he's also performing our wedding ceremony."

I settled down a bit.

"Are you still with the Romance Guild?" I asked.

"Yes. They've been so fantastic to me."

"Cool. So, uh, Laesa. Are you sure you want to get married? I mean, with all our differences and such. I still do! I just want you to be certain."

"Oh, I'm certain. I love you, Hank."

"Thanks. I love you too."

"Everything has finally turned around for me. I can get emotional release from my acting and not force you to come to my shows at greasy diners. I'm able to contribute to our relationship."

"I liked watching your shows. But what am I contributing to the relationship? You're visiting me in the hospital and I didn't even get you a ring."

"Hank. You're my hero. I had heard about you...doing things and fighting people, but I thought it was kind of exaggerations. But when I saw what you did with my own eyes, it was like watching a hero from mythology. I would be crazy not to marry you."

"Oh. Thanks. Did you see how I sat on the gun to prevent them from shooting you guys?"

"I did. I never would have thought of doing that."

"Well, that wouldn't have worked if you tried it. It's my mutation. One of my mutations."

"Yes, you're a mutant. An Ontakian mutant. That's amazing! Not only are you great to be with, you can protect me from anything. You're always saying how dangerous Belvaille can be."

"Yeah. Maybe after we get married we should move. I could probably get some of my friends to come. Cliston would *love* to be around real culture and society. And Delovoa doesn't care where he is. He probably *wants* to move, so many people dislike him here. MTB just wants to be a cop somewhere. Garm will never leave. But I guess I could make some new assassin friends. Sure. Why not? I'm a likeable guy."

Laesa stared at me.

"Hank. The dramatic industry is here. I've finally broken in. I plan on having a long and vibrant career. I'm not leaving."

"But it's dangerous. Like you said. I barely saved you last time."

"But you're Hank! Who better to look out for me than someone with a negative ten Trouble rating?"

"I have a negative *three* Trouble rating," I said.

"I think it's ten. I looked not long ago."

"You shouldn't even be able to see my profile. You're on the actor side of Scanhand," I complained.

I reached over and got my tele. My attributes had changed again.

My Toughness was a yellow nine. It used to be a purple eight. My Smarts were a green six, down from a blue seven—I kept getting dumber. My Trouble rating used to be a pink negative three, and now it was simply a picture.

"What's a shoe mean?" I asked.

"What?"

"My Scanhand Trouble rating lists a shoe."

I held it up to Laesa.

"I'm not sure. Maybe it means you're capable."

"A shoe?"

"You need shoes to do things."

"I don't. My feet get dirty, but I do fine barefoot."

"Maybe that's what it means, then. That you don't need shoes," she pondered.

"It doesn't make sense. And since when did you use Scanhand?"

"Always," she said, confused.

"Why didn't you tell me about it?"

"I thought everyone knew. I've been on it for a few years at least."

"This is stupid. Why even *have* attributes if they are just going to put pictures?"

"It helps people know what to expect," she said.

"What are your attributes?" I asked.

"I'm not supposed to show. You aren't in a Guild," she said politely.

"Who runs Scanhand?"

"I thought the Guilds did."

"No. They wouldn't know anything about gangs. It's probably Cliston. Some other personality he forgot to mention. Scanhand Cliston. He's always doing stuff like that. You know he's written like thousands of books?"

"No, I didn't know that," she said. "He's a really good agent and butler."

"Yeah," I admitted begrudgingly.

"Oh. We're getting married in five days. Do you think you'll be out of the hospital by then?"

CHAPTER 25

I was still in the hospital, but I was able to sit up in bed and eat my food with my own mouth instead of through a tube. I wanted to stay here as long as possible because I still felt Delovoa's gizmo chewing my insides, though it was not as bad as before.

It also allowed me to avoid most of the commotion surrounding my wedding. Cliston would stop in every three hours or so to confirm details about things on which I had no opinion. I kept telling him to check with Laesa, but he said he was *my* butler until the wedding.

Laesa stopped by a few more times as well. She already had a job lined up after our nuptials. A major tele feature. She wasn't the lead, but she had second billing, which I think meant they paid her twice. Acting was confusing. But on reflection, it wasn't any more or less confusing than the criminal world. The stuff we did hardly made any sense to outsiders either. If it did, no one would need my services.

Laesa said she would pay for my hospital stay. Once the medical staff found that out, I got much better food than I normally received. I wasn't complaining, but it sucked they had been giving me lousy food before they knew I had a famous wife-to-be.

MTB came by and said there had been less murders of a less violent nature and asked if I knew anything about it. I did not, but I said I would take credit for it with Garm.

Garm also came by and said she already heard about the reduced crime from MTB and that I couldn't take credit for it. She then fired me because I hadn't done anything and I was getting married, after which I was even *less* likely to do anything.

Oh, well. I guess I didn't have to bother with the Entertainment Extermination any longer. I just needed to keep Laesa safe so she could earn our money.

I was thinking about all this when Rendrae came in.

"Hank. How are you doing?" he asked.

I looked around the hospital room as if it should be obvious.

"I brought you a gift," he said.

He handed me a very large box that was extremely light. I figured it was a joke present and the box was empty. I opened it and it was stuffed full of greenish-orange squares that carried a putrid aroma.

"What's this? Dried vomit?" I asked.

"It's plant synth-protein. Zero calories. Zero fat. Zero carbs. High in fiber and nutrients. You'd be in the hospital a lot less if you were in better shape. Take it from me. My nutritional habits almost cost me my life." The skinny Rendrae smiled, pounding his hard stomach.

"I'll burn so many calories *chewing* this that I'll actually starve to death. I'm doing fine on my own diet."

"I believe you could lose some weight. It can't be healthy to have a tongue that weighs a hundred pounds."

"I'm dense—I'm...anyway, thanks. I'll do something with it," I said, trying to stave off Rendrae giving me health pointers.

"I've been doing a lot of work on the gang war since you've been goofing off."

"Why does everyone think I *like* the hospital?"

"You're here often enough. But I've laid down a bunch of spies and informants to get to the bottom of the Entertainment Extermination."

"Movie Mayhem would be a better title, I think."

"I'm not looking for a *writing* partner, I'm looking for my *street* partner to help me with legwork and breaking heads. Garm isn't going to be happy if you keep slacking off."

"She already fired me."

"See? I learned what the core problem is. The gangs are operating without motive or direction. They are executing these attacks blindly. We have to—"

"Yeah, it's Scanhand. That's where they get their jobs," I interrupted.

Rendrae stopped and stared at me.

"How did you ascertain that?"

"This guy I talked to."

"What guy? Were you talking to people behind my back? We're a team."

"It was just some guy that MTB captured."

"You're working with MTB now? You trying to scoop me?"

"*Scoop* you? Is it showbiz talk?" I asked.

"What is the source of your information? Give me a name."

"Grassly. But also Borgin Two-Eyes confirmed it."

"I met Borgin Two-Eyes. He has *four* eyes! I don't recall him saying that."

"You were cowering against the wall, you might not have heard. He said he didn't know who was paying them. People post jobs to Scanhand. Or gangs have their services bid on. That's why this 'gang war' isn't playing out like a gang war. To get to the bottom of it, you need to find out who is hiring them and why."

"You already said it was Scanhand," Rendrae huffed.

"That's just the tool. Someone is coming up with a huge amount of money to pay these mercenaries."

"Who are some of your ideas?"

"I'm fired. I don't have any ideas."

"So you're just going to quit? That's not like you."

"It's exactly like me. I'm not getting paid. I'm in the hospital. I'm getting married. Pick any one of those."

"Your Damakan wife might be next!"

"I'll devote all my attentions to defending her," I said.

"Like you did with the others? Or was that just half your attentions? You're bulletproof. But you can't *catch* bullets. Or explosions. Or toxic gas. Do you really think you'll be able to guard every production she's in?"

"No," I admitted. "But what can we do?"

"Well, who do you think has the money to be renting all these gangs through Scanhand?" he asked.

"Procon Hobb has enough money to pay everyone on Belvaille to commit suicide using a rubber hammer."

"He's not a Procon! That word doesn't even have a definition."

"I think it means 'giant mutant frog that has enough money to pay a city to commit suicide and also owns your newspaper.'"

"Partially owns! Who else?" he asked.

"Gax."

"The Marquor of Lunacy?"

"How many other Boranjame do you know?" I asked.

"I don't even *know* that one. Why would he want a gang war?"

"I don't know anyone who wants it. The Navy? They've messed around down here before."

"This strikes me as very subtle for the Navy," he said.

"I agree. And they could just take Belvaille if they really wanted it. I don't think they do."

"What about Garm?" he asked. "She could have hired you as cover—knowing you wouldn't discover her because you keep getting hospitalized."

"Garm would never waste money. And while Garm is certainly rich, she doesn't have the cash to pay all sides in a gang war."

"So who does that leave?" he asked.

"I don't know. You'll have to ask around. Do some reporter stuff."

"What about you?"

"I'm getting married in two days. Come to the wedding. It should be fun. It's at your boss's church. Cathedral. Procon Hobb."

"He's not a Procon and he's not my boss! You mean to tell me that you, Hank, are okay with a gang war tearing apart this city as long as it doesn't affect you or your Damakan wife directly?"

"I'm getting married, man. What do you think I can do?"

"I think this Damakan wife has got you forgetting your priorities. The Hank I know doesn't let his space station fall into anarchy."

"We might not even live here after we're married. Might pack up, take Cliston along, and move to somewhere quiet. That also has show business."

Rendrae's thin jaw hung open. His teeth were sparkling white.

"I mean, we'll probably stay. Belvaille is really hot as far as dramatic work right now," I continued.

"You better pull yourself together, Hank. Your wife is an actor. The life expectancy for that career is woefully short at the moment."

"I know. That's why I want to move. And even without the gang war, Belvaille is dangerous. I have to think about someone besides myself now."

"Well you certainly aren't thinking about me!" Rendrae said.

"Why would I? I'm not marrying you. I'll try and help on your story after I get hitched. I can't make any promises, because I want to work security on Laesa's shows if I can."

Rendrae was fuming. He grabbed his box of vegi-crap and shoved it up by my chin.

"Here. Eat this. Maybe it will unfat your fat head!" He said, then he spun on his shapely legs and marched out of the room.

I started to feel great that night and even my stomach stopped hurting. I went home and was tremendously happy to be back.

But the next day my lips and tongue swelled up to quadruple their normal size. I looked like a fish with gigantism.

When doctor Delovoa stopped giggling at me, he said it was probably his Dredel Led nanobot that had finally dissolved into a poison. Apparently, it made your lips and tongue enormous. At least to me. He said it would wear off in about ten hours—if I didn't die.

The good news was I didn't have to answer any more wedding questions from Cliston because my tongue was too large to reliably speak. This made Cliston very cross. But he went on and got my wedding organized and gave me periodic, lengthy updates.

The night before my wedding my lips and tongue were almost back to regular size, and I could at least talk.

Delovoa was over at my apartment. As my Alternate Man, he was supposed to bathe me.

"Like, with water and soap?" Delovoa asked Cliston.

"It is a ritual cleansing. You aren't supposed to use soap, you're supposed to use the sap of a Thimiferous tree," Cliston said. "Though I couldn't procure that so I made you some brown sugar water instead."

"I'm not getting naked in front of Delovoa," I said.

"I'm not touching your 'little shotgun' with any kind of water," Delovoa replied.

"You're then supposed to dress him in four robes. One signifying the darkening of his past. One representing the opening of his future. One—"

"Skip to the first non-awkward thing he's supposed to do," I told Cliston.

"Awkward by what measure, sir?"

"Our measure. Us. You know us," I said.

Cliston was silent a while.

"Would you gentlemen care for drinks?" he asked finally.

"Are we supposed to drink?" Delovoa asked.

"No. But everything else is awkward," he said.

"Yeah, let's get a little toasted. Not much. I'm getting married tomorrow," I said. "And Cliston said there's all kinds of symbolism."

"Good, then I'll get ripped. Maybe it will make sense when I'm hungover," Delovoa said.

"Don't throw up at my wedding," I warned.

"I know who you're inviting. I'll probably be the only sober one there," he said.

Numerous drinks later, I was buzzed and Delovoa's eyes were all looking the same direction. Which meant he was hammered.

"You know, it's not too late to get out of this. We could take a tour of the galaxy. You've only met like, what, *five* Boranjame sitting on this space station. Go out and meet fifty!"

"They're scary. I don't wanna meet them," I said.

"We've been on this dumb city almost our whole lives," he said.

"Yeah."

"I thought you never get married."

"Me neither," I said.

"I thought I get married."

"Me neither," I said.

"No. No. I said, I think, I thought, I would get married," he stumbled.

"You?"

"Yeah."

"Delovoa?"

"Yeah."

"Who...who going to marry you? You crazy and ugly. Crazy ugly."

"Nyah. I don't want to marry no one. I just wanted a wedding. Big cake."

"You...can get cake without a wedding. I do. And you don't like no one, Delovoa."

"I like...some. You okay."

"Thanks," I said.

"You know. I'm pretty sure I be dead without you, Hank."

"Yeah."

"No. No. I mean it," he said.

"Yeah."

"I'm. I'm be serious. You stick up for me."

"I know. You dead."

"What about you? You think you be die without me?"

"Nah."

"Hank?"

"Yeah?"

"Hank?"

"Yeah?"

"Wait. Lemme. Let me talk. Let me talk."

"Alright. Alright. You talk."

"Shushy! I...I...don't like Laesa," Delovoa said.

"I know. She don't like you."

"What? Why? That's mean. Why?"

"I don't know. You just...you kinda weird, Delovoa."

"What?"

"I'm weird. Not like...you weird. You *really* weird," I said.

"What?"

"It okay. Okay. Don't worry."

"You think...Cliston likes me?" Delovoa asked.

"Not really."

CHAPTER 26

My wedding day didn't start out like I thought it would. I wasn't woken up by Cliston. I wasn't dressed by Cliston. I didn't have my food prepared by Cliston.

Cliston had been working all night preparing the actual church for the wedding. He wrote me a 148-page manual of what I was supposed to do. It had a separate manual just with illustrations and a separate glossary of terms. It detailed how I was supposed to dress and the cultural significance of each garment and color; how to make my food and the nutritional ramifications of each selection; how to get to the church and the traffic patterns of Belvaille stretching back fifteen years; and nearly every probable or improbable event that could possibly happen from now until the day I died.

The time it took him to write this you'd think he could have just whipped me up some food or laid out my clothes.

I did my best to follow the instructions on what I was supposed to do, but it was far too complicated. Cliston's methods were great for Cliston or some unlikely Cliston-like creature. But the reason he was the best butler in existence was because no one else could do all these small details as perfectly as he did.

I showered and ate some dry space station rations. I used to love rations. They were a perfect food designed to be stored and shipped across the galaxy and keep whole populations alive. But I had since been introduced to butler-created recipes. My palette had evolved. Now I could taste the chemicals in the rations. There were hints of nitrates, an impression of wet cardboard, and an aftertaste that was reminiscent of a particularly abrasive dish soap. I suppose everyone changes. Even me.

Here I was getting married. Living in stately apartments that used to be City Hall. I had a Dredel Led butler. The police chief was one of my best friends. I somewhat regularly spoke with Boranjame. And I hadn't done anything technically illegal in years—though that was partially because of Belvaille's absence of laws.

If I had told my young self this would be my future life, I wouldn't have believed a word of it. I would say time got away from me, but I remembered everything. Not the names, of course. Or the dates. Or a lot of the finer details. And I probably mixed up some of the rough outlines. But I remembered the broad strokes. I'd done a lot. I'd lived a lot.

It was time to get married. Laesa was a great woman. Not great as in there would be statues of her. Who would want to be married to that? But great for me.

Still, it was a big decision. I couldn't say I'd really thought a lot about it. Was this cold feet? Was this what everyone went through? I was getting married!

The doorbell rang and I didn't pay any attention. Cliston always got the door. It rang about ten more times in rapid succession.

I walked over to answer it.

Delovoa was standing outside, his ugly body swathed haphazardly with three robes of conflicting colors. He waved a huge stack of papers in my face.

"How am I supposed to follow these instructions? Cliston wrote me a damn encyclopedia," he said.

Delovoa tried to storm past me, but his robes were tangled around his legs so he had to kind of hop-scoot.

"Are we going now?" I asked.

"Yes, but I have to walk inside first. Look around. And slap you." Delovoa slapped me with his be-robed hand.

"Is the slap some ceremony thing?"

"No. I'm just mad you're making me do this," he said.

We went downstairs to Delovoa's creepy van.

We got in and Delovoa drove us away.

"Are you hungover?" I asked him, after last night's drinking session.

"No. I took out one of my brains. So don't ask me anything about smells or the relationship between shapes because I don't know."

"Shapes? Don't you need that to drive?"

"Not really. Besides, I'm still a better driver than you," he said.

I sat there quietly for the rest of the trip, not wanting to disturb my chauffeur who was operating on two-thirds of his normal brains.

We got to the address and parked in front of the building. Delovoa actually parallel parked without hitting the curb or the two nearest cars. Everyone had to show off.

"It doesn't look like a church," I said, standing outside the tall, imposing building.

"How many churches have you seen in your life?" Delovoa asked, next to me.

"The Sublime Order of Transcendence kind of had churches," I said, referring to an old cult that had existed on Belvaille in times past.

"That was just a money-making scheme."

"Then I guess just this one. But it still doesn't seem very church-like, does it?"

"How should I know? Come on."

I had invited nearly everyone I knew to my wedding, which was a lot of people, but I wasn't certain how many would show up. Just to be sure, I had MTB as my head usher and appointed the toughest, roughest guys as backups who could be entrusted to keep the peace.

We walked up to the front door and MTB was standing there looking sour next to a five-foot pile of guns.

"Void, MTB, did you bring enough weapons?" I asked.

"Cliston told me to frisk everyone and take their arms," he replied.

"Don't they have a coat room?" Delovoa inquired.

"This church is for lizards. I guess they don't wear coats.," MTB said.

"Have there been any fights?" I asked.

"No. Cliston's been serving food and drinks."

"Drinks? Is he crazy?" Delovoa asked, alarmed.

"I think Cliston put something in them to calm everyone down. Some kind of herb-infused beer."

Delovoa and I shared a concerned expression.

"It's not too late to run," Delovoa said.

"Come on," I answered.

We went inside and were greeted with an enormous main room filled with pews. Along the back wall were dozens of stained glass pictures of Procon Hobb doing all kinds of stately Procon Hobb things. The pews were packed with Belvaille's thugs and criminals. Many of them appeared to be asleep.

"I knew no one could be as 'nice' and 'proper' as Cliston! That herb beer must be poisoned," Delovoa said.

"Good afternoon," Cliston answered, approaching from nowhere.

"Gah!" Delovoa jumped.

Cliston was wearing his priest outfit, which was a perfect and handsome interplay of overlapping robes of various shades and materials that hinted at the complexity of the universe. On seeing him, I realized what Delovoa's outfit was *supposed* to look like. Delovoa appeared as if he rolled around in a dozen colored sheets that bunched up on his body.

"Is everything okay, Cliston?" I asked.

"Ahead of schedule and no complaints," he replied.

"Did you have to use the ushers on anyone?" I asked.

"Several guests became slightly unruly over some apparent business disagreements but I took care of things myself," he said.

Cliston examined Delovoa's swirling toga maelstrom.

"You are not dressed according to my specifications," Cliston stated severely.

"Don't kill me. I'll fix it, Cliston!" Delovoa replied.

"No. *I* will fix it. The Alternate Man is not going to spoil this event," Cliston said.

Cliston *picked up* Delovoa and hurried away.

"Isn't he supposed to call me 'sir'?" Delovoa asked, as he was rushed off.

The crazy thing about the church was that it was lit with *candles*. Candles and big oil lamps. I thought they were very realistic imitations at first. But, no. Those were real live candles and sconces of oil lanterns and even oil chandeliers. As if a church dedicated to you wasn't enough, having it filled with consumable light sources showed just how unbelievably wealthy Procon Hobb was. He had to ship all that here. Load up freighters full of lamp oil and fly it across the galaxy just so he could set it on fire. It would probably be cheaper to literally burn money instead of spending a billion credits to make the biggest fire hazard on Belvaille. If we had building codes, this place would be shut down for sure.

As I was gawking at the lights, one of my ushers approached. His name was Kramfaze and I knew for a fact he had been shot at least fifteen times in his life and yet he still enjoyed being a gang heavy. For some people—like me—it's all they knew how to do; for other people, it's an adrenaline high; for Kramfaze, I think he enjoyed getting shot. Still, he was a cool customer and I trusted him to keep the peace—unless someone pulled a gun and then he'd probably run in front of it.

"Cog-a-jations, Hank," he stumbled. He could talk fine, but he probably never said "congratulations" before. It wasn't a common word on Belvaille.

When Delovoa and I were drinking last night, we tried to come up with the shortest sentence that had never been spoken before on the Belvaille. We settled on: "Morality obligates me to decline fornication."

"Thanks, Kramfaze. Where am I supposed to go? Up there?" I said, pointing to the front of the church.

"No! Only Cliston goes up there!" He answered, concerned. "You go to a side room and wait. Says 'goom' on the door.

"Goom or groom?" I asked.

Kramfaze shrugged.

"Does one letter matter?"

"No," I agreed.

I walked away from my usher and he called after me.

"Don't come out of that room until Cliston says it's okay. Trust me, you don't want that Dredel Led pissed off."

I went down the hall and found the room I was supposed to wait in and I began waiting. There was another set of instructions that Cliston had set out that detailed the actual service. The collection of pages was about the size of a large pillow.

I sat down, made myself comfortable, and began flipping through.

About ten minutes later, Delovoa came in, out of breath, and dressed perfectly in his assortment of robes. Even with his monstrous face and hands peeking out, he looked almost respectable.

"Wow," I said. "You totally screwed up that outfit on your own."

"Cliston practically strangled me," he said.

"Have a seat."

"Not a chance! He warned me what would happen if I got even a single wrinkle in this. I'm going to stand until this wedding is over. And then one more day to be sure."

"Suit yourself. Do you know what we're supposed to do when the wedding begins?" I asked.

"You have to do some acting."

"What?" I skimmed through the manual that was on my lap.

"Yeah. It's a celebration of emotional exposition."

"How do you know that?" I asked.

"When he wasn't choking me and twirling me around, he talked about what I was supposed to do."

"What do *you* have to do?"

"I'm not allowed to say, but I have to go practice in a minute."

"Did he say what page this acting stuff was on?"

"No. Let me remain here peacefully a moment and forget angry Cliston. I might have to take out another brain after that traumatic experience," he said.

The door to the room opened and my uncle Frank came in.

"What's up, dumbass?" Frank said to me by way of greeting.

He was dressed in his usual dingy clothes and even had a grease smudge on his face. There's no way Cliston knowingly allowed my uncle inside.

"I thought you said you didn't invite Frank," Delovoa said.

Frank turned casually to face Delovoa.

"Beat it, nerd. I want to talk to my nephew alone."

When Delovoa didn't move, Frank took a menacing step closer to him.

"I said leave. Before I stick my hand down your throat and pull your butthole out of your mouth."

Delovoa left without hesitation or comment.

"What do you want?" I asked.

Frank walked over and pulled up a chair and sat down. He didn't like the armrests, which were too narrow for his muscular frame, so he snapped them off.

"How is life, Hank?"

"Life's a game. And I'm losing," I said automatically. "Wait, that's not true. I'm getting married! Life is fantastic."

"For some reason, people think I have some pull with you. That you listen to what I say."

"Every time I listen to you I regret it," I replied.

"That's what I told them. But here I am," he shrugged.

"Well?" I asked.

"Okay, kid, let's get out of here."

I couldn't believe my uncle. All of a sudden he wanted to be pals.

"I'm not hanging out with you. The ceremony starts soon."

"I know. I'm taking you out of here. I thought you might be running some kind of grift I couldn't figure out, maybe taking this dame for her money or family connections. But I checked her out, she's got nothing."

"Not that I care, but she's starting to make serious money," I countered.

"She wasn't when you got engaged."

"Maybe I'm in love. Did that ever occur to you?" I asked.

"Kid, our kind doesn't do this."

"Do what? Have normal relationships? Not blackmail and use their nephews?"

"That's right," he said. "Marriage exists for a lot of reasons. But all those reasons have to do with evolution. *We* didn't evolve."

"Speak for yourself. I even carry a handkerchief," I began.

"I'm not talking about you and me specifically. Our species."

"Right. I'm supposed to find some nice Ontakian gal and repopulate our race? Here's some news, Uncle, our home world is destroyed. My chances of meeting a decent Ontakian woman just went from lousy to astronomical."

"When I say evolve, I mean our species was created in test tubes. Ontakians never developed all these crazy social customs that other races took tens of thousands of years to build. Everything we know and needed was implanted into us."

"I had parents. I wasn't created in a test tube," I said.

"Yeah. Ontakians got like five generations of actually making our own babies. That's the blink of an eye as far as evolution goes. You ever think about your parents? How your dad sacrificed himself to give you a life and your mom stayed on Ontak to fight? Does that sound like a happy family to you? They just happened to be two people who had a baby. Ontakians don't *do* marriage."

"You saying my parents weren't married?" I asked slowly.

"How should I know? If they were, I never went to a wedding. I think Ontakians just kind of agreed they were married at some point."

"That's ridiculous," I replied.

"It worked for us. If people got fed up, they stopped being married. We weren't designed to be sappy and sentimental. You, me, and your parents were designed for combat. The fact we can even get along with normal people without ripping their heads off is a testament to our good natures. But you're living in a dream world if you think you'll settle down and be content. Ontakians don't die of old age. We die fighting."

"Great speech, Frank. But I'm in love with Laesa."

"The fact you've come this far means you're either having the first-ever Ontakian mid-life crisis, or that Damakan witch is controlling you."

"Controlling? Why would *anyone* go out of their way to marry me? She could get someone wealthy," I said.

"Maybe she doesn't want that. Maybe she wants someone exciting. To her, you're probably a real-life action hero. But she'll get tired of it quick or you'll end up getting her killed. Bulletproof people need to hang out with other bulletproof people or it's going to end in bullet holes. That's just common sense."

"Frank, you have never done anything for me. You tell me bits and pieces of my childhood like you're dispensing top secret evidence. You've caused nothing but trouble since I've known you and I honestly wish we never met. I know a lot of really selfish people, but you're the only person who would throw me off a cliff without a second thought if you could make a single credit from it. I have to think you're talking to me now because you expect something out of this. Like you're worried I won't give you any more money. Or help you in your shifty deals. You can't possibly convince me you have my best interests at heart. It would be the first time."

"You're wrong, kid. Maybe I'm just old. Your father and I were born in test tubes. We were combat models, top to bottom. But when he knew our home world was doomed, he chucked everything to give you a chance. I never had kids, but I can see why he done what he done. I never did you any wrong that I knew you couldn't handle. But this, this is too much for you. This will tear you up more than any armor piercing missile. This isn't a trip to the hospital when you're done."

"What exactly do you think Laesa *is?* I'm confused."

"I think she's a Damakan. And she has focused every ounce of her ability on making you fall for her. It couldn't have been easy. Everything I hear, she's not a good actor."

"She's a great actor," I said.

"Like every species, some are better than others. You're a better combat model than your father and mother put together."

"You always do this! Trickle out bits of information from my past to jerk me around. I can't believe anything you say."

"I know that girl is trouble. Big trouble."

"You've never even *met* her."

"She was working piss jobs until recently. And she only moved up because of Cliston—who happens to work for you."

"He's a talent agent. He doesn't work for me."

"Cliston is a Dredel Led. He's a lot more complicated than you think," Frank said.

"I know how complicated he is. But talent agent Cliston barely even likes me. He wouldn't do me any favors."

"He would. Especially if he knew you were in deep. Maybe Laesa threatened him."

"*Threatened Cliston?*" I asked, stunned. "That is the most idiotic thing I've ever heard in my life! Wait, wait. Let me record this. I want to watch it to remind me how screwed up you are."

I took out my tele and started recording Frank.

"So, Frank. Please explain how little Damakan Laesa Swavort threatened the 10,000-year-old Dredel Led, Cliston. Who, if he had an evil circuit in his body, could kill every single person on this space station. Hell, he's probably written *manuals* on how to exterminate space stations."

"I don't mean she physically threatened him."

"Damakan abilities don't work on Dredel Led," I said, still recording.

"No. But they work on you. And Cliston cares about you."

"Yeah. He's my most favorite Dredel Led butler."

"What if Laesa told him she would destroy you if Cliston didn't help her career?"

I switched off my tele. Frank had a poker face.

"This whole time you've been throwing stuff against the wall, seeing what you could make stick. It was comical in a way. Good old ruthless Frank. Always dependable. But I ain't laughing now."

"I'm not either, kid."

"You need to get out. Get out of this church. Get out of my sight," I said.

"I'm not going without you."

I took a step closer.

"You're going. You can walk out, or you can drag what's left of your body out that door. I don't want to kill you on my wedding, but you and I are through. Get out. Now!" I said.

Frank sat there in his busted chair, cool as liquid nitrogen. He stood up quickly, and I instinctively took a step back, putting my arms up for a fight.

"Alright. But I warned you," he said. Then he turned his back and walked out.

CHAPTER 27

The time for the ceremony had come and I stood at the front of the cathedral.

Cliston was at a lectern in his tall hat and robes. The building was designed for lizards of various sizes and shapes, but I noticed a lot of people sitting in the pews were uncomfortable.

Garm flashed a wry grin and nod. Poor gal, probably still hot for me.

Delovoa, as my Alternate Man, stood in his straightened robes and played a complicated musical instrument. It had strings, a bellows, and electronics.

"I didn't know you could play music," I whispered to him.

"Shut up. Don't mess up my concentration," he hissed.

Delovoa was only playing about five different moves over and over again. He was mouthing along some instructions that Cliston must have relayed, and his three eyes were blinking to the rhythm. The music itself sounded complex but eerie.

Cliston was too tall for the lectern, it being designed for the diminutive, administrative-type lizards who served Procon Hobb. It only came up to about his waist. But Cliston appeared so majestic and serene that every wedding from now on would probably require a Dredel Led minister in a reptile cathedral to be considered official.

Without any pomp or notice, Laesa joined me at the front of the church.

She was radiant!

She wore her hair in pigtails. Her dress was comprised of tight, white leggings. Garters. Lacy panties. A long, sheer, skirt kind of thing that hung down behind her. And a white, half-bustier top with a plunging neckline that showed off her cleavage. It was a bit risqué but perfect for a Belvaille ceremony.

She took my breath away. I had never seen Laesa Swavort look so unbelievable. She didn't even glance at me and stood facing Cliston. But I couldn't take my eyes off her.

If that wedding ring she gave herself was true, we had a thousand years of bliss ahead of us. I couldn't wait.

I was only briefly aware of the scene. I knew this was an important event in my life, but it felt like a dream. Not a dream where I was walking around in my underwear or a dream where I was trying to run but couldn't. The kind of dream where everything you think will happen, does happen, no matter how ridiculous, and no one thinks it's ridiculous. Everything was wonderful.

"Oi, yoze, Hank! I got a question," MTB yelled at the rear of the church, snapping me out of my dream.

I turned to see him standing at the back of the pews in the middle of the aisle.

"Dude. I'm getting married up here! Do you mind?"

"I know, I know. But Hank. Are you friends with Kaxle?"

"What? No. I hate that guy," I yelled back.

"Yeah. I thought I remembered you saying something like that." MTB began running away from the exit. "Gate crasher!"

The main stained glass window of the cathedral featured an image of a saintly-looking Procon Hobb. The glass shattered as Kaxle came *flying* into the church! Kaxle hovered uneasily in the air, the bottoms of his enormous power armor legs spouting jet flames that must have been ten feet long.

The engines cut off abruptly and Kaxle fell to the floor with a crash. He landed poorly and began to topple over in the cumbersome battlesuit. But then a high-pitched whirring noise kicked in and Kaxle immediately righted himself. Either Delovoa had installed new rocket boosters and a gyroscopic balance in that armor, or Kaxle had recently discovered more line items on Delovoa's infinite invoice.

It figured that my wedding would begin with violence. Or end with violence. Or have violence at the reception. But this ceremony was a terrible place to attack. My audience was comprised of every hitman, thug, strong-arm, and malcontent that we could fit inside. It would be safer to attack a bomb factory than my wedding.

I expected my audience to joyfully rise and hammer this Rough Boy into submission. But they didn't move.

Cliston, in his role as wedding planner, had calmed down the hundreds of competing gang members from hundreds of different sub-species of Colmarians. He couldn't drug them all, they had different physiologies. So he got some drunk, others drugged, overfed some, and entertained the rest. He so bedazzled and besotted them, that they were currently about as useful as a straightjacket on a stripper. This was Cliston's soft power at its finest, but it was lousy timing.

When I beat Kaxle before, it was only because he had fallen down and the massive armor was incapable of getting up on its own. But as Kaxle took several strides toward me, I could see he was moving more confidently and with less hesitation.

"According to Damakan matrimonial law, I hereby certify a grievance to this proposed union. May the opposed thespians forthwith elucidate their emotional pretext," Cliston loudly proclaimed.

Kaxle looked at Cliston. I looked at Cliston. He spoke so authoritatively you simply had to acknowledge him.

"You may begin," Cliston stated.

Delovoa and Laesa were backing away but Cliston hadn't flinched.

"Cliston, get behind me," I yelled.

"No. I must adjudicate this Damakan petition," he replied.

"You're not a Damakan. You're not even a Colmarian!"

"I will file that as a separate grievance," he stated.

If Kaxle cut loose with his barrage of fireworks inside this building, it would cause massive casualties. And the fireworks were the least of his weapons. If he fired the freeze cloud or mortar it would be even worse.

"Garm. MTB. Delova. Get Laesa and get everyone out of here!" I screamed.

I rushed at Kaxle, tearing apart my suit with my efforts. My shoes splintered into confetti. Kaxle roared and raised his monstrous metal claw.

CHAPTER 28

Everyone I knew was at this wedding. Well, not everyone. I knew a lot of people. All the people I liked were here. Well, I didn't *like* everyone—sometimes you had to invite important jerks or they'd get offended. And some people I *did* like didn't come because they were busy—or because they didn't like me in return.

In any case, I would be unhappy if everyone inside the building was murdered.

But Delovoa was dragging Laesa toward the exit. And Garm, MTB and my ushers were trying to pull the drugged audience to safety. I had to keep this Rough Boy occupied while they cleared out.

I knew I couldn't outfight Kaxle. Not in any conventional way. But my mind was racing on how I might deal with him. Or at least slow him down. Outside his armor, Kaxle was *nearly* as strong as I was. But he was much lighter and less resistant. *In* the armor, he was impervious, weaponized, and powerful.

Every joint on Kaxle's armor needed a motor to move. I evaluated which mechanisms were the biggest. The pneumatic pistons that bridged Kaxle's forearms and biceps were huge, as were the motors at the tops of his shoulders. The leg servos were massive, but those were just so he could move around all that hardware.

I got the sense that Kaxle could lift his arms very forcefully, but he couldn't actually push or pull very well. On a normal Colmarian, our chests are about our strongest muscles on our upper bodies. But the battlesuit didn't engines on the front, instead, that area was covered with armor. So Kaxle couldn't actually punch very hard without twisting his waist or swinging an uppercut

Kaxle lowered his left claw and extended his bladed flingers. I knew he was going to use that powerful bicep piston to try and rip me open.

It was counterintuitive, and quite insane, but I rushed closer. I got right up to his chest, almost in kissing distance.

Kaxle swung the claw upward, but I was too close.

He bodily bumped into me and it was like an immovable object hitting an immovable object. We proceeded to not move.

If that robotic claw had been attached to his real, biological arm, he could bend the wrist and stab my back. But the armor couldn't dream of behaving that way. It could only move in very broad, linear strokes.

Pressed up against Kaxle. Leaking motor oil and axle grease were smearing across my tuxedo. I saw a couple frayed wires sticking out of the armor that were belching sparks. This was a true Delovoa invention. If I had an extra thirty minutes, I could probably just wait around and the power armor would explode all by itself.

But I didn't have that luxury. I had to protect Laesa.

And then get married.

"Hank! No now. Not yours in time," Kaxle yelled in my face.

"Your mother!" I replied. I wasn't sure what he was saying, but I assumed it was an insult.

Kaxle tried to swivel and get away from me. But his feet and legs, which were reinforced to carry that weight, and housed rockets capable of flying, were not nimble enough to sidestep. The armor was really good at stomping forward, turning in place, and stomping forward some more. Maybe it could back up, but knowing Delovoa, that probably wasn't a major concern. And what criminal asks for a powered battlesuit that has a reverse gear?

"I stronger than you. I can fly!" Kaxle snarled.

"I can fly too!" I yelled back. "Like your mother," I added for good measure.

"Only when you're in outer space," someone in the audience corrected. There were a lot of murmurs of agreement that I could hear above the din of battle. Here they were, facing imminent destruction in an alien cathedral, and they decided to stick around, spectate, and give commentary.

"Hey, shut up!" I said.

Kaxle moved his arms to try and bear-hug me. His right cannon was so wide and his left claw so thick, that he kept bumping them into each other, unable to embrace me.

He began roaring in frustration and each turn of his arms and rise of his shoulders squirted more oil at me. It sounded comical, but it burned my eyes and it was getting really hard to see.

"Here you go, sir," Cliston said, reaching in and wiping off my face with a handkerchief.

"Cliston! Butler Cliston! Is Laesa safe?" I asked.

Cliston replaced his minister hat abruptly.

"Each of you must mirror the other and portray the inner plangency that has beget this discordance," Cliston intoned.

"What you say, Cliston?" Kaxle asked.

"Yeah, quit interrupting us," I added, as if Kaxle and I were discussing philosophy.

"Hank," Laesa called. I couldn't tell where she was.

I had to get Kaxle out of here. But he had other ideas. Dropping his cannon arm, he hugged me with just his left, clawed arm. The motors spun and gears whirred.

The arm pressed against my back, smushing me up against Kaxle. The taste of oil was in my mouth and in my nostrils. As the air was pushed out of my lungs and I began to realize that getting close to Kaxle had been a bad move. But then I heard the armor's shoulder gears slipping.

It was like *wrrrr, wrrr...clack! Wrrr, wrrr...clack!*

My face was turning red but at least I wasn't being squashed. He couldn't pull his arms in with enough force to actually crush me. The armor wasn't designed for it. Delovoa had neglected to add that line item.

"Hah. Thak," I said to Kaxle. I was trying to say, "Hah, I have thwarted your nefarious plans, you cantankerous contraption." Well, I was going to say *something,* maybe not that exactly. But something cool.

This was usually my sweet spot. I was a wrestler. I couldn't punch people very well. I didn't know where anyone's nerve clusters resided. Every time I tried to kick someone I ended up falling down. I wasn't even a good shot with a gun.

But I could grapple. I could pull people around like a tow truck on a joyride. But Kaxle's armor had enormous legs and feet. I think even with a running start I couldn't knock him over.

While he used one arm to hug me he had his cannon arm completely free. I was obviously too close for him to aim it directly at me, but he could shoot the floor. Or the walls. That would hurt the both of us. More urgently, it would hurt everyone in the building. But I couldn't break free from his grip and I couldn't budge him from this spot.

"Clist-Cliston," I gasped.

"Do you have a further grievance to register, entertainer?" the minister asked.

"Help."

"I'm afraid I can't take part," he replied.

Great. I was going to die up here. Before my honeymoon. Before I was even married. I had access to a super robot, but he was stuck in the wrong personality.

"Butler Cliston," I said.

He didn't reply.

"There's a spot. On the floor," I managed.

"Where, sir?" Cliston chirped, alarmed.

"Behind. There. No. Further. Down." I said.

Cliston bent over to inspect the ground at the microscopic level. It seemed amazing that he was not concerned about the dripping oil or blood from our fight. But Cliston was weird.

I saw this done in a tele movie with a lot of slapstick comedy. What I had done was manage to get Cliston on his hands and knees positioned behind Kaxle. I pushed Kaxle as hard as I could, my back screaming in protest.

Kaxle went to reposition his leg to stabilize himself and bumped into Cliston. Cliston was a Dredel Led robot. I'm not sure what he was made out of, but it wasn't feathers.

Kaxle tipped. I heard his gyro spinning to try and rebalance. He let go of me and that allowed me to push even harder. The gyro couldn't cope and Kaxle fell backwards, his legs coming down hard on Cliston. Kaxle was so heavy the tile floor shattered.

"Cliston!" I yelled.

I pulled on the arms of my butler and minister to try and extract him.

"Sir, there is no spot," Cliston said.

"I know, Cliston. Sorry. I had to get away."

I managed to yank Cliston free. His robes were torn and his torso had a lot of scratches, but he seemed okay.

"Sir, I have to tell you that to secure this church, we had to put down a sizeable security deposit. Your efforts are getting us dangerously close to forfeiting our funds."

Kaxle was on his back, flailing. The gyro couldn't lift him from the ground.

"I wish Delovoa hadn't run off. He could tell me how to deal with this stupid armor," I said.

My tele rang.

"Sir, your tele."

"I don't have time for that! I have to—"

"Hank's tele, Cliston speaking," Cliston said, having removed my tele and answered before I could finish complaining. "Sir, it's Delovoa."

"What?"

I grabbed the tele.

"Hank," Delovoa said calmly. "Great wedding. What entertainment is planned for the reception? A live volcano?"

"Did you get Laesa out?" I asked.

"I'm fine, thanks. She's fine as well."

"How do I fight Kaxle?"

"It's powered by Keilvin Kamigan fuel cells."

"So can I like, hotwire that or something?" I asked.

"Stop trying to be smart, Hank. You're not smart," Delovoa barked on the tele.

"So what can I do?"

"Overload the batteries. I didn't put any resistors or circuit breakers in the armor because...well, because I didn't feel like it."

"How do I do that? I'm not a Keilvin Kamigan," I said.

"No, stupid, but you invited one to your wedding."

There Zzzho was, "sitting" at a pew. Just a small cloud of red gas and purple lightning bolts. He hadn't bothered leaving because he likely wasn't concerned about the fight. It's not as if Kaxle and I were wielding dangerous air filters.

The problem was, Zzzho didn't have ears. Or a mouth. Or eyes. Or an anything. How could I communicate with him?

"Zzzho!" I yelled in frustration.

A moment later, a small gas cloud was in front of me.

"Hey," I said. "Can you hear me?"

"Yes," he replied. His voice came from the church speakers. I hadn't really noticed, but the ceremony was being amplified through the building. Zzzho must be plugging into the audio system, his body stretched out beyond what I could immediately see.

"Zzzho, I need your help," I said.

"I can't," he replied.

"You don't even know what I need."

"I'm not Zzzho. I'm Zzzha," he replied.

"You're...one of the other guys—gasses? Zzzho's friend?"

"Yes."

"You have to work on that name, buddy. But can you charge, overcharge, that armor? Like plug into the batteries and make them more—like not work?"

"I can try," he said.

Kaxle had his cannon barrel flush with the floor and was trying to use it to hoist himself up. The triple-barreled cannon turned. I heard the *clunk* of ammunition being loaded.

Oh, no.

A big *whump* of exhaust shot across the floor as Kaxle fired pointblank at the tiling. The recoil was enough to push him upright and the whirring gyro stabilized him. He hadn't fired a mortar shell and they certainly weren't fireworks. It didn't do "much" except launch a massive power armor mutant about four feet into the air.

But he was now standing. And angry.

Suddenly, the sparks that had been sizzling on the armor glowed blue and arced against anything metallic within a dozen feet. The motor oil spewed out in thin jets. The gyro screamed so loud I thought the windows would shatter. The triple cannon spun faster than I could see.

Zzzha had succeeded. The armor was overcharged and Kaxle looked concerned that his metal coffin was misbehaving.

"Hah, you don't have any surge resistors in that armor," I said, pointing. "Maybe next time you should make friends with people I like to refer to as—"

Kaxle fast-walked over to me, swung his cannon arm like a club, and knocked me thirty feet away before I could finish gloating.

I smacked into the wall just underneath the enormous stained glass window with a Kaxle-sized hole in it. My journey had caused me to plow through an elaborate altar. Lots of candles. Gold and silver sculptures. I couldn't tell what religious purpose it served because it was now a heap of junk I happened to be sitting on.

I wobbly returned to my feet, leaning heavily against the wall for support. On rising, my shoulder bumped an ornately framed picture of Procon Hobb. It was holographic, and expensive. It tilted and fell. I tried to catch it, bobbled it from one hand to the other, and my movements caused me to accidentally knock over a crystalline vase and bowl that had been resting on an ivory stand. The picture hit the floor and cracked. The vase and bowl shattered.

"Sir," Cliston announced, suddenly at my side. "I've calculated that our security deposit has nearly been exhausted. If you could refrain from destroying anything more, you might enjoy a more financially stable married life."

"Tell him that!" Kaxle had his back to me. He probably punted me away so far he didn't even see where I went. "The Keilvin Kamigan thing didn't work," I yelled.

My tele rang.

"Hank's wedding and arena fight, Cliston speaking. Yes? Very well. I will relay that. Are you enjoying the ceremony so far? Thank you. They were imported from the Rettosian colony. Yes, they moved and created a new habitation. Very exclusive. I'm not sure. I could inquire if you like."

"Hey! Is that Delovoa? What did he say?" I asked.

"He wanted me to tell you that the Keilvin Kamigan overcharge idea didn't succeed," Cliston replied.

"I *know* that. Why did you say arena fight? You usually don't make jokes."

"No, sir. I have taken the liberty of billing this event as a duel. We have most of the station's bookies in the audience. The house, that is, your wedding, stands to make a sizeable chunk of the gambling proceeds."

"Were you planning this all along?"

"No, sir. It has taken me quite by surprise. But it is my belief it will help offset the damages that are being done to the building. If you are uncomfortable with this arrangement, I can refund all wagers."

"No. Might as well. What are my odds of winning?"

"I don't set the odds. But from what I gather, they aren't good, I'm afraid. But there is a high probability of you surviving, sir."

"Well, there's that. Alright then."

I moved to head off Kaxle.

Kaxle stood at the front of the church trying to control his hyper-charged armor. The cannon was still spinning, the left leg was bucking, his clawed arm swung like a windmill and seemed about ready to tear Kaxle's arm from the socket.

Since he was facing the other way, I thought this was my opportunity to get in a cheap shot.

I reached down and picked up one of the shattered tiles from the floor. It was some kind of fake marble and fairly heavy. Not that I needed a weapon to bash against Kaxle, but there was so much gear on his back that I couldn't hit his head without some extra reach.

I hefted the tile for an overhead smash against the back of the mutant's skull.

"Kaxle! Behind you," gang boss Podiver Vance yelled. He was standing up at his pew, his nine-foot, gangly frame looking both too tall and too thin to contain that much of a jerk.

"Come on, man. You're a guest at my wedding," I complained.

If it had been any other city in the galaxy, the person would have realized their social blunder and at least blushed. But Podiver Vance merely shrugged his spaghetti arms indifferently. He must be wagering on Kaxle to beat me in this fight and didn't care who knew.

Kaxle, now alerted, turned around. His legs stayed planted and his torso twisted. His spine was either more flexible than mine, or was broken in half.

With his detestable claw, he grabbed me about the waist. This all happened so fast I still had the tile hoisted above my head.

I half-heartedly brought it down on Kaxle's face. It shattered into fragments, but didn't appear to do any damage.

"Hah," I said triumphantly. "You got dust all over your fur. You look ridiculous."

Kaxle's face went from annoyed to alarmed. Not because of tile dust, because the engines on his legs activated and I got the idea it wasn't by choice. The Zzzha overcharge was still wreaking havoc with his systems.

Correction, one engine was firing. The other was sputtering. My pants caught on fire as flames leapt up from the floor.

Kaxle couldn't maintain his grip on me and he cartwheeled sideways three times in the air and blasted through a door to an adjoining hallway.

I had cuts around my midsection from the claw, but I seemed mostly okay, assuming no nanobots had been inserted. Watching Kaxle somersault like a professional gymnast despite being a massive mutant in a monster machine left me somewhat dazed.

I looked at my wedding crowd and saw Cliston walking amongst the gamblers and bookies who were yelling and wagering heavily at the latest turn of events. Podiver Vance seemed particularly disappointed and slumped in his pew, his knees poking up past his chin. People were speaking on their teles and there was even a small whiteboard erected with colored figures and odds. Not sure who brought that, but it was a lousy wedding present.

Laesa had returned!

"Hey, get out of here," I said to her.

"I have to be here for the wedding challenge," she said.

"It's not a challenge. It's just Kaxle being an ass."

"If I leave the building, I'm automatically married to the challenger," she added.

"Cliston!"

My priest and butler and fight promoter looked up.

"That is correct. If she exits or you exit, the challenge is validated."

"What a stupid culture. No offense, Laesa. Stay put."

I hurried after the rocket-assisted challenger into the next hall. Going around a corner I was immediately confronted by flames. His rocket legs had not merely displaced him, Kaxle was currently being dragged face first along the corridor.

The engines oscillated power and direction seemingly at random. The carpet, which looked pretty expensive at the corners still intact, was crumpled and tattered. That Delovoa-designed armor seemed to specifically seek out the most expensive stuff to destroy.

I covered my eyes to shield them from the jet exhaust and carpet fibers.

The rockets straightened and Kaxle shot down the hallway and blew through another door. I hurried after him.

The next room was a small antechamber, with a tall ceiling. Inside were a bunch of lizard people. They seemed to be engaged a ceremony of some sort. I couldn't say they looked surprised or shocked or angered to see us. But that's only because they looked like lizards.

"Hey," I shouted at them urgently. "This isn't the time or place to be having a baptism! Can't you hear what's going on? This is a wedding. Get out of here before you're killed!"

The lizards hurried away through the door we burst through.

Kaxle had his head smushed up by the rafters as his jets continued to flare. He couldn't physically push against the strength of his rockets.

I couldn't very well fight Kaxle while he was flying. The force of the exhaust was pushing me away and I was clear across the room.

I began coughing. The room was not especially ventilated and a mutant was flying his personal spaceship in the corner.

The jets finally shut off and Kaxle, face and fur bloodied and ragged fell to the ground. His gyro kept him on his feet, but he didn't look well. One of his fangs seemed broken, not sure if it had always been like that.

"So," I began, but then my throat caught. There still wasn't a lot of air in here.

As for the power armor, it was acting like a drop of cooking oil on a hot plate. It was sizzling. It vibrated all over. As if every gear was turning a centimeter back and forth a few thousand times a second.

Kaxle stretched his jaw. Rotated his teeth over and around. Licked at the blood in his mouth. I got the idea he was going to say something.

"*Raaawwwrrr!*"

Right. This was a creature. He might be in a high-tech deathtrap, but he was still a dumb beast.

He swung his claw in front and above him. He was attacking the ceiling that he had been smushed against. He was swung again. It was just blind rage. Animal rage.

But I could *use* this. I couldn't fight Kaxle muscle-to-muscle. I couldn't out-mutant him. Not in that armor, anyway. But I had a mind. A brain. I was far more intelligent.

Kaxle swung again. His claw sparked uselessly against the ceiling.

I faced him, my knees bent, my arms curled, hands flexing. My voice coughed a low, thoughtful cough.

I walked to the left as Kaxle took jerking, halting steps to my right. He roared again and took a swipe once at the air, at the floor, at the ceiling.

I needed to focus. He couldn't walk fast in that armor. Especially in this cramped room and that even more cramped hallway. He couldn't walk backwards.

That's it, *think.* I didn't have to punch him. Or grapple him. This sputtering, roaring creature was past the point of deduction. He was trapped inside that armor like it was a cage. Like at a zoo. Or a pet store. A *bad* pet store with a disinterested, teenage clerk that didn't like animals.

Kaxle swung and stomped and circled me. Blood was in his eyes, his fur was soaked and matted with it.

Keep him on edge. Keep him frothing. Kaxle could have never thought of using a Keilvin Kamigan to supercharge his opponent's armor. I did that! I mean, Delovoa told me. But I asked. Used the recourses available.

"I'm better than you, Kaxle. Your mutation owns you. Corrupted you. Turned you into a brute. Governed by violence."

Kaxle howled. It was long, undulating, and sent a chill up my back. I had to stay out of his reach.

"See?" I continued. "You don't even know you've lost. But you can sense it. Can't you? Your pathetic mind is struggling against that reality. But it's there. You're just too stubborn to accept it."

Kaxle whipped both his arms around in a fury. Good. I had to keep him angry enough that he didn't use his cannon. Make him want to stab me, crush me, anything. But if he fired that mortar in this tight room, it might kill us both.

"What you have to understand, Kaxle—" I began.

"Hank," Kaxle interrupted.

"Yeah?"

"You talk too much."

Kaxle swiped again at the ceiling and the roof collapsed!

On me.

I had been circling around and apparently didn't notice he had not been swinging blindly, he had been cutting the supports. Only part of the roof came down. Kaxle was fine.

I was on the floor and had a mound of metal and masonry on my back. I could see out of one eye, and could breathe, a bit, but I couldn't move.

Okay. That was pretty smart. Maybe Kaxle wasn't as dumb as all that.

"Kaxle?" I wheezed. "I usually don't do this, but I'm willing to call this a draw. Hell, I'll even write a nice entry about you in Scanhand."

I was prone. Defenseless. I expected to be stabbed or shot or poked. Instead, I heard the power armor fitfully walking away.

"Kaxle. Hey. Kaxle!"

He was gone, making his way down the next hallway, tripping over the crumpled carpet and banging on the walls to keep his balance. Probably ruining priceless frescos as he went.

"Well, crap."

I felt like buried treasure. Except not very valuable. Maybe someday I would be discovered and displayed in a museum. I couldn't do much more than blink my eye and flex one butt cheek. However, my eyelashes weren't long enough to dig me out and my butt wasn't nearly as big as everyone teased.

Much to my surprise, chunks from the pile on my back began to be removed. Piece by piece.

"Hello? Cliston? Garm? Podiver Vance?"

After a short while, I was able to push up and help dislodge the debris.

It was the lizard people. Not sure if it was the same ones I met when I came in, they all looked the same. Except I noticed that several of these lizards were missing limbs.

"Did Kaxle chop off your arms?" I asked, even though I didn't see any wounds.

"No. Someone froze us in the city and removed them," one of the lizards replied.

Oh, crap. Delovoa did that. He told me and I forgot.

"I don't know anything about that," I said quickly. "Thanks for digging me out."

"You must stop him," a lizard implored me.

"Delovoa? I'll tell him to stop stealing your body parts. What's he going to do with them, anyway? They're too small," I said.

"No, Kaxle. This building is sacred. You must preserve it," the lizard continued.

"Right. The church," I said. I stepped around the pile I had been trapped under and moved back toward the hallway. "Hey, maybe when you're doing renovations, make the ceilings so that they don't come crashing down if someone sneezes, huh? For a sacred building it sure is flimsy."

"This church is rated to withstand hurricane-force winds," my lizard savior replied.

"*Winds?* This is a space station. Like there's ever going to be a hurricane here. Make sure it's mutant resistant. Or bomb resistant. Or plasma weapon. Something practical."

I was beaten. Tired. Out of breath.

As I stepped back into the main room of the church, the wedding guests who saw me enter pointed, cheered, and modified the gambling odds.

Kaxle was standing at the very front of the pews, his back to me. He seemed to be trying to make impromptu repairs to his battlesuit. He was banging on one knee that was locked in the bent position. The armor had clearly suffered damage. A rainbow of colored fluids was seeping out. Numerous panels were dislodged or broken all over it. The back was smoking. And the claw had lost almost all of its metal blades, after ripping apart the ceiling.

"Sir, did you cause any further destruction while you were visiting the baptismal?" Cliston asked politely, after seeing me approach. "This facility has experienced tremendous depreciation since the start of your wedding. Procon Hobb will seek reimbursement."

"No, I didn't do nothing."

"I wanted to advise you that some of your guests have retired, sir."

"Good, at least they'll be safe."

"Pardon me, I believe I phrased that poorly. I meant to say they're dead, sir."

"How did they die? We weren't even in the room."

"I believe there was a disagreement over toilets."

"What?" I asked, distracted from Kaxle for a moment.

"Yes. They couldn't agree on the order of who would get to use the toilets first. It became rather heated, I'm afraid."

"Well, I guess they knew the dangers when they came to a wedding. Kaxle," I shouted.

The mutant in question slammed his leg into shape and turned around.

"Hank. You so stupid," he said.

"No I'm not. You are," I replied.

The wedding guests cheered at the witty banter. With Kaxle's armor damaged, I thought I might have a chance of beating him.

I rushed him. He brought his clawed fist down on my head with the force of a mutant in power armor. The lack of blades had not mattered in the slightest.

I fell to my knees and briefly blacked out. Blood was coming out of my ears and nose, and I think I nearly bit off my tongue.

Three barrels were inches away from my face. Big barrels. Cannon barrels. Seemed like an unsafe place to put them.

I pushed on the cannon, trying to steer it away from my head. We were grappling. Muscle versus machine. Both of us grunting and groaning with exertion.

"Hello. I realize you aren't technically a guest today, but would you care for something to drink? Or other refreshments?" butler Cliston asked Kaxle.

"Yes," Kaxle said with difficulty. "Please."

"Be back in a moment," Cliston replied.

I kept tilting the cannon arm upward. Kaxle hammered at me again and again with his busted claw. He was tired. He hit my shoulders. My neck. My face. They weren't gentle taps. I didn't giggle. But the armor wasn't responding well. The gears were stripped. The battery low. And the animal inside had just about had enough.

I reached up and grabbed a patch of his fur from his lower neck and pulled off a clump. Kaxle snarled in pain so I grabbed another fistful.

"Hah!" I said. "You're going to be cold."

Kaxle, using his broken claw, punched me straight in the mouth. All my front teeth shattered.

I backed up and spit. Tooth fragments and blood sprayed the floor.

"Stho what," I lisped. "I can regrow teeth. Can you regrow fur?" I asked, holding up my handfuls of Kaxle-hair.

"Of course. But not here for you, Hank," Kaxle said.

"*What?*" I screamed. "You always do this! This is my wedding! If you're here for one of my guests, settle it afterwards. Why did you make me kick your ass all over this church?"

"You didn't kick my ass. I kick yours," Kaxle said.

"Shut up and fight," someone in the audience yelled. Lots of people agreed. They were wagering on the outcome.

"You know, forget it. If you want one of my wedding *guests*, help yourself. I won't stop you. Who are you here for? I'll even point them out."

Kaxle scanned the audience for his target.

"Laesa," he said.

I stood there, my broken mouth agape.

"Laesa who?"

"Laesa Swavort. Damakan. *Her!*" Kaxle yelled. He pointed his claw at Laesa, who was cowering by the front pew.

"Hank?" she asked.

"No. She hasn't done anything. We're getting married. You can't! Fight me! I'll kill you! *I'll kill you!*"

I rushed at Kaxle, grabbed hold of his cannon arm and tried to stop him. I hit him. Kicked. Even attempted to bite his carbon carbon-steel power armor with my toothless mouth.

It took Kaxle two big steps to reach Laesa, as he dragged me along. I was a whirlwind, attacking Kaxle every way I possibly could.

Cliston lifted Laesa to her feet and was trying to pull her to safety. She didn't understand. She was still trying to stay, to prevent the marriage challenge. She couldn't comprehend the danger.

Kaxle raised his massive fist and brought it down hard on my defenseless Laesa.

It didn't matter that his armor was damaged, his claw blades were broken, or that I was pulling with all my strength to stop him. He was a powerful, mutant bruiser. To a normal person like Laesa, his punch was like being hit by a speeding truck.

Laesa was killed instantly.

CHAPTER 29

Laesa and I—when she was alive—had watched *countless* tele movies where a wife or daughter is killed and it sends the hero on a murderous rampage to exact revenge. It was a very common plot device. The shows had names like "Clenched Fist of Fingers," "Salty Bloody Bloodcake," or "Forever and Ever and Ever and Ever Dead."

Even at the time, I never much cared for those programs. You'd think being on Belvaille, the Damakans would know a thing or two about crime and violence. But they didn't. Or at least they chose not to show it. The movies were unrealistic and stupid.

Either those characters in the tele programs were complete psychopaths who had been *praying* someone they knew was killed so they could finally let loose, or Damakan movies were just bad fiction crafted by an innocent species that didn't understand how people truly behaved.

When Laesa was killed, I didn't attack Kaxle. I didn't hunt down the Rough Boys. I didn't run out of the church, grab a couple machine guns, and start shooting every drug dealer and jaywalker in sight.

My wife was murdered. I broke down and cried.

The next seven weeks after that were a blur.

"Seven *months*, sir," Cliston corrected.

I scowled at him and stumbled to the front door. I didn't feel like listening to Cliston lecture me on things. He had been doing that a lot. Lecturing about my hygiene or how much time had gone by or how I should stop sleeping so much.

"Shall I expect you back for dinner, sir?" he asked.

I left without a word because what use was it? I couldn't talk Laesa back to life and I couldn't talk away the pain I felt.

I walked to The Club to get drunk. I'd been drunk a lot lately. Pretty much the whole last seven weeks. Months. Whatever.

"Hey," Fample said at the coat check.

"Hey," I replied.

"No, stop," he clarified.

I kept walking.

"Stop him," Fample yelled at his security guards.

"*You* stop him," they replied.

"Hank, you stink. Take a shower. I'm running a business!" Fample added.

I settled into a first-floor booth in the corner. I grabbed the closest overhead light fixture and twisted it. I wanted to drink in the dark. The waiter didn't bother bringing any sausages or sandwiches. I went straight to the hard liquor.

It was a few or more days later and I finally had to use the bathroom. I hadn't moved from my spot in The Club. It was open all night and day, but I would technically get sleep when I periodically blacked out.

I got the sense they were bringing me less alcohol. And they piled up garbage around me before they took it out to the dumpster. They were trying to get me to leave, but it wasn't working.

I stood up from the booth and my pants stuck to the seat, ripping off. I shrugged. It was too hot in the city anyway.

I made it most of the way to the bathroom before I relieved myself against one of The Club's support beams.

"Hey!" the support beam yelled at me. I didn't know they could talk. And had red hair.

"Hank?" someone called from behind.

"I'm bitsy," I said. "Bitsy," I said again.

When I was less busy, I turned around and saw a bunch of familiar blurry faces.

"Droll Bloobooboo?" I asked.

"Yeah, it's your old buddy. Roll Bungalow," he said.

"And Ulteem."

"And Podiver Vance. Hi, Hank."

There were other names and blurs, but I blacked out momentarily. When I woke up, I was on the floor surrounded by legs and socks and shoes.

"I'm in Bootville," I laughed.

"Hank, we need to talk to you. Do you have a moment?" Podiver asked.

"No," I said, indignantly. I flopped on my back to try and get up, but failed. Bootville had powerful gravity.

"We want you to come back to work," Roll said.

"Work?" I asked.

Roll crouched down next to me so I could see his knees.

"Yeah. Things have...things have gone to hell. We all agree on that."

"I don't," I said.

"How would you know? You been inside a bottle for months," Ulteem accused. I could see he had on his fake head that he used when he wanted to persecute someone.

"Seven days," I countered.

"Look, we need the old Hank. We need you to work your magic. Belvaille is in bad shape. Even *you* must have seen that," Roll said.

"You want me to start...killing people?" I asked.

"No! We need you to put an end to it. It's madness. Worse than ever," Podiver—I think—said. He was so tall, his voice was from far away. So it was either Podiver or a ventriloquist who was using a lifelike Podiver mannequin.

"You many can," I stated.

"Hank," Roll's knees continued, "come on. We're willing to help you out if you can help us out."

I moved to my stomach and stood up, only falling four or five times.

"Who should I kill?" I asked.

"This guy is useless. I told you," Ulteem said.

"No one, Hank," Roll said. "Come on. Let's get you something to eat."

"Pfft. Food is gross. Don't you want me to kill anyone? Anyone at all?"

"How about yourself?" Ulteem grumbled.

I reached in my jacket and pulled out my shotgun. I was amazed it was still there. Amazed it was in my hand.

"How about I kill some Damakans? You all kill Damakans, right?"

I was floating the barrels of my gun around past the various gang bosses who were staging this intervention.

"You all were there. My wedding. You just...sat there and watched," I said.

"What are *we* going to do against Kaxle? You couldn't even stop him. We aren't muscle," Ulteem said.

"No. Never you. Always someone else. But it *is* you. You make it...make it dead. Make her dead. You killed Laesa!" I shouted.

"If anyone made Belvaille what it is, it's you," someone said.

I fired my gun. Fired again. I wanted the gang bosses gone. This was my murderous rampage. I was finally seeking vengeance for Laesa's death.

I tried to reload my gun but I realized it wasn't a gun. I was holding a rotten sausage that was covered in mold and sticky napkins. I didn't know how to load a sausage.

"Out! Out!" Fample yelled. I was also on the floor again. And everyone was gone. And I think it was tomorrow.

Four security guards were trying, and failing, to drag me out of the The Club. It's not that I was putting up a fight. I was dead weight. Truly dead. Fample was still screaming at me between my black outs.

"Banned! Banned for life! Your life! Everyone's life! My great-grandfather put up with you! My grandfather! My father! My—" Fample grabbed his tiny chest, overcome with emotion. His eyes were wide. He fell against the wall and slumped to the ground.

"Hah," I said, pointing, as the guards continued to heave on me.

It took them some hours to get me out the front door. They even hired some contractors to knock out part of the doorframe to make room for me.

I decided to pass out in front of The Club and catch a little shut eye. And this way everyone would have to walk around me to get into that lame establishment.

I woke up a few days later when a car ran into me.

As far as alarm clocks went, it was still better than Cliston yelling at me. I took a moment to count my arms and legs and fingers but somehow ended up with twenty-five and I knew that wasn't right. Still, it was better to be ahead than behind, right? I looked at the driver who was lying on the ground. He had gone through the windshield and was only a short distance away. I would normally be mad, but I was quite hungover, and it was too much effort. Besides, the driver looked familiar.

"Rendrae? When did you buy a car?" I asked him.

"Hank?" he replied weakly.

I pulled myself out of the auto wreckage and then helped Rendrae up.

"Thad Elon, you smell," he said.

I dropped him.

"What the damn hell are you doing driving on the sidewalk," I demanded.

"It's not the...this isn't the sidewalk," he said. "You were in the middle of the road."

I looked around, ready to argue. But it clearly wasn't the sidewalk. I wasn't even near The Club. Where was I?

"I was sleeping," I said finally.

"You were walking."

Rendrae collected himself and stood up.

"Maybe I was sleepwalking," I ventured.

"I've been looking for you for months. Where have you been?" Rendrae asked.

"Here."

"In the street?" he asked, confused.

"No. The Club, mostly. I just left. I think I'm going to drop my membership. Tired of that place."

"I went to The Club. They said they haven't seen you in weeks," Rendrae said.

"Who said that? Fample? He's lying."

"Fample is dead. I went to his funeral last week."

"You got any money I can borrow?" I asked.

"Hank. We were supposed to solve the gang war, remember? It's escalated. Everything is falling apart."

"Is that a 'no' on the money?" I asked.

"I realize...your wedding didn't work out. I'm sorry. Really. But people need your help. *I* need your help."

"Didn't 'work out'?" It's not like we got a bad wedding cake or the DJ didn't have our favorite song. My wife was murdered!"

"I realize that, Hank. But innocent people are being murdered all over the city."

"No one on Belvaille is innocent," I sneered.

"Was Laesa? Because a lot of her Damakan brethren have been killed. And if you don't care about that, a bunch of gang members. City workers. Bartenders. Shop owners. If you care about *any* group of people, some of them have been killed."

"I'm not a reporter. You don't need my help."

"Hank, I've been personally attacked a half-dozen times. Shot at. Laid up in the hospital twice. People don't want this story reported. I can't even talk to anyone anymore. Everyone is paranoid and shooting first. You're the only one I know who can ignore that and *force* people to talk."

"It's Scanhand. That's where the jobs come from," I said.

"But we don't know who runs Scanhand. I have a feeling it's Garm, but I can't prove it. She wants to land Navy troops here. They're going to take over."

I had to snort.

"Garm would suffer from that more than anyone."

"But that's how desperate things are. I'm surprised you aren't aware of this."

"Rendrae, I just don't care. I don't. Not at all. I'm done with this city. The vermin here watched my Laesa get killed. She could have lived her life in peace anywhere else in the galaxy. She had to come to Belvaille to get murdered. Marrying me got her killed."

"No, Hank. The gang war got her killed. You can help stop it. Prevent it from taking others."

"Why should I? This city has taken everything from me. Let it tear itself apart. I hope it does," I said, and I began walking away.

"What about my car?" Rendrae yelled.

"Sir. Sir. Sir. Sir," I heard Cliston saying.

He was shaking me. Hard. He might have been doing this for minutes, hours, or days. It was impossible to tell.

"What?" I asked, trying to go back to sleep.

"You cannot sleep on the floor, sir."

"Why not?"

"Because you have soiled yourself and I need to clean the carpet before it permanently stains."

I turned on my side to examine the carpet.

"That's not soil."

"In any case, I must wash it."

"You're always trying to impress people, Cliston. I don't care if it's soiled."

"I do. And I am your butler. And per our *signed* agreement, I am in charge of the household. Now move! Sir."

I got up because I knew Cliston wouldn't let me rest. As soon as I rose, Cliston was on his knees, scrubbing.

"I have hot coffee on the kitchen table and I've drawn up a bath for you," he answered, without looking up.

"I don't want coffee. Or a bath."

"If you wish to remain miserable, that is entirely your right, sir. I simply request that you not vomit or urinate on the rugs. The proteins are difficult to remove."

"Tell me, honestly. You didn't like Laesa, did you?"

Cliston slowed his scouring but didn't stop.

"I am terribly sorry for your loss, sir. I have stated that many times and I mean it most sincerely."

"But did you *like* her?"

Cliston faced me, absently brushing and spraying while he did so. His red eyes glowed.

"I can't say, sir."

"Can't or won't?"

"I prefer not to."

"You gave her a job because of Garm, didn't you? I asked her to talk to you and get Laesa work. Was that what happened?"

"You will have to speak to Laesa's former talent agent, I'm afraid."

"Don't give me that crap. I know it's you. Pull the plug or turn the dial or whatever you got to do. I don't care what persona you use but answer me."

Cliston sighed. An affectation he rarely used. He stood up. Removed his rubber gloves. Took off his apron. Folded it and put it underneath his arm.

"You want to know what I thought about Laesa Swavort?" he asked.

"Yes. Tell me the truth. Not as a butler. Not as a fight promoter. Or racecar driver or jellyfish or anything else. Tell me as my friend."

The air was still. I could hear the bubbles from the carpet cleanser popping at our feet.

"Very well. Laesa was a horrible person. I could find almost no redeeming characteristics about her. And as an actor, she was a third-rate talent."

I was stunned. Shocked. I thought I was beyond such things. Beyond being moved at all. But I was wrong.

"Cliston. You and I are quits. We're through."

"Then I have to mention that you owe me for eight months of rent. I have been deferring your share of the costs until now, but if we are going to terminate our agreement, I will require immediate payment."

"Oh. Can you let me slide a bit longer?"

"Of course. But I will be keeping your belongings until I am repaid."

"That's fair. Coffee in the kitchen?"

"Yes."

I turned to go get it. I figured it would be the last Cliston luxury I'd ever have.

"And Hank, I *am* sorry for you about Laesa's passing. But I do not personally miss her."

CHAPTER 30

I wasn't living exactly day-to-day.

Once Cliston had kicked me out of the apartment, time seemed to completely change. I lived by the hour. That's as far ahead as I ever thought. What was I going to do for the next hour?

I'd never really contemplated suicide before. Never crossed my mind. I'd been in a lot of agony a lot of times, and even then, it never occurred to me. You either had the capacity to consider a life of *no life*, or you didn't. I didn't. Suicide had to be the ultimate in long-term planning. An irreversible retirement strategy. I didn't even have a savings account, so that's about how good I was at thinking about the future.

Besides, it's hard to kill people. Really hard. People think it isn't. You point a gun in the general vicinity of someone and they drop dead instantly, quietly, and painlessly. I'd killed a bunch of people and it was almost always difficult. Hell, people *tried* to commit suicide all the time. Most of them failed. I even met a guy who wanted to end it by sitting *on top* of a bomb and he still survived. He gave up on the prospect of suicide after that. Not because he was suddenly happy, it was just a lot harder with no arms and legs.

Even if I wanted to, I would have an uphill fight to bring about my own death. About 99% of the things I could do to end my misery would just make me more miserable. And then I would slowly heal. If I jumped off the latticework, would I die? Or would I just break a thousand bones and be tortured for months of recovery?

I happened to be surrounded by the most efficient killer in the universe: deep space. But you couldn't just roll down a window and climb out into the void. Space was rather dangerous to a space station. So we did a whole lot to keep it out there and us in here. I would have to get a lot of help to override the airlocks. And even then, I'd be in space. Who knew what would happen? My mutation might kick in and I'd start flying around in a panic and crash into spaceships and generally have a bad time.

And I was quite capable of having a bad time *inside* of Belvaille without any help. Still, the fact that I was thinking about the impossibility of suicide was closer than I had ever been to it.

Cliston had me locked out of my apartment and it was unlikely I would ever go back. He had all my stuff, but that's all it was: stuff. It didn't matter. In my new life, dignity had become a luxury I could no longer afford.

You had no idea what kind of a luxury it was until you were struggling to survive. If you were bleeding out your eye sockets, you didn't worry if you're also passing gas in public. If you were suffocating, you didn't notice or care that your clothes were wrinkled or you had a booger in your nostril. You couldn't even recognize the *concept* of dignity until more pressing concerns were addressed. And while you were busy addressing them, dignity was the first thing to go.

I found places around the city where I could get free water. Fancy houses that watered their plants. Buildings with outdoor spigots. A few hidey holes in the sewers that had fresh pipes.

I located places to eat. Mostly outside restaurants. Dumpsters and trash cans. Even on a space station we wasted an awful lot of food. I never did, but other people. I also got a handout now and then. If I had dignity, I wouldn't accept such charity. But going four days without food, I accepted just fine.

The heat was bad. Damakan heat. You'd think I would get used to it, being in it every minute of every day, but I never adjusted. I discovered every hidden spot where there was shade or a few-degrees-lower temperature. The station's climate wasn't perfectly uniform. Architecture created artificial temperate zones, not to mention the imperfect distribution of our life support systems. I had nothing but time to find where there were gaps and pockets.

The latticework above and to the side of the heaters blew out cold air from the heat exchange. I'd sleep there sometimes, but it was a long way up and a quick way down. I even siphoned some of the extreme air conditioning the coroner's office used to keep their corpses from spoiling until Muck-Mock chased me off.

If Belvaille had gutters, I'd be sleeping in them. But we didn't.

I was kind of a bum. I only say kind of because...well, I guess because I was a dangerous bum. Bums could be dangerous, right? If they were crazy or desperate enough. I was a mutant Ontakian bum. If I was panhandling somewhere, you couldn't just ignore me. I was too big. You couldn't call the cops on me because they didn't have the hardware to push me around and I was friends with them from before I was a bum.

I was kind of like Wallow, the dead Therezian. He keeled over dead years and years ago and was still there. He blocked the street and we couldn't move him. Instead, traffic moved. People relocated. That was me. If I felt like sitting down, or lying down, or passing out somewhere, well, that's where I was. Walk around me.

Shop owners or gang members or movie producers would give me a bit of money or food or water so I would leave. I was a nuisance, but I was cheap.

That was my life, an hour at a time. I didn't talk to no one. Didn't do anything, really.

The Club had nixed me, so I couldn't get discount booze from them. This was a problem, because I wanted to drink away my troubles. But my liver must have weighed about two hundred pounds and was, by all accounts, in good working order. I couldn't afford alcohol. Not in the quantities I wanted.

I didn't use drugs. I didn't really like them. But I saw my only option to forget my troubles was to try and stay in a drugged haze.

I headed to southwest Belvaille.

"Anyone here a drug dealer?" I yelled.

Several people with greasy skin and greasy hair seemed to teleport out of thin air. They hadn't, of course, they merely had the ability to blend in with their surroundings. The surroundings currently being dominated by rubbish and derelict vehicles.

"You got cash?" three of them asked at one time. They were jittery, and paranoid, and looked everywhere except right at me. Drug dealers were, in my estimation, their very own biological species.

I held up my wad of crumpled, donated money, which got them interested. I picked the ugliest guy to transact with. Ugly people couldn't coast through life on charisma. An ugly guy who was also a bad drug dealer was like a toilet that didn't flush. People didn't keep toilets around for their aesthetics. They either worked or were removed.

He walked me over to his office which was a washing machine at the side of the road.

"Hey, Hank," someone said good-naturedly.

I hadn't heard anyone call my name in what seemed like years. The man who called to me was sitting by some steps that led up a narrow building.

I couldn't place the man at first. Looking at him, I thought I was already high. His eyes were a bit crooked. His nose was off-center. His upper lip was misaligned with his lower. His hair was choppy and different colors.

"Holy crap," I said. "Lagla-Nagla?"

"How you doing?" he asked.

Lagla-Nagla was the "lopsided man." Like every facet of him was just...wrong. As if he were constructed out of a 10,000-piece jigsaw puzzle with 3 pieces missing and the gaps were smushed closed. He wasn't bad-looking per se, he was off-putting. Delovoa was hideous, but it was so glaring that you could tune it out after a while. Lagla-Nagla was like having a hair in your eye. You kept trying to blink him into focus and it didn't work. Even his mannerisms, speech, and movements were off-kilter.

Lagla-Nagla was competent and friendly, but he was eventually fired from every job he ever had because he made everyone so uncomfortable. In consequence, if there was a job on Belvaille, at some point Lagla-Nagla worked it. He was a good resource to talk to, but I usually looked at the ceiling when he was around because he gave me vertigo.

"What are you doing here?" I asked him.

"This and that. Selling drugs, mostly. How about you?"

"Nice. I'm a hobo. But I'm also looking to score some drugs."

"Really? I can help you out if you'd like," he said.

"Sure."

"Sorry, he and I go way back—" I began to say to the drug dealer I was with, but he had vanished. Become one with the scenery again.

I walked over to Lagla-Nagla and handed him my cash.

"Last I heard, you were playing glocken," Lagla-Nagla said, as he walked up the stairs and I followed.

"That was long ago. I'm just doing bum stuff now."

"I was a vagrant for a while. But I wasn't very good at it," he said.

"It's not easy," I agreed.

There was a padlocked door on a landing with no railing to the side. Lagla-Nagla opened the door and we walked inside a hall and up more concrete stairs.

"Easier for you, probably. You can just take stuff if you want it. People would kill me."

"I try not to steal," I said.

A dim light illuminated a small apartment. It was living quarters. If Lagla-Nagla wasn't a vagrant, he was only a few steps removed.

"I remember you being decent and moral. Otherwise you could kill me and take my drugs," he said. Then he stared at me.

"I'm not going to kill you and take your drugs," I replied. "What made you become a drug dealer?"

"I was working in the dramatic industry for a while."

"Like moving stuff around?" I asked.

"Sort of. I was a dolly grip. After that I did camera adjustment."

"You operated the tele cameras?" I asked, surprised.

"No, only Damakans do that. They had me stand in front while they were setting up. They would calibrate the lights and cameras using me."

"Because of your weird facial features?" I asked.

"They didn't say. But then everyone started getting killed. I'd seen enough of that and got out."

Lagla-Nagla was a survivor. Anyone that looked like him and survived was a survivor. Then again, if you tried to shoot him, you'd probably end up running out of ammo before you ever hit him.

"My wife was an actor. She was killed," I said.

"Acting is a tough business," he agreed.

"Yeah."

"I figure I'm going to lay low for a few months," he said.

"Why a few months?" I asked.

"All this violence will be straightened out by then."

"How can you be sure?"

"Just the way things work," he said with a shrug.

"So about some drugs."

"Yeah. What kind do you like?"

"I don't know. I'm new at this. I like getting drunk. I don't like hangovers. I want to forget my wife died brutally in front of my eyes and I'm doomed to an unfulfilling life of despair."

"How much do you weigh?"

"That's rude."

"Most drugs are based on body weight. I just need an estimate."

"3300."

"Pounds?"

"I don't know it in kilograms," I said.

"Hank. To be honest, most drugs aren't going to work on you."

"Why?"

"You're too big."

"I'm too fat to get high?"

"You're not fat," he said politely. "Drugs are designed for people who aren't Super Class glocken players."

"I'm also a mutant."

"What's your mutation?"

"I can fly. But I can also heal wounds and illnesses and I'm really dense."

"Drugs are probably a bad idea for you," he said, scratching his lopsided ear with his lopsided hand.

"Why do you say that?"

"You should be saving the world. You're wasting your time getting wasted."

"Kaxle murdered my wife," I explained.

"He's a jerk. I used to work with him before he got mutated."

"You used to work with everyone. I want some drugs. I'm tired of saving the whatever. I couldn't save my wife."

"Okay, okay. Here. I guess you can try and inhale this," he said, handing me a plastic pipe. "Press the back while breathing in."

"Will it get me high?"

"Not high enough that you forget your wife."

"Then what's the point?"

"I want to test if it has any effect. If not, I'll try something else. But I want to take it slow," he said.

"You sure are a conscientious drug dealer."

"And you're a conscientious drug customer. You could have killed and robbed me, which is what most druggies would do."

"I'm still learning."

I clicked the button a dozen times while sucking in. Lagla-Nagla's mismatched eyes went wide and he grabbed my arm.

"What?" I asked, holding my inhaled breath.

"You were supposed to take a little puff. You emptied it," he said, shaking the pipe.

"So what will happen?" I asked, still holding my breath.

"You should be dead. Do I look, you know, strange or wavy?"

"You always do."

"Look at the wall. Can you see anything?"

"Chipped paint. Mold," I said.

"You feel different? Lighter? Or bouncy? Like you can fly?"

"I *can* fly. But only in space."

"I don't think it worked," he said.

Lagla-Nagla pulled out some hidden caches and began rifling through them. I was still holding my breath. I finally exhaled and a blue plume of smoke enveloped the room.

Lagla-Nagla panicked and ran out of his apartment.

"What?" I called.

"I'm not a trillion-pound mutant! Is the smoke dissipated?"

"How can I tell?"

"What's it smell like?"

"I lost my sense of smell when I became a bum," I said.

"Wave around the air for a bit. I don't want to die."

I waved my arms but didn't feel it was very effective.

"I think it's safe," I said after a while.

Lagla-Nagla slowly returned, sniffing with his different-sized nostrils at each step.

"I got one thing that might be effective. Most people don't like it." Lagla-Nagla went to a corner and moved some junk around and retrieved a small box.

"Why do you think I'll like it?"

"Because it may actually do something. It's called Thad Alien."

"Thad Elon," I corrected.

"No, it's called Thad Alien."

"Did the god Thad Elon invent it? Because I don't trust him."

"I don't think anyone knows who makes drugs. But I can't imagine a god would bother inventing a narcotic."

"You'd be surprised. He did all kinds of annoying things. What's the drug do?" I asked.

"It takes like, the path of least resistance."

"What's that mean?" I asked.

"Everyone is different, right?"

"I don't know. I think most people suck," I said.

"But I mean biologically. Some people can drink one booze for ages and not get drunk, while other people can't even take a sip. Some people get high off Straight Z and others are mutants who weigh 1,497 kilograms."

"Will it get me high?"

"Maybe. It hits everyone in their most vulnerable spots. No two highs are the same and it will be different each time."

"Can you get addicted to it?" I asked.

"In a way. You can get fifty different addictions to the same drug. But you can't ever satisfy the same addiction twice."

"I don't know," I said.

"You want to forget your wife?"

"I want to forget everything."

"Then have some Thad Alien," he said.

Lagla-Nagla handed me a pill the size of a small car.

"I can't swallow this," I said.

"You chew it."

"Do you have anything else?" I asked.

"Hank, I think you could snort up all the drugs on this entire street and not notice it. Drugs are just drugs. They can't beat mutations. This is your best shot."

I shrugged and stuffed it in my mouth.

"Eck! It tastes terrible."

"Yeah, like Thad Elon," he said.

"How do you know what he tastes like?"

"He created the Colmarian Confederation. Of course it leaves a bad taste."

I was now a Thad Alien addict.

* 271 *

Because of its peculiar properties, I was in a constant state of withdrawal even as I was in a near-constant state of intoxication. I was taking it as much as I could. If I had only worried about hours at a time before, I wasn't even thinking that much now.

I'd find some out of the way spot, make myself comfortable, and dream away entire weeks. The drug wasn't very popular. Most people didn't like how strong it was. Not to mention the inevitable withdrawal. But I liked both aspects.

My favorite hallucination was one where I was so euphoric, I was absolutely certain I had been reunited with Laesa. I would hold her close and we would dance. But because of my perpetual withdrawal pains, I envisioned us dancing in hell. I liked the pleasure of being with Laesa and to punish myself for being unable to prevent her death.

But the high would eventually go away and I was left with only cascading layers of withdrawal suffering.

I had lost so much weight I was probably well under 3000 pounds. My skin hung loose in areas. I could actually see one of the scars on my face by stretching my skin and holding it up in front of my eye.

While I stayed in different places, my main "home" was in the sewer. It was merely the space where two levels of the sewer overlapped and weren't filled in. It was cool down here and I had access to water. I would have gone deeper in the sewers where it was even colder, but it was too noisy.

"Cliston is going to be envious when he learns you've gotten yourself a swanky new apartment," Delovoa said one day.

I was just coming around and saw the scientist standing at the entrance to my underground domain.

"Is one corner for mucous and another corner for feces? Or have you thrown such tired decorating clichés out the door?" he asked.

"Don't...have a door," I mumbled. My voice was weak from disuse.

"I guess you're right. Must be a nice neighborhood."

"No."

"Talk. Talk. Talk. That's all you do, Hank."

I hadn't seen Delovoa in a long time. He looked the same.

"Get any more mutations since we last talked? You always seem to be getting new ones," Delovoa asked.

"No."

I thought that was the end of the conversation, so I went back to staring at the floor.

"You might be wondering what I'm doing here," he said.

When I didn't answer, Delovoa squatted next to me and continued.

"Cliston is beside himself with nothing to do. He started cleaning *my* apartment. He's even remodeling the whole building. *All* of City Hall. You have any idea how big that is? It will take him a thousand years."

"He won't care," I said.

"He really misses you."

"He didn't like Laesa. Said she was a monster."

Delovoa's three, misaligned eyes searched my face.

"But Laesa is, regretfully, gone. Maybe it's time for you to come back," he said.

"Can you make Thad Alien?"

"It's pronounced Thad Elon."

"Not the guy. The drug."

"Is that what you're taking?" he asked.

"Only thing that works."

"Seems pretty wonderful," Delovoa said, examining my underground hovel.

"Can you make it?"

"I wouldn't know where to begin."

I sat up so fast that Delovoa retreated in worry. I began picking through my meager things until I found some crumbs of a pill. I held it out to him.

"Can you make this? Please?" I asked.

"Hank. I'm not going to feed you drugs."

"You did before," I said.

"Yeah, but that was when we were experimenting on hidden formulas from long-lost civilizations. That was exciting. This has you living in a sewer."

"I could force you to make it," I said threateningly.

"Could you? Could you leave this fantastic home and keep a gun, or handful of slop, to my head for the days and days it would take me to analyze that compound and attempt to recreate it? I'd like to hope that you could, but seeing you here, I think you would lose interest after we took a few steps."

I sat back down.

"How did you find me?" I asked.

"See? That's a good question. That's using your higher brain functions. You're unscannable, remember? I just look for areas I can't scan and one of them is you. There are other Ontakians running around Belvaille, but they usually are— running around, that is. Not lying in one place for days. And you're more impenetrable than the rest."

"You talk to Frank?"

"Another question! Two in a row. I've spoken with him a bit, yes."

After a few moments of silence passed, Delovoa spoke up.

"You missed the opportunity to ask how Frank is doing. Or if Frank is still a jerk. Or if Frank is still your uncle. Any of those would have been fair."

"Did you like Laesa?" I asked Delovoa.

"Ah," he said, and held up a finger. "Before I answer that, Hank, I am going to move a bit over here. No reason. Things seem very interesting at this particular spot. That happens to be out of striking distance."

"So?" I asked.

"I...did not, in fact, care much for...the person who you...might be..."

"Laesa. My wife."

"You weren't—I mean, that's not precisely how marriage works—generally speaking. You know, the whole ceremony—I don't make the rules, you understand— it's just you didn't actually, *quite* become husband and wife. I mean you *should* have! I was there. I was the Alternate Man. Strumming and playing and running for my life and everything."

"Why didn't you like her?"

"Hank. She was a Damakan."

"So? I'm an Ontakian. And you're whatever thing you are."

He took a huge breath. A bit of ooze squirted from his neck where he had a metal plate bolted.

"Laesa was using her ability on you. She didn't love you. You didn't love her."

"Of course I did. How can you say that? I wanted to marry her."

"I've known you for centuries, Hank. I've seen you in love. It's a clumsy, embarrassing thing. With Laesa, it was totally different. You weren't yourself. You were talking about marriage a week after you met Laesa."

"Because I loved her."

"Hank, just...*think!* She used her ability on you."

"I heard this before. Why would she?"

"Because you're Hank! Because no one would mess with her. Because you were friends with me. Because you were friends with Garm. Because you were friends with Cliston. Because Boranjame call you on the tele and invite you to dinner. Because anyone who has been alive in the last thousand years and has read what passes for a newspaper, has heard of you at least once. Any of those reasons."

"She didn't need me. She wanted to act. She should have gone for a Damakan director."

"Cliston said she wasn't very good at it."

"What does he know? He's a robot. He doesn't have a heart," I said.

"He knew she was controlling you. And that he had better give her a job so she wouldn't *kill* you. That's what he knew!"

"He's lying," I said.

"Of course. Why hadn't that occurred to me? Cliston, the big, fat-face liar. That master machine of deception."

"Do you believe him?" I asked.

"We *all* knew this. We talked about it over and over."

"Who is we?"

"Everyone. Everyone you know who can be trusted. Okay, I guess that isn't a lot of people. But Cliston. Me. Garm. MTB. Zzzho."

"What would Zzzho know about it?"

"Well, clearly not very much because he's radioactive steam. But we asked him anyway."

"You talked about Laesa? Behind my back?"

"Technically, behind *her* back, but yes. You couldn't see what was happening because you were...mystified. We kept trying to get you away from her. MTB learned how to bowl. He *hates* bowling. Laesa was dangerous," he said.

"Laesa would never hurt me. She wouldn't hurt you guys."

"We knew what she was capable of because she flat out *explained* it. She told Cliston she would turn you against him unless he got her good acting roles."

I was startled.

"Did she say anything to you?"

"Yeah. She said, 'Stay out of my way.' So I stayed out of her way as much and often as possible."

"Did you give Kaxle weapons on purpose? To kill Laesa?" I asked.

"As if Kaxle needed power armor to kill a small Damakan? I sell weapons, Hank. I've been doing that my whole life."

"Okay. Did you kill the actors I was protecting?" I asked.

"Me? Kill actors? I enjoy watching tele programs more than the average person. I've sent so much fan mail that I got a threatening letter from a Quadrad agent hired to kill me if I kept doing it."

"If what you say about her was true, why didn't you tell me earlier?" I asked.

"We did. A *lot!* You couldn't even hear us. Laesa's been gone nine months now and you still don't believe me. She kept twisting and twisting and closing you off."

I sat brewing for a while.

"I need to think," I said.

"Think, yes. Thinking good. Drugs bad. You have so few brain cells as it is. But understand that I'm not making this up. I'm not that creative."

"I don't know about that," I said.

"Why would I invent this story now that she's gone? Why would Cliston? Why would Garm? Why would everyone you know be in a conspiracy against your ex-not-wife?"

"I don't know."

"You could have used your tele. Instead of coming over in…person—if that's what you still are," Garm said.

We were standing outside her telescope administration buildings. I had walked over here a week or so after speaking to Delovoa. Her security wouldn't let me in the building. They paged her.

"I sold my tele. Or lost it. I can't remember," I said.

"You look worse than I've ever seen you. And I've seen you after a train dragged you across the city."

"You look nice," I said. "Did you lose some medals?"

"Shh. I've been slowly taking them off and hoping no one will notice. I was having back issues."

"Delovoa said you and Cliston and MTB were plotting about Laesa."

"*Plotting?* We were plotting about you. How we could pull you back to reality. Yeah, we were. I can forgive you for being seduced. Damakans have some kind of species-wide mutation or something. We've never seen that before. It's not your fault."

"Did you kill her?" I asked.

I wasn't sure what I would do if Garm admitted it. If she denied, could I believe her? Garm could have anyone on the station killed. She'd more than proved that. The idea she was formulating some complex plan about Laesa was a lot less believable than Garm simply ordering Laesa's assassination.

"I didn't kill Laesa, Hank. I wouldn't do that."

"You're a Quadrad."

"By birth, by death. I give you my solemn word. I swear by the Quadrad. By my children and grandchildren. I did not plot, nor influence, nor institute the death of Laesa," she said rigidly.

"Okay."

"I *wanted* to. It would have been incredibly easy. Would have saved me hours and hours of hanging out with Delovoa. But you were under her spell for so long, that it became real. More than real. We had to think of a way to sever the relationship."

"What did you come up with?"

"We tried all sorts of things. Remember you and I kept talking about taking a vacation?"

"No."

"To another System. I said we had a hint on Ontak and where your relatives could be."

I searched through my memory. It sounded familiar. But I had been in a drugged haze for so long that everything seemed disconnected. I couldn't remember what was a hallucination.

"But we didn't go anywhere," I said.

"No. Every time we tried a new angle, she would block you. She'd spend the night and you'd forget everything except your name."

"Did she ever threaten you? Say she would hurt you? Or me?"

"Hurt *me?* That's not likely. I never spoke to her as Garm. I used disguises. I'm not so stupid to be alone with a Damakan who had a grievance. She threatened Cliston."

"Do you believe him?"

"Do I believe *Cliston?*" she asked, not comprehending.

"Yeah."

"I...do not believe that Cliston is even *capable* of making something up. Maybe there is a Tall-Tale Cliston persona who can do that. But I made sure to speak to butler Cliston and talent agent Cliston."

"Talent agent Cliston isn't exactly friendly."

"No, he's not. Because he ruthlessly utilizes his position and ruthlessly tells the truth. He was scared of Laesa. Scared for you. We all were."

"But she was killed. Was that a coincidence?"

"While you've been adding layers of grime and stink to your body, a *lot* of Damakans have been killed. This is Belvaille. People die. People around *you* die. Check Scanhand."

"And you didn't have anything to do with it?"

"I swore. I gave you a Quadrad oath. You want me to hold up my pinky, too? We were going to kidnap you. Before the wedding we were working it out. You're not an easy person to kidnap. If I had ten other Quadrad I could do it. But I was working with a butler, a pink cloud, a psychopath, and a street cop. How would we move you? How would we keep you sedated?"

"Thad Alien."

"What's he have to do with anything? Is he here?" Garm asked, looking around worriedly.

"No, the drug."

"I don't know anything about drugs. Hank, Laesa was cunning. Ruthless."

I shook my head at the concept.

"I know. I know. It must be impossible for you to imagine," Garm said.

"I can't stop feeling what I'm feeling. I'm doing everything I can not to rip your arms off for talking bad about Laesa," I said.

"And *that's* why she had you. What better bodyguard in Belvaille is there?"

"But I couldn't save her," I said.

"She wasn't worth saving! That's what we've been trying to say forever. She was a grifter. A cheat. A scammer."

I held up my hand and turned my head.

"I get it. I can't...I just can't process it right now."

"Let's go. Take a vacation. *Real* vacation. Grab your friends—except Delovoa. See the galaxy."

"You're Adjunct Overwatch."

"I'm a *Quadrad*. This," she said, holding up one of her many uniform citations, "is merely a disguise. Besides, we may lose control of the station to the Navy."

"Because of a gang war?"

"Because of everything. Dramatic revenue has bottomed. Popular shows have been disrupted or cancelled. Port facilities are in jeopardy. No crews want to lay over anymore. They know there's a chance they'll get shot in the crossfire."

"You'd actually leave Belvaille?" I asked.

"If I was a rat, I would already be on another boat. But to move my artwork alone would take a year of carefully doctored manifests and diverted traffic."

"I'm not ready. I'll...I'll talk to you later," I said.

I stumbled away, confused and disoriented.

The universe had smacked me around quite a bit since I dared to be born. And over my life I'd experienced some brutal situations that toughened me so much that I worried if I was still capable of compassion. But as course as I was, I still couldn't cope with the loss of Laesa. Despite everyone telling me to the contrary, I couldn't believe that what I felt for her was false or an illusion brought about by her unique species.

I decided to relocate. Move to a new home. That is, I found a new place to squat. Hopefully one that would have less visitors spewing harsh realities at me.

I was now at the very west of Belvaille. I dragged over an old car, turned it upside down, and I slept inside. Flipping it over was to discourage anyone from tampering with it. Would be my luck to have someone steal my house. Probably my uncle, who would try and sell it back to me at three times its value.

I was in an alley at the very edge of the space station. There was a wall that bordered Belvaille. Not really a separate wall, per se. It was an extension of the metal roads and the metal infrastructure, the very bones of the city. It was quite sturdy and built when the space station itself was constructed.

My car-home was flush up against the wall. If the wall didn't exist, and the shield protecting Belvaille didn't exist, I could literally roll out of bed into outer space. Obviously that couldn't happen, but it occupied a lot of my thoughts to imagine I was only a house-car's length away from the void.

I tried to resume my Thad Alien habit as soon as possible. They called being strung out on Thad Alien, Thad Ailing. But that was too many puns for me so I refused to say it. I now had about two dozen distinct withdrawal symptoms all competing with my emotional misery.

I couldn't even sob, because I was dehydrated and my eyeballs hurt. I couldn't sleep it off, because I had insomnia. I couldn't eat away my anguish because my stomach ached, I had diarrhea, swallowing made me dry heave, and I was hallucinating that my hands were monsters trying to steal my teeth.

I couldn't get over my withdrawal because none of my old dealers would sell to me. Not even Lagla-Nagla. They told me to go away. They were out of stock. Or busy. Sometimes, they would see me and simply run away.

Finally, I found out what was going on. MTB had come by and threatened them. Rounded up every Thad Alien dealer in the entire city and given them the business. His police force was now my personal drug rehab. In a city full of scumbags, a city built on crime, I couldn't find anyone to sell me narcotics.

I was shivering in my car-home. It must have been 100 degrees in this far-flung Damakan land and I was freezing. My feet were hot, though. My ears ached. I couldn't see out of my left eye unless I closed my right eye. Nine of my toenails had stopped growing and were stubby and chipped, but one had grown about quadruple speed and stuck through my shoe. I had to wear gloves because I was afraid I was going to try and bite off my monster-possessed fingers. Drug withdrawal was a serious, fulltime business.

You need to get up, I thought to myself.

But why?

Because I would like to talk to you.

I *am* talking to me.

"I am outside. This is Procon Hobb," I thought.

"Oh crap," I said aloud.

I peeked out the car window. There were a bunch of big lizards standing in the street. Just what I needed.

I opened the door and fell out of my home.

Procon Hobb had six guards with him. Large, muscled, bipedal lizards who carried advanced polearm-type weapons. They immediately lunged forward and stuck their electrified blades in my face.

It was a bit silly. As if I was going to attack Procon Hobb. As if *anyone* was going to attack Procon Hobb, a ten-foot immense lizard that resembled a squatting frog, except with clawed, carnivorous arms. Not to mention he was telepathic.

"Sorry I broke your church," I said.

Hobb made a motion and his guards backed off. There were two smaller attendant lizards who misted water over Hobb's massive form.

I picked myself up and tried to dust myself off, but I wasn't covered with dust, I was covered with grime.

"How are things?" Hobb thought at me, using my own internal voice.

"Things?" I gazed around at the city. "Things are fine. I'm terrible, however."

"You need to get back to your life, Hank," Procon Hobb thought.

"Do I? Is that what you're here for? A pep talk?" I asked.

"No," he thought.

"I'm tired of people telling me what to do. Telling me who I should love. My whole life, all I've done is help other people!" I shouted. But when I said it out loud it sounded absurd. "Okay, maybe *half* my life was spent helping others. But that's still hundreds of years. Probably a bit less than half. Most likely a third was for other people. Two-fifths at least."

Procon Hobb held up a massive claw that was about the size of my torso. He really was enormous. And probably as wide around at his base as he was tall.

"You should resume your old ways," he thought.

"I should? And why should I? So I can get smacked around some more? So I can be a flunky for everyone? Including people like you? Oh, you think you're some high and majestic guy. But I've saved your life along with everyone else's. You know what I got for it? Do you know? You can read minds, right? You know what I got? Go head, ask me," I yelled, crossing my arms, then uncrossing them, because I was still hallucinating that my fingers were monsters and I didn't want them to bite my armpits.

Procon Hobb stood there getting misted by his servants. He blinked one bulbous eye. Then another. His eyes were solid black. Each was larger than my entire head.

"Do you know anything about me, Hank?" he thought.

"You're like a priest. A rich priest. Who owns planets. And talks in heads. And used to own the glocken team I played for. And has fights at the arena. Oh, and owns *The News*," I said.

"But do you know anything *about* me?"

"Sure. All the stuff I just said. And you're like a lizard. Amphibian. Frog-lizard. Giant frog-lizard," I shrugged.

"I am like you."

I glanced at his submissive servants and then back to my house-car.

"I don't see the resemblance," I said.

"I came here as a nobleman. When all you needed was to be wealthy to earn that title. When everyone else vacated this city, do you know why I chose to remain?"

"No."

"Do you know why I bought the Belvaille Glocken Team?" he thought.

"No."

"And the reason I purchased *The News?*"

"Are you going to keep asking me why you paid for stuff?"

"I did all those things...because they were enjoyable," Hobb thought.

"Holy crap, you're just like Thad Alien!" I said.

"The narcotic?"

"No. I mean Thad Elon. The creator-god. He caused the civil war because he figured it would be amusing."

"Yes. It is written that he created the first mutant of my species."

"Man, that guy gets around. He created damn near everything."

"My species are normally like them," he thought, and he motioned toward the small attendants and the much larger guards. "But I am like you. A mutant."

"Oh. That's what you meant."

"I suspect the first mutant of my kind decided to further utilize his size and abilities, and he declared himself a god. Thereafter, every single one of us is considered his descendent and treated the same. I was born this way. And I was told from a very early age that I would eventually become spiritual leader of numerous solar systems once the existing lord passed."

"Sounds like a tough life," I said.

"It was. Though I understand your sarcasm. Trillions of souls rely on my every word and react to my every whim. If any of my servants commits even the most minor infraction in my presence, they are ritually executed. Because I am not allowed to witness imperfection."

"Then you should probably look the other way. I'm not operating at my usual perfection right about now," I said.

"Hank," he thought at me. "I am on Belvaille to escape those things. I have told my people I am on a sacred quest. I am capable of communicating telepathically across the galaxy."

"I use a tele. But I lost mine. Or sold it," I said.

"I tire of being a god. Do you realize that I have no achievements to call my own? Everything has been given to me as it was given to those who came before me. Have you any comprehension of what that is like?"

"Not really. All *this* is my own doing," I said, showing off my ratty clothes and living conditions.

"I did not build a church on this station. My followers did. Even here, I cannot escape them. I have no choice."

"Just kill a bunch of them. Tell them you're not a god. They'll take the hint and leave after a while," I shrugged.

"They would not, unfortunately. When I started the Belvaille Glocken Team, which you played for, that was the first vocation I had ever undertaken. And then you ruined the Championship," he thought.

"I was trying to stop a *real* god from mutating the whole System."

"You failed."

"Yeah, but I didn't know I was going to fail. Or I would have played your dumb game."

"Now I am banned for life by every major sports league in the galaxy. I had put together a brand-new team from nothing and was poised to win the most prestigious sporting event in existence. Something I could truly call my own."

I didn't bother pointing out that he had very little to do with our team's victories. He hired a top-notch coach and general manager who hired top-notch players and made top-notch strategies. We never even *saw* Procon Hobb. But apparently, he heard my doubts.

"I paid for it all. If it was so easy to do, others would have done it. That victory would have brought me prestige and personal satisfaction. My species would finally become known as more than the 'reptiles' of this foolish empire."

"Not sure what you want me to say, Procon Hobb. I'm sorry you have trillions of people believing you're a deity and dropping down cathedrals everywhere you take a crap. However, if you want to kick me while I'm down, I guess that's your right."

"I want you to fight Kaxle in my arena," he thought.

"You came out here to get me to do an arena fight? Is this another rich-person hobby you've taken on?"

"Yes. It will be a great battle. It would bring spectators from across the galaxy."

"I can't believe you. I suspected you were going to give me some religious talk to turn my life around. Mention my greater purpose. Metaphysics. But you're just a pampered underachiever," I said.

"I can help you," he thought.

"I'm sure you can. But I don't need your money! I mean...I need drugs. Drug money. I guess *some* money would be nice."

"I can give you information in exchange for your participation in the arena," he thought.

"Information? What can you possibly tell me? Unless you know the location of where I can find a warehouse filled with Thad Alien."

"I know who killed Laesa Swavort," he replied.

"So do I. Kaxle. The guy you want me to fight. But just because the movies work like that doesn't mean I do. Kaxle is an ass and I hate him, but I don't have a murderous desire to see him dead."

"Kaxle was performing an assignment," Hobb thought.

"Exactly. It was a bad job to take, but it was a *job*," I replied.

"But who gave him that job?"

"Scanhand," I said.

"But who created and runs Scanhand?"

"No one knows."

"I do," he thought.

"Was it you? Is it like a religious thing? Frog thing?" I asked.

"No. I do nothing whatsoever for religious reasons."

"But did you create Scanhand?" I asked. "Because I don't think posts should be anonymous. There's a lot of bad stuff about me that isn't true. My Trouble rating is now a picture of used toilet paper."

"I know who created Scanhand and continues to operate it," he thought.

I stood contemplating that for a moment.

"Eh, so what? It's annoying. It sucks. But life sucks. Scanhand is just a big pile of life."

"If you confront the owners of Scanhand, you may find out who hired Kaxle. And why," he thought.

That hit me hard. For so long I had chalked it all up to randomness. Meanness. The terrible state of the universe in general and this city in particular. When I was feeling really low, I even considered her death a payback for my lifetime of transgressions. I had been so close to happiness and it got snuffed out because I didn't deserve to be happy.

But Procon Hobb was saying there might actually be an explanation for Laesa's death. Nothing could justify it, but maybe it could help me understand and punish those truly responsible.

Hobb picked up on that last part.

"That is correct. There is a party out there who orchestrated her death. Don't you wish to avenge her?"

"Just like a tele movie," I said breathlessly.

"I will also give Rendrae his share of *The News* back," he thought.

"Who?" I asked, confused.

"Rendrae. He has been bothering me about that inconsequential paper. And he may be of use to you. And I will give Cliston a greater share of the proceeds from the fight," he continued.

* 283 *

"What fight?" I asked. I wasn't used to thinking about non-drug issues and this was all happening too fast for me.

"Your battle with Kaxle," he thought. "With your share of the purse, you will be able to buy copious amounts of drugs. If you so choose."

Procon Hobb was a terrible negotiator. I could barely keep up with how much stuff he was offering me.

"I can afford to be generous," he thought. "I own solar systems."

"I've already fought Kaxle," I said.

"The city feels you are even. You won the first fight. He won the second."

"Sorry about your church," I said automatically.

"It isn't *my* church. It is a church *of* me."

"Yeah," I said, like I knew the feeling. "Do you know who hired Kaxle? Can you save me some time and effort?"

"I do not. Nor do I care. My interest is promoting a worthy fight. A new occupation for me," he thought.

"So because you're banned from owning any sports teams, you're trying to invent an entirely new sport? Why don't you actually do something religious? Go around doing...nice stuff. You got the money. There's plenty of people, even on this station, who could use your help."

"Every single day, tens of thousands of my own people are sacrificed in my honor. I have ceased being burdened by that. You, and the Colmarians of this space station, are not even of my species. Your hardships are of no importance to me," he thought.

"Right," I said quickly. "Um, sure. I guess. It might take me a few months, though. I'm still kind of addicted."

"I do not wish to wait."

"You don't understand. I'm in no shape to go confronting anyone about anything."

"I can tell from your mind you are dealing with issues. Chemical dependence. Heartache. Loneliness. Hunger. Mild psychosis," he thought.

"And that's just the good stuff. Unless some of your followers on Belvaille happen to run a drug rehab clinic specializing in mutants on Thad Alien, I need time to sort this through."

"As I said, I do not wish to wait," Procon Hobb thought.

It felt like someone shoved a hot fork into my brain! Blinding pain consumed me. And just as quickly as the sensation came, it vanished. I didn't even have time to raise my hands to my head or scream.

More importantly, I felt okay. Not great, but okay. My withdrawal symptoms were all severely diminished. My fingers were no longer monsters.

"What did you do?" I asked.

"Restored homeostasis of your mind."

"Explain what that is," I said.

"I choose not to. However, you are now free to find the cause of Laesa's murder and then fight in the Arena," he thought.

"Huh. Alright. I guess. I mean, are the Scanhand people on the other side of the galaxy? I'll need some money to get there. How do we do this?"

"You may require assistance. But they are close."

CHAPTER 31

I was in my spaceship, the Suckface.

Despite being homeless, in the strictest sense, I was still rich. I owned a spaceship! And it wasn't just any piece of repurposed junk floating out here, it was an original Colmarian Navy Logistics Corvette. I could probably sell it for...I had no idea. Who the hell buys Navy Logistics Corvettes? Besides me. I don't even know. Maybe the PCC Navy. But I'd have to fill out forms for years and years.

When the Belvaille System emptied out except for passing trade ships and the PCC Navy, I had a bit of a problem. Where should I put the Suckface? I couldn't just stick it in the closet of my apartment. Or park it on the street. I couldn't even park it at the port.

Despite Belvaille's ports being massive and technologically advanced, no one was okay with me leaving an empty corvette there for years at a time. The port berths were constantly being used, updated, repaired. The fees for merely *docking* were astronomical, to have my ship sit there it would be cheaper to abandon it. Hell, it'd be cheaper to ram it into a Navy warship, have them fine me, and then confiscate it.

But I had a unique ability that many people in the galaxy didn't: I could make friends with weirdos.

Zzzho was my regular pilot. My only pilot. I actually knew nothing about my own ship. He's the one who talked me into buying it. He provided the fuel and know-how. I provided the...name for the ship. And I guess I acted as ballast when I was on board.

What we did was, we anchored the Suckface *fairly* near Belvaille, but out of the way of any ships that needed to use the ports or Portals. I had to get clearance from the Adjunct Overwatch, but that was easy.

Every once in a while, Zzzho would go out and recharge the batteries and make sure the ship was okay. How did he get out there? He was Zzzho. A Keilvin Kamigan gas cloud. Space was no more dangerous to him than a hot shower was to me. Less. I could slip in the shower. He couldn't get around very fast, but the ship was nearby.

Currently, I was in the crew compartment of the Suckface with Rendrae, who was doing sit-ups, as the ship flew on its journey.

Zzzho was piloting. Zzzha was operating the stealth systems. And:

"What's your name?" I asked. "The other Keilvin Kamigan."

"Zzzho," came from the speakers.

"Is that Zzzho answering or are you also called Zzzho?" I asked.

"I'm also named Zzzho."

Rendrae laughed.

"You can't do that. Even Zzzha is a terrible name. Come up with something else," I said.

"Why? Colmarian names aren't unique. Zzzho sounds nice."

"Because we can't tell you apart except by your names and you went and made them the same," I said.

"We've gotten used to Zzzho, but I don't know how the city is going to feel about having multiple Keilvin Kamigans," Rendrae said warily.

"Why? We're about the friendliest species in the galaxy," some cloud said.

"Most people have never interacted with your kind," Rendrae stated.

"He has a point. The rest of us Colmarians had to coexist. Make bathrooms we could all share. Planets and filtration systems. But you all were always off by yourselves on the planets everyone else *wasn't* on," I said.

"It wasn't by choice. We just didn't want to fight. How could we?" Zzzho said. "Other than electrocute you."

"What?" Rendrae asked, alarmed.

"Nothing," I said quickly. "If you all were different colors or had different voices or *anything* we could use to tell you apart, it would be better."

"We look nothing alike, actually," a Keilvin Kamigan answered unhelpfully.

"You aren't getting anywhere, Hank," Rendrae said.

"It's a long flight. Nothing better to do than debate gas cloud proper names," I replied.

We were on our way to visit the Historians. They were a group of hermits who lived at the edge of the System, assuming our System had an edge, which it didn't, really, since it didn't have a star.

The Historians collected data. History, I guess. They sprang up after the civil war when we came very close to losing everything. They decided to intercept tele messages and record the comings and goings of our entire society, all of the PCC, so that we would never lose important information from our past. They were located in the Belvaille System because they used our city's telescopes and the Portals.

I had negotiated deals with them before. They shared some of their data in exchange for some of mine they didn't already have.

Procon Hobb had—

"He's not a Procon!" Rendrae shouted.

"He's willing to give you back your newspaper. The *least* you can do is call him by whatever silly name a ten-foot mutant telepath deity wants to be called by," I replied.

"He'll do that if you fight Kaxle. Are you capable of staying sober that long?" Rendrae asked.

"I barely have any withdrawal after he blasted me. He has the potential for a really good career doing that. That is, if he was the kind of Procon who didn't own solar systems. Or he was interested in working. Or he cared about curing addiction in people. Or cared about anyone. He's probably not going to do it."

Anyway, Procon Hobb had explained that the Historians had created and managed Scanhand. I never would have guessed that in a billion years. The Historians were, you know, historians. An online job database didn't fit their profile.

Speaking of profiles, not only would I look to see who hired Kaxle to kill my wife, I would try and get my Scanhand values corrected. Or at least see who wrote all the bad stuff about me.

"I still don't know why we have all these Zzzhos here," Rendrae muttered.

"Zzzha, how are you doing on our detection?" I asked.

"I'm scrambling all frequencies and even masking the gravitonic wake of our ship. It would take someone running into us for them to find us," he replied.

"Excellent. Pilot Zzzho, is there any chance of a ship running into us?" I asked.

"Don't be stupid, Hank," Zzzho replied casually. "PCC requires all those freighters to have their courses set. And the warships maintain regimented patterns. We're the only ones flying without clearance."

"Sensor Zzzho, how are you doing on the scans?"

"Good, Captain. I have scanned every Navy vessel and transport in range. I know the crew numbers, propulsion, armaments, defenses, and if the ships have any major weaknesses like compromised hulls," he said.

"Great. File that," I said confidently.

"File it? How?" he replied.

"I don't know. In files," I said.

"You planning on starting a war?" Rendrae asked.

"No. That's important information, right? We should keep it," I said.

"This is the pilot speaking. You probably don't want to store that information anywhere. Especially on the Suckface that sits empty all the time. And none of *us* wants to be caught spying on PCC ships."

"I accept your recommendation, pilot. Sensor operator, don't file it. Forget everything you saw," I amended.

"Yes, sir," Zzzho replied.

"You're no captain. You don't even have a home," Rendrae said.

"So? It's my ship," I said. "And when we reach the Historians, let me do all the talking. Not only as captain, but because I'm a master negotiator. They are an odd bunch of guys. And one gal."

"I still don't know why I have to come along. This is a lot of travel time. I need to reorganize my newspaper," Rendrae complained.

"You don't own it yet. And *Procon* Hobb hinted you should come. This is a long enough journey that if I suddenly found I needed a skinny reporter, I wouldn't be able to turn around and get you. Go back to doing your gymnastics."

"Guys, we're about thirty minutes away from the Historians," Zzzho said.

"Thanks, Zzzho," I said.

"I'm Zzzha."

"Use different speaker settings at least," I said.

I wanted to sneak up on the Historians because I felt the creators of Scanhand wouldn't be forthcoming on their own. We would surprise them and *make* them talk. It was a long, long flight, even with Zzzho stepping on the gas. We were able to fly much faster than the normally restrictive PCC speed limits because we were cloaked. Otherwise, it would have been a full day's journey.

"Remember, I'll handle the Historians. If I have to bash a few heads, just know it's for a good cause. Keep your mouth shut, Rendrae, and pretend you're my backup. These guys get uptight about visitors so don't expect friendliness," I warned.

"I'm a reporter. I am familiar with hostile interviews, Hank."

"You better be," I said direly.

"What's that mean?"

"It means...nothing. I don't know. I'm just talking."

"Master negotiation," he said.

"The Historians are in a small ship, so it will be tight quarters," I explained.

"No, they moved years ago. They live on Floloria now," Zzzho said.

Floloria was the old Rettosian space station. But the Rettosians all left ages ago. I had completely forgotten about it. Floloria was much smaller than Belvaille, but it still couldn't be cheap to try and move a whole city through space. Which is probably why the Rettosians didn't even bother. Not to mention it had been severely damaged in the past.

"Sensor Zzzho, are there people there?" I asked.

"My name is just Zzzho. Scanning. There are sixty-three lifeforms. They all conform to the broad definitions of Colmarian. None are Rettosian."

"Sixty-three? They're adding to the headcount. Last I was here they were only a small group," I said.

"That space station could easily house tens of thousands of people. I don't know how they can even maintain it with that few," pilot Zzzho said.

"Isn't that the place you fought Thad Elon's scientist?" Rendrae asked.

"Yeah, I killed a bunch of people there. Hey...Zzzho that is operating the sensors, do you scan any...unscannable areas?" I asked. "It would be like—"

"I know what unscannable means. No, everything is visible. They have no defenses. Just a standard navigation shield. Place is mostly empty."

"Why would they need a whole city?" Rendrae asked.

"I'm thinking for the Scanhand database," I said.

"You know the database is electronic, right?" he asked.

"Yes. But it needs electricity." I pointed at the space station.

"Hank, this *ship* is more than enough to run Scanhand," Zzzho said.

"How many databases have you created, Gas Man?" I asked.

"Do you want me to land or not?" Zzzho asked.

"Yes. No! Can we cloak in?" I asked.

"I've already passed our acknowledgement and transmitted our mission and occupants," Zzzho said.

"Why did you do that? I wanted to sneak up on them," I said.

"Hank, we can't surprise land on a space station. We'd smash into the shield. They have to give us permission. It's not a public park. It's an extremely complex city that exists in outer space."

"Is the station still called Floloria?" I asked, wanting to sound like a captain after I failed to understand how spaceships worked.

"The facility is designated as Floloria. It's a lot of paperwork to change a ship name. To change a space station marking is almost impossible in PCC space," Zzzho said.

"This isn't actually PCC space," I stated.

"Yeah. It's just filled with the PCC Navy and PCC Portals and the *parts* of Belvaille that are PCC," Zzzho said.

"Sarcasm sounds ridiculous on those speakers," I replied.

"Landing!"

I walked out of the Suckface and felt immediately worse. You would think I would feel better being out of the very cramped, gas-filled corvette. But the artificial gravity and life support on Floloria were definitely substandard. I was used to Belvaille.

"There's no one to meet us. That seems suspicious," I said.

"Someone is coming. Don't start shooting anyone," Zzzho called from the external speakers.

The Historians usually wore big fish-bowl helmets with single lenses on top and all manner of contraptions and gizmos. This one was wearing rough pants with a dress shirt and had brown hair. He was riding a bicycle.

"Hello, Hank," he said on approach. He looked youthful. Friendly.

"Greetings, Historian. Please take us to your leader," I said.

"Everyone is a bit busy at the moment. But if you'll kindly grab a bike, we can see who is available," he replied. Off to the side of the dock were dozens of bicycles.

"Hank is too heavy for those and I don't know how to ride," Rendrae said.

"Don't you have any cars?" I asked.

"We try and cut down on extraneous machinery. We spend too much time as it is repairing things. But we can walk," he said, dismounting.

The Historian walked at a fast pace and Rendrae and I followed. The Zzzhos were left back on the Suckface.

"How did you all come to reside on Floloria?" Rendrae asked.

"We bought it from the Navy," he said.

"Floloria wasn't the Navy's to sell," I said.

"They were maintaining it. It was dangerous to leave it floating around the Portals and trade lanes. We took it off their hands."

The city was still very much old Floloria. It was a narrow residential space crammed with buildings. The flowing, flowery, three-dimensional script that was the Rettosian language was mounted on some buildings.

"What do you do with all the space?" Rendrae asked, taking notes and snapping pictures.

"We now have room to store actual hard copies," he replied.

"Hard copies? Like rocks?" I asked.

"What? No. We store important physical writings. And art," the Historian said.

"Where are your hats? Your big dome things. Metal bowls," I asked.

"I'm sorry. I'm not entirely sure what you're inquiring about."

"What's your goal here?" Rendrae pressed.

"We can be a research institute. We've been getting donations from across the empire. Even some things from other empires."

"Are you sponsored by the PCC?" Rendrae asked.

"No, they have offered. Repeatedly. But we want to maintain strict neutrality. We don't want to be at the mercy of changing political climates. We *have* accepted several cash grants from the Post-Colmarian Confederation Colmarian Confederation, but we made it clear that we weren't beholden," the Historian said.

"Is that your only source of income?" Rendrae asked.

"No, we make records available, for a fee, and we have other generous patrons who have given funds."

"History can be twisted and used out of context for political purposes. If you provide information, how do you stay clear of politics?" Rendrae asked.

"We don't seek to *control* information. We seek to preserve it. A hammer can be used to build or to harm," the Historian stated.

"You could hit someone with a hammer," I pointed out.

"Reporting on history makes you part of it. Whether you like it or not. There are no such things as neutral tools if they are made available to those who aren't neutral," Rendrae said.

"We have an Ethics Department. We regularly evaluate and question our role here," the Historian replied.

After what seemed like an infinity of walking and talking, we finally reached a large building filled with:

"Wow! *Books!*" Rendrae exclaimed.

I had never seen so many. It even smelled weird in here. They had row after row after row of big, upright furniture that held all the books.

"Look at all those paper-binder-cabinets," I remarked.

"Bookshelves," Rendrae corrected.

I blinked. I had never seen a bookshelf before. Let alone a whole building of them.

Another Historian approached us. He had silver-gray hair and a trim beard. He's the kind of guy that you could imagine as soon as he hit puberty and scraped together a little money, he went straight out and got himself a savings account with a respectable interest rate. He carried in his bare hands numerous bound books. Probably worth a fortune.

"Hello. You're Hank, right?" the man asked.

"I am. Captain of the Suckface," I said importantly.

"Since my captain isn't going to introduce me, my name is Rendrae."

"You wouldn't know of another Rendrae who once lived in Belvaille, would you?" the older man asked.

"I'm the only Rendrae I know of on Belvaille."

The man smiled politely.

"The Rendrae I'm talking about died some years ago. He was a reporter who worked at a publication called *The News.*"

"I didn't die. I was sick. Went away for rehabilitation. It's a long story," Rendrae said.

The two Historians looked stunned.

"You are Rendrae of *The News?*" the man asked again for confirmation.

"Partial-owner. I don't wish to associate myself with the current incarnation. But for centuries I was the editor, publisher, distributor, and reporter at *The News*."

The older Historian whispered to the younger man, who nodded and took off running.

"Crap," I said.

I pushed Rendrae out of harm's way and reached into my jacket for my shotgun. But then I remembered I sold it for drugs. I pulled out something hard I found in my pocket. It was a piece of candy I must have put in my coat weeks ago. I took off the wrapper and popped it in my mouth.

"Alright. Eat suck, suckface!" I declared.

I tried to punch the Historian, but I lost my equilibrium. The gravity and thin air and long walk conspired to make me miss my swing by a mile. I fell on the floor.

"We're huge fans of yours," the Historian said to Rendrae, ignoring my outburst.

"Me?" Rendrae asked, surprised.

"Absolutely. You recorded every aspect of Belvaille meticulously for generations. We strive to reach that same level of comprehensiveness in our own records."

"I was merely a current events reporter, not a historian." Rendrae blushed.

"Accurate reporting is what *becomes* history. When you—when we thought you had died—we struggled to come up with a replacement for *The News*. Without you, we were missing out on so much information."

"Scanhand!" Rendrae gasped.

"Yes, we had no choice but to rely on self-reporting. We couldn't match your breadth and access or talent. So we created Scanhand to let the populace fill in events we were losing."

"But you have jobs and assignments in it. Much more than daily news," Rendrae said.

"We had to give them an incentive to publish. The profiles and job boards were a means to make the system popular. So they would fill in details and keep it current."

"Oh. To give them access to the job functions, you made it so they unknowingly provided you with information. Historical information. But you don't record any photos. Or videos. Those things are very important," Rendrae said.

"Maybe in another society those features will work. But on Belvaille, we found that when we allowed rich media, it became almost entirely pornographic."

"You're using Scanhand in other Systems?" Rendrae asked.

I picked myself up from the ground, but no one noticed or cared.

"We've started pilot programs elsewhere, yes. They have different names and uses. We have a very small staff here and make do with intercepts, donations, and subscriptions to local news. Scanhand was our first attempt at what we call, 'distributed reporting.' But there are quite a few regions of the galaxy with no interest in factual reporting."

"Terrible," Rendrae said.

"Yes," the Historian agreed glumly.

"Yeah," I echoed.

"The others would *love* to meet you! We've archived every single edition of *The News* ever published and we use it as a benchmark to rate the level of reporting in other regions of the galaxy."

"That's very flattering," Rendrae said. "Why is Scanhand anonymous, if I may ask? A byline is important for accountability."

"And lies!" I said.

"We experimented with having attribution but found that it quickly descended into falsehoods or people were afraid to add information. We've calculated that with the input being anonymous, we still maintain an almost 92% accuracy rate."

"No way. How can I be vomit-level Trouble?" I asked.

Rendrae and the older Historian began to walk away together.

"I'd caution you against using me as a litmus test. I'm the first to admit there were times when I had to sacrifice journalistic integrity or even took *biased* views with a goal to swaying popular opinion," Rendrae confessed solemnly.

"We understand that. Even Dredel Led journalists add commentary. Every time information passes along to another source, it becomes filtered through their perspective. That's why it's imperative to get facts as soon as possible to limit distortion."

"Who killed Laesa?" I yelled at the retreating duo.

The Historian turned back to me, puzzled. Rendrae gritted his teeth and lowered his hands at me as if I should calm down.

"I'll take care of it, Hank. Wait here. Don't do anything," he said.

I sat down on the carpet and watched them go.

"I'll take some food if you have any," I called. "Rude."

CHAPTER 32

I woke up in bed.

My bed. In my apartments. The sumptuous sheets pulled up to my chin. Cliston's unmistakable, yet subdued, interior design skills were evident all over the bedroom in functional, yet decorative, furniture.

Had it all been a dream? I had the groggy, morning mind of someone who had overslept.

I remember being married—almost. And Laesa's death. And I was a junkie hobo.

As I was trying to clear away the deep sediment from my consciousness, Cliston walked in carrying a tray of food. It smelled remarkable.

"Cliston," I said with a relived smile.

"Hello, sir. Would you care for me to draw a bath for you?"

"Too tired. Let me hang out in bed for a while."

"Very good, sir. You sound rather fatigued."

"Yeah, I am. Crazy. Crazy dreams."

I looked over at the inviting tray of food that was placed on the table next to the bed. There was a particular fruit that caught my eye. Luscious, purple, inviting.

"Hey, is that from your trees?" I asked.

"The arboretum? Yes, sir. It is."

"I guess they aren't poison after all," I said.

"It is, sir. But it is less poisonous than the drug you were addicted to. And it helps cleanse that other product from your system."

At that moment, Rendrae walked into my bedroom munching on some horrific-looking vegetable.

"Skinny Rendrae!" I exclaimed. "Then it all really happened. The wedding. Kaxle. Living in the sewers."

"Afraid so," he replied, mouth full of half-chewed crops.

Cliston cleared his robotic throat.

"Rendrae, you seem to have misplaced the saucer I gave you for your food. Shall I fetch you another?"

"Sorry, Cliston," he said.

"How long was I asleep?" I asked.

"Generous calling it sleep," Rendrae answered. "You passed out as soon as you got back in the ship. I guess whatever mutation Hobb used to help you beat your drug addiction, has a limited duration."

"Procon Hobb," I said.

"You've been asleep several weeks. Off and on, sir," Cliston stated delicately.

"I didn't get the information from the Historians," I lamented.

"I did. I explained it to you, but you were already suffering your relapse. You ready to hear it again?" Rendrae asked.

"I'll leave you two alone," Cliston said.

"No. Cliston, could you stay, please?" Rendrae begged.

"I'm not going to punch you. I'm dead tired."

"You *say* that. But Cliston's input may also be of use," Rendrae replied.

I sat up in bed. Cliston adjusted the pillows for me.

"I'm sorry I was a dick to you. You didn't deserve it, Cliston," I said, looking him square in his glowing eyes.

"You had your reasons, sir. All is forgiven. I've missed your robust companionship," he said.

"Is that coming from talent agent Cliston or priest Cliston or what?" I asked.

"From your *friend*," he said.

"The Historians have access to see who posted everything in Scanhand," Rendrae began. "According to their records, Risky Jerv is the person we should be concerned with."

"Risky Jerv. The name sounds familiar, but I don't know him," I said.

"If I may, sir. Risky Jerv is the President of the Comedy Guild."

"What's that have to do with Laesa? She wasn't in the Comedy Guild. She was in Romance," I said.

"Examining Scanhand, I found that there were *hundreds* of contracts issued by the various Presidents of the Damakan Guilds. It wasn't a gang war. It was a Guild war," Rendrae said.

"We didn't recognize it because we never had one before," I replied.

"There's more," Rendrae said warily. "While the other Guilds hired gangs to attack rival productions, *every* contract for murder was created by Risky Jerv. All of the killings were handled by one particular assassin."

"Who?" I asked.

"Laesa."

I blinked.

"Laesa who?" I asked.

"Laesa. Swavort. Sh-she was at your wedding," Rendrae said.

"*My* Laesa?"

"Yes," he said.

I laughed.

"That's ridiculous! How could she *kill* anyone?"

"I believe she was capable, sir. At least mentally," Cliston said.

"Name *one person* she killed," I asked.

"Weelon Poshor. Gordle Maytop. I spoke to talent agent Cliston about this while you were recovering. Basically, every actor or set or production you were hired to protect, she went after."

I was in a daze.

"Sir, you told her who you were guarding. You gave her times you would be there. The route you would take. Where you would be. She had inside information."

"And the access codes to their homes," Rendrae added.

"No. That's not possible. Scanhand must be wrong. It's totally wrong about me. It's wrong about Laesa," I said.

Rendrae carefully walked closer and showed me his tele.

"There is footage from security cameras. The Historians had access to it," he said.

"Security cameras? There are no security cameras here," I said.

It was true. Belvaille never had surveillance. There was never a need. If someone was robbed, you knew who robbed you once they tried to sell your stuff. People were beaten and murdered in the city, but it wasn't personal, it was business. It was never difficult finding out who was responsible. They often told you, to make sure you got the point.

The only place that Belvaille had security cameras was at the port. At quarantine. And that wasn't even to keep out criminals. It was to track if someone had a noxious disease that the station's life support couldn't deal with.

I looked at the video. It was from the inside of Weelon Poshor's home. There were four different cameras I could navigate between.

MTB hadn't found this security footage video. I hadn't found it. It had never occurred to us that someone was recording the activities *inside* their own home.

There I was. Walking around. Fumbling with the security door. Sweating. Eating. Falling asleep on the couch.

Weelon Poshor came in later. He acted up a storm at my slumbering body. Yelled. Told me I was worthless. Useless. He was going to fire me. I didn't wake up or even flinch. I was out cold.

Then he went upstairs.

Laesa came in the front door. It was Laesa. It was.

She checked on me. Whispered. Talked. Tried to push me. When I didn't stir, Laesa called up to Weelon Poshor. Simply hollered out his name.

* 297 *

He came downstairs dressed how I discovered him later. He walked right up to Laesa. He didn't even react when she took out a gun. It wasn't cocked. The safety was on. She corrected those things while he stood there. He wasn't surprised. Or irritated. He was nothing. He was a Damakan waiting for another Damakan to give him emotions.

Instead she blew him away. Shot him over and over.

Stabbed him.

Poured water on the floor around the body. Then she left.

I watched the video from every angle available. I tried to find something, anything, that would make me understand. Find even the smallest gesture on her part that I could claim showed she cared about me.

But there was nothing. I'd witnessed many, many murders in my life and this was the only one I'd seen where there was a complete lack of emotion from both the killer and victim. Even when Laesa stabbed Weelon Poshor's corpse, she was a mask of indifference. As if she was daydreaming about something inconsequential.

I watched the video for two hours straight.

There was a point, very early, when there was nothing more I could learn. The edited video was short. Only about five minutes total. I had long ago memorized every detail. But I wanted to watch Laesa. I wanted to *see* her. Even if it was in the act of committing a murder.

This was the proof I needed. This is what everyone had been trying to tell me. Not only was Laesa gone. She was never here. Not the way I understood.

"I am sorry, sir," Cliston said, when I finally put down the tele.

Rendrae came back into the room a few moments later. I gingerly returned his tele to him. I couldn't bring myself to say thank you. The words died in my throat. As if he were somehow vaguely responsible for Laesa being a killer, instead of merely discovering the fact.

"I'm sorry, Hank," Rendrae said.

"I wasn't asleep on the job. Laesa cooked me a meal. She *never* cooked. Why would she, I had Cliston. She must have put something into my food," I said.

"You could not have known, sir," Cliston said.

"But I don't understand. Was Laesa some Quadrad-level double agent this whole time? Was I a cover for her work as an assassin? Was she even a real Damakan?" I asked.

"She was a Damakan, sir," Cliston said. "Of that I am sure."

"So who hired Kaxle to kill her? That's what I wanted to find out from the Historians. Not the details of your stupid Entertainment Extermination Guild war," I said.

"Laesa had a contract put on her by the same guy she was working for: Risky Jerv. He hired her to kill everyone you guarded, then hired Kaxle to kill her. If anyone knows why, or what's behind this, it's the Comedy Guild President," Rendrae said.

CHAPTER 33

"Does Risky Jerv have enough money to create all these gang contracts? Just one Guild?" Rendrae asked Cliston, showing a list from Scanhand.

"The amounts you're talking about would take everything Risky Jerv had and then some. He might have tapped some of his Guild members for funding," talent agent Cliston said.

"Entertainment business is down. For all the Guilds. What do you think he hopes to gain? It did nothing but hurt the entire industry," Rendrae asked.

"I don't know. There is certainly competition between the Guilds," Cliston said.

"I thought the Guilds all worked together," Rendrae replied.

"They do. I never witnessed more than a polite rivalry. Damakans are a cooperative species by nature. The Guild Acting Rewards is about as cutthroat as they get, and that's only for a handful of trophies once a year," Cliston replied.

"Risky Jerv and the Comedy Guild decided to use Scanhand, which is anonymous, to murder talent. If we can give proof of this to the other Presidents, what will they do?" Rendrae asked.

"I can't say. He would lose his Presidency for sure. But other than that, their entire species has little exposure to violence," Cliston said.

"And they settled on Belvaille. This must have been a shock for them," Rendrae said.

"I understand it was. *Is.* It's why they have been so easy to attack and they had to rely on locals to protect them. Technically speaking, it wasn't Risky Jerv who created a Guild war, he hired people who did it," Cliston answered.

"I'm going to meet with Risky Jerv," I said suddenly.

"Okay! Face first. The Hank way," Rendrae said, punching his hand. "When are we going?"

"I'm going alone," I replied.

"Sir, I strongly advise against such a course," Cliston said, switching back to my butler.

"I concur. You'll be walking into a *Guild* of Damakans. Just one actor managed to enslave you," Rendrae said.

"Kid, the Guild Presidents aren't in their positions because they are good administrators. They are in that role because they are great *actors.* It's what

Damakans respect most. Risky Jerv convinced his fellow thespians to give him leadership. Your butler is immune to Damakans. Take him with you," Cliston the talent agent said.

"I'm relatively immune as well. I've seen a bunch of Damakan shows and they did nothing for me," Rendrae said.

"He knows you're immune," I said, pointing at Cliston. "And he *doesn't* know you," I said, pointing to Rendrae. "But more importantly, he knows *me*. He knows Laesa conned me. I can get Risky Jerv to talk. He'll feel safe with me alone, but not with either of you."

"Do you expect to punch him in the throat and *make* him talk?" Rendrae asked.

"No. He's not a Belvaille hoodlum. There's something bigger at play. And...I have to do this," I said.

"What are you going to do against an acting master?" Rendrae asked.

"I'm afraid I have to agree with Rendrae, sir," my butler added.

"I can't explain it. But I need this chance to...set myself free."

"This is *my* story, remember?" Rendrae said.

"My wife was murdered. My life was destroyed. You can have your damn story. It's a lot more than that to me," I replied.

"You also promised Procon Hobb you would fight Kaxle in Cheat Hall," Rendrae added.

"I thought you said he wasn't a Procon."

"He is if he gives me back *The News*. And in exchange for tipping us off about the Historians, you owe him a fight. And you can't do that if you're dead."

"Your concern for me is heartwarming. But I need to know. This will hang over me the rest of my days if I can't sort it out," I said.

"I believe I understand you, sir. If you are certain you must pursue this on your own, we will of course let you," Cliston said.

"What if he dies? I'll never get my newspaper back," Rendrae pleaded.

"I have yet to see anything capable of killing Hank," Cliston stated calmly.

That was flattery. Cliston and I had both witnessed many, many things capable of ending my life. But his support felt good.

"You'll get murdered if you try and go into the Comedy Guild alone," Rendrae said.

"Just because Risky Jerv paid for gang violence doesn't mean the entire Guild is some kind of fortress," I said.

"While you were on chemical holiday, some of us were out beating the streets. These are dangerous times. I've been threatened and attacked, just for asking questions. This isn't only the Comedy Guild, it's every Guild. They utilize gangs for security. And since no one knows who is working for whom because of

Scanhand, they're all on edge. Everyone knows you, Hank. They see your wide load walk up and they'll evacuate the building. If he knows how to jog, you'll never get close enough to interrogate him," Rendrae explained.

"Cliston, can you arrange a meeting?" I asked. "Say you got a hot new actor he should check out. Invite him to the Artistry Agency. That will separate him from his security."

"That might work," Rendrae replied, rubbing his chin. "Cliston is considered neutral since he represents people from all the Guilds."

"I don't like the idea of messing up my reputation by having you kill a Guild President. I'll get blacklisted," Cliston said.

"No one will find out. It's almost certain that either I or Risky Jerv will die. If he dies, he won't be able to tell anyone. And you can say he never showed up. On the other hand, if I get killed, your agency will get noticed in Scanhand for removing me from Belvaille. As of this morning, my Trouble rating is an animated green butt. I think it's a butt. In any case, it's not good."

"If you're gone, how will we deal with Risky Jerv? He's still a threat to the whole dramatic industry," Cliston asked.

"You said it would take all his money for these contracts. That means he can't continue the Guild war for much longer. As for dealing with him if I die, hire Garm."

"The Adjunct Overwatch?" Cliston asked.

"Sure. I think she secretly always wanted to be the one who finally killed me. She'll be plenty mad at Risky Jerv if he beats her to it. And it will get the Navy bookkeepers off her back."

Cliston made an exaggerated show of thinking about things. He swiveled his head slightly. Shifted the weight on his legs. Made deep breathing noises with his electronic mouth. All of it quite ridiculous since he probably made his decision in a split second.

"Agreed. I'll set up a phony audition and let you know. Should I talk to you or your butler?" Cliston asked.

"Keep it in the family. Talk to yourself," I said.

Cliston arranged the meeting and I had nearly a week to prepare.

Laesa had taught me a lot about acting. She told me that acting was a balance of intellect and emotion. The one fed the other. You couldn't be *truly* sad during a scene, even one that called for you to appear sad, or you'd be unable to improvise. She said it was similar to how I went about fighting people: I allowed fear and adrenaline to give me a boost, but never overwhelm me so that I was mindless.

Risky Jerv was a frightening adversary. He wasn't a ferocious monster or machine gun robot. He was an actor. The Guild President for a race of actors. It was like facing the official Angry Person of my own Ontakian species.

A Damakan tele commercial for feminine hygiene products could cause me to get sentimental. That's how powerful their broadcast empathy was. Laesa was, by all accounts, a feeble actor. But she easily manipulated me. There's no telling what would happen confronting a skilled thespian like Risky Jerv.

I kept replaying all my conversations with Laesa in my head and tried to see through what she had been saying and doing. Discover the hidden meanings and ulterior motives. Then I borrowed her strategy and began writing a script for my encounter with Risky Jerv. Hit the major beats. Started with the introduction. Popped out the surprises. Got it flowing like a genuine Damakan production. What should I wear? What about props?

No gun. I didn't need one to deal with a Damakan. And I worried he would make me use it on myself. I bought a knife. I didn't actually own one. Except Cliston's kitchen knives, and I didn't know where he kept them.

I practiced my speech in the sewer. The same place I had been living during the low point of my drug frenzy. That depressing environment helped me remember what I was facing. I tried to research Risky Jerv, but there wasn't much out there on him. He became Guild President as soon as they invented the Guilds, so there weren't any recordings of his acting. Talent agent Cliston had met him before, of course, but he couldn't give me any insights into the Damakan's personality other than to say he was charming and humorous. All the Guild Presidents were like that because they were playing the *role* of Guild Presidents. Who knew what they were really like?

For my script, I ended up making a branching narrative. Since I didn't know what Risky Jerv's motives were or how he would react, I worked out multiple contingencies. It would help me improvise if I had to.

I then recorded myself giving my speech and hammered out the timing and movements. It had to appear fluid and unrehearsed. So I kept rehearsing until I knew everything by heart.

I spoke with Cliston two days before the meeting to design a wardrobe. A regular costumer would need months. But this was Cliston. He chose subdued colors offset with lots of hard, geometric angles in the stitched patterns. The clothes were loose yet flattering. He even made an ingenious system of chillwipes hidden throughout the suit which would keep me comfortable in the hot agency.

I added a final, personal touch to my suit.

On death, everyone on Belvaille was cremated. Purified completely. The life support of a space station could never compromise, and every stray organic molecule was viewed suspiciously. I had bribed and threatened Muck-Mock after my failed wedding.

Pinned to my lapel, I had a lock of Laesa's hair that I had kept, in violation of every quarantine procedure ever created. The hair was hardly noticeable under my double chins, but it helped remind me what I was doing. An emotional touchstone, as Laesa might have said.

On the eve of the meeting, I went up and met Cliston at the door to the Artistry Agency.

"Risky Jerv is in a back conference room waiting for my mystery actor. I let the staff off early and cancelled all other appointments. You have the entire floor to yourselves," Cliston said.

"Great. Thanks. Did he look suspicious? Or armed?" I asked.

"Armed? He's a Damakan Guild President, not a guerrilla fighter."

"Did you lower the temperature?"

"Yes, but only five degrees. Any more and he might suspect something. This is a Damakan office, after all," Cliston said.

"Fair enough," I said.

"Try not to get any blood on the carpet. I had new material put in," the talent agent said.

I looked down at the rug.

"How much did it cost?" I asked.

"Just shy of two million."

"For that?" I asked.

"It's self-cleaning."

I scuffed it with my shoe.

"If it's self-cleaning why do you care?"

"I'd rather not test the claims. Most manufacturers probably aren't anticipating buckets of blood," he replied testily.

"Okay, I'll try not to get any Damakan spills on it."

"I was talking about your blood. You have a habit of leaking everywhere."

"You said he wasn't armed."

"I didn't frisk him. I didn't even meet him. My receptionist got him situated and then went home for the day."

"So he could have a bunch of security guards with him?"

"No, because then my receptionist would have said, 'Risky Jerv and five men carrying machine guns are here to see you,' when she told me of his arrival."

"But he *could* be armed?" I asked.

"He *might* have a nuclear weapon in his undershorts, yes, Hank. But I believe it would be quite irregular."

"Thanks, sarcastic Cliston."

"Sir, what time should I expect you home and what would you care to eat?" butler Cliston asked.

"I don't know. Not sure if I'll be alive. Prepare something easy to chew. And have the first aid ready."

"It is always ready, sir. If you would like me to accompany you, I would be more than happy to assist in whatever ways I can."

"No. Thank you again, Cliston."

"Very well, sir. I wish you the best of luck."

Cliston left by the elevator.

I walked to the back of the agency offices. Cliston had placed him far from the exits, which could end up hurting me if I needed to escape. I looked through my script one last time in my tele as I walked.

I had memorized it forward and back. I made plans for every eventuality I could imagine. It was the most I had ever prepared for a meeting. Probably the most I had prepared for anything whatsoever.

The conference room was walled with thick, frosted glass. I could see a blurred shape inside, so presumably he could see me.

I touched the lock of hair on my lapel, put my hand on the doorknob, turned, and walked in. I closed the door immediately behind me.

Risky Jerv was seated at the conference room table. He had gray hair, wore lightly tinted sunglasses, and had a well-manicured goatee. He wore a bright yellow, five-piece suit with a black tie. He had on gloves that were covered in glitter. If he was carrying a weapon, it was well-hidden in that stuffy outfit. He had copious wrinkles around his mouth and was currently grinning at me. He probably assumed I was Cliston's great new acting prospect.

"Hello, Hank," Risky Jerv said, with a pleasing, yet strong, voice. "Would you care to have a seat?"

My script was ruined. Already I had encountered a response I hadn't expected. I thought I would have to explain who I was and how I knew him. But Risky Jerv knew me. Knew me on sight. He did not seem alarmed whatsoever. I cleared my voice.

"Risky Jerv."

"I should have guessed Cliston was up to something. He told me not to soil his carpet, which seemed an unusual request."

"Don't blame him. I made him set up this meeting. It's entirely my doing."

"We rely on Cliston's impartiality, but none of us quite trusts him. He's a machine that merely pretends to have feelings," Risky Jerv said.

"I'm not here to discuss Cliston," I said, trying to find a thread of my script to wind back into. "I'm here to talk about the gang war you started."

"I know why you're here," he said calmly.

"You do? Because even I'm a bit confused."

"You aren't here because of some Damakans being killed," he replied.

"I am, actually."

I was blinking my eyes rapidly, trying to figure out his scheme.

"You are here because of Laesa. Because you still love her. You have a clip of her hair right there on your coat," he said. It wasn't a taunt. It wasn't an indictment. It was simple fact.

As soon as he said it, he hit me to the core. He was absolutely right. I still loved her. I hadn't even admitted that to myself. Or understood it.

"You don't know what you're talking about," I said, trying to recover.

"You are Hank, the Hard Luck Hero."

"Don't believe what you read in Scanhand. That thing is filled with lies," I said.

"The lifelong bachelor had finally decided to settle down, only to have his wife-to-be killed on his wedding day."

"A murder *you* paid for," I said, pointing.

"Yes. Yes, I'm afraid I did," he said.

Risky Jerv spoke with almost no emotion. He was polite. But nothing more.

"So why do *you* think I'm here? So I can take my revenge on you?" I asked, flexing my hands menacingly.

Risky Jerv cracked a slight smile.

"You want to know about Laesa. Try and understand why she betrayed you. And prove that you still have what it takes to be a menacing presence on this city by confronting me," he said.

My mouth dropped open.

Laesa could do profiles on people she met. Tell what they were thinking, what their motivations were, just by observing them. But it took time. What could Risky Jerv, the Guild President, do? Could he read my mind like Procon Hobb?

"No, don't worry, I can't read your mind," he said. "In fact I'm surprised you were able to see me this soon."

"What do you mean?" I asked, confused on so many levels.

"I assumed you would be devastated by your loss. Severe emotional withdrawal. Perhaps drug dependence. Shirking of personal connections and responsibilities. Sleeping under bridges."

I stared at him.

"Bridges? Belvaille doesn't have bridges. What's there to bridge?"

"Oh, of course. In vacant buildings, then. Or the sewer—if this city has one."

I wanted to leave immediately. I had hopelessly underestimated this situation. Risky Jerv knew everything about me with just a glance. And in a few words, he had caused all those emotions to come rushing back. I wanted to crawl into the sewer and cultivate more Thad Alien withdrawal. Yet all I knew about him was he apparently liked to wear the color yellow.

"Trust me, this is not my first choice for an outfit," he said, picking at his jacket. "But when you're the President of the Comedy Guild you're expected to dress a certain way. Vibrant. Madcap. If you would like to leave and reschedule this meeting for another time, I completely understand."

"No!" I said.

I slammed my fist on the table and my hand went straight through. I hoped my show of strength had made an impression.

"Cliston will be upset about his table," Risky Jerv said mildly.

"I don't care!"

I was spinning. Lost. And what was worse, he could see it. Could read me completely. But he didn't appear arrogant. Or mean. He seemed entirely at ease. Restrained, even.

"I suppose I shouldn't be surprised you found me out. And that you recovered so quickly. Laesa spoke of you quite often," he said.

That gave me something to grab hold of.

"Was this when you were giving her targets to kill?" I asked.

"Sometimes. But she did have a great deal of respect for you. You are assertive. Forceful. In control of your destiny. Characteristics she wished she had."

"She used me," I said.

"Indeed. But don't underestimate your influence on her, Hank."

"And I assume you're going to say that she loved me?" I asked.

"No. She couldn't love you. She couldn't love anyone," he said.

I wanted to jolt Risky Jerv. Try and get the upper hand. Throw something out that would surprise *him* instead of the other way around.

"She hated those actors," I said.

"Which actors?" he asked.

"Her targets. The ones you had her kill."

"Why do you believe that?"

"They were stabbed. Not all of them. She had taken steps to misdirect us. But there was no point stabbing them when they were dead. For her to bend over their bodies, after she had gunned them down..."

"You think she despised them?" he asked.

"Yeah. She did."

"No, Hank. She wasn't capable of such extreme emotions on her own. If anything, she envied them."

I shook my head.

"Envied their careers?" I asked, confused.

"We do not understand one another at all. My species does not relate to Colmarians and your kind does not appreciate Damakans," he said.

My eyes must have flicked for a millisecond.

"Yes, I know you aren't a Colmarian. You're an Ontakian. It is too bad that *my* species was not as warlike as yours. Maybe we could have fought off the advances of the PCC."

"How did you know I was an Ontakian?" I asked.

"Laesa told me."

I was shocked. I had made her promise not to tell anyone.

"Don't be concerned. Who could I tell? Damakans wouldn't know a Colmarian from a Boranjame," he shrugged.

"Boranjame eat planets. Colmarians just mess them up."

"You should be proud you aren't a Colmarian. They are an odious species in a horrible empire."

"Yeah," I agreed.

I couldn't get over how deadpan he was.

"Were you and Laesa lovers?" I asked.

"Nothing of the sort. I think I need to take a step back and explain a bit about our species and my assessment of the Post-Colmarian Confederation Colmarian Confederation."

"I don't give a damn about your political views," I said. "Tell me about Laesa. Were you controlling her?"

"It will be so much easier if I go through everything," he said.

"You expect that you're going to talk and talk and act and act and somehow *convince* me that murdering Laesa Swavort was some great thing to do?" I asked in disgust.

"No, I don't believe I will be able to do that," he said solemnly.

"Then why the hell should I care?" I yelled.

"May I ask you a question?"

Just like that my legs got pulled out from under me. I had been on a nice, steady pace. Getting angrier and angrier. But it didn't accomplish anything. Risky Jerv wasn't flustered. He didn't fear for his life. And to top it off, he had information I wanted.

"Yeah. I guess. Sure," I said, defeated.

"Why do you think I had those actors killed? Those productions attacked?" he asked, staring intently at me.

"Market share. You take out the other Guilds then you're the big boss. You call the shots."

For the first time, Risky Jerv didn't seem to have predicted that answer. He was surprised.

"You think I had Damakans murdered for no other reason than to—I don't know—become a more influential Guild President?" he asked.

I didn't answer.

"Does that kind of thing happen around here? Do people murder each other just to get ahead in their employment?" he asked.

I thought of the countless gang wars. Civil wars. Galactic wars.

"Yeah. That's usually why they do it," I said.

He shook his head in disbelief.

"Most certainly we do not understand one another. It was a dark day indeed when the PCC came to visit my world."

I was about to say something but Risky Jerv held up his hand and I kept silent. Like I was a child who had been shushed by an adult.

"The PCC is currently at war with the Dredel Led, isn't that right?" he asked.

"More or less. I don't think there's a lot of fighting, but we aren't friendly."

"My native language doesn't have a word for 'war.' We only recently discovered that concept. We have no tribes. Or countries. No battling religions. Maybe it is that constant strife that has enabled the other species to become so technologically advanced. It is your constant broiling emotions that you harness to great heights. We should have never joined this empire."

"Everyone joins the PCC. Basically, any species that isn't important enough to have their own empire joins us. We get all the castoffs and riffraff."

"Why wasn't that explained to us?" he asked.

"Because it's not a very good sales pitch."

"Damakans weren't advanced. Aren't advanced. I know that. But we had other things. It was preposterous to ever believe that we could coexist in this empire," Risky Jerv said.

"The PCC has at least 50,000 unique species. You think no one else had assimilation problems?"

"It is far worse than that. Damakans cannot exist in the PCC. It will destroy us both."

I snorted.

"Don't pretend you're some innocent species caught up by the big, horrible PCC. You may not have grown up with the concept of war but you've managed to become a criminal mastermind all the same. You're coping with the change just fine. Now get to the point and explain before I pull your spine out through your mouth," I said.

Risky Jerv cracked a weak grin.

"You can't threaten me, Hank. I thought this was clear. I quite expect you are capable, both physically and in temperament, to inflict grievous injuries against me. But I am not *able* to cower in fear from those threats. You are not a Damakan. This is not a Horror Guild production. Only a Damakan acting could make me emotional."

I sighed and tried to cool down. Blowing my temper wasn't doing anything.

"Tell me why you used Laesa. What did you promise her?" I asked.

"Do you know why there are no murderers among my species?" he deflected.

"Who are you trying to fool? You have murderers. *Laesa* killed people. *You* made the contracts," I said.

"We have the capacity, but it is incredibly rare. What do you think we do to murderers in Damakan society? How do you suspect we punish them?" he asked.

I didn't want to play along, but I didn't have much choice.

"I don't know. Kill them?"

Risky Jerv flashed a brief look of surprise.

"*Kill* murderers? We truly do not understand one another," he said sadly.

"Okay, I get it. You all are wacky and strange and Colmarians are evil. How does this apply to Laesa? I'm running out of patience," I said.

"It is all connected, I assure you. In those uncommon cases where a murder was committed and the perpetrator caught, the punishment was always the same. Nothing."

"What? You just let them go? Does that prove you're some kind of enlightened people?"

"On the contrary. When we help one another experience emotions, we receive a kind of emotional payment for lending the help. There is no word for it in Colmarian—or I do not know it. The audience passes back that sensation, quite unconsciously. Even if they aren't Damakans."

"And?"

"We did not develop violence because we are too civilized, we avoided it in the name of self-preservation. To murder is to cause harm to countless people beyond just the direct victim. Friends. Family. Associates of the person slain. Even if they don't know it was you, a Damakan killer will *feel* that pain they caused until memory of the victim is completely forgotten by everyone alive. In consequence, a Damakan murderer never knows a moment of peace. They invariably commit suicide to escape the anguish. No punishment we could devise as a society would match what they already experience."

"Then why would Laesa become an assassin if she was going to be bombarded with sadness forever? Why would *you* do it?" I asked.

"Every species has its outliers. You, as I understand, are not a typical Ontakian."

"I'm not fat. I'm a mutant."

"I, too, am an outlier. I'm able to transmit emotions to extremely large groups. But we also have individuals who are not gifted, but instead...impaired. Laesa was one such person."

"Don't try and say she was a psychopath. I knew her better than that," I said.

"You didn't know her at all, Hank. As you are aware, Damakans get emotional stability from other Damakans. Each individual has his or her own needs. Some can function perfectly fine having merely a handful of acquaintances. But some Damakans require more emotions than even a large network of family and friends can provide. They are emotional vacuums. You might consider it similar to someone who was starving to death even after eating a full meal."

"Laesa wasn't like that! She was always happy and bouncy."

"Her behaving in that manner was not a display of *her* emotions. It was to provide those emotions to others. To you. She was not sad. Or angry. Or hurt. She was *negative* those things. Your people do not have this condition. You can be tremendously delighted or moderately at ease, for instance. But Damakans can not only be at zero emotions, we can be at a deficit."

It hit me.

"*You* acted for her. *You* were her emotional source," I said. "That's how she could be with me romantically. Because she was getting regular emotional feedback from you."

"The times she told you she was at 'acting classes' or 'rehearsals' she was often with me. I poured everything I could at her and it was never enough. But it kept her grounded."

"Why didn't she tell me about it? I told her all kinds of stuff wrong with me. I've got more health *issues* than I got health. I know she needed to hang out with other Damakans to be normal. Why the big secret?" I asked.

"I don't believe she fully comprehended what was wrong with her. I believe she came to Belvaille with the design of securing a larger emotional network, though tele acting, to satisfy her. I only discovered her condition by accident when I gave a speech to some young people and she was present. I could tell by her emotional feedback that she was out of the ordinary."

"So you promised her big acting roles? And that if she got them, it would keep her healthy. From all those billions and trillions of viewers giving emotional feedback," I said.

"You are correct. That is what I offered. I didn't suspect it would provide her much relief because she wasn't able to influence enough people. It was irrelevant if her performances were broadcast or not."

"You took advantage of a sick person. You lied to Laesa and raised her hopes."

"Yes, I did. Someone like her, on our home world, would have been the responsibility of the entire community. We would have pulled together to ensure she had sufficient feelings to cope and prosper. In the PCC, she was adrift. It wasn't possible for her to organically create an emotional framework large enough to sustain her."

"But even with your promises, why would she murder? She'd feel that guilt you were talking about for the rest of her life. You were *adding* to her problems," I said.

"Her condition made her ideal. Even applying my considerable acting skills I could barely affect her. Whatever passive feedback she received from her crimes, she would not even notice. She may well have been born for this. The first Damakan serial killer."

I pounded the table with my arms and split it in half. The crash knocked Risky Jerv out of his chair and he fell to the floor gripping his leg in pain. I reached down, took hold of his neck, and hoisted him up. I was going to push his face through the frosted glass wall and see if that changed his expression.

"You admit all this and don't show the slightest bit of concern. *You're* the serial killer. Not her."

"I can't show concern, Hank. I can't conjure up guilt on my own. I could act it, make *you* feel guilt and force you back into the hole of your despair. But that emotion wouldn't truly belong to me."

"Could you do it before I crushed your skull?" I asked.

"Yes. I could."

"Why don't you, then? Is this amusing for you?"

"Because you of all people should be able to appreciate my actions. You have done heinous things on behalf of others. Things I can scarcely comprehend. But you had personal reasons. Justification."

I slammed him against the wall. His collarbone snapped. His eyes rolled back when his head hit the glass wall. But after a few moments of dizziness, he once again appeared unbothered.

"If Laesa was the perfect stooge, why did you have her killed? Had she served her usefulness? Did you find someone else to abuse?"

"She got work," he said.

"Work? Killing other people?"

"No, acting. I had not thought it possible. Laesa was a very poor actor. But I didn't understand your connection with Cliston. I didn't know your butler was also the talent agent. If Laesa started getting broadcast roles, the lack of emotional payoff would make her understand that I had been deceiving her. My plan was in jeopardy."

Bashing Risky Jerv around was unsatisfying. He didn't react. I let go of him and stepped away. He slid down the wall and sat on the carpet.

"Did you put Laesa up to dating me? Was that your idea?" I asked.

"No Damakan has experience with murder. None have ever gotten away with it. We had to consult experts."

"So you tapped me?"

"No. We looked through Scanhand."

"And you saw me listed. That figures," I said.

"Actually, we went with other options first. There was someone named Frank."

"That's my uncle! Laesa dated him?"

"I spoke with him. But I recognized he was far too untrustworthy."

"So then you went to his nephew?" I asked.

"We didn't know he was your uncle at the time. He seems to take great pains to hide that fact. We spoke to Kaxle."

"Kaxle? He's not even a person!"

"I felt he was too unstable to risk," he said.

"But you hired him to kill Laesa."

"Yes. I did. There was no need for subterfuge or subtlety at that point."

"When did you settle on me as Laesa's future boyfriend?" I asked.

"You were about the eighth or ninth person we spoke to. We were anxious about your Trouble rating."

I don't know why, but that hurt. I wasn't even in the top five list of chumps they had pursued. Risky Jerv picked up on my thoughts.

"As I said, she came to admire you, as much as she could admire anyone. I have as well. Which is why I'm speaking to you now. We could never have put this together without your assistance."

"She could have gotten door codes and locations from anyone," I said. "Why did she have to charm me? Hell, I would have told you everything for a few credits."

"It wasn't merely where to find the targets. We had no idea how to actually murder someone. Even the most basic steps. How does one go about such a thing?"

"It was me," I said numbly. "I trained her how to be a criminal."

Laesa had often asked about my work. Never about negotiations, but about combat. Hurting people. Killing people. I assumed she was merely curious. That she was using it as fodder for her acting career. I told her where to get guns, how to use them, how to plan it, everything.

She was trained by an experienced murderer: me. Not knowingly, but that hardly mattered. Her Damakan victims didn't have a chance.

"You claim to have no crime. No war. Nothing bad. But you've just admitted to doing terrible things to innocent people. Damakans. Why?" I asked.

"In four days, the Guild Acting Rewards will be given out. I've ensured that the Comedy Guild will sweep the highest honors."

"You want...statues?" I asked.

"All the Guild Presidents made a secret deal with the Navy. Whatever Guild achieves the most rewards will set the scheduling for *all* future programming. That Guild will control the entire dramatic industry in the PCC."

"This *is* about you! You did all this to decide what brand of stupid tele programs gets made? Laesa *died* for that?"

"It wasn't for the Comedy Guild. I'm not doing this for me. Guilds never existed before we came to this loathsome empire. I did it for the galaxy."

"How humble. Now I *know* you're crazy," I said.

"I argued with my fellow Damakans for years. I told them that our acting was dangerous to Colmarians. But they couldn't see it because it's not dangerous to us. We don't know what it's like to have *real* emotions. To be gripped by the heat of passion as you are. Colmarians cannot control themselves when faced with Damakan broadcasts. It is immoral to force emotions upon the galaxy."

"I think you're overestimating your abilities. Not everyone is a fan of Damakan drama," I said.

"The most popular tele programs among Colmarians always involve death and destruction of the foulest sort. Those shows are the province of the Horror Guild. I knew they would win the competition if no one stopped them and then the Horror Guild would control Damakan programming. The galaxy is already a vile place full of needless brutality. If we flood the empire with lurid tales performed by Damakans capable of *instilling* those feelings, how much bloodshed will that cause?"

"But you didn't just attack the Horror Guild."

"No. I attacked them all. I had to be certain. When I couldn't convince the other Guilds to create less offensive programs in order to spare the Colmarian people, I began discussing the issue with Laesa. She agreed to help me," he said.

"What are you going to do? Stop all tele programs? They aren't going to let you close up shop. You've created the demand," I said.

"I realize that. But I'm in the Comedy Guild. If Damakans *must* create programs and broadcast emotions, we will shower the galaxy with laughter and joy. If we *have* to manipulate you, we will force you to be happy."

"But you also benefit. You're the President of the Guild. That's no coincidence. You'll be the most powerful person in the industry. The whole empire will be hooked on your product."

He smiled weakly.

"I am not Laesa. Although I did not directly commit the attacks, the murders, I can *feel* them. The injuries sustained, the lives that have been lost. It is a grief that expands daily. I did not do this for me. I will not live to see it."

Risky Jerv slowly picked himself up from where he had been sitting on the carpet. It was then I noticed that his left leg was turned at an odd angle. When I broke the conference table, I must have also broken his leg. He winced setting his chair upright and taking a seat. Looking at him, you would think he was dealing with nothing more bothersome than a mild insect bite, not multiple broken bones.

I didn't know what to think. I couldn't tell if he was acting or not. Was this another performance or did he believe what he was saying?

"This is not a performance," he said.

"You say that, but how do I know?" I demanded.

"Because you are unsure. If I was acting, you would *believe* it. I can't halfway act. Or partially broadcast emotions. But I want to tell you that I *do* feel Laesa's loss. It emanates from you with every pulse of your heart."

"You should! You caused it. All of it."

"I did. And I apologize. Though I understand that word is appallingly insufficient. The feedback from her death is with me every moment. Not as strongly as with you, but I am burdened by many others. My kind have no ability to process that grief," he said.

"I took a lot of drugs for a long time."

"That would not help me," he said.

"Didn't do much for me, either. I...I don't know. This is a lot for me to sort through," I said.

"The last thing I ever wanted to do was create more suffering. But I saw no choice. Colmarians routinely destroy one another without any pretext. When driven to emotional frenzy by Damakans, how much worse will things become?"

"So let me get this straight. If I killed you now. *Right now.* Would you care? Would it do anything? Or would I be putting you out of your misery?"

"Everything is in motion. The Comedy Guild will be triumphant at the Guild Acting Rewards. From my understanding, this is similar to Therezians," he said.

"What about Therezians?"

"The Colmarian empire found their species and determined their physiology made them too dangerous to be permitted to roam freely. Damakans aren't giants with incredible strength and durability like Therezians, but we are no less deadly," he said.

"You're not toxic waste. You're actors. Good actors, but still actors," I said.

"I read in the news that a young man watched a Damakan police drama and acted out one of the scenes in his home town. He killed eight neighbors."

"Maybe he was already screwed up. Some irrational, mentally ill people *may* be incited by Damakan dramas."

"And how many such people exist in the galaxy? Millions? Billions?" he asked.

"Probably. But the universe can't be made safe for the most vulnerable while still accommodating everyone else. It's not possible. Crazy people are going to be crazy no matter what they watch. We can't build a society that caters to lunatics."

"What about the inhabitants of this very space station? Just using Scanhand, I managed to perpetrate a crime wave."

"Yeah, but we were crummy long before you all showed up. If anything is proof that Colmarians can handle broadcast emotions, it's Belvaille. There's a whole lot of maladjusted psychopaths that live here and a whole lot of weapons. According to you, we should have killed each other years ago, when you broadcast your first action movie," I said.

"But you've assaulted actors and productions."

"Yeah, because you *paid* us. You mentioned the Guilds made an arrangement with the Navy. I thought they didn't do anything more than collect the profits."

"They have left the industry alone, for the most part. But once we create and record a program, we have to coordinate with the Navy to use their transmission equipment."

"What equipment? On their ships?" I asked.

"I'm not sure what they do. A simple tele is far beyond any technology I can decipher."

"Who did the Guilds make this secret deal with? Did a delegation come from one of the capitals and speak to you?" I asked, trying to understand.

"There are Navy personnel on this space station already. We specifically work with their liaison. I believe the military title is Adjunct Overwatch."

"Garm? You're talking about Garm? A woman? Garm?" I asked hurriedly.

"Yes. That is her name. Do you know of her?"

"Hold on! Hold on! Black hair? Only talks about money? Medals all over her uniform? So many ribbons it's like a parade exploded in front of her?"

"We only met in person once. But your description is accurate."

"She *knows* about this deal? Garm? Where the winner of the most GuildARs gets to decide the industry content?"

"She administers the Navy broadcast facilities. Apparently, it was burdensome to deal with each Guild and fashion a slate of programs. She told us we had to nominate *one* Guild to oversee all Damakan productions. That way the Navy would only be involved in transmission and not any of the day-to-day issues."

"And you all decided on the Guild Acting Rewards?"

"It was her suggestion."

"Garm came up with the idea? Why?" I almost screamed.

"The Guild that won would prove they already had the skills necessary to create the empire's tele programs. It would show they could create popular entertainment."

"But you're cheating! You killed Damakans."

"I explained why," he said.

"Garm knows you've been attacking the other Guilds?" I asked.

"I don't see how she would have that knowledge. From my estimation, she wasn't particularly concerned about anything we did. The Navy wants to have as little to do with us as possible."

"You big dummy! Garm *is* the Navy. Garm is a friend of mine. I used to date her. Dated her granddaughter. She had me searching the city to try and find *you!* When it was her stupid idea that started this whole mess."

"I do not follow what you're saying. The Comedy Guild will score the most Guild Acting Rewards and supply the Navy with Belvaille's programming schedule. Those shows will be pleasant and uplifting. It will be of benefit to the entire galaxy."

I was sputtering, stamping my feet, trying to talk as my brain did backflips.

"I can call Garm up right now and have her cancel the Guild Acting Rewards. When I tell her what you did, there's no way she'll let you win. She was at my wedding!"

"The Adjunct Overwatch made a *formal* Navy agreement with all the Guilds. Swore us all to secrecy on our proceedings. She was extremely strict about it. Said it was 'Top-Secret-Confidential-Hush-Hush Level 9.'"

I almost had a heart attack.

"That was a joke! Don't you all know jokes when you hear them? You're in the damn Comedy Guild. Does 'Hush-Hush Level 9' sound like a real Navy term?"

"I wouldn't know. Damakans never created weapons, let alone a military structure to use them," he said.

"Holy crap. You turned this city upside down for nothing. Absolutely nothing. You got tons of people killed in this ham-handed, Gang-Guild war. And you murdered Laesa. You can forget your Guild Rewards. You can forget everything. All I have to do is tell Garm and you're done."

"But why would you?" Risky Jerv asked.

It was so ignorant I almost laughed.

"Didn't you hear what I said?" I yelled.

"I did, Hank. But did you listen to *my* words? If you can convince the Adjunct Overwatch to renege on her agreement, it will be disastrous. The galaxy will be forced to endure Damakan manipulation of the most negative sort. It will be a constant barrage of emotional torment. Do you wish to see the PCC unravel? I thought you had personally struggled to prevent such catastrophes. I'm trying to save Colmarians, and by extension, my people," he said.

"You're horrified at Colmarian savagery. But you deceived and killed an unhealthy Damakan. Got her to eliminate some of your most talented citizens. You've done everything you accused Colmarians of."

"I only did it to protect them," he pleaded. "We will be easy victims of Colmarian aggression. Aggression that we inadvertently caused with our tele programs."

"You don't kill innocents to protect them. If your objective is to save little children, you don't start by making a bonfire out of little children."

"I've read your stories. I've heard them from Laesa. You've hurt and even killed innocents on many occasions," he said.

"I'm a *criminal!* I'm a bad guy. I'm an outlaw according to the PCC. Don't use me as a guide on how to create a harmonious galaxy."

"You've repeatedly made the decision to do dreadful things in the name of helping a larger whole."

"But I made damn sure I understood the choices first. You've been in this empire for a few decades. You looked at our worst examples and decided that's who we all are. But it's not."

"I believe it is the right thing. I've witnessed what can happen," he said.

"You're right about a lot of things, Risky Jerv. Colmarians, and even Ontakians, are emotional. Far more emotional than Damakans," I began.

"I did not mean to imply that it is a weakness. Our species evolved differently. You have abilities we can't begin to approach. There will never be Damakan soldiers. Or brilliant Damakan mathematicians uncovering the mysteries of space. We are a simple race that happens to possess a biological quirk the PCC felt they could exploit. But our societies should never have been brought together."

"You said we will never understand one another. But I think you made some fundamental miscalculations about Colmarians," I said.

"In what ways?"

"Laesa is gone. She isn't broadcasting emotions at me any longer. But I still care about her."

"Yes. You engaged in self-destructive behavior at her passing. Imagine if you experienced emotion like that every night watching the tele."

"But that's what you don't get. Maybe Laesa got me first interested using her abilities. But I loved her because of *me*. That's from here," I said, tapping my chest. "People fall in love with the wrong people, for the wrong reasons, all the time. It wasn't a Damakan that made that possible. It's because I cared for her," I explained.

"I believe you're missing the point. If Laesa had incited you to violence instead of trying to court you, how much damage would you be causing to this very day?"

"It's not the same," I said.

"They are all emotions."

"We aren't gibbering madmen. We have a vast, collective empire. That was built with logic, not emotion. Yes, the PCC is backwards. But Colmarian is just a word. There is no one Colmarian species. It's an amalgamation of 50,000 unique races that more or less cooperates. That alone is amazing."

"Don't tell me every atrocity Colmarians perpetuate is done logically. That you engage in purely intellectual mayhem," he said.

"No. We have crimes of passion. But Damakan shows cannot create the same emotional intensity as real life. We know it's fake."

"That is not true. I've witnessed it time and again. Stolid businesspeople brought to the pinnacle of fear by a clever show. I've seen hard men weep openly at hackneyed dramas."

"But do they stay like that? Do they go home crying? Cry for a week? A month? I admit I've been swept away by Damakan programs. But then they're over. And I go back to being me. We don't watch horror movies and then commit horror. It's a break from our reality. We aren't slaves to them."

"I have made a long study of your Colmarian culture. Experienced all your stories and poetry and movies. All Damakans have."

"I know, I know. Hank the Fat Mutant of Belvaille."

"Wait. That's *you*?" he asked.

"No. I mean, I guess it is. But it's not true. None of what they taught you is true."

"*Hank the Fat Mutant of Belvaille Consumes a Giant.*"

"I didn't eat a Therezian. Those are just stories. Lies. Well, entertainment," I said.

"Most Damakans were delighted by the breadth of Colmarian history. The eons you've spent with mass murder. It is good material for drama. I alone seemed to realize what it meant for a culture to embrace such a savage personality."

"That's not our culture," I said.

"Of course it is. Belvaille has done nothing but confirm that. There is violence every single day on this space station."

"Yeah, because someone screwed up. Or is mad. Or wanted to rob someone who didn't want to be robbed. But no one gets shot because they watched a violent *theatrical piece*."

"The dramatic Guilds created programs that draw largely on Colmarian history. Your crimes and carnage, mistresses and massacres. The PCC empire has embraced our programs. If you are suggesting that our media doesn't truly represent the Colmarian society, why have our shows become so popular?" he asked.

"Because you guys are damn good! Yeah, the PCC probably discovered your planet and was like, 'Meh, these people have nothing. Not worth our time.' Then you wacky Damakans put on a school musical or something to welcome the space aliens and every sailor was so blown away they immediately quit the Navy and opened an improv theater."

"Precisely. Colmarians are too susceptible."

"I was exaggerating. You have to understand, we don't use stories the same way you do. To us, they're entertainment. Or they have moral lessons. Or they're a temporary escape from our boring, mundane lives."

"You are a mutant murderer! How can you say your life is dull?"

"Because it's *my* life. I get tired of it. I get stressed out. I want a break now and then. Damakans use drama to feel emotions they don't naturally have; we use them to escape the emotions we *do* have. If I'm depressed, I can't simply decide to stop being depressed. I have to replace it with something else. Damakan programs do that for us."

"Are you willing to risk flooding the galaxy with negative emotions? Do you believe that Colmarians—or Ontakians—can resist the influence?"

"Do your worst. On me. You can act, right? You can project emotions. Make me mad. I got anger problems already. I have a dead wife and I'm talking to her killer. If I can resist, that will prove others can as well. It will prove we know the difference between reality and Damakan fantasy."

"If I do this, and you kill me in your fury, you must swear to allow my efforts to succeed. To assist Damakans in bringing cheer to the empire. And to protect my people. We are not able to protect ourselves. Do you swear it?"

"I do. I swear it," I said.

Risky Jerv was seated. His collar bone broken. His leg broken. He wasn't a threat at all.

But he began talking. Emoting. Gesturing with his hands. He was insulting me. Insulting Laesa. Talking about how he used me. Sneering. Cackling.

It was subtle at first, but I myself being pulled. I *knew* he was doing it. I repeated the mantra in my head that he was doing it. But it didn't matter. I bared my teeth like an animal and my fists clenched so hard I dug my fingernails into my palms.

There was an Ontakian drug called daxapronal that was designed to make my species become focused warriors. It worked differently on me and I merely became a raging maniac. I felt very similar under Risky Jerv's taunts.

I turned in circles and stomped on the floor with every step. Punched at the air. Shook my head. Tugged at my hair so hard I thought I'd pull it out of my scalp.

Risky Jerv continued his japes. Raised them to extremes. I was furious. He was cutting me, and everything I cared about, to ribbons. He searched out every dark crevice of my mind and not only laid it bare, but spit on it and set it on fire.

I finally had enough and turned toward the seated Damakan.

I leaned over and put my face a few inches from his.

"You, my friend," I said, tasting the words, licking my teeth, "are a fantastic actor!"

I stood up straight and smiled. My jaw hurt from clenching it. My muscles were rigid. My blood pressure was high.

But I knew it wasn't real. What he was saying wasn't real. He killed Laesa, but his death wouldn't resurrect her. He did it, all of it, because he was trying to help. He was wrong, misguided, but pulling off his toes and shoving them up his nose wouldn't avenge Laesa. It wouldn't save me. Risky Jerv was a little man who was lost and confused in an enormous galaxy he never knew existed.

He stopped acting and watched me. I paced around, still hyped from my experience. Damakans would be fantastic cheerleaders. I wanted to beat his face in, but *I* was in control. Me. I wasn't a puppet. If I ultimately punished Risky Jerv, it would be on my terms for my reasons.

"You were right," he whispered.

After that, neither of us said anything for what felt like hours. I daydreamed, pushed into my subconscious by the Guild President's theatrics.

I snapped out of it when I heard a thump.

Risky Jerv was on the floor, curled into a fetal position, save for his broken leg.

I walked over to him, warily. I wasn't sure if he was going to try a different angle on me and portray tragedy and sorrow. I didn't have any tissues handy, but I could use my shirt.

Risky Jerv was crying. Sobbing, his faced shriveled and creased. But I didn't feel anything other than caution. And my chillwipes had worn off and I was getting warm. Also I was a bit hungry.

"I killed them," he said. "So many of my people!"

"Then you understand us?" I asked.

"I don't. I'll never understand. I'll never bring them back. They're gone. All the things they could have been. I feel all of them. I am so sorry. I was a fool. An arrogant fool!"

He was pathetic. Shaking and oozing. It wasn't a Damakan act, because I felt nothing other than he deserved it. Now that he realized he had been wrong, that he wasn't saving the galaxy from ruin, he had no justification for his actions. He was absorbing the full force of the blowback. All the sorrow from everyone connected to the Damakans who died.

And these were actors who were broadcast across the galaxy. There were billions of people who experienced that loss, however slight. All that grief and disappointment poured into Risky Jerv.

"Colmarians—and Ontakians—may be barbarians compared to your species, but it's not easy for anyone to take a life. To deal with it, you have to rationalize, deny, or shut some of yourself off. Do that enough and you close off so much that you aren't you anymore."

"Hank. How do you cope?" he asked.

"Living by a set of principles. Doing penance when I can. Laesa asked me once how I dealt with it. Was it okay to win at any cost? I didn't get what she was asking at the time. If I knew what she was planning, I would have responded very differently. There are some costs that are too high. It isn't a victory if you destroy yourself or go down a hole you can't climb out of."

Risky Jerv reached out toward me.

"Your loss. For Laesa. It is inside me. When will it stop?"

"Stop? It will never go away completely. It will get less over time. But she will always be there. The pain, but also the good times."

"Can you forgive me?"

He writhed on the carpet, his broken leg twisting and clacking.

"I can. But I'm not a Damakan. It won't do anything for you."

"Please. Make it stop," he said.

"You want me to kill you?"

"Yes! Please. I was wrong. Horribly wrong. Help me."

I took the only weapon I brought to this meeting from my coat. A regular knife with a six-inch blade. I dropped it next to Risky Jerv.

He scooped it up like it was an heirloom of incalculable importance. His whole body was trembling. He turned the blade in his hand. Held it like a dagger. The realization of what he had to do was competing with his sorrow.

He brought the knife down...on his thigh. Poking it.

He then poked his arm. His chest. His stomach. His skull.

The knife fell from his hand and he fell back to the carpet.

"Ow," he said, sobbing.

"You don't know how to use a knife?" I asked.

"Bread," he cried. "Cutting...vegetables."

Man, these guys really shouldn't be on Belvaille.

I hated Risky Jerv for what he had done to Laesa. But as I stood there, watching him bleed from a dozen little cuts, I couldn't feel anything except pity.

There was a Hank who believed that everyone should get what's coming to them—and a little more on top of that. And Risky Jerv earned this. Death by dehydration. From crying. I could see myself ordering some food, getting comfortable, and watching Risky Jerv suffer for the next four days as he withered away.

But I wasn't trying to impress anyone. Risky Jerv wasn't a gang boss that I had to make an example of. More importantly, Laesa's ghost wasn't standing over my shoulder, asking for revenge. She had been sick and wanted to be made well.

I said I dealt with my crimes through atonement. Saving the galaxy erased the times I robbed defenseless grandmas.

This was a situation where I would choose my path. The person I most despised in the universe was at my mercy, begging for release.

I picked up the knife and used it.

Quickly. With as little pain to Risky Jerv as I could manage.

And that was it.

He was gone.

There was no triumph. No sense of clarity or salvation. I was the same Hank I started with. But at least I wasn't any worse.

I killed someone who made a mistake. A terrible series of mistakes. I believed in forgiveness, but some mistakes were bad enough you didn't get a second chance. If you jumped off a building wondering if you could fly that's a mistake that you only got to make once.

I started to leave the conference room when I spared one last look back.

"Damn," I said.

There was blood all over the carpet.

Cliston would be furious after all the warnings he gave about his precious rugs.

Screw it. Cliston said the carpet was stain proof. Or self-cleaning. He could deal with it. I was done.

CHAPTER 34

I had known Garm for a long, long time. For whatever reason, it never registered to me how vindictive she was. I suppose because I was smart enough to never betray her.

I had a policy that if anyone shot me, I had to give them some sort of payback. Even though I was bulletproof, I didn't want people thinking it was okay to blast me. Bullets hurt. And there were weapons a lot deadlier than firearms that I didn't want pointed at me. MTB had taken my policy and made it more severe. If anyone harassed or slandered him, he'd smack them around so they wouldn't do it again in the future.

Garm had a policy that if anyone did...*anything* to her, she would not only have them assassinated, she would wreck their businesses, ruin their families, humiliate their friends, and if they happened to own any pets, she would have them stuffed and mounted on a wall—a dirty wall.

Garm didn't play around. She destroyed her enemies. She didn't always handle it herself. In fact, she'd probably hired me to do it a thousand times at least. Garm didn't like dealing with the same problem more than once. So she removed any chance of it being a problem ever again.

When I explained to her what Risky Jerv had done, her immediate reaction was to cancel the GuildARs. She called up the Guilds and told them the deal was off.

She was about to disband the Comedy Guild and banish all its members from Belvaille when I stopped her. It wasn't their fault. It was Risky Jerv. He was a first-generation Colmarian who had failed to comprehend how our universe worked. A lot of people lost their lives because of that confusion, including my Laesa, but Risky Jerv had also died.

I recommended that Garm create an association that would handle the production slate for the dramatic industry. Garm immediately thought about money and who should head that association. How much would gang bosses pay to have a piece of that?

But no, I told her to make it be the Guilds. Damakans. They should run it.

Risky Jerv was right about one thing, the less direct interactions Damakans and Colmarians had, the better. I promised Garm that Belvaille could find a way to siphon money out of the dramatic industry, but we had to let Damakans be Damakans. And to do that, we had to protect them from Colmarians.

Let them observe us and create entertaining stories based on our significant flaws and features. We'd buy those stories. Sell them. Trade them. Exploit them. But if we ever turned Damakans into Colmarians, it would be a sad day for the galaxy.

Garm finally agreed. She was happy to move on.

In some ways, Risky Jerv had succeeded in his plan. We would still be broadcasting Damakan programs throughout the empire, but his species would be handled with care, at least on Belvaille.

Maybe things *had* to happen like they did. If Risky Jerv had come to us and said that his people needed protection, we wouldn't have cared. Enough money had to get disrupted and enough people had to die for us to appreciate this lesson.

The dramatic industry resumed operation almost immediately. I figured I would have to explain what happened, but no one cared. Not even the gangs cared. There had been an unorthodox gang war for months, but as soon as the funding was cut off, it ended and Belvaille's criminals went looking for other revenue sources.

With the resumption of the dramatic industry, Garm was in the clear with the Navy. They were so happy they gave her a new commendation. She got to wear a sword. And by "got to" that meant she was required to display it. But it wasn't just any sword. It had a particular length and style that was designed on some central PCC planet according to central PCC racial characteristics. The long sword dragged on the ground behind her. Some of the gangs started referring to her as "Sparks" because of the perpetual metal scraping.

This was all well and good, but I still owed a fight to Procon Hobb.

I had to battle Kaxle in Cheat Hall in repayment for tipping me off about the Historians being the source of Scanhand. It would also secure Rendrae's ownership of his precious newspaper. Through talent agent and fight promoter Cliston, I let Procon Hobb know I was ready.

The arena match was scheduled for six months later, giving time to both train and advertise. Not to mention get Belvaille in order.

I was sitting around watching the tele one night when a commercial came on for the match. Kaxle the Ferocious versus Hank "Stank Delicious" the Fat Mutant of Belvaille. The commercial had short interviews with the two combatants, which were clearly Damakan actors. I'm not sure why they didn't use us. They didn't even ask me. The Damakan Kaxle wore a cheap fur costume that was hardly realistic. But as an actor, he was so convincing at being Kaxle that I was terrified watching. The Hank actor was so good that I was immediately hungry after he spoke. Procon Hobb paid for the commercials and was running them regularly.

People began to pour into Belvaille in order to watch the match. No one knew Kaxle. And only a small number knew me. But people were excited. This was the first main event for arena combat in modern history. The sport was practiced all over the empire but was only marginally legal and lacked production value. Procon

Hobb was attempting to take arena combat mainstream. He would finally have an achievement, however useless, that he could claim as his own.

After solving the Damakan Guild war, Scanhand listed my Smarts as nine. My Toughness was ten with a gold star next to it. For my Trouble rating, I had apparently broken the system, because there was a stack overflow error message. When you tried to click on the details, the application would crash, and in some cases, it would cause irreparable damage to your tele.

I viewed the fight as a necessary assignment to keep Procon Hobb and Rendrae happy. But now I believed this was a good opportunity to rehabilitate my reputation.

Not only that, but Kaxle had killed Laesa. Yeah, it was set up by Risky Jerv. But Kaxle actually did it. I had gone through every stage imaginable dealing with my grief. At this point, Laesa's death had been over a year ago and I was almost back to normal. And my back-to-normal self was very interested in getting payback on Kaxle.

I intended to win the fight.

By cheating.

Because I was pretty confident everyone else, from bookies, to Kaxle, to spectators, were also going to cheat. This was Belvaille. I wasn't going to be the only one playing by the rules. Besides, did anyone actually expect me to *not* cheat in the arena I personally made famous for cheating?

Over the preceding year, Delovoa had completely repaired and upgraded Kaxle's armor. I got the details of the design from my idiot friend and it was pretty sobering.

With no assistance on either side, fighting in a big, open field, Kaxle, and his Delovoa-built, multi-weapon power armor, would easily triumph over me. I was heavy. I could heal. I could fly in space. But Kaxle was outfitted to fight a war. Kaxle had used the last of his Gang-Guild war money to pay for his armor. And Delovoa made the mother of all invoices. My only hope was that Kaxle would be so confused by all the options available that he couldn't decide.

But I possessed something that Kaxle did not: I had friends. Very talented friends. We would meet at my apartment every night and go over strategy. I had an expert assassin, city administrator, and Navy liaison, complete with sword, in the form of Garm. Cliston was an authority on every skill no one even knew existed. MTB and his rugged police force were the designated security at the arena. Delovoa was the designer of Kaxle's armor and was not above killing everyone on Belvaille if it would result in increased scientific knowledge—or if he did it by accident.

Adding to them, I was friends with gas-cloud taxi drivers; I had a long history with the only legitimate reporter on Belvaille; I was technically a member of the Ontakian society in exile and one of their main citizens was my uncle Frank; and

I had association with countless thugs, counterfeiters, forgers, gamblers, prostitutes, drug dealers, vagrants, and mischief makers who called Belvaille home.

I thought about contacting the Boranjame royalty who had his own ship near Belvaille. The Marquor of Lunacy, Gax, the Unfathomable and Disreputable. But all I had to do was say his name out loud to remind myself why one did not drop in on a Boranjame without a prior invitation.

One of my biggest concerns about the fight was handled long before it began. I had dealt with Kaxle enough times to know that he was *always* with the Rough Boys. The two other mutants might not be anywhere as scary as Kaxle, and their armor not as advanced as his, but they were going to join the arena fight despite the fact they weren't supposed to. So I was going to have to deal with them along with Kaxle.

But Cliston had started getting job offers. Not as a talent agent. Or butler. Or fight promoter. People wanted to get married.

There were a few other ministers on Belvaille but only Cliston was fluent and capable of performing ceremonies for nearly any Colmarian or non-Colmarian species. You would think his last wedding would have dissuaded clients. The one where my bride was killed and I became a hopeless drug addict. Not to mention a bunch of the guests were murdered and the church destroyed.

Quite the opposite. Cliston had chaperoned the deadliest wedding in Belvaille's history. Why would any self-respecting gang member settle for another preacher?

In any case, when the two less-rough Rough Boys weren't hanging out with Kaxle, they were hanging out with each other. And it turned out they wanted to get married. Wanted Cliston to marry them.

Cliston suggested the date and time of my arena fight was when he could conduct the ceremony. It meant I wouldn't have access to Cliston's bountiful skills during the match, but it removed two Rough Boys from the equation.

I wasn't terribly pleased that those Rough Boys were getting happy, mutant matrimony after they helped Kaxle fight me the first time. So I asked Cliston to botch up the ceremony somehow. Fight promoter Cliston agreed. Even my butler agreed. But neither was performing the wedding. The best I could get from preacher Cliston was a vague assurance of spiritual castigation. Which sounded like a polite no.

As preparations for the arena battle were escalating, I went searching for Belvaille's most persistent blue-collar worker.

It took longer than I expected to find him. By my count, he had held twenty-three different jobs since I last talked to him. Lagla-Nagla, the lopsided man, was now assigned to Wallow. I got a cab ride from Zzzho to my old street and met him there. When I walked up to the dead Therezian sprawled across the road, Lagla-Nagla was standing on Wallow's thigh operating a large vacuum cleaner.

"That's a weird job," I said, as I approached.

"Hi, Hank. If it pays, it's not weird."

"Are you concerned that a big corpse is dirty?"

Lagla-Nagla turned off the vacuum so we could talk. I was standing just under him on the road. The leg was so big, it would be a decent fall if Lagla-Nagla slipped off. But he had several ropes securing him.

"Kids have been hanging around here. They leave a lot of trash and campfires and started putting up graffiti."

"Who decided you should be picking up litter on a deceased giant?" I asked.

"Procon Hobb. With your arena match coming up soon, they wanted to show the city in its best light. Besides, this might be a tourist attraction one day. There aren't many Therezians left."

"He's not exactly left either. But I get what you mean. When you sold me drugs, you had mentioned that you used to know Kaxle before he was mutated. Is that right?" I asked.

"I worked with him. I would guess on...three different jobs. Over the course of ten years. But I work with a lot of people."

"Tell me what you know. I'm trying to make a personality profile," I said.

"I have to get this thigh cleaned and then sweep out the glass between his toes. I think the kids throw bottles at his feet."

"I'll help you. There's probably some of my dried blood still between his toes and it will bring back memories," I said.

Lagla-Nagla was on a ladder with a rope around his midsection working from the bottom of Wallow's left foot. I climbed up some debris from a smashed building and then I was on top of Wallow's ankle.

"Kaxle was a mean little guy," Lagla-Nagla said.

"That's no surprise."

"He had it tough here on Belvaille."

"Everyone has it tough. Did he have a bull's-eye tattooed on his forehead or something?"

"No. None of this will get back to him, will it? Kaxle could rip me in half and not even notice. I don't like making a practice of gossiping," Lagla-Nagla said.

"I always get gossip from you."

"Yeah, but about gang bosses. Or nobles. Not monsters."

"I won't say a word." I put my hand over my heart, but Lagla-Nagla couldn't see me because Therezian toes were in the way.

While there was trash on top of Wallow, he was otherwise extremely clean. His skin was harder than any surface on the space station. You could use the harshest solvent or tool you had to clean him. There was no concern about doing any damage to the body. Especially since he was dead.

"Kaxle was really small. Like the size of a Po or one of Procon Hobb's slaves."

"They're not slaves. I think technically those lizards worship him," I said.

"Same difference. But whatever species Kaxle was—"

"He wasn't Colmarian?" I asked.

"Yeah, he was Colmarian. But that doesn't mean anything. Kaxle was stubby. And kind of plump. He couldn't move very well. He would kind of hobble side-to-side when he walked."

"Okay, I get you. He was kind of handicapped?" I asked.

"I think the term they use now is 'jack fracked,'" Lagla-Nagla said delicately.

"*Who* uses that term? That doesn't sound polite."

"I didn't say it was polite. I just erased a bunch of graffiti that used 'jack fracked' a lot."

"So Kaxle was gimpy?"

"Right. But you know how it is. Our personalities are formed from our frailties," he said.

I thought about that in relation to my own life as I picked up some glass and put it into a trash bag. The glass couldn't cut my hands but Lagla-Nagla had to use a broom.

"That's pretty insightful," I said.

"Yeah. That was another bit of graffiti I saw earlier. I almost didn't want to remove it, but it was on his eye."

"Someone put graffiti on Wallow's *eyeball?*" I asked, shocked.

"Sure did. The white part. It's one hell of a climb up there," he said.

Wallow was lying in the street, but parts of his arms were still on buildings and his whole upper body was leaning against several, which propped him up a bit. This immediate area was deserted because of Wallow. He blocked the street and there was a concern the buildings would collapse and the body shift. And who wanted to live near a gigantic corpse?

"You're saying Kaxle got picked on? And that made him mean?" I asked.

"No, he did the picking. He started fights with anyone he saw."

"I thought you said he was frack fracked, or whatever. How did he beat up people?"

"He didn't. He got his ass kicked every time. But he kept at it."

"Was he trying to prove himself? You all work for a gang?" I asked.

"This first place was back at a nobleman's spa. You know, when Belvaille had nobles. The noble had these consorts—"

"Music concerts?" I asked.

"No. *Consorts*. Like, fancy hookers," he said.

"Okay, gotcha."

"But he was into these Neflorns. The species was aquatic. Underwater. They would gum up the filters and fans in the hot tub. I had to clean it out."

"Sounds kind of gross."

"Like I said, any job that pays is a good job," he replied. It was that attitude which made Lagla-Nagla Belvaille's serial worker.

"Was Kaxle doing that with you?"

"No, he did other stuff, but at the same boss. The noble, Ziferon del Morshinon of Porinis-Gail—"

"Man, I'm so glad I don't have to remember any of those titles anymore," I said.

"Me too. But everyone there hated Kaxle and Kaxle hated everyone. I must have seen him get in twenty scraps."

"Were people making fun of him?"

"No. Not at all. He'd find a reason to start brawling. I could never figure it out because he was so bad at it."

"He ever fight you?" I asked.

"No. I don't do that nonsense. Not when there's a paycheck on the line. He would talk to me. Kaxle would say this new guy was eyeing him funny. Or flexing on him. Or some other reason to start throwing punches. I'd tell him to ease off or he was going to get canned."

"Did he get fired?" I asked.

"Yeah. He lasted a few months. Then I got transferred to another noble not long after," he said.

"You work with him at your next job?"

"No, no. I didn't see him for years," he said, and I heard him stop brushing glass, so Lagla-Nagla must have been concentrating. "You had just started Super Class. We were in construction, helping build a stadium."

"You built Cheat Hall?" I asked, surprised.

"Yeah, it wasn't called that then. They needed every bit of labor to put that up."

"I was surprised when I saw all those workers. You would think they would have robots or something. But it was people on scaffolding straight up to the latticework," I said.

"Robots? No one's going to use Dredel Led in PCC territory."

"I don't mean Dredel Led. Just robots, you know? Like automation."

"Robot is a Dredel Led far as most people is concerned. Cliston is the only one people can stand. He's like the exception."

"You know Cliston?" I asked.

"Everyone knows Cliston. I worked at his teeth place cleaning the floors and emptying the trash."

"Teeth place? Cliston is a dentist?" I asked.

"No. You remember that species that came here with the really big heads?"

"That describes a million varieties of Colmarians."

"But it was one ship and they stayed for a year. They had *huge* heads. And really big teeth. Like the size of your fist."

"No."

"You'd remember if you saw them. Anyway, they had like, writing on their teeth. Pictures and stuff. Scrimshaw. Cliston would do that for them. Make designs and pictures," he said.

"Would they hand Cliston these teeth to work on?"

"No, it was the teeth inside their mouths," he said.

"Didn't that hurt?" I asked.

"I never heard no screams or nothing."

"Was Cliston any good at teeth-writing?"

"I can't say from personal. But the big heads seemed to like it plenty. His waiting room was packed every day," he said.

"And he's still doing this?" I asked.

"No, no. This was years back. But I worked for Cliston again making baskets—well, Cliston made them. I'd help split big strands of rope into smaller strands. Other people did reeds. Some others sorted glass pebbles."

"When was this?" I asked. I couldn't believe Cliston was working odd jobs behind my back.

"Decades ago. Cliston opens a shop every few years. But only for a little while."

"Is it always teeth and baskets?" I asked.

"No. Different every time. Stuff you never heard of. But he seems to make money."

I shook my head thinking about it. I thought Cliston only wrote books and pamphlets. I guess it made sense that he would *use* his skills now and then. Or that he would have to *do* things to get those skills in the first place.

"Anything else about Kaxle?" I asked.

"Yeah. He hated you."

"Me? Did I do something to him?" I asked. I didn't remember a Kaxle, but this was before he was mutated.

"No. He just thought you were a phony."

"Phony? Like how?"

"Phony tough guy, I guess. He always said you weren't anything special. When you were playing glocken, he thought you were holding the team back," Lagla-Nagla said.

"He was probably right about that. How often was I a topic of conversation?"

"Not much. But whenever you played a game or did a deal in the city people were talking about. He just didn't like you."

"That stayed consistent even after he became a Rough Boy. You recall anything else? Like his family?"

"He didn't talk personal. It was all about who he was going to beat up."

"Okay. Hey, this was a big help."

"Did you discover any secret profiles?" he asked.

"I got to dwell on it. I'm not a Damakan. I can't do it on the spot."

"Sorry about your marriage," he said.

"Were you at the wedding?" I asked, not sure if I invited him.

"I was, I was. I was parking cars. A valet. A lot of your friends are bad tippers," he said.

"Yeah."

"But a few are really good tippers. So it kind of evened out," he added.

"Good. Thanks again for your help, Lagla-Nagla."

"Not a problem. Let me know if you need anything else or Cliston is starting any new businesses."

CHAPTER 35

Emotionally, I was ready for the arena fight. The memory of Laesa was no longer a jagged piece of iron in my chest, poking me with every breath I took. I didn't think about her all that much, honestly. I know that sounds terrible. But when people say they dwell on some loss or love every single day, it sounds romantic, but they are either full of crap or permanently scarred.

We move on. It's what we do to survive.

I was old. My mutation, and modern science, had allowed me to live for...I don't even know how long at this point. But I didn't ponder my sorrows—I was too busy making new ones. I would think of Laesa in the *good* times. When I wanted to.

Mentally, I was also ready for the fight. I knew what I needed to know. I had prepared. I left room for creative improvisation. Because that's what I was good at. I wasn't good at planning out every minute detail. At some point I started second and third-guessing myself and I'd screw up my plan if I tried to overthink it.

If I wasn't a bulletproof mutant, maybe I would plan more. But if I was a Therezian, maybe I would plan less. Maybes don't matter.

The night of the Kaxle arena fight came and everyone on my team went to their assigned duties.

Cliston had to perform the wedding ceremony for the two Rough Boys, so he was gone early. He said he would be available, on a limited basis, via tele.

The stadium was raised over the city, sitting on supports just above some buildings. But it wasn't designed to handle this many pedestrians. They were clogging up the roads.

It was a nightmare getting into the arena. People were yelling at me or cheering me or spitting at me or trying to throw drunken punches in my general direction. I found the ordeal was sapping my energy. The good news, I suppose, was that Kaxle would have to go through at *least* the same thing. In his armor he was far more recognizable, not to mention larger and more cumbersome.

It took about two hours just to get on one of the roads that fed into the stadium itself. It was claustrophobic walking up the enclosed tunnels that were choked with representatives of every single species in the PCC. I was stepping on tentacles, getting jabbed with horns, and tasting ammonia in the air. It was a mess.

Finally, I teled for MTB to send some cops to escort me inside or the fight would never begin. And then he'd have to put down a riot.

The cops displayed an excess of enthusiasm.

They dropped a pile of concussion grenades and tear gas into my tunnel. And beat and clubbed anyone who got in their way. That filtered away everyone except me, and a few weird species who enjoyed the taste of tear gas.

"Hey, kid. MTB said you needed a hand," Frank stated, wearing his red policeman's uniform.

This had been my suggestion. I was concerned that I would be attacked by the fans and spectators during the match. That might be okay during a normal night when there were only a few hundred fans armed with pistols, but who knew what a hundred thousand visiting fans from across the galaxy would be packing? I wanted MTB's police to control the stadium. But to do that he would need each officer to be armed with a tactical nuke or he had to get more manpower.

MTB never had enough police. Because no one wanted to be a low-paid cop that everyone disliked when they had the option of being a highly paid criminal that only some people disliked.

I reached out to my brethren, the Ontakian species. Ontakians were a slave race that had been custom designed by the Rettosian empire. Belvaille had about the largest collection of Ontakians left in the galaxy since our home world was destroyed. When the Rettosians left this System, most of the good jobs vanished for Ontakians.

I suggested that MTB recruit the combat-model Ontakians still on Belvaille as police. They were perfect for the role. In fact, they were literally built for it. They were resistant to damage, strong, and they would be as uncompromising or flexible as MTB desired.

Frank negotiated on behalf of the Ontakians. And one of the conditions was that he be made a lieutenant on the police force. Not second-in-command, but not far behind. I pleaded with MTB to refuse. There was no telling what harm Frank could do if given even the slightest amount of authority.

But MTB was so smitten with the idea of having a capable police force for the first time ever, that he agreed.

So when I was "rescued" from my traffic jam at Cheat Hall, it was by an army of Ontakian combat-model police, led by my uncle.

The new recruits didn't have to be trained—they were born trained. They didn't have to be armed—they didn't need weapons. Practically overnight, Belvaille's police went from a joke to an effective organization you dared not cross.

"You could have used sirens to disperse them. Those are paying customers," I said to Frank.

"Yeah? I could have also tickled each one and read them bedtime stories. This was a lot easier. Come on. Need to get you to the locker rooms before the next wave comes."

I was flanked by Ontakians. I felt more protected than the King of the Galaxy.

"There is no such thing," Frank said.

"Shut up, this is my story," I replied.

They escorted me to the locker room where I had some trainers, some police, as well as MTB, Garm, and Delovoa.

"What's the crowd in the stands look like?" I asked.

"Low-rent hicks from the sticks," Delovoa said.

"Really? They came all the way to Belvaille?" I asked.

"Ticket prices are a third what a typical Super Class glocken game goes for," Garm said. "Not only that, but space travel has gotten a lot cheaper over the years."

Garm wasn't wearing her Navy uniform, of course. She was off duty.

"Are the other Rough Boys coming?" Garm asked.

"No, they're getting married to each other. Cliston is handling that," I said.

"Is it Rough Boys as in unorthodox, unrefined, or rough as in coarse and bumpy?" Delovoa asked.

"I don't think it's any of that," I said. "Does everyone know what they're supposed to do?"

"I'm still confused on what my role is," Delovoa said.

"You built Kaxle's armor. You're my technical advisory board. And you're to work with Garm as a floater. Dealing with any mischief that MTB and his Ontakian police can't handle," I said.

"And how do you expect me to handle it if they can't?" Delovoa asked incredulously.

"I told you to bring some fancy inventions. What are those?" I asked, pointing.

Next to Delovoa were some gadgets and a floating drone that looked heavily armed.

"I didn't know you meant weapons! I brought my remote-control pillow-fluffer and eyeball sharpeners," he said.

"You're a weapon designer. Why would you bring non-weapons?" I asked.

"I devise *other* things. I thought you were going to have an auction or something. I've had these sitting around forever," he said.

"People can fluff their own pillows," I yelled.

"What if they don't have hands?"

"Then how are they going to use a remote control?" I asked.

Delovoa looked the device over. It was covered in small buttons.

"Their feet," he replied smugly.

"Just...help out Garm," I said.

* 335 *

"Help her do what? I'm not a Quadrad," he complained.

"Give her tax advice. Be a cheerleader. I don't care," I said.

"Do you need any pillows fluffed?" Delovoa asked her. Garm chose to ignore his presence.

"I think my new recruits can deal with most anything this audience can come up with," MTB said rather cockily.

"Great. But Garm, you're backup. And Delovoa is your backup," I said.

"Don't mess up my city. Everything is in working order and the Navy has finally taken us off their list of problem areas," she said.

"That's got to be a huge list in the PCC," I replied.

"So big it's worthless. But it's still a list we were on," she said.

"Imbecile Navy and its imbecile lists," Delovoa teased.

Garm finally looked at him.

"If I kill you right here, about a thousand times more people will be happy than sad," she said.

"I'll be sad. Or at least unhappy. Wait until the arena match is over," I said.

"Besides, MTB will arrest you with his new super soldiers," Delovoa countered.

"I'm not going to arrest the Adjunct Overwatch. She could chop off both my arms and drop them on the ground and I couldn't even give her a ticket for littering," MTB corrected.

Garm smiled at Delovoa, who smiled back with his rusty metal teeth.

"Enough! Be pissy on your own time. I'm trying to survive this fight," I said. "Call Cliston to make sure he's on schedule. Give me updates on Kaxle's location and preparations. Keep the audience under control. Get everyone else in position."

My crew of trusty companions grumbled and muttered as they went about their tasks.

I had my trainers check my joints, tendons, and ligaments. They confirmed they were all bad. I had them rub down my feet and shoulders, but they lacked the mechanical strength of Cliston, so they didn't do much more than hurt their hands.

I spent most of my waiting time in meditation. Not in the spiritual enlightenment sense, but just thinking about Kaxle and his personality profile.

The start of the match kept getting postponed. Procon Hobb was contacting me telepathically to let me know Kaxle wasn't ready.

I called up Cliston. I didn't know the tele number for preacher Cliston, but I had the tele for butler Cliston. It was the same number, but I had to call my butler first and he transferred me. Yeah, it was stupid.

"Are the Rough Boys getting any calls?" I asked.

"Yes. I believe your adversary for tonight's bout is speaking to them. I can only hear the responses, but they are saying they will try and hurry over when they are complete here," he said.

"Stall them! Last thing I need is two more armored mutants showing up," I said.

"How might I stall them? I have the evening's activities planned perfectly."

"Make it imperfect. You're Cliston. Think up some weird Cliston stuff. Have them do ceremonial dances. Or ceremonial speeches. Make them take a math test to prove they are ready to be married. Don't make it official until you get word that I'm done with this fight. Is that clear?" I asked.

"Respectfully, I don't work for you, Hank. I'm merely keeping you appraised out of courtesy to your butler and because you used my services for your own, unfortunate, wedding," preacher Cliston said.

"Thad Elon's Frosty Nutsack, Cliston. If you mess this up, I will get Delovoa to modify my body so that my sphincter empties out directly on the floor with every step I take. You'll be constantly scooping up my wet crap!"

There was a slight pause on the line.

"You'll be pleased to learn that I *just* thought of four hours of entertaining activities I can use to extend the wedding." Then he thought to add. "Sir."

"Thanks, Cliston."

I wasn't going to go out on the field until Kaxle was there. It wasn't an ego thing. I had a few tricks ready and I didn't want to tip my hand.

Frank, MTB, and the police were talking back and forth in abbreviated, military fashion on the tele. They sounded like they had the stadium under control. Anyone who got too rambunctious was given a stern warning. Anyone who ignored it, was beaten to a pulp by Ontakians who were slightly high on daxapronal. It was a damn expensive drug to acquire now that the Rettosians had shipped out, but it was worth it to keep the fans subdued.

Procon Hobb told me to go out on the field. I said no. Well, I *thought* no. I wouldn't go out until Kaxle did and I was happy to wait all night. I knew he was stalling to try and wait for his companion Rough Boys to finish their wedding so they could help out. But that wasn't going to happen.

Finally, Kaxle couldn't delay any longer and took the field. I heard the thunderous response from the audience.

I suited up and went out.

Kaxle stood across from me at midfield. The crowd cheered, booed, and threw things, before they were smacked around by the police.

Kaxle's armor was completely changed. In Delovoa's redesign, the cannon had been removed. Kaxle, having frozen, and fireworked, and exploded himself with that cannon, realized it wasn't very useful on a space station. His suit was now fully enclosed, armored, and equipped with claws on both arms. It was also significantly more agile and lighter than it had been, having lost its big armament. He couldn't fly, but he had life support, and no obvious weak points. His previous armor had been a mismatch of metal plates and colors that looked like a tractor had collided with a tank. His new armor was white, like his fur. It was sleek, elegant, and terrifying.

Delovoa had truly outdone himself. The armor must have cost millions of credits. I know, because he billed Kaxle for slightly over five million.

Fortunately, the claws no longer had nanobots that ate away your insides. Delovoa said he felt bad about my hospital stay. But honestly, I think he simply ran out of the parts to make them.

In my estimation, Kaxle was more dangerous than ever. His previous armor had been clunky and cumbersome, with firepower so excessive it was just as harmful to himself as anyone else. Now, all his natural abilities were heightened.

It was going to be tricky. As in damn near impossible.

My outfit was strange for this setting. I was wearing body-tight insulated layers of synth clothing. Designed by Cliston, of course. My skullcap had an integrated tele I could use to communicate with my team. I had dark, radiation-proof eyewear, and several spare sets of glasses, in case the first got damaged.

It was agonizingly hot in my gear. Which was why I had waited so long to put it on and come onto the field. It was made worse by the ridiculous Damakan climate in the city.

"Keilvin Kamigans, proceed with plan," I said into my tele.

My gas buddies, Zzzho, Zzzha, and Zzzhi—yeah, that was his new name— were up on the latticework. I couldn't have done this next part without Delovoa and Garm. I was somewhat worried about making the call so early, because I couldn't undo it. The Keilvin Kamigans were now out of tele contact, since they couldn't hold teles with their nonexistent hands.

Belvaille had tremendous environmental controls. It had to, we were in space. We couldn't put some plywood on the roof if we sprung a leak. We also had to deal with the 50,000 species of the PCC, any one of which might have a homegrown virus or bacteria that could kill us all with one sneeze. I'd never known anyone to have even a common cold since I'd been on Belvaille because our systems were so robust. The Keilvin Kamigans plugged themselves in to those systems.

Delovoa once told me that Keilvin Kamigans were the most efficient batteries in the galaxy. It's why a species that was less substantial than fog, with no ability to manufacture, or mine, or create technology, was still valued and respected.

Keilvin Kamigans powered everything of importance in the PCC. My own spaceship, the Suckface, relied on Zzzho as an energy source. It took almost nothing from him. He said it would be like if I had to *fart* into a gas tank a few times a year—though I'm not sure he understood what farts were.

Now my gaseous friends were shoving themselves wholly into Belvaille's latticework systems. Three Keilvin Kamigans was a lot of juice, but for a city the size of Belvaille, it still wasn't that significant. They were only working with the machines directly above the stadium.

Immediately, the lights' intensity increased almost a thousand percent! Not only that, the lights normally put out a tiny amount of ultraviolet radiation as a side effect. It didn't matter at its usual level, but it was enough now to lightly burn your skin. Garm was covered in what looked like half an inch of sunscreen.

The increased light blinded everyone. Except me and my team, who were equipped with sunglasses.

Kaxle roared and covered his helmet with his metal claws.

I charged across the field toward him.

At this point, people in the audience would normally be yelling and cheering, but no one could see the action. They were screaming in the agony of scorched retinas and mild sunburn.

My charge wasn't very fast, because *I* was not very fast. And I was hot. But as I moved, the air started to turn cold. Not just lower than Damakan temperatures, it was getting nippy. The Keilvin Kamigans were also overloading the air conditioning system above the stadium.

The space station's atmosphere was complicated. As cold air blew directly down from the latticework, there were still eddies and currents of hot air swirling around, creating mini-weather zones. But the temperature gauge began inexorably heading south within the arena.

The humidity control was the final system the Keilvin Kamigans affected. Normally, Belvaille was bone dry. If you needed moisture, you had to put drops in your eyes, or nose, or mouth, or have attendants, like Procon Hobb's, constantly spray your whole body down with water. But our hijacked systems slowly began to pump out more water into the air.

Delovoa and I had gone over the design for Kaxle's new armor trying to find something to use. One thing about suits, whether armor or business, was that they're hot. Adding personal air conditioning in the battlesuit was too bulky and easy to damage. Delovoa had created room in Kaxle's armor to add chillwipes or layers of clothing. So Delovoa was sure that's what Kaxle would do to compensate for the stifling conditions in a Damakan-heated arena.

But now the temperature was dropping, humidity rising, and the light was blinding. Kaxle had no protection against those conditions.

Already I could feel the cool air filling my lungs and against my face as I neared my opponent.

Kaxle was still protecting himself from the harsh light. He probably figured the latticework was malfunctioning. It had never been used as a weapon before. If this was a normal city, I'd be in all sorts of trouble for commandeering the very systems that kept us alive in deep space. But Belvaille wasn't a normal city.

I rammed into Kaxle as hard as I could.

This was a test. It would tell me if I had any chance whatsoever of beating Kaxle tonight.

He staggered! My blow was enough to make him take several steps backwards and even steady himself as he went down on one knee.

The old armor would have been laughingly immobile if I ran into it. His new suit was more flexible, but it offered a lot less protection. The pistons which powered the joints were no longer exposed, but they had to be miniaturized, so they could fit inside the plating.

Kaxle thrashed around with his whole upper body. His helmet went side to side as if he was trying to shake off the glare like some pesky fleas. Bestial Kaxle was frustrated and reacted accordingly

"I smell you, Hank," Kaxle purred.

He sprang from his crouched position and ripped upward with his right claw. Kaxle tore a gash across my entire midsection all the way up to my face!

I would have lost my nose if I hadn't tilted my head back a millisecond before he hit. My sunglasses were cut almost perfectly in half.

Kaxle hadn't been shaking like an animal. He had been trying to gather my scent. He was forcing air into his armor by moving around.

Without sunglasses, the latticework lights screamed down at me and I fumbled to get one of the replacement pairs I had stored.

But Kaxle wasn't letting up. I hadn't moved from my initial hit so Kaxle did a scissor swing with both his claws, aiming for my neck.

Only the fact I was reaching down for sunglasses, which changed my profile, saved my head. My left shoulder took a huge hit but Kaxle's other hand missed completely. The difference in impacts made his attack have less force because he was unbalanced.

So much for my great plan. In two seconds I lost my vision, a chunk of my torso, and my shoulder.

When we met to prepare, Delovoa kept talking about those claws. The metal they were constructed with. Or something. I didn't care. I knew they weren't as powerful as the previous ones. To me, they were just big knives, and I wasn't much concerned about knives. Once I knew the cannon was gone, the nanobots were gone, the jets were gone, the armor plating was thinner, and the pistons were weaker, I thought this was my fight.

But Kaxle was mutant-strong and mutant-fast, and his power and speed were enhanced by the armor. The best carbon-steel blades would shatter if Kaxle used them on anything firmer than a wet marshmallow. He was simply that strong and fast. But Delovoa had built something special with those claws. I hadn't paid any attention because they didn't seem dangerous.

However, my gaping chest could attest to the danger of Kaxle and his metal fingers.

I put my arms up and covered my head and neck. Kaxle slashed two more times but he hit poorly, smacking me with his wrist and forearm instead of the claws. He could smell me, but that wasn't the same as seeing.

My own synth outfit was surviving well despite being completely unarmored. Cliston had taken a look at Delovoa's battlesuit design and tailored my clothes to resist slashing. They didn't block the attacks at all, but the stuffing didn't spill out and the incisions resealed themselves.

I shoved Kaxle. It was a desperation move to try and buy me some time and it worked better than I anticipated. I was blinded by the light as much as he was, but I felt him give way and fall to the ground.

I moved backwards and to the side. My mistake had been to stay in one place after he sniffed me out. Super mutant or not, presumably his nose wasn't as good as sonar, especially when he was wearing an enclosed metal helmet. I started fitting a new pair of sunglasses to my skullcap and turned on my tele.

"Delovoa, he can still smell me. I thought you said his air was filtered," I asked.

"Delovoa is at the concession stand," Garm answered through clenched teeth.

"What? Delovoa!"

"They got caviar and champagne," Delovoa said, clearly eating. "Ah! That's good. They even have pretzels."

"Never mind the food. What about the armor?" I asked.

"The respirator only removes *toxins*. He's not in a self-contained breathing unit. As stinky as you are, you're not mustard gas. Your scent won't be filtered," he said.

"What about the station's life support? It's hardly changing," I replied.

"We're trying to change the atmosphere in a square kilometer of airspace. Give it at least ten seconds."

"I'll be dead in ten seconds!" I said.

"Then I won't buy you any caviar. Oh, wow, they've got roasted duck anus," Delovoa said.

With my sunglasses replaced I could again see. I tried to blink away the sunspots.

Kaxle was more acrobatic in his smaller armor but getting up from his back was still not a fluid process. I should have attacked him, but I was still half-blind and wasn't sure how quickly Kaxle would recover.

Once he was back on his feet, he shielded his eyes, turned around to face me, squatted, and jumped. A claw passed six inches from my forehead and his other claw stabbed my right thigh.

He pulled out and swung, but I blocked it. I pushed him away again, but this time he kept his balance.

He circled left, shaking his helmet to gather air. Then he turned, sprang at me, and uppercut with both claws, which caught me under my left forearm and my right side. Before I could even process that, he cocked his arms back and tried to scissor off my skull again. I unlocked my knees and dropped, using gravity to help instead of fighting against it. The lethal blow was only a glancing shot to the top of my head.

My opponent liked to lunge. I had not known that about his fighting style. In preparation for this match, I had asked around town to get information on how he brawled. However, the people who had fought Kaxle tended to be dead or unable to speak due to traumatic injuries.

Kaxle could jump quite far, even in his armor. That fact made me underestimate his reach and allowed him to close distances instantly. He would wait until there was a gap between us, lunge, take two swipes in the air using his accelerated speed, and then another two when he landed. Then he'd back off, sniff, and repeat.

He did this two more times and on each occasion I was unprepared. Because he made feints and starts and switched up his strategy. And I was a slow learner.

Despite my synth outfit looking fine, I was a mess of cuts and punctures underneath. I felt I was only delaying the inevitable. My movements were slowing down and getting sloppy. Kaxle was going to connect with a kill shot any moment if I didn't turn things around.

Then it started raining.

It wasn't *really* rain. We were in space. But the Zzzhos had overloaded our environment systems and the humidity was at epic levels. We had created a cold front surrounded by the Damakan heat on all sides. Globules of water splattered and misted and fogged in swirling patterns.

If Kaxle could smell me in this, I needed to buy some better anti-perspirant. Presumably in the afterlife, since I would be dead.

I walked backwards, zigzagging. I was practically tiptoeing, to mask my sound. It was foolish, since the stadium was pumped with music and tens of thousands of spectators. Even if I wore trash cans for shoes and danced on an aluminum floor, Kaxle would have a tough time hearing me over the ambient racket.

The mutant wolf in question shook his head rapidly. Swung his body. Then he tilted his neck back and began to sniff. I couldn't hear him sniffing, but it was clear that's what was going on. Either that or he was gargling inside his battlesuit.

Other than my draining blood, conditions were improving for me. The rain was picking up and the temperature continued to drop. I was wearing insulation, Kaxle was, we suspected, wearing street clothes or cooling products under his armor.

"MTB, status on the crowd," I asked.

"Hey, kid, they're fine," Frank answered.

"Bystanders blind," MTB said. "He was asking me, Frank. And don't forget to use radio protocol."

"This isn't a radio. It's a tele. You don't want my nephew to get killed because you all take too long, do you?"

MTB sighed. He was already regretted hiring Frank. I told him so.

"I told you," I said.

"Hank, did you make your squatface war cry?" Delovoa asked, chewing food on the tele.

"Suckface. No, I'm losing. Hey, unless it's urgent, don't talk unless I talk."

"You *are* talking," Delovoa said.

"Don't respond—just be quiet," I said. "So when is the armor going to be affected by the weather?"

Silence.

"Who you asking?" Frank said.

"Why would I be asking *you*, Frank, about complicated battle armor you had nothing to do with when the inventor of the armor is on the line?"

"I don't know. That's why I thought it was weird you were asking me," he said.

"Delovoa!" I shouted.

"Am I allowed to talk now, oh Lord?" he replied.

"Yes!"

"You still have a long while. I would guess another hour or two," he said.

If Delovoa was in front of me, I would have punched him in his ugly, duck-butt-chewing face.

"Two hours? I've never even heard of a roving street battle lasting that long. Arena fights last a few *minutes* at the most. You said it would take seconds," I said.

"About that. I think I was wrong. I kind of guessed on my calculations."

"Why would you *guess*? Hank's life is on the line," Garm said angrily.

"Many apologies! I've never modified the weather on a space station before. No one has. You know why? Because space stations don't *have* weather. I invented a brand-new field of science and you want me to be a seasoned expert," Delovoa huffed.

"I can't hold him off that long," I said.

"By the way, the name of the new science I created is called Hankface-the-Fatface," Delovoa said.

"This crowd won't sit here patiently," Frank said. "You better wrap it up soon. Sports fans who spend three months travelling to *watch* an arena match want to see what they paid for. Right now, they can only see your latticework supernova."

I made a call to Cliston.

"Cliston, how far along is the wedding?" I asked.

"Nearly done. How is the arena?" he asked.

"Would I be calling if it was going well?"

"I would hope so. You said your butler should prepare a festive party in celebration of your victory. And that *I* should perform a ceremony at your funeral if you lost," he said.

"Stall the Rough Boys a bit longer. The weather isn't cooperating."

"Even if we end on schedule, they would have to reach the stadium. With all the traffic, I anticipate that would take a considerable while."

"I don't want to risk it. Maybe they have a jet car somewhere. No matter what, don't let them say 'I do' until my fight is over."

"They will not say 'I do' in this wedding. They wrote their own vows. They end with 'Oi, yoze.'"

"Alright. Don't let them say that either," I replied.

"I will do my best, but I am running out of religious assignments. They are currently performing the Anutsian ritual scrubbing of the lavatory."

"You got them cleaning the bathrooms?" I asked.

"Yes. Procon Hobb should be pleased."

"Wait. You're having the wedding at the *same* church I used? I thought it was destroyed."

"They repaired it while you were a drug addict. Besides, it is the only church on Belvaille that can seat four hundred and twenty-three guests."

"Is that more people than my wedding?" I asked.

"You would have to consult your wedding planner," he replied delicately.

"*You're* my wedding planner."

"Not at this moment. Excuse me. I need to resume my responsibilities. Best of luck to you."

The priest ended the call.

"Ha, ha," Delovoa laughed on the line. "Cliston hung up on you."

I called Cliston back.

"Cliston! Listen. We're friends. *Good* friends. You've saved my life a lot of times. And we accept each other's quirks. But when it's an emergency—like now—I need to know I'm talking to *one* Cliston. If we're in our apartment and I yell 'fire!' I have to know you'll help out. I can't be worried that I'm suddenly dealing with a Cliston personality who is a pyromaniac. You bring a lot to our relationship, but so do I. I haven't gotten you killed, and I expect the same in return. Just because I'm a mutant head-cracker doesn't mean you're better than me. I might be a criminal, according to the PCC, but you're a Dredel Led. The PCC is at *war* with your species. A real war. However much they dislike me, they aren't targeting me with military vessels—at the moment. So, you know, we're in this together and I need you to maintain your end. If you can't deal with that, maybe we should reevaluate where things stand between us."

Silence.

Everyone on the call held their breaths. Not even the police were communicating to one another while they waited for Cliston's reply.

Finally, someone broke the quiet.

"Did he hang up again?" Garm asked in a nervous whisper.

"No. He didn't answer. That was a voice message for him. But he'll listen to it later," I said.

"Ha, ha!" Delovoa laughed. "Your butler doesn't answer your calls."

It's intriguing how some skills never go away. You learn them once and they are lodged in your brain, your nervous system, your muscles. Walking took *ages* to figure out. But it's super easy once you know it.

Swimming. Riding a bicycle. Those are skills that never go away—so I've heard. I was always too heavy to swim or ride a bike.

My point is, some skills stay forever, and some decay over time. The rate at which they go away depends on the skill in question.

Fighting. That was one of those skills that decayed. I hadn't really noticed that before. I was often fighting, so I didn't get an opportunity to forget how.

But I hadn't been in a fight since my wedding more than a year ago. As coincidence would have it, it was with the same guy I was currently dealing with.

Since that time, my fighting skills had atrophied. It wasn't just muscles and twitches and such. It was strategy and tactics. And plain old common sense.

For instance, I forgot that during an arena fight, you shouldn't call up your butler and leave him long voice messages when the only thing keeping you from being murdered was the fact your adversary couldn't locate you because he was blinded.

Me blabbing incessantly on my tele was enough for Kaxle to approach and make a precise lunging attack without me realizing.

Next thing I knew, I was on my back pressing my hands to my gut. I was sure if I removed them, my intestines would escape, happy to be free from a lifetime of overeating.

Kaxle loomed over me, his claws dripping blood. *My* blood.

I couldn't see his face under his armor, but I was sure he was smiling, his fangs glistening.

My tele was filled with chatter. Garm. MTB. Frank. The police. Delovoa. Even Cliston had broken character so he could speak. They were yelling and arguing and conveying information. All in a futile attempt to save me. It was a dull buzz I barely noticed.

"You have any last words?" Kaxle said to me.

He was poised. Powerful. Ready to dispatch me with those special claws I should really know more about.

Last words...

In the history of Belvaille, no one had ever asked that. I must have witnessed at least a thousand murders in my life. Not once was the victim asked to give their last words.

The killer, or killers, or me, had already chosen the person to die. We had already confirmed that their *life* was not worth sparing.

If it had been decided that everything that person might accomplish was not of sufficient value to allow them to live, why the hell would we care about a few syllables they could conjure up before death? Someone facing doom, their mind *choked* with adrenaline, was not capable of profound thoughts or phrases. The last words of a dying person were worthless.

So no one ever asked for them on Belvaille. Kaxle was officially the first monster to do it.

It wasn't that Kaxle was particularly clever or progressive. There had been an early Damakan murder-rampage-revenge tele program called, "The Sins of Your Brother Who is Being Shot Repeatedly." It was a classic movie that spawned a whole genre with its success.

In that show, the brother was asked for his last words and he said all kinds of amazing things that led us deeper into the story.

Well, every single murder-rampage-revenge program that came after, and there were a lot, had a last-words scene. At least one. Some had dozens, last words being spoken so frequently that you wondered if anyone was left alive to hear them.

Culture affects the real world. Even exaggerated, Damakan attempts at culture.

Here was Kaxle, a real-life killer, about to real life kill me, and he was repeating lines written by a Damakan who had probably never killed more than an insect.

My mind was in the same region as *any* person facing their own destruction after suffering grievous injuries. I was distracted by excitement, fear, and pain. I was in a stadium filled with screaming sports fans. And my tele blared disjointed conversations into my ears.

And it was still raining on a space station.

If I was asked for my shoe size right now, I probably wouldn't have been able to give a meaningful answer.

But I had seen the same programs that Kaxle had. At first, I was really annoyed by the last-words scenes. What a pointless, unrealistic thing to ask.

However, the scenes kept coming up again and again, and I started to wonder what *my* last words would be. I spent a lot of time thinking about it in the shower, or before I dozed off to sleep. When I finally came up with an answer, it became a kind of mantra for me. I'd ask myself for my last words and then reply. Over and over in my head.

It was this repetition that imprinted the words into my subconscious and allowed me to respond to Kaxle despite my present situation.

"You have any last words?" Kaxle said to me.

"Bela-Tore Jangle-Flot," I replied immediately.

My tele went quiet. Everyone shut up all at once.

"What?" Kaxle asked. He must have thought my brain melted.

"Bela-Tore Jangle-Flot," I repeated.

"W-what's that?" Kaxle asked.

"Where I stored my money. The source of my power. The start of everything," I stated serenely.

Kaxle and I had become a Damakan drama. It was now his turn to say his lines and he didn't know the part.

"Which...uh, which thing? Start of what power?" Kaxle asked.

"All of it," I said, no hint of confusion or fear in my voice.

I had spent a long while thinking about the concept of my last words. I finally decided there was no value in being philosophical. Why leave my killer with a life lesson? Like I gave a bloody crap if the person about to murder me would go on to better things. There was nothing I could do or say that would make Kaxle change his ways or forever declare that I was an amazing guy—that he killed. Bestowing wisdom upon Kaxle with my last words was the absolute least important objective, out of a universe of possible objectives, I was interested in accomplishing.

I'd never been dead before. For all I knew, it could be an eternity of awesomeness and comfort and good times. But it's something you only got to do once. You don't get to be dead for a few months and then say, "You know, this isn't for me," and go back to being alive.

I avoided everything you couldn't take back. Everything permanent. I didn't have any tattoos or cosmetic surgery. I didn't have any children. I'd never gotten a mortgage or long-term loan. Hell, I never even wrote my name in a bathroom stall indicating I was a source of good times, because I couldn't be sure how long those words would hang around—we didn't have a lot of janitors on Belvaille and Lagla-Nagla could only get around so fast.

I invented my last words because if I was ever asked to give them, it meant I was about to die. And I didn't want to die. I had rehearsed my last words a thousand times at least. Because if I was ever called upon to answer, I'd have to recite them perfectly, through a curtain of dread.

The purpose of my last words was to stall for time. Confuse my foes and possibly save my life.

The Keilvin Kamigans had been steadily changing the environment controls over the stadium since we began the fight.

We had talked about what might happen next, but I wasn't prepared for it.

I had seen it in tele programs hundreds of times. Seen it in photos. Read about it. But I had never personally witnessed it.

Snow.

It was snowing on the space station Belvaille.

The stadium spectators, which had been at a fever pitch of discontent, suddenly turned confused. The rain they could handle. That merely heaped on more annoyance. But these were largely space-faring citizens. Snow was hardly unique in the galaxy, but there were enormous swaths of the empire which had never once encountered it in person.

I was one such person. It was...beautiful. I was on my back, holding my guts in, and I felt like I was witnessing magic.

Kaxle stepped back. Stepped back more. Then more. His mutant-animal mind couldn't grasp snow. To someone who gathered all their life experiences in artificial environments, snow was a bewildering appearance.

And it was everywhere. The sky was full of it. It collected on the ground and coated everything that would sit still for a moment. And it kept coming in sheets. It seemed like the air was more snow than air.

You assumed—or I assumed—it would stop momentarily. Because that's what stuff did. But this wasn't confetti. Or balloons. Or glitter. Or any of the similar things we might have seen in the past. The snow kept going and going, inexhaustible.

I thought the snow would diminish the stadium's supercharged illumination. But if anything, it was even brighter. I had on my sunglasses but the light felt like it was coming from all sides, instead of just the latticework overhead. It was as if the snowflakes were overeager light bulbs trying to force their way in through any gap where my glasses didn't perfectly touch my skin.

How did people get used to snow? I kept flinching. I had a lifelong habit of blinking whenever I caught focus on an object coming toward my eyes. Even if I knew it was only a bit of frozen water flakes.

It was against every instinct I had, but I removed my hands from my wounded stomach. I expected a jack-in-the-box of intestines to shoot out, but there was nothing. Not even a dab of blood. Cliston's resealing synth clothes remained intact and were acting like a pressure bandage.

I leaned to my left and put my right arm on the ground. Half my forearm disappeared into the snow. It was piling up that fast. But my clothes were warm and I had far bigger concerns than numb knuckles.

As pretty as the snow was in the air, on the ground, however, it was wet stuff. Slushy. It might be sub-freezing temperatures up near the latticework, but the city floor and its structures were far removed. It would take them days, or even weeks, to cool down. They had absorbed Damakan heat for years.

Delovoa said Kaxle's battlesuit wasn't able to handle cold. I asked what that meant in specific terms, but he wasn't sure. Delovoa didn't plan out mistakes ahead of time. He just built stuff and waited for the inevitable catastrophes—which always happened to someone other than himself. We suspected that Kaxle would have taken steps to keep himself cool in the armor, so now he was probably frigid.

If we were keeping score, Kaxle had torn a bloody gash across my stomach and I'd made him chilly. So far, he was winning.

The spectators had also adjusted. They created makeshift tents and umbrellas to filter out the light and weather and now they were back to their rambunctious selves.

"What are the chances of the crowd attacking?" I asked on the tele.

"It's a damn natural disaster up here and the snow ain't stopping. I got binoculars and I can't even *see* you guys," Frank answered. "Unless someone smuggled in a snowplow, half these people will be lucky to get out of here without frostbite."

"Good," I said. "About them not attacking. Not frostbite."

But that was my only bit of welcome news tonight.

Kaxle was done admiring the snow and no longer seemed concerned about the nature of Bela-Tore Jangle-Flot. I probably should have come up with less silly sounding last words.

Kaxle was about thirty feet away from me. At this distance, in the light, in the snow, in his white armor, he was difficult to see. I'm not sure if he could still smell me, but I crossed to my left, a bit to the right, then back to the left to try and confuse my location.

I experienced intense pain from my slashed gut that radiated down to my thighs and all over my back. But I resisted the urge to put my hands over my midsection. If Kaxle could see me, I didn't want him to know how injured I was.

Kaxle lunged, covering at least half the distance between us in one standing jump! He landed in a crouch, pushed out to lunge again, and his legs shot out from underneath him.

He slipped. Apparently, running and jumping in a metal battlesuit, on wet snow, was harder than anyone guessed—though no one bothered to guess.

Instead of a graceful attack, Kaxle went hurtling through the air, his arms and legs flailing wildly. He bounced off my right shoulder and splatted into the snow. His momentum was enough that he twirled away, making two complete circles across the field and ending up more than a dozen feet away.

I moved to take advantage of my fallen enemy. The first step I took, I fell down. Apparently, walking as an incredibly heavy Ontakian, on wet snow, was harder than anyone guessed.

Snow was confounding stuff.

Out here on the field, it was deep and wet enough that moving took considerable effort, but it was also slippery as hell—assuming hell was made out of wet snow. Which, I was beginning to feel, was a really good choice of building materials if you were constructing eternal damnation.

"Does anyone know how to move in snow?" I asked in my tele.

"Jet pack? Boat? Ice skates?" came some of the useless replies. I wasn't the only one with no experience in arctic combat.

Kaxle rose, fell, rose again.

I moved, wobbled, slipped, and caught myself.

It was a good thing no one could see this fight. We probably looked like two enormous and bloodthirsty toddlers attempting their first steps.

After a series of failures in our ambulatory efforts, both of us macho, mutant brawlers decided to *crawl* toward each other. A few yards apart, Kaxle began to stand up and so did I.

The snow, on average, was up to my waist. But it wasn't uniform. There were streams of water cutting through the drifts where you could almost see the grass, and in other areas it piled to over twice my height. It was a mess.

Kaxle tried to lunge at me, his arms wide, claws ready. He tilted forward and stayed like that. The snow was too deep for him to jump in. It was ridiculous.

I took a big step and my foot didn't sink all the way to the ground. I wasn't ready for the elevation and I almost fell over.

Why did anyone like this stuff?

It took an exhausting minute for Kaxle and I to reach one another.

We grappled.

I grabbed him! He grabbed me!

And that was it.

I couldn't get any leverage. He couldn't get any distance or momentum. I was bulletproof, he was in a battlesuit. Not only couldn't we maneuver, we couldn't take a single step. And the snow kept coming.

I couldn't begin to push him, he was wedged solid. And so was I. He scratched at me, but this close, it was ineffectual.

After about thirty seconds of bopping at each other, I actually sat down. Not on the ground, I just dropped my knees a few inches and my butt compressed the snow enough that it supported me.

"Kaxle," I said.

He kept trying to hit me.

"Hey. Kaxle. This isn't working," I said.

He finally stopped.

"Why we fighting in this? This is stupid. What is it?"

"Snow."

"Snow what?" he asked, clearly frustrated.

"I...huh? Hey, Kaxle. You killed Laesa," I said.

"Who?"

"Laesa Swavort. Damakan," I said.

I was in a blizzard and he was wearing armor that restricted his movements. I couldn't be sure, but I think he shrugged.

"I kill lot of Damakans," he said.

"She was my wife."

"You married?" he asked, surprised.

I've learned that not every action had a deeper meaning.

Sometimes...people died because they died. Maybe they were murdered. Or they got cancer. Or it was simply their time. The universe didn't reach out and take a life in order to make some profound statement. A masterstroke chess move that would become clear in another million moves. The universe had a lot of stuff to do. And individual lives weren't that important.

I wasn't sure what I hoped to accomplish by talking to Kaxle. I did my personality profile on him and came to the conclusion that he was pretty simple.

Kaxle had a chip on his shoulder the size of a decent asteroid because of his lousy childhood. But beyond that, Kaxle was a killer. He killed people because he was good at it, maybe liked it, and he was paid. That's all. There wasn't a lot of other things going on with Kaxle. I had met his exact personality on Belvaille countless times. If I lived, I expected to meet countless more. Kaxle was standard issue.

Maybe it would be nice if you could have Belvaille crime without killers. Just the *soft* crimes like counterfeiting, theft, blackmail, and loansharking. But for as long as I'd been doing this crap, the soft crimes led to hard crimes. Without at least the *threat* of violence, it all fell apart. No one was going to pay, they'd take back their stolen goods, free the kidnap victims, or confiscate your printing press and fake artwork.

There would always be a need for the Kaxles to keep crime operating. He wasn't the engine. Or the fuel. Or the gears. He was the floor supervisor who fired you if you didn't put the fuel in the engine and oil the gears. But that meant there would always be a need for me as well—or at least people like me.

Great. So we were both useful mutants.

In spite of our tremendous value to the Belvaille economy, neither one of us was gaining an advantage in our arena battle. The weather had worked. Kind of. But it had worked on me as well.

"Kaxle," I started again.

"What?" he replied, annoyed. Kaxle didn't like to talk and fight. I preferred it. His voice was still a growl, but it was a shivery growl. He was cold. Far colder than I was in my cozy synth outfit.

"Who do you think is going to win?" I continued.

"Me! I going to kill you."

In an attempt to prove his words, Kaxle swung. One of his claw blades went up my nose. Just the end of it. Then he tried to stab my face with only a few inches of movement.

I sniffled and brushed his hand away.

"Maybe. But you're using armor," I said.

"So? I bought it."

"Yeah. But do you want to be known as a rich mutant guy?"

"You're rich."

"Would I be fighting in the snow if I was wealthy?" I asked.

"What is this damn stuff? It's freezing."

"Yeah. But what I'm saying is, do you want to prove you're the strongest mutant on Belvaille? The toughest guy?"

"I am."

"Maybe. Or maybe your armor is," I said.

Kaxle stopped jabbing at me for a moment.

"You use things. Plasma. Dredel Led."

"Where are they? Have you been shot with any plasma Dredel Leds? Led? I thought this was a mutant fight. I thought you wanted to see who was best."

"Me. I stab you good. You're hurt."

"Maybe. Or was that your armor that stabbed me?"

"You're using snow," he accused.

"I didn't make it. I can't move the same as you," I said.

"Who make it?"

"I don't know. Probably some...bad people," I said, unable to come up with a better excuse.

"You. Me. We're the bad people," Kaxle said, which struck me as a poignant reply.

"I think you're a little guy. You can't beat me without a battlesuit. I'm using my mutation. You're using Delovoa's armor," I said.

"It's mine."

"I know. But he built it."

"It's mine."

"Okay. That's true. But if you beat me—I'm saying *if*—people will be like, 'Kaxle had to use armor. Hank was fighting with his *bare* hands.'"

"*Who* say that? Tell me who?"

"I don't know. People. You know?"

"Which?"

"Any! Someone in the audience," I said.

Kaxle turned his helmet to the stands.

"I can't see them. They can't see me," he said.

"But they know you came with weapons, right?"

"No. Armor."

"But it's a weapon."

"Armor is armor. Weapon is weapon," he said.

"But if someone hits you in the face with a vibro shield, that's a weapon. Like if it breaks your lip."

"Won't break *my* lip," he said.

"If a damn Therezian swung a vibro shield at your face it couldn't break your lip?" I asked, irritated.

"Look at Wallow in street. Vibro shield wouldn't fit his hand."

"What are you, 12 years old? A Therezian with a Therezian-sized vibro shield, then."

"Wouldn't break my lip. Would kill me," he replied.

"Okay! So it would be a weapon. Even though it's a shield."

"Guess," he said begrudgingly.

"So my point... Man, what *was* my point? Oh! You've got a weapon. A big weapon. I'm unarmed. I'm fighting you with my skills. My talents. My experience."

"You're fat. And I cut you hard," he said.

"Maybe. But maybe I'm better than you and you're scared to fight me. That's what I think. I think you're a little man. A tiny little man in a big metal suit. You're a coward."

I was using his personality profile. From what Lagla-Nagla told me, I thought Kaxle was still dealing with inferiority issues. Most professional legbreakers had similar stories. Well-adjusted, happy people almost never became hired muscle. Kaxle was a short guy from a tall species in a criminal underworld. Just because he mutated into a monster didn't mean he switched personalities. You couldn't mutate away from your history. It was always there.

Delovoa said the armor was capable of being put on—*and taken off*—by the user. That meant Kaxle could ditch his high-performance gear any time he wanted. I was trying to goad him into taking it off.

From my profile of him, Kaxle wanted to be the big man. His mutation had given him his fondest dream. What every downtrodden boy dreamt of—minus the fur. No one would pick on Kaxle ever again. He was the apex predator. But that wasn't enough. He had to *prove* to everyone he was powerful. And even that wouldn't satisfy him, because there was a never-ending stream of people to convince. New crooks were born every single day and it seemed half of them came to Belvaille eventually.

Like I said, Kaxle was standard issue. If I had a credit for every time a gang boss started a war because of personal hang-ups then I'd have enough credits to hire all of Cliston's personalities at once.

My taunts were quicker than I imagined. I heard a string of pneumatic *pops* and Kaxle was more or less outside of his armor. He took a few moments to shrug the pieces off. But more urgently, he tore away the chillwipes that had been freezing him solid.

Kaxle had expected to be fighting inside a metal suit under Damakan heat. Instead, he was in a snowstorm. Kaxle wore an entire set of underclothes made out of refrigerating chillwipes!

I liked to think it was my personality profile and negotiator skills that had tricked Kaxle into taking off his armor, but he was looking for any excuse to get at his chillwipe clothes. They were actually frozen to his fur and he roared in pain removing them. Kaxle's fangs were as white as ever, but his gums were no longer blood red, they were dull pink from nearly freezing to death.

"Stupid," I said.

"*You* stupid."

Kaxle was fast and strong and brutal. But no one was fast when they were up to their chest in slush. And no one could be brutal when they were suffering from hypothermia.

I put both my arms around Kaxle's neck. He instinctively tried to dodge, but there was nowhere to go. He couldn't tunnel away quick enough.

I then tried to haul myself out of the snow using Kaxle as leverage. I was putting all my weight on his shoulders.

It pushed him down. And down.

He bit at my neck. Tried to scratch my back. But he was not exactly in fighting form. His arms were numb and clumsy.

Kaxle sank into the snow and in another...I don't know...hour, he would be completely buried.

It was a fairly slow process but I didn't have anything better to do.

"I should kill you, Kaxle, but I won't," I said.

His teeth kept coming, but they couldn't find purchase. He was getting mouthfuls of synth padding and snow. Cold or not, Kaxle should have never taken off those damnable claws.

His lower body tried to resist my weight, but it wasn't happening. I could beat damn near anyone wrestling. And this wasn't even *proper* wrestling with moves and counters. We were testing which of us weighed more. You didn't need a neutron scale to figure out who was going to win that contest.

"Someone who lived in darkness might think a candle was bright. Obviously, it isn't. But you don't know that until you compare it to a flashlight. Kaxle, having you around on Belvaille reminds people how smart I am. How stable I am. You're a candle. I'm a star."

"Y-you talk lots," he said, his muzzle struggling to remain above the surface of the snow.

What am I doing? I thought to myself.

I'm fighting and beating Kaxle. The monster who murdered Laesa.

But you are cheating.

Oh, crap, I thought.

"Hank," I said to myself with my inner voice. "You have broken the rules."

"This is an arena fight, Procon Hobb," I said, as I knew that was who was speaking to me with my own mind. "The stadium itself is called Cheat Hall."

"It is not! It is the Procon Hobb Sporting Hall and Participation Arena," he thought.

"Alright. Well, I'm participating and sporting."

"This fight was to be between you and Kaxle alone. You have assistance," Procon Hobb thought.

"I do?"

"I can sense them."

"So? It's a fight. A *good* fight," I thought.

"It cannot be viewed. The outcomes of many wagers are in question and will be litigated. This will befoul the reputation of arena combat for years. And you are breaking the rules," Procon Hobb replied.

"What *rules*? This is Belvaille."

"I sent your promoter the designated materials," he thought.

"You did? You know, I don't care. I'm going to beat Kaxle. We can have a rematch someday. But it's cold and I outplayed him. If you don't like it, that's your problem," I thought.

"This is not the fight I anticipated. I will not have it," he thought.

I was about to mentally argue, when my inner voice started speaking another language. *Screaming, numerous* other languages. At the same time.

This was not merely my mind wandering, which could be disastrous in a fight. I could literally not think. I couldn't shout down the voices in my head. I couldn't even understand them.

It was like an intense strobe light in my eyes. But instead of disoriented, I was almost entirely paralyzed. I couldn't process incoming information.

Was I being attacked? Was I falling? Was I on fire? I had no idea. Even if I knew, I couldn't respond. I couldn't issue orders to my body.

Procon Hobb had confiscated my brain.

Kaxle got out of my grip and was kind of swimming away in the snow. Not quite hopping, not quite doggie paddling, it was a weird hybrid only utilized by wolf mutants on snowy space stations.

When Procon Hobb built this stadium, he put in all kinds of ludicrous things because he's a ludicrous frog-lizard.

"I can hear you," he thought at me.

"I know," I thought back.

The liquid part of the field began to drain away. There was still plenty of snow, but the water at the bottom was being siphoned out by a complicated series of overflow pipes. Not sure where the stadium emptied out, considering it was elevated above the city. It probably just rained cold snowmelt on the very confused citizens below.

Not only that, but the roof began to close.

Cheat Hall had a retractable roof. Because...I don't know why. The roof was probably a small caliber shot away from the latticework itself. Why it needed a roof was anyone's guess, but it was threatening to block the overloaded environmental systems.

I was standing there, *watching* all this happen. People were driven to murder from hearing voices in their heads. I was being prevented from murder by voices.

Out of the chaos of my mind, I somehow heard Laesa! It was as if she was speaking to me directly from the afterlife. Her voice was clear, and calm, and wonderful, and it cut through Procon Hobb's domination.

She asked me a question.

Laesa wanted to know if I was interested in watching a tele program about a group of girls learning the meaning of sisterhood as they came to grips with their own budding sexuality in a post-Civil War farm that grew and harvested beautiful flowers that they sold to crippled orphans.

No. I absolutely *did not* want to watch such a show. Ever. I would rather remove my own teeth using plastic explosives.

When Laesa was alive, I routinely watched such programs. Or something similar. Because doing so made her happy. Sitting there with Laesa, I had to cope with some truly horrific entertainment. To cope with them, I learned to tune them out. We could do that. Just ignore half of our sensory input. It seemed a crazy skill to have, but it was easy. We did it all the time.

"Then what's the problem?" Laesa asked me.

I turned off my mind.

Procon Hobb's voices were only voices. I tuned them out like they were one of Laesa's painful tele programs she wanted to share with me.

"Hey. Bat-nat-grot. Guys. Procon mat-mot-hote Hobb is messing with me. Ma-ma-my mind. Help," I said. I had trouble speaking on the tele because I would intermittently pick up Procon Hobb's babble.

"He's the promoter," MTB said.

"N-not him. Get capsule. Castle. Kaxle," I replied.

"Garm, if this roof keeps closing, we're going to have to deal with the crowd. You go after Kaxle," MTB said.

"Got it," she answered. "Delovoa, get with me."

"I'm not a fighter. I'm here for the champagne," he said.

"Come on or you'll be drinking it through a straw when I'm done with you," she snarled.

"How *else* do you drink champagne?"

The sky roof was halfway closed. The light was still overpowering, and it was still pouring in snow, but the water from the field was draining. Thick snow was almost to my neck in places, but there was no longer a river of water underneath.

Procon Hobb was still broadcasting into my brain. I had it down to a dull roar, but he would occasionally throw me by making Hank-like thoughts. Like, "Maybe I should kneel down to achieve a tactical advantage."

And I'd wonder if that was me thinking that. But Procon Hobb kept his own vocabulary and manner of speaking, even if it was *my* voice. So I tried to filter out everything that was gibberish or sounded too educated. My own internal dialogue existed somewhere in between.

At this time, I would have been easy prey for Kaxle. But he wasn't taking advantage of my scrambled thoughts. I suspected it was for a number of reasons. Namely, he was cold, without a battlesuit, buried in snow, and because he didn't know that a giant, mutant, frog-lizard telepath was molesting my mind.

While Procon Hobb flipped through the radio stations, I could barely concentrate. I reached down to try and make a snowball to throw at Kaxle, but I forgot how. Forgot how to reach down.

I could sense things were about to escalate. This was that high-energy pivot. When the glass teetered on the edge of the table. When the firing pin moved forward to strike and ignite the primer. When Cliston twitched ever so slightly, indicating that his internal sensors detected that my food was ready to be served.

What happened was, the roof on the stadium closed completely.

And it went dark. Totally dark.

The stadium was filled with snow, angry fans, and not one photon of illumination. It was phenomenal how fast those angry fans transmogrified into terrified invertebrates simply because they couldn't see. They couldn't see earlier, but too much light was a universe away from too little light.

The jeers and taunts and curses were swapped almost instantly with screams.

Even Belvaille's criminal natives, who enjoyed operating in low light as much as any nocturnal swamp creatures, were uneasy in pitch blackness. Especially in a cramped and frosty building with gambling outcomes hanging in the balance.

"Bust out the brights," MTB said on the tele.

"For those of us Ontakians that don't speak MTB, what the hell did you just say?" Frank asked.

"Light some damn flares before this crowd tears itself apart," MTB yelled.

Dots of orange, yellow, and red flares popped up in the stands. They were tiny, and at this distance, they provided almost no visibility on the field. They were like dying stars viewed through a smog-filled atmosphere. But they were reassuring nonetheless. You could hear the crowd hysteria reduced a few notches.

I moved haltingly, my mind trying to ignore Procon Hobb's stampeding babble. I concentrated on my mantra. What are your last words? Bela-Tore Jangle-Flot.

I said it over and over again to try and drown out Procon Hobb's voices. By doing that, however, I was blocking out everything. I had turned on autopilot.

It was dark. I plodded forward through snowdrifts. I was attempting to maintain my balance and make contact with something. With what, I wasn't sure. I didn't think about it. I didn't think about anything.

What are your last words? Bela-Tore Jangle-Flot.

Laesa said that you needed to rehearse a part. Study the character so much that you could improvise. If you were given ad lib material, you could integrate seamlessly. Because you *were* that person.

I was now acting.

I was acting like Hank. A Hank who was in an arena fight in the snow with the lights off. It was a very convincing portrayal. If the GuildARs hadn't been cancelled I might have won. If only someone could see my performance.

No one could, of course, but someone could *smell* it.

I didn't hear him. I didn't hear anything except my mantra and Procon Hobb trying to boil my cerebellum. But someone or something was cutting me.

I think.

I felt pain. If I had to say where, specifically, I'd have to answer "approximately everywhere." I kept going. My mind was unfocused. I swung my arms loosely, kept my eyes closed, and repeated my mantra.

Kaxle was using the blackout to work me over. He found every weak point I had and made a few extra. He took his time.

I couldn't fight him with Procon Hobb screaming at me. Or in the dark. Or buried in snow. Any *one* of those conditions would make me unable to deal with Kaxle. All three at once meant I was simply waiting to die.

At some point I stopped walking and fell down. Not by choice. Not even by accident. My muscles or tendons or bones had been broken. It took me a while to notice.

Kaxle's beating suddenly stopped. I could hear something. Something besides a stadium of fans screaming from the dark tundra. Something beyond my mantra or Procon Hobb.

I knew the sounds intimately. Even still, it took me a moment to decipher them. I wasn't often on this side.

It was Garm! She was clobbering Kaxle. Or at least preventing him from clobbering me. How she managed to get down here, find us in the dark, and do battle with the ferocious mutant was anyone's guess.

"Hello, Hank. You look terrible," Delovoa said.

I managed to turn my head and I saw a small, glowing, blue circle in the dark.

"Yeah, my eyeball sharpeners," he said. "I forgot they grant almost perfect night vision. Of course, they'll carve out your eyes if you leave them in too long."

"What?" Garm yelled.

I saw another blue eye bobbing and jumping and cartwheeling to the side.

"Relax. I estimate we have another fifteen—or five—minutes," Delovoa said.

I had to help them. Even with night goggles I didn't believe Garm could hold off Kaxle alone. Besides, my butt was getting cold lying in the snow. Kaxle must have torn off the back of my pants.

I struggled to my feet. Procon Hobb was still mentally dictating at me, but he was either getting bored, or sitting inside my brain for this long was making him claustrophobic, because it wasn't as bad as before.

In this ocean of terrible noises, it was pretty amazing to actually hear a truly terrible noise.

I looked up and saw a white lightning bolt slowly travelling across the sky. Not only was that peculiar because it was moving at a walking pace, but Belvaille obviously had no clouds, and the roof of the stadium was closed.

The lightning forked. Splintered. Meandered. And then it finally joined up again.

A chunk of the roof collapsed!

A shaft of light poured into the stadium along with an avalanche of snow. The hole was well off to the side so there was no immediate danger.

"Oh yeah. With the roof closed, the snow must be piling on top. I bet it's not rated to withstand a blizzard," Delovoa said.

"Probably rated for a hurricane," I added, remembering the lizard cathedral.

I could see somewhat. My mind's eye had drawn a picture of the battleground I was fighting on and the sudden flash of light made it clear that what I had envisioned was completely wrong.

Garm was facing off against Kaxle who could suddenly see as well as smell her. As quick and agile as she was, the deep snow was severely limiting Garm's movements. Kaxle had an easier time being much stronger and heavier.

Kaxle snaked his arm out and grabbed Garm by the front of her snow suit.

"Eat pillow fluffer, fluffface," Delovoa said. He threw his invention at Kaxle where latched onto the mutant's chest and began gently massaging him. "Sorry, that's all I got," Delovoa apologized, seeing the item fail to be of use.

But the minor distraction allowed Garm to duck down and out of her coat and spring away from Kaxle. She would be freezing cold in a moment, but it was better than being dead.

My mind was still playing catchup while Procon Hobb yelled at me. It was one thing to stumble around in the dark, but processing and reacting to combat was a whole other deal.

Kaxle roared in anger at Garm's escape and tossed aside the metal contraption on his chest. He took a look at me and decided I was no immediate concern. He then lunged at Delovoa, grabbed the scientist by each of his arms, and tore them completely off his body!

"Delovoa!" I yelled.

"Hey, those cost good money," Delovoa said, annoyed. He then attempted to kick Kaxle, but the mutant had already moved.

Another piece of the roof fell, this one only ten yards away from us. The snow that accompanied it was far worse than the concrete debris. All of us, including Kaxle, had to hustle away to prevent being buried. In fact, it wasn't snow at all that was falling.

"With the roof closed, the environment systems are blocked. They're not making snow anymore. It's ice," armless Delovoa stated. He did not seem terribly concerned about missing his limbs. He actually twisted his torso like a hyper child, causing his empty sleeves to flop around.

I stared at the mountain of ice underneath the hole. It was easily thirty-five feet tall at the peak and probably the same distance wide at the base.

Kaxle snarled and swiped at my face with his claw.

"Are you blind, man?" I demanded. "We're going to get crushed if we don't get out of this stadium."

"It's a trick. You did this," he said.

"It doesn't matter who did it. None of us can survive twenty tons of ice falling on them from the latticework," Garm said, rubbing her bare arms to try and get warm.

Kaxle was unsure.

"Admit I won," he said.

"Listen. Look," I said, pointing to the stands.

There still wasn't much light coming in, but we could hear the fans. They were screaming. Trying to run away. No one was remotely interested in our fight.

"We probably should have thought of a way to tell the Keilvin Kamigans to stop," Delovoa said. "This building is going to fall."

"We have to get underground. The locker and training rooms are beneath the floor and should be safe from the roof," I said.

"You don't understand, Hank. It's not just the roof. This whole stadium is coming down. The facility is elevated. The supports can't handle this much weight. We must escape," Delovoa replied.

"It took five hours to get everyone in here. We can't run past an arena of stampeding people," Garm said. "I'm calling the Navy."

"No Navy," Kaxle barked.

"I can't believe I'm saying it, but I concur with the monster," Delovoa said. "What can the Navy do? Shoot the building? Process out forms?"

"The Navy owns maintenance shuttles that can operate inside Belvaille atmosphere. They're really slow. But they can land in the center and evacuate us."

"Tell MTB, Frank, and the police to gather here," I said.

"No cops," Kaxle growled, but everyone ignored him.

As Garm spoke on her tele, I realized the next moments were going to be risky. And if Procon Hobb really tried, he could prevent me from leaving.

"Procon Hobb. I know you can hear me. Quit messing with my brain," I said.

"You have ruined another of my ventures as you ruined my glocken team. I will ensure you suffer in the most calamitous and grievous manner possible," he thought.

"I'm not sure if you can see from where you're sitting, but I assume you're in the stadium somewhere. Not only is the roof caving in, but the extra fifty feet of ice is going to cause the whole arena to collapse to the city floor. If you're here when that happens, you're going to die. If you meet us down in the center of the field, we can rescue you by shuttle. But *only* if you stop messing with me and if you agree we are square. That means no calamitous grievances. No suffering of any kind—other than my usual amount.

The voices in my head went silent for a moment.

"I will join you momentarily," he thought.

With my brain free, I was in full control of my senses. Huge pieces of the ceiling were hanging off and ready to fall at any time. Rivers of ice poured through the holes already created with new leaks appearing all over.

The stands were emptying fitfully, as frenzied fans attempted to dig their way out of ice and snow and past their fellow sports enthusiasts.

Kaxle huffed and puffed in front of me, pacing a path clear in the snow. Even with the building about to land on his head, it seemed like it took all his control to hold off attacking me.

"I beat you," Kaxle said finally.

"Whatever," I replied.

When MTB and his police team reached us, Kaxle finally backed away and gave me some breathing room.

"Can the shuttle carry this many people?" I asked Garm.

"Three are coming. It's enough, even with Procon Hobb. But we can't take any fans or they'll riot," she said.

"No one is crazy enough to run down to the center of a collapsing arena," I said.

The building shook. It was like an earthquake. Or I assumed it was like an earthquake, because I had never experienced one before. A dozen more pieces of the roof fell, dumping a few icebergs into the stadium.

"That ceiling is getting weaker with every fracture. Not to mention if it gives out directly overhead, we're doomed. How long will it take those shuttles to get here?" Delovoa asked.

"Soon. They had to come all the way from the port," Garm replied.

Procon Hobb arrived with two lizard guards in tow. They moved slowly. Not that Procon Hobb ever moved fast, but I suspected this cold wasn't happy times for them. Were they cold-blooded?

"No, we're not," Hobb thought at me.

"Anyone seen my arms?" Delovoa asked, looking through the snow.

"Any casualties in the stands?" Garm asked MTB.

"We won't know for sure until we can mount some rescue efforts," he replied.

It was long minutes before the shuttles flew through holes in the roof. They were smaller and louder than I imagined and looked like rectangles affixed with jet engines. They didn't move or land gracefully, all three cocking at odd angles as they plopped onto the snowy field.

The doors opened and we filed in with as much politeness and serenity as the occasion called for. That is, we rushed the doors and piled in, jostling one another.

The pilot in my shuttle took the time to organize us to maximize space and then strapped us all in. He had trouble with Procon Hobb, who was much too large to be strapped, and then he had trouble with Delovoa, who had no arms to be secured. Kaxle refused the restraints and I was also left standing.

"I'll have us out of here in a moment, folks," the pilot said.

"Delovoa, those stupid eye sharpeners wrecked my vision. I'm seeing double," Garm said, as the pilot fastened her buckles.

"Lagla-Nagla?" I asked.

"Hi, Hank," the pilot said cheerfully. His lopsided physical features were confusing Garm.

"You're a Navy shuttle pilot?" I asked.

"Nah, the ship mostly flies itself. I just buckle stuff down and punch a few buttons. Besides, I'm just backup. All the regulars are watching your fight," he said.

"Well, you might finally have a permanent job as this stadium is about to fall on them," I replied.

"Who wants a permanent job?" he asked distastefully.

It had never occurred to me that Lagla-Nagla actually liked perpetually switching careers. I thought he was always fired because of his off-putting manner and appearance.

"You big people are going to need to hold on to something. These seatbelts are mostly designed for cargo," Lagla-Nagla announced.

"Hey, LN," Kaxle said to Lagla-Nagla, which is the first almost nice thing I ever heard Kaxle say.

"Howdy, bud. Haven't seen you in a while. Hope you're well."

"What's that supposed to mean? You trying to start crap?" Kaxle threatened, reverting to form.

"Don't attack the pilot," Garm said.

The shuttle took off. Ours was the last one off the field, as it was the one filled with the oddball-sized creatures, myself included. The doors on both sides remained open because there wasn't enough space to close them. My right arm and leg were hanging out and half of Procon Hobb's...everything, were out the other side.

"Admit that I beat you, Hank. Put it in Scanhand," Kaxle said, as the shuttle was rising. We were at least a hundred feet up and snow and ice were pattering off the top of the ship.

"Wait until we're on firm ground," I said.

Bracing himself with his arms against the ceiling, Kaxle pushed his way across the shuttle to stand by me.

"I wasn't even hurt. Not hardly. I took off my armor because you was scared. I'm the best mutant. I'm the strongest on Belvaille," Kaxle continued.

"Take it easy back there! This crate ain't designed to fly in bad weather. Or any weather," Lagla-Nagla called from the front.

"Yeah, calm down," Garm shouted.

"For the record, Procon Hobb was telepathizing my brain. That's the only reason I had trouble fighting you. I been trouncing punks like you for centuries. You're nothing special," I said.

I don't know what I was thinking. I let Kaxle rile me when it was totally insignificant what he thought.

Kaxle launched himself at me and grabbed my throat! His momentum caused the aircraft to tilt dangerously as we attempted to fly through the snowstorm.

His claws were digging into my neck and his weight was pushing against me, threating to catapult us both out the open door. I had my left hand holding onto the overhead safety bar. My feet were attempting to find purchase on the icy metal flooring.

Garm repeatedly kicked Kaxle in his side, but she was secured to her seat and couldn't get much force. Delovoa did his part by squealing in despair.

As the shuttle rocked back and forth, even Procon Hobb, who was squished into the shuttle, was losing his hold. His guards unfastened their harnesses to try and protect their religious lord. They should have worried about themselves. As the shuttle bucked, both the lizards were flung out of the craft. I saw one of them tumble through the snow and out sight. We were hundreds of feet above the stadium at this point and there is no way he survived the fall.

Kaxle was berserk. He was going to kill us all and he didn't seem to care.

My feet slipped and my legs dangled out of the side. The sudden extra weight on my hands caused the metal bar I was holding onto to bend and break. I was unsecured and began falling!

I clawed and grasped and panicked worse than I ever had. I didn't have a fear of heights. But I sure as hell had a fear of plummeting into a collapsing arena. It was a very specific phobia.

My grasping hands found purchase and held on. I was clinging onto Kaxle's furry leg. That wet pelt was my lifeline.

Kaxle and I together had essentially been the counterbalance to the massive Procon Hobb's weight in the shuttle. But as the frog-lizard swayed, and we hung out the door, the entire shuttle was thrown sideways.

I could hear the engines howling in protest. This shuttle was designed to carry heavy equipment high up on Belvaille. It wasn't prepared to fly while carrying fighting mutants of extraordinary girth.

As hardy as Kaxle's fur was, it couldn't begin to hold my weight and I was ripping out tuft after tuft as I scrambled to stay alive.

I'm not sure what possessed me. Perhaps being this close to another creature was reminding me my mutation needed to heal. Perhaps I was tapping into a subconscious ability I never knew I had. But I bit Kaxle on the back of his leg. Hard.

I do a lot of eating on a regular basis. It had never really occurred to me I had a strong mouth. But Kaxle's screaming was almost louder than Delovoa's high-pitched whine.

With the extra grip provided by my teeth, I was able to adjust my hands and find a better purchase. One hand was on the step to the shuttle and another on the fur at Kaxle's midsection.

Warm blood poured into my mouth from the bite. I had to say, it had a surprisingly pleasant flavor. Kind of a semi-sweet, after-dinner appeal with a heady meat texture. I probably wouldn't want to have it every day, but it wasn't gamey at all. As the thick liquid passed over my tongue and to the back of my mouth, I could even detect earthy notes and a dash of citrus acidity. Kaxle must eat a lot of fruit. Which was good, because I needed the vitamins.

Was it really cannibalism if I ate Kaxle? Yeah, he was a mutant and I was a mutant, but we were mutants of different subspecies. And even if it *was* cannibalism, it was only his leg. And maybe his foot. That's not even ten percent cannibalism. Low single digits. I could live with that.

The shuttle rose though one of the holes in the stadium and we could see the city. That is, we could see it if we weren't in the snow clouds, surrounded by the arctic.

On top of the arena, rising almost up to the latticework itself, was ice. It was a glacier. Must be damn near all of Belvaille's water supply frozen up here.

There was no way the stadium could survive that weight. It's amazing it was still standing right now.

Kaxle kicked me in the face with his good leg, trying to dislodge my teeth. But my mutant strength, my hunger, and my fear, made me far stronger than anyone in the city. If I was going to fall, I was taking Kaxle's leg with me. At least I could plunge to my death doing what I loved most: eating. And it wasn't a bad last meal, all things considered. Cliston would have added spices and paired it with a nice wine, but sometimes simple food really hit the spot.

I looked up and saw Procon Hobb looming behind Kaxle. The shuttle was turned completely sideways now. If Hobb slipped, he would kill us all.

Procon Hobb reached out to us with one of his massive claws.

He was going to push us!

He grabbed hold of Kaxle and pulled him inside the shuttle like he was a small doll. A small doll with a larger doll holding onto the first one with its doll teeth.

Procon Hobb set us down on the center of shuttle and the craft leveled off, more or less.

I reluctantly released my grip on Kaxle. I had two massive bunches of fur in each hand and a mouthful of blood. As I swallowed, I detected an intriguing flavor I couldn't quite identify. What was it? Delicate but undeniably hearty.

"If you all are done. I'll have us down in a minute," Lagla-Nagla said.

"Fly clear of the stadium. Land us by the telescopes," Garm answered.

Kaxle punched me and clawed at my head. Our brush with destruction hadn't pacified him in the slightest.

"I'll kill you! You tried to eat me," he screamed unreasonably.

The shuttle shook as Kaxle thrashed about.

As I was being battered, I saw a muscled, scaly arm pass in front of my eyes. Procon Hobb took hold of Kaxle about the chest. And then squeezed. It was one quick motion and faster than I would have thought possible. Kaxle squirted between the fingers of Procon Hobb.

The frog-lizard god then flung Kaxle's corpse out the door and waved his hand in an attempt to remove the remaining pieces. He spoke to me casually.

"What a nuisance. The way I see it, we *were* even. You damaged the Procon Hobb Sporting Hall and Participation Arena yet provided me this transport to safety. However, I have now saved your life. Once I build a new stadium, you owe me a fight."

I stared at the hulking form until Garm gave me a kick.

"Yeah. Yeah, sure," I said.

Armless Delovoa was still screaming.

"Cinnamon. Smokey cinnamon," I said, smacking my lips. "That's the flavor I couldn't recognize."

Delovoa predicted the stadium would fall sometimes over the next two to three days as the ice melted and the building supports weakened. In actuality, it took less than three hours.

Most of the fans made it out in one piece. It had taken much longer to fill the stadium, but there were no tickets to check and they were going downhill, driven by panic. Most of the injuries were caused by the force of the crowd.

After the collapse, the Navy sent recovery crews to help. This was an organizational activity they were honestly proficient at. And it went a long way to enable cleanup and rescue of survivors.

Still, even with hundreds of emergency personnel assisting, many of Belvaille's high-ranking gamblers died in the stadium destruction. Not *in* the stadium, however.

Apparently, once they left the building, they stood around taking wagers on what piece of the structure would fall off next. When the entire arena crumbled, it completely destroyed everything within ten blocks, gamblers included.

CHAPTER 36

I took my time recovering in the hospital.

Cliston paid for my medical expenses. He made a lot from my arena fight, despite its disastrous conclusion. "No refund in case of cheating, death, accidental or purposeful spectator mutilation, or building annihilation," was clearly indicated on the tickets. Procon Hobb and Cliston were experienced fight promoters and knew me well.

Regardless, thousands of fans complained to the Navy and even organized a class action lawsuit. They each kicked in a hundred or so credits to fill out the official petition. The petition was created and sponsored by Garm who took the money and bought herself a new bracelet.

I didn't make anything from the fight. Or not much. I used a portion of the proceeds to buy a pint of blood from the two surviving Rough Boys who had since been married. I couldn't shake the craving I had developed ever since I tasted Kaxle's blood and hoped theirs was the same. But the other Rough Boys were inferior vintages. I could *barely* finish drinking it. I was thinking maybe I got a bad batch and I should try again, but they went off on their honeymoon to another System.

Over my recovery, I spent many hours reading *The News*. Rendrae posted article after article on the Entertainment Extermination and its aftermath. Procon Hobb had kept his word and given ownership of the paper back to Rendrae. All the fluff and gossip were quickly removed from *The News* and Rendrae returned the publication to hard journalism—a move which reduced the readership by about 90%.

Delovoa was in high spirits despite being dismembered. He viewed his condition as a chance to start over and get only the best. He also swore that *this* time he was going to plan out his body instead of adding as he went along. But rumors about Delovoa and his peculiarities had travelled great distances—aided by Scanhand. Consequently, Delovoa found that no one wanted to hang out with him because they were afraid of losing appendages.

The Keilvin Kamigan Triple-Zs had stopped pouring down cold and snow half a day after the arena collapsed. They were hard workers. They took that dedication back to driving taxis and freight across the city. If it was a car or truck on Belvaille, it was probably operated by a talking cloud. They swore there was only three of them, but they seemed to be everywhere.

Cliston closed his Artists Agency as, soon enough, there weren't many artists left on the city. He was back to being my butler and writing the occasional industry-defining handbook.

Belvaille had played out its monopoly on Damakans. Once cities, planets, species, empires, saw how lucrative and effective Damakans could be, the actors were hired away to perform across the galaxy.

That was the Colmarian way.

Damakans were now officially Colmarians and they would be scattered across the empire like every other Colmarian, used where they were most useful. Or, as was often the case in the PCC, used where they were *least* useful.

We halfheartedly tried to keep the Damakans here, but it didn't work too well. Belvaille could *broadcast*, but we didn't actually have much in the way of money. Some megacorporation could enlist Damakans to put together employee-satisfaction films and double productivity. Or a planetary warlord could have them perform in his private luxury gardens. Belvaille couldn't compete on that scale. We were merely a space station.

The dramatic industry still existed on Belvaille, but it became lowest-common-denominator fare. Our shows still managed to get some viewers, despite our low production values, but they were no longer the best, or only, source of Damakan entertainment.

But that was fine. Belvaille, in its history, had never been a producer of quality products. We were not the haven of intellectuals or artists. We were the home of criminals.

Belvaille had been given a once-in-a-lifetime gift. By pure luck, we had possessed nearly every Damakan that existed off their home planet. We didn't know what the hell to do with them. We didn't even recognize what we had. We nearly killed them out of existence by our own dumb instincts and greed. If they had landed somewhere else, who knows what could have been created. The best Belvaille did with a race of emotion-controlling actors was to broadcast a ton of corny action programs that weren't destined to survive the test of time.

Belvaille did crooked stuff and did it well. But not *too* well. Just lousy enough to get by. That was the Belvaille motto. Or, if it wasn't, it should be.

I put off looking at it for about a month, but I finally broke down and opened Scanhand. My attributes had been changed yet again. My Toughness was a ten. My Smarts was a ten. My Trouble was...a zero.

Not a bleeding zero. Or a snot-covered zero. Or a zero that exploded and destroyed your tele. I clicked on the comments. The first comment was highlighted and stuck to the top so that it would always appear first.

Hank is indeed all sorts of trouble. But what joy would life hold for its practitioners if it was too easy?

Signed, Thad Elon.

Then it said, "The Scanhand Administration Staff has researched the above comment and its ownership and determined that it is legitimate."

Thad Elon left me a comment!

The Creator God of the galaxy personally left a comment on Scanhand. About me.

Last I saw of Thad Elon, he had been sealed inside a black bag and sent adrift in deep space in the general direction of nothing. How did he return so fast? It had been years, but still, it *should* have been eons.

I got a lot of work requests from that comment, but no one, not even people who had met and fought Thad Elon, ever specifically asked me about it. It was too big and too scary to wrap your head around. It wasn't even whispered in the dark corners by drug addicts hooked on his namesake.

Thad Elon was alive and well somewhere. And he had access to a tele. Any way you looked at it, that meant bad times ahead.

With Kaxle gone, I was the toughest mutant on Belvaille. But that might only be because no one ranked Procon Hobb.

After a long time, I started flirting with women again. Not that I was any good at it. I tended to offend more often than I enticed. But it showed recovery. I'd never get over Laesa completely. But I didn't want to. Life, and living, wasn't something you "got over." You carried it with you until it was gone.

I had a good run so far and I was still going.

As I walked out of the hospital, having recovered as much as possible with tubes up my nose, one of the medical technicians said "good day" to me. Normally, I'd answer, "The day ain't over yet. Wait and see." But I stopped myself. I looked around at the city that lay beyond those glass doors. At the opportunities that were ahead of me and I replied:

"You know, it *is* a good day."

THE END

Printed in Great Britain
by Amazon